"...A HEIG
CEPTION, A
SENSITIV
LARGED COMPASSION
AND THE DIVIDENDS OF
JOY AND DELIGHT AND
RELEASE FROM TERROR
AND SORROW..."

Thus the editors of this superlative anthology
describe what we seek when we turn to the short
story for our reading pleasure.

*This collection has been assembled to satisfy
that desire to the full. There is rich diversity
here. The stories come from many different
lands. Their moods are different, and their
styles. Each, however, plays its integral role
in the total design: each "adds its unique dimension to the color and texture of the human experience. We may start where we will; we may
turn in the direction we choose; the pieces of
the kaleidoscope fall into place in any number
of fascinating ways."*

ABOUT THE EDITORS: ABRAHAM H. LASS
is the principal of Brooklyn's Abraham Lincoln
High School, one of the largest public secondary
schools in the country. In addition to anthologies
of plays and stories, Mr. Lass's published work
includes HOW TO PREPARE FOR COLLEGE
and THE COLLEGE STUDENTS' HANDBOOK,
which he co-authored with Eugene S. Wilson of
Amherst College. His syndicated column on college admissions problems has appeared in many
newspapers, including THE NEW YORK POST
and THE BOSTON TRAVELER, and Mr. Lass
is now writing a biweekly column on college for
THE NEW YORK TIMES. NORMA TASMAN
is chairman of the English Department at Sheeps-
head Bay High School in Brooklyn, New York.

Other Collections of Short Stories

The Secret

Sharer
and Other Great Stories

edited by

ABRAHAM H. LASS
and NORMA L. TASMAN

A MENTOR BOOK from
NEW AMERICAN LIBRARY
TIMES MIRROR
New York and Scarborough, Ontario
The New English Library Limited, London

Library of Congress Catalog Card Number: 69-17924

ACKNOWLEDGMENTS AND COPYRIGHT NOTICES
(The following page constitutes an extension of this copyright page.)

The editors wish to thank the following for permission to reprint the short stories listed:

"Waves of Darkness." Reprinted by permission of Cord Meyer. This story was originally published by the *Atlantic Monthly*.

"His Excellency." Copyright 1954 by Marc Slonim. Reprinted by permission of Simon & Schuster, Inc.

"A Summer's Reading." Reprinted with permission of Farrar, Straus & Giroux, Inc. from *The Magic Barrel* by Bernard Malamud. Copyright © 1956, 1958 by Bernard Malamud.

"The Rocking-Horse Winner." From *The Complete Short Stories of D. H. Lawrence*, Vol. III. Copyright 1933 by the Estate of D. H. Lawrence © 1961 by Angelo Ravagli and C. Montague Weekley, Executors of the Estate of Frieda Lawrence Ravagli. Reprinted by permission of The Viking Press, Inc.

"A Wreath for Miss Totten." Copyright 1948, 1949, 1950, 1951 by Hortense Calisher. From *In the Absence of Angels* by Hortense Calisher, by permission of Little, Brown and Co.

 MENTOR TRADEMARK REG. U.S. PAT. OFF. AND FOREIGN COUNTRIES
REGISTERED TRADEMARK—MARCA REGISTRADA
HECHO EN CHICAGO, U.S.A.

SIGNET, SIGNET CLASSICS, MENTOR, PLUME AND MERIDIAN BOOKS
are published *in the United States* by
The New American Library, Inc.,
1301 Avenue of the Americas, New York, New York 10019,
in Canada by The New American Library of Canada Limited,
81 Mack Avenue, Scarborough, 704, Ontario,
in the United Kingdom by The New English Library Limited,
Barnard's Inn, Holborn, London, E.C. 1, England.

FIRST PRINTING, FEBRUARY, 1969

4 5 6 7 8 9 10 11 12

PRINTED IN THE UNITED STATES OF AMERICA

To
BETTY, JANET, and PAUL
and ARNOLD

TABLE OF CONTENTS

Foreword

There are many ways to read this collection of short stories. And all of them are right. One obvious way, of course, is to start with the first story and go on to each of the others in turn, reading them in the order in which they appear. But few of us would care to sample with such formality the variety of stories presented in these pages. Nor is it necessary or even desirable to do so. Every story in this anthology is complete in itself and independent of every other story, except that each adds its unique dimension to the color and texture of the human experience. We may start where we will; we may turn in the direction we choose; the pieces of the kaleidoscope fall into place in any number of equally fascinating ways.

The short story demands only our time and our attention. In return for these, it shows us our world and our own lives in ways we may not have seen them before, with freshness compounded of new views of the familiar, and strangely familiar views of the new and unknown. The short story forces us to participate in lives that were never lived, and it enables us, through this participation, to recognize that our experience has meaning, both because it is ours and because it is, in some mysterious way, common to all men. The fictional lives we encounter in the short story become, for a time, our own lives—with one important difference: when we finish the story, we leave these lives behind, but distill from them a heightened perception, an increased sensitivity, an enlarged compassion—and the dividends of joy and delight and release from terror and sorrow.

The short story is a unique art form. Its impact is immediate and concentrated; the moment in the story is *now*, often with only hints of what went before and only a suggestion of what comes after. The unanswered *why* generated by the story sends us searching deep into our own experience and understanding. In a very real sense, then, it is the reader who completes the story.

The stories in this collection are alive with the force of the contemporary and with the perennial vitality of the significant, relevant past. They have something to say to all of us in our time. We hope the reader will find them as fresh and as exciting as we have.

A. H. L.
N. L. T.

Brooklyn, New York

Waves of Darkness

CORD MEYER, JR.

"Waves of Darkness" takes place during World War II on an island in the Pacific. The hero is a young American lieutenant surrounded by an untiring enemy hunting him down relentlessly. What does a man think of when he is waiting in the darkness for the death that has come to his buddies and to millions of other soldiers? The answer is here in the simple, highly charged prose of "Waves of Darkness," a vivid picture of what happens to men on the battlefield, and what goes on in their minds as they fight for their lives in a world where "one moment you lived, and the next you were snuffed out like an insect."

CORD MEYER (1920–) was born in Washington, D. C. He is a graduate of Yale University. From 1942 to 1945 he served with the U. S. Marine Corps in the Pacific. From 1947 to 1949, Mr. Meyer was president of the World Federalists. He is at present with the Central Intelligence Agency.

"Waves of Darkness" received an O. Henry prize award for distinguished writing. Mr. Meyer has written one book, Peace or Anarchy, *and a number of articles which*

have appeared in The New York Times *and* The Atlantic Monthly.

Waves of Darkness

They lay in a hole just wide enough to lie in side by side, and not more than a foot deep. They had arranged that one should keep guard while the other rested. Every two hours they changed.

Lying on his stomach the lieutenant was able to prop himself up with his elbows to see over the mound of dirt. He held the Thompson gun in his arms and kept two grenades in readiness by his right hand. The even breathing of his friend comforted him with the knowledge that he was not alone. During the day, physical action and the necessity for decision occupied his mind. Now he had nothing to do but wait and watch. Each minute of waiting made the next more difficult.

He tried to remember the surrounding terrain as it had looked before the light failed. He looked for the broken stump of a coconut tree and the large boulder whose relative position he had deliberately impressed on his memory as he dug his hole. He had memorized the harmless shadows so that he might know the shadows of the real enemy for whom he waited. A heavy layer of clouds obscured the tropic stars and he could see nothing but the formless night, isolating in worlds apart each small hole with its occupants.

He continued to stare into the blackness with wide-open, unblinking eyes, and found fear crouched menacingly at the end of every corridor of thought. He deliberately attempted to lose his fear, and the hysteria that mounted in his heart, in another emotion, and strove to awaken lust by summoning up pornographic memories. It proved a poor substitute, and he could find hardly a passing interest in the indecent scenes that he paraded before his mind's eye.

Then he attempted to rationalize his fear. What was

he afraid of, he asked himself. Death, was the simple answer. He knew that it might come at any moment out of the dark, carried on the bayonets of a banzai charge or dealt skillfully by the well-placed hand grenade of an infiltrating scout. He could not deny this fact on which his fear nourished and grew. It was inevitable that the enemy would attack during the night. They must know how thinly the line was held and that they would never again have such an opportunity. It was merely a question of time.

Most of his companions had a superstitious faith in their own luck. No matter how great the odds, the vast majority of his men always preferred to believe that though others might fall, they would not. It was only on the basis of this conviction that they found the courage for the risks they had to take. He preferred to think death inevitable. By absolving himself of all hope prior to each battle, he had found himself prepared for the most desperate eventualities. Now, with an effort of the will, he urged his mind down this accustomed path of reasoning. He stripped the night of its hideous pretensions to find only death, an old familiar companion. Though his fear remained, it became controllable, and this was all that he asked.

He turned his head sharply toward the sound of a gun fired offshore. An illuminating shell burst overhead with a soft popping sound, like the breaking of a Fourth of July rocket. For fear of being silhouetted against the light, he allowed only his eyes and the top of his helmet to project above the rim of dirt. He knew the shell was fired from a friendly destroyer lying off the beach, but it must have been ordered because of the suspicion of enemy movement. With a scarcely audible hissing the flare settled slowly down.

The blasted coconut trees cast deceptive shadows that danced in slow rhythm as the flare swayed to and fro in its descent. The unearthly, pallid light accentuated rather than dispelled the threat of horror that the night held. It was impossible to distinguish shadow from substance. Every small depression in the ground was filled with darkness, and the line of thick jungle growth some sixty yards ahead presented an impenetrable question. He could make out nothing for certain. Each natural object assumed enormous and malevolent proportions in the shadows that lengthened toward him. He felt as if he were lost in the evil witch forest of some ancient folk tale and he shivered involuntarily.

With his finger on the trigger, he longed to let go a burst of fire in defiance, but restrained the impulse. In the game he played, the one who first revealed his position became the hunted and was lucky to escape with his life. The flare settled on the ground and burned up brightly for a moment. Then the night surged back. It was as if he sat in a theater where the scenes are silently shifted in the dark. Even more than before, the darkness seemed a curtain behind which some fantastic tragedy waited. Again the destroyer fired and a shell burst.

He glanced behind him and saw the village they had paid for so dearly during the day. It sprawled desolately beneath the uncertain light. No roof remained, and only a few of the walls stood upright, like the remnants of a decaying skeleton. It seemed an archaeological curiosity from the long-vanished past instead of a place where men had lived forty-eight hours ago. When the naval bombardment began, the natives had fled to the hills and left their town to the foreigners who fought in a war the inhabitants could not understand and the outcome of which could leave them no different than before. He guessed that there were many who had fought bravely, on both sides, who understood it all no better than the natives and had as little stake in eventual victory. The flare sank to earth behind the village. Ghastly, still as the dead that lay among its wreckage, he saw it in the flare's sick light as the symbol of all war.

The ship fired three more shells at irregular intervals. He waited for the fourth in vain. Each silent minute seemed a tiny weight added on a scale that slowly tipped toward destruction. He allowed himself to think of the dawn and looked hopefully for the long, thin streak of gray in the east, as if by some special dispensation the sun might rise six hours early. The day appeared infinitely remote, and he thought of it as one dreams of some distant and charming country which one has no real hope of ever seeing.

The small sound of a stick broken near-by focused all his senses. He twisted his body quickly and brought the Thompson gun to bear in the direction from which the sound came. He held his breath and the blood drummed in his ears. His friend felt the movement and inched over onto his stomach. Together they stared fruitlessly into the blackness. Gradually the tension left his limbs, and he allowed his breath to escape softly.

"Guess it was nothing."

"Sand crabs probably. What time is it?"

Cupping his watch in his hands, as if the slightest wind might blow out the light, he made out the tiny green figures. It was four minutes past one.

"Past time. Your turn," he said.

He felt for the two grenades and put them into the hands of his friend. Without words they traded weapons.

He rolled over on his back. Unbuckling his chin strap, he rested his head in the leather harness of the helmet and stretched out his legs. There was hardly room for them, and he pushed his feet into the soft dirt at the end of the shelter trench. His breathing came easier. He was aware that there was just as much danger as ever, but he liked the feeling that he was no longer directly responsible. There was nothing now that he could do to prevent their being surprised, and his eyes closed. He did not attempt to sleep. Perhaps after two or three nights like this one, he thought, he would be tired enough. But not yet.

A cold, thin rain began to fall. He buttoned his dungaree jacket to the throat and hugged his body. There was nothing to do but lie there under the open sky. The earth in the narrow hole turned slowly to a sticky mud, and his clothes clung to him. A long spasm of shivering shook him. He wondered whether it was caused by cold or fear. The rain seemed a wanton addition to his misery. Slanting down, it pinned him to the earth.

For a moment he was overwhelmed by self-pity.

But gradually the rain no longer seemed directed especially against him. He felt its huge indifference and imagined how the tiny drops fell on all that lay without shelter beneath the night. The rain merged with the saltier oblivion of the sea, each drop leaving a transient ripple on its broad impassive face. It seeped down to the roots of the tropic plants and nourished that abundant life. With an equal carelessness it streaked the dirt on the faces of the living and washed the blood from the bodies of the friends he'd lost. He imagined the rain falling through the dark on their upturned, quiet faces.

2

Slowly he went over in his mind the names of the men of his command. Of the platoon of forty-four who had climbed up the steep beach in the morning, thirty remained to dig their holes in the evening. The bodies of the others lay behind to mark the path of the advance.

The lieutenant could form no continuous picture of what had happened. With terrible clarity a particular scene would present itself, only to be replaced by another equally sharp but unrelated vision. It was as if he watched magic-lantern slides whose logical order had been completely disarranged.

He saw himself crossing a rice paddy and signaling his first squad to follow. There was the familiar whistle of an approaching shell and he flattened himself. When he looked up, the three men who had been carrying the machine gun lay sprawled in the open field. He ran back but they were past help. In the awkward attitudes of death, they looked like small boys who had flung themselves down to cry over some little sorrow. He wondered at the brute chance that chose them and left him alive.

He saw again the still body of one of the enemy collapsed against the wall of a trench with his head thrown back. The man was obviously dead, but in a moment of childish bravado he lifted his carbine and fired a bullet through the throat. The body did not move, and the high-cheekboned Oriental face continued lost in its impenetrable dream. A thin fountain of dark blood sprang from the hole in the throat and spilled down over the wrinkled uniform.

He stood staring and ashamed, feeling that he had wantonly violated the defenseless dead. One of his men walked past him and stood over the corpse. Casually and with a half smile he swung his rifle butt against the head, which wobbled from side to side under the impact. Jocularly, as if death were an intimate joke they shared together, his man addressed the corpse. "You old son of a bitch," he said, and there was a note of admiration in the remark.

He remembered standing behind a tank trying to direct its fire. A great bull whip seemed to crack by his ears and he fell to the ground as if some enormous hand had jerked him roughly by the shirt front. Scrambling to cover, he ripped open his dungaree jacket and found only a small welt. With resignation, for he understood that he could not continue to escape, he climbed to his feet. The bullet had torn through his breast pocket and cut the tip of the cigar he carried there. Though his fingers trembled, he lit the cigar with a melodramatic gesture and pretended a courage that he did not feel.

The day came crowding back. Again he was lying beside Everett, the youngest man in his platoon, under the remorseless sun. The boy had been shot through the abdomen and chest. A medical corpsman joined him and together they attempted to stop the flow of blood. Because of the continuous enemy fire, they had to keep close to the ground while they wound the bandage around the body. The flies gathered. The boy's head arched backward. His mouth was wide-open, gasping for air. Both the lieutenant and the corpsman knew in their hearts that there was no hope for the wounded man, but they tightened the bandages mechanically, as one might shut a house at evening to keep the night out.

"I've got to leave," he said to the corpsman, who kept waving the flies away with one hand while he felt the failing pulse in the boy's wrist. "Has he got any chance?"

"Always a chance, Lieutenant," was the cheerful reply. "Now if we had him on a good clean operating table we'd bring him round in no time." The corpsman smoothed the hair back from the wet forehead with a tender gesture. Then, realizing there was no operating table and no need for professional optimism, he shook his head wordlessly and finally added, "I'll keep the flies away. They bother him."

When some time later the lieutenant returned, the corpsman had gone to other duties and Everett lay dead and alone, the bandages dark with his blood. He had liked Everett best of all his men, and because of the boy's youthfulness felt particularly responsible for him. He remembered a letter he'd had to censor, which Everett had written to his mother just before the landing. It was full of hope and assurances that there was no need to worry. Now the body was covered with flies and already he thought he could detect the odor of decay. He caught the slight form under the armpits and dragged it to where a low bush cast a dark pool of shade. The feet, dragging limply, left two furrows in the sandy soil. Opening the pack, he took out the poncho and wrapped it carefully around the body, and stuck the rifle, bayonet first, into the earth as a marker for the burial detail.

Out on the oil-smooth sea the battleships and transports stood silhouetted against the burning sky. As he stared at them, he was surprised to find his vision blurred with tears. An unreasoning indignation shook him against all who had placed Everett where he lay. For the frightened enemy that shot Everett and was probably already dead he had pity. "But I wish," he thought, "that all those in power, countrymen and enemy alike, who decided for war, all those who profit by it, lay dead with their wealth and their honors and that Everett stood upright again with his life before him."

3

Then the present claimed him. His friend was shaking him gently by the shoulder and whispering, "Listen." The rain had stopped but the earth still smelled of it. Then he heard. Overhead there was the beating of tremendous wings. He twisted quickly onto his belly and pressed his face into the dirt as the night's stillness exploded. The shell landed well to their rear. Then, like pond water gradually rearranging itself after it has been disturbed, the fragments of silence fell back into place.

Quickly he buckled on his helmet. He listened. Sharp and distinct came the sound for which he waited. It was the crack of a gun, but the pitch was higher than that of the destroyer's and the sound came from inland. Slowly he counted the seconds before the shell reached them.

Then again the great wings beat overhead, only this time louder and more insistently. "The angel of death passing," he thought. The shell crashed to their rear still, but closer.

"Goddamn them, George. They're walking the stuff in on us."

"Must have somebody spotting for them right near," was the almost inaudible reply.

Because the unknown and imagined were more terrible than the known, he found relief in the certainty that the enemy's plans were no longer a total mystery. After adjusting their artillery fire onto the thinly defended line with a single gun, they obviously intended to open a barrage with all their batteries and probably follow it closely with a banzai charge.

The distant gun fired once again. The enforced inaction became almost intolerable. They must cower in their holes while the invisible enemy deliberately found the mathematical formula for their destruction. Each explosion closer than the last was like the footfalls of some enormous beast. The shell crashed in front of them this time instead of behind. The trap was set. In order to spring it the enemy gunners had only to split the difference between the range settings on the last two shots.

"Bracketed," George said.

It did not enter his head to pray. His mind was washed vacant by fear, and long fits of trembling ran through his body as he clutched the wet earth. The enemy batteries opened fire simultaneously and sent their shells curving through the night. Enough presence of mind remained for him to raise himself just off the ground with his elbows and toes in order to avoid the dangerous shock of a near miss.

The barrage fell on them. It ripped and plowed the earth into smoking craters and lit the night with the hot flash of the explosions. The deep roar of the shell bursts mingled with the high, despairing wail of jagged splinters of steel flung at random against the night. Indiscriminately the shells dropped.

A near miss erupted in a geyser of flame and sound close to their hole. His head rang with the concussion, and the fine earth sifted down over their bodies. The stinging smell of the high explosives lingered in his nostrils for a moment to remind him how tenuous was his hold on life. The casual purposelessness of the destruction appalled him. One moment you lived and the next you were snuffed out like an insect—no courage, no skill, no strength, could make one iota of difference. He pinned his faith on the narrowness of their small hole and endured, helpless and insignificant.

As suddenly as it had begun the barrage lifted. Softly he worked the bolt of his weapon back and forth to assure himself it was ready. "If they're going to come, they'll come now," he thought. By contrast the silence was more profound than ever and stretched like a precarious bridge from minute to minute, until the beating of his heart seemed to fill the world. The darkness pressed down on him, and the air itself seemed too thick to breathe. Tightening his grip on the weapon, he noticed that his hand was wet and slipped along the smooth wood of the stock.

"What in hell are they waiting for?" his friend murmured.

He did not answer. With a detachment that astonished him, he found himself suddenly able to look down on the spectacle as if he were no longer involved in it. On the one side, he saw his countrymen lying in their scooped-out holes with their backs to the sea, each one shivering with fright yet determined to die bravely. On the other, the poor peasantry from which the enemy recruited his soldiers were being herded into position like cattle, to be driven in a headlong charge against the guns. For a moment it appeared impossible to him that what was about to take place could actually occur. Adult human beings of the civilized world did not slaughter one another. There must be some mistake which could be corrected before it was too late.

What if he should get out of his hole and explain the matter reasonably to both sides? "Fellow human beings," he would begin. "There are very few of us here who in private life would kill a man for any reason whatever. The fact that guns have been placed in our hands and some of us wear one uniform and some another is no excuse for the mass murder we are about to commit. There are differences between us, I know, but none of them worth the death of one man. Most of us are not here by our own choice. We were taken from our peaceful lives and told to fight for reasons we cannot understand. Surely we have far more in common than that which temporarily separates us. Fathers, go back to your children, who are in need of you. Husbands, go back to your young wives, who cry in the night and count the anxious days. Farmers, return to your fields, where the grain rots and the house slides into ruin. The only certain fruit of this insanity will be the rotting bodies upon which the sun will impartially shine tomorrow. Let us throw down these guns that we hate. With the morning, we shall go on together and in charity and hope build a new life and a new world."

4

A single rifle shot interrupted his imaginary eloquence. "What a fool I am!" he thought. Suspended in that last moment when the whole black wall of the night seemed a dam about to break and engulf him, he felt utterly helpless. All the events of the past seemed to have marched inevitably toward this point in time and space, where he lay shivering between an implacable enemy and the indifferent sea. To object or to struggle was like shouting into a big wind that tears the words from the corners of one's mouth before even oneself can hear them. He, his friend, his countrymen, the enemy, were all dying leaves cast on the black waters of some mysterious river. Even now the current ran faster and the leaves whirled toward the dark lip of destruction.

The echoes of the rifle shot were lost now, and the wave of silence mounted and hung poised. Catching his tongue between his teeth, he held himself rigid to prevent the trembling. Then, at last, the night was fulfilled, and the listeners had their reward. A long-drawn-out cry of furious exultation rose from the line of jungle growth, wavered, then rose higher in barbaric triumph.

"Now," his friend breathed.

A crescendo of rifle fire swept down the line in answer. The steady rattle of machine guns sounded in his ears. Rocked by conflicting emotions, hoping all, fearing all, confused by the roar of sound, he knew nothing but that he must defend himself. An illuminating shell burst. In its brief light he could make out figures stooped and running. Smoke swirled from his machine guns and obscured the scene with monstrous shapes. Flame from the muzzles leaped against the dark. Holding his weapon ready, he could find nothing to shoot at. The strange foreign voices, high with excitement, seemed all about him.

A bullet snapped overhead. He ducked instinctively. Nearby, a man screamed in the universal language of pain and he could not tell if it was friend or enemy. All human thought and emotion withered and died. Animal-like, he crouched, panting. Like a cornered beast run to earth at last, he awaited the fierce hunters. He could hear them at their savage work, uttering harsh, short cries of triumph, and he imagined them plunging the long bayonets through the twisting bodies of his companions. He could see nothing.

Then a voice began shouting, running the words together in an incomprehensible stream of speech. The firing faded to sporadic rifle shots.

"They're falling back," whispered his friend incredulously.

It was true. The high tide of the attack had rolled to the edge of the foxholes, wavered while a few grappled hand to hand, and then drifted back into the dark. In the battalion combat report long afterward it would read, "In the Battalion's first night ashore, C Company repelled a local counterattack in its sector and suffered minor casualties." For him, there had been such noise, confusion, and terror that he knew nothing for certain except that by some miracle he survived. He had not fired a shot. Gradually the tension left his limbs and he was aware again, almost gratefully, of physical discomforts, the wet clothes and the mud. He would have been willing to believe the attack a fevered nightmare if it had not left behind it appalling evidence. The cries of the wounded rose in supplication or diminished to low continuous moans of incoherent agony.

His watch showed half past one, and his friend shook his head in disbelief. Settling himself on his back again he could feel his heart still pounding. It seemed longer than ever to the dawn. The enemy might well attempt another mass attack, and the danger of infiltration was continuous. Looking up into the apex of the night, he noticed that the clouds were thinning and that a few stars shone with a cold, implacable brilliance. Full of a sweet regret, gentler times came back to him when in another land the stars had seemed close and warm. Now it appeared as far to that land as it was to the stars, and as improbable a journey.

5

Abruptly, a heavy object bounced in the hole and rested against his right leg. It lay there and gave off a soft hissing sound. Though he moved with all the speed in his body, he felt in a dreamlike trance and seemed to stretch out his hand as a sleepwalker toward the object. His fingers closed around the corrugated iron surface of a grenade, and he knew that it was his own death that he held in his hand. His conscious mind seemed to be watching his body from a great distance as with tantalizing slowness his arm raised and threw the grenade into the dark. In mid-flight it exploded and the fragments whispered overhead. Another bounced on the edge of the hole and rolled in. He reached for it tentatively, as a child reaches out to touch an unfamiliar object.

A great club smashed him in the face. A light grew in his brain to agonizing brightness and then exploded in a roar of sound that was itself like a physical blow. He fell backward and an iron door clashed shut against his eyes.

He cried aloud once, as if through the sound the pain that filled him might find an outlet to overflow and diminish. Once more a long, rising moan was drawn from him and he lifted his hands in a futile gesture as though to rip away the mask of agony that clung to his face. Then, even in that extremity, the will to survive asserted itself. Through the fire that seemed to consume him, the knowledge that the enemy must be near-by made him stifle the scream that rose in his throat. If he kept quiet they might leave him for dead, and that was his only hope.

There was no time yet to wonder how badly he had been hurt. Like a poor swimmer, he struggled through the successive waves of pain that crashed over him. There would be a respite and then, again, he would be engulfed, until the dim light of consciousness almost went out. He pressed his hands to his temples, as if to hold his disintegrating being together by mere physical effort. His breath came chokingly. He allowed his head to fall to one side and felt the warm blood stream down his neck. There were fragments of teeth in his mouth and he let the blood wash them away.

It did not seem possible that anyone could have done this to him without reason. In a world on the edge of consciousness, he forgot the war and kept thinking that there must be some personal, individual explanation for what had happened. Over and over he repeated to himself, "Why have they done this to me? Why have they done this to me? What have I done? What have I done?" Like an innocent man convicted of some crime, he went on incoherently protesting his innocence, as if hoping that heaven itself might intervene to right so deep a wrong.

At last he became calmer. Hesitantly, he set out to assess the damage done his body. The pain was worst in his face, but to investigate it was more than he yet dared. His right arm moved with difficulty, and blood slipped down his shoulder. It seemed that his ears were stuffed with cotton or that he stood at the end of a long corridor to which the sounds of the outside world barely penetrated.

From a great distance he heard a heavy thud on the ground, as of a fist pounded into the earth. There was another even heavier, followed by silence. He attempted to form the name of his friend with his lips. "George," he tried to whisper, but no sound came. He could see nothing, but in the loneliness of his pain reached out his hand. It seemed that a gradually widening expanse of darkness separated him from everything in the world, but that if he could only make contact with his friend it would be easy to find the way back. His fingers touched a dungaree jacket and felt the warm body beneath it. His hand moved upward, until suddenly he withdrew it. There was no need to search further.

A flood of the kindest memories obliterated momentarily the knowledge of his own misfortune. The empty body beside him had housed the bravest and the simplest heart. Between them there had been an unspoken trust and the complete confidence that comes only after many dangers shared together. If he had met him years later he would have had to say simply, "George." They would have shaken hands and the years between would have been nothing at all. Now, cold and impassable, stronger than time, stood death, and a hopeless, irremediable sense of loss flowed through him. The noise that at first had attracted his attention must have been the last despairing movement of his friend. Gently, he wiped the blood from his hand on his trouser leg. A long spasm of pain recalled him to his own condition.

Gratefully, he noticed that the edge of the pain was dulled. It continued to flow through his body, but his conscious self seemed to be slightly removed from it. The occasional rifle shots appeared to come from further and further away. His right arm had lost almost all power of movement. With care, he rested it across his stomach. While sufficient strength remained, he determined to know the extent of the damage done his face. Truth was never more terrible than at that moment when, fearfully, he raised his left hand to trace the contours of his personal disaster. As delicately as a blind man touches the features of one he loves, he ran his fingers over the lineaments of the face he did not know. Though there was considerable blood, the bones of his chin and nose seemed intact.

Then at last there was no choice. The fear whose existence he had refused to admit grew monstrous and possessed his mind. Tightly he cupped his hand, without touching the eye itself, over his left eye and suddenly withdrew it. He repeated the process with the other eye. There was no change in the even texture of the dark. It remained impenetrable, unrelieved by the slightest glimmer of starlight. One hope remained and he clung to it as the condemned believe to the last in the hope of pardon. It might be that the clouds had returned and that the complete blackness was not his alone, but shared by all. There was a way of finding out. For a moment he hesitated, and then with cold fingers touched his left eye.

There was no eye there, only a jelly-like substance peculiarly sensitive to the touch.

A long sigh escaped his lips. The evidence was undeniable and the sentence pronounced. He did not care to investigate the other eye. Even the idea of touching again that useless jelly revolted him. With slow reluctance his mind accepted the full meaning of his loss. The emotional portion of his being continually revolted against the real event and kept asserting the reality of a world where such things do not happen. It was an almost irresistible temptation to reject the whole experience as an illusion. He felt that he would almost welcome madness if it could save him from his empty tomorrows. But little by little his reason forced him to understand.

"Blind," he whispered at last. "Oh, my God, my God." It was not a prayer so much as the expression of the bitterest despair. In all its poverty his life as it would be appeared before him. All other things, he felt—the mutilation of his face, the loss of his limbs—would have been endurable, but not this: the dark dragging hours, the mocking blackness of his nights, the loneliness of a world where people are only voices which if beautiful are more bitter to hear, the unassuageable regret provoked by every memory of the lighted past, the cheerful self-sacrifice of kind relations to goad the sense of his own parasitic uselessness, and always the mind growing more deformed in its crippling attempts to escape the dark of prison.

6

The memory returned of how as a boy he had almost drowned. It seemed that again he struggled upward through the black water. An illusory hope filled him that he could break the confines of the dark that pressed down on him as the ocean had so long before, but the excitement passed quickly. Above this ocean no sunlight flashed on white waves. It was infinite, and extended in blank perspective from that moment to the day of his death, when, he thought, one form of eternal night would be exchanged for another devoid of anguish and regret. Behind the sightless eyes, his mind would burn down like a fire in a room the guests have left until, mercifully, darkness was all.

There was nothing in those weary years that he wished to have, nothing for which he cared to wait. He felt a strange and brotherly companionship with the dead. The fact that such friends as he had known were gone seemed a warm assurance that death could be no terrible disaster. Their presence in that other world into which he drifted lent it a familiarity that the world of the living lacked, and took all fear from the journey he was about to make. Deliberately, he felt for his weapon.

He could not find the gun. Perhaps the explosion had blown it out of reach. The difficulty he had finding it allowed him a moment of indecision. What a spectacle he would make in the morning! The others who had died had done so bravely in the performance of what they had considered to be their duty. Death crowned their boyish honor, but would remain his shame, for he perceived well enough that he wished to die because he could not endure the pain and feared the dark years to come. He guessed that many during the long war had endured a life more unbearable than his. If they had not been happy, they had been admirable by the courage that they brought to their misfortune, and the knowledge of his own weakness was bitter.

A solitary, stubborn pride refused him the oblivion for which he longed, just as so often before, far more than any fear of social disgrace, it had forced upon him the consistent series of decisions that led inevitably to where he lay. Why did he enlist in so dangerous a service? Why did he refuse the job with the artillery or with the regimental staff, where one could afford to hope? Asking himself these questions, he knew there was no logical answer.

Certainly he had always expected this, or something like it. Not because he believed the war was fought for any cause worth dying for. Rather, he saw the war clearly as the finished product of universal ignorance, avarice, and brutality. A little out of adolescent vanity, but more because he had failed to become a conscientious objector, as he ought to have done, he chose to accept the consequences in an effort to redeem by personal valor a lost consistency of purpose. From the monotony and occasional violence, he had saved only his courage intact, and now he stood to lose it in a final ignominious act. Giving up his search for the weapon, he accepted his dark fate.

7

There was no way to tell the passage of time. It might have been hours or minutes since he had been hit. Whenever he tried to move his right arm the blood would start running again. Body and mind seemed to be drifting further apart. It was not the pleasant sensation of slipping gradually off to sleep. He seemed to fight the slow effect of a drug that paralyzed his limbs but left his mind active.

Occasionally he would test himself by raising his left arm. It became heavier, and the translation of wish into action grew more difficult. All sounds reached him from very far away, as if he were listening on a faulty telephone connection. Like one dying of cold, he abandoned himself to the slow change that was taking place, and hoped that death would not be too long in coming. He was sure now that he was dying, and was grateful that nature would accomplish what he had hesitated to do himself.

In the certainty that he would soon leave the world, he looked down from a great height and was glad that he was done with it. With a new severity, he contemplated the few short years of his life to discover some strand of meaning running through the trivial sequence of days and nights stretching back to the earliest memory. There was nothing in those transient joys to interest him, and even the moments of love or insight that he had once valued seemed entirely inconsequential when weighed against the vast extent of the descending night. Life seemed so poor a thing that he smiled to himself at having feared to lose it.

There was no hatred in his heart against anyone, but rather pity. He considered the shortness of man's days, the pointlessness of his best hopes in comparison with the certainty and conclusiveness of death, and could see him only as a poor creature struggling for a moment above a forever escaping stream of time that seemed to run nowhere. It would have been better for man, he felt, if he had been given no trace of gentleness, no desire for goodness, no capacity for love. Those qualities were all he valued, but he could see they were the pleasant illusions of children. With them men hoped, struggled pitifully, and were totally defeated by an alien universe in which they wandered as unwanted strangers. Without them, an animal, man might happily eat, reproduce, and die, one with what is.

Above him he imagined the imperturbable stars swinging on their infinite wanderings to God knows what final destination, and the knowledge of how slight a ripple there would be when he slipped beneath the surface of reality reconciled him easily to oblivion. Part of a prayer from his schooldays returned: "When the shadows lengthen and the evening comes and the busy world is hushed, and the fever of life is over, and our work is done, then in thy great mercy, O Lord, grant us a safe lodging and peace at the last." A safe lodging he would have as his body decayed to feed the rich jungle growth, and his mind the peace of nothingness as its precarious balance dissolved like a soap bubble into air.

Without hope or fear, he waited for death. It was a long time later, he guessed, when he felt a tear run down his cheek. Where his right eye should be there was a smarting itch that made him wish to rub it.

Surprise wakened him from the dreamy state into which he had fallen. There must be more of his right eye left intact than he thought. In the depths of his consciousness stirred an indefinite hope. He tried to work the lid but there was no movement. The beating of his heart echoed the expectation he hardly dared admit. Starting to raise his arm he let it drop. What difference could it make? Bereft of all desire and convinced of the futility of existence, he had no cause now to disturb that profound indifference. It was his strength. Hope was weakness and could bring only a vain regret and the despair he had renounced. Reasonably he knew all this, but it did not stem the rising flow of excitement.

With gentle, inquiring fingers he touched the tissues of the right eye. It was swollen shut, but beneath the dried blood on the lid he could feel the rounded form of the eyeball. Hardly aware of the pain, he forced the lid open roughly and searched the blackness above him for a sign. Gone was all indifference. Light was life, and the possibility of hope both intoxicated and appalled. All that he was, hung poised in dreadful suspense on the frail miracle he awaited.

Then down the long corridor of the night it swam into his vision. Out of focus, it trembled for a moment hazily, and then burned steady and unwinking. Fearing that he might have created it out of the intensity of his wish, he let his lid close and then forced it open again. The star still lay in the now soft and friendly dark. It flooded his being like the summer sun. He saw it as the window to Hope. Another appeared, and another, until the whole tropic sky seemed ablaze with an unbearable glory. Joyful tears rose in his heart. Gently, he permitted the torn lid to shut. Warm on his cheek and salty in his mouth were the tears of his salvation.

Mateo Falcone

PROSPER MÉRIMÉE

Mateo Falcone moves quietly, almost coldly toward the final, chilling act of this story, propelled by primitive loyalties into what he feels every father must do when the terrible time has come.

Few stories have the power of "Mateo Falcone" to hold the reader in their grip almost against his will. He can struggle against the central thesis, but he succumbs at last to the elemental force of the characters and setting.

While Mérimée's literary contemporaries were still wedded to ornate, heavy prose, he was writing in a lean, hard, supple style. In his spare laconic descriptions and dialogue, his unflinching, unsentimental treatment of life as he saw it, there are remarkably vivid foreshadowings of Hemingway, Camus, and other moderns. In "Mateo Falcone," Mérimée is at his best, dealing with simple people reflected against a wild landscape and an unrelenting social system.

PROSPER MÉRIMÉE (1803–1870), accomplished French man of letters, historian, and linguist, owes his reputation largely to his nouvelles (long short stories), the most famous of which is Carmen, the source of Bizet's opera

*of the same name. Mérimée's stylistic objectivity and his
psychological penetration had a marked effect on the course
and form of the short story in France. "Mateo Falcone"
is universally acknowledged to be one of the world's great
short stories.*

Mateo Falcone

Coming out of Porto-Vecchio, and turning northwest toward the interior of the island, the ground rises somewhat
rapidly, and, after a three hours' walk along winding
paths, blocked by huge rocky boulders, and sometimes
cut by ravines, you come to the edge of a wide *mâquis.*
The *mâquis,* or high plateau, is the home of the Corsican
shepherds and of all those who wish to escape the police.
I would have you understand that the Corsican peasant
sets fire to a stretch of woodland to save himself the
trouble of manuring his fields. If the flames spread further
than they should, so much the worse. In any case, he is
sure of a good crop if he sows on this ground, which has
been fertilized by the ashes of the trees which grew on it.
When the corn has been harvested, they leave the straw,
because it takes too much time to gather it up. The roots
of the burned trees, which have been left in the ground
undamaged, put forth very thick shoots in the following
spring, and these shoots, before many years, attain a
height of seven or eight feet. It is this sort of undergrowth which is called a *mâquis.* It is composed of all
sorts of trees and shrubs mingled and tangled every
whichway. A man has to hew his way through with an
axe, and there are *mâquis* so thick and tangled that even
wild rams cannot penetrate them.

If you have killed a man, go into the *mâquis* of Porto-
Vecchio with a good gun and powder and shot. You will
live there quite safely, but don't forget to bring along a
brown cloak and hood for your blanket and mattress.
The shepherds will give you milk, cheese, and chestnuts,
and you need not trouble your head about the law or

the dead man's relatives, except when you are compelled to go down into the town to renew your ammunition.

When I was in Corsica in 18—, Mateo Falcone's house stood half a league away from the *mâquis*. He was a fairly rich man for that country. He lived like a lord, that is to say, without toil, on the produce of his flocks, which the nomadic shepherds pastured here and there on the mountains. When I saw him, two years later than the incident which I am about to relate, he did not seem to be more than fifty years of age.

Picture a small, sturdy man, with jet-black curly hair, a Roman nose, thin lips, large piercing eyes, and a weather-beaten complexion. His skill as a marksman was extraordinary, even in this country, where everyone is a good shot. For instance, Mateo would never fire on a wild ram with small shot, but at a hundred and twenty paces he would bring it down with a bullet in its head or its shoulder, just as he fancied. He used his rifle at night as easily as in the daytime, and I was given the following illustration of his skill, which may seem incredible, perhaps, to those who have never travelled in Corsica. He placed a lighted candle behind a piece of transparent paper as big as a plate, and aimed at it from eighty paces away. He extinguished the candle, and a moment later in utter darkness, fired and pierced the paper three times out of four.

With this extraordinary skill Mateo Falcone had gained a great reputation. He was said to be a good friend and a dangerous enemy. Obliging and charitable, he lived at peace with all his neighbors around Porto-Vecchio. But they said of him that once, at Corte, whence he had brought home his wife, he had quickly freed himself of a rival reputed to be as fearful in war as in love. At any rate, people gave Mateo the credit for a certain shot which had surprised his rival shaving in front of a small mirror hung up in his window. The matter was hushed up and Mateo married the girl. His wife Giuseppa presented him at first, to his fury, with three daughters, but at last came a son whom he christened Fortunato, the hope of the family and the heir to its name. The girls were married off satisfactorily. At a pinch their father could count on the daggers and rifles of his sons-in-law.

The son was only ten years old, but already gave promise for the future.

One autumn day, Mateo and his wife set forth to visit one of his flocks in a clearing on the *mâquis*. Little Fortunato wanted to come along, but the clearing was too far off, and moreover, someone had to stay to look after the house. His father refused to take him. We shall see that he was sorry for this afterwards.

He had been gone several hours, and little Fortunato lay stretched out quietly in the sunshine, gazing at the blue mountains, and thinking that next Sunday he would be going to town to have dinner with his uncle, the magistrate, when he was suddenly startled by a rifle shot. He rose and turned toward the side of the plain whence the sound had come. Other shots followed, fired at irregular intervals, and they sounded nearer and nearer, till finally, he saw a man on the path which led from the plain up to Mateo's house. He wore a mountaineer's peaked cap, had a beard, and was clad in rags. He dragged himself along with difficulty, leaning on his gun. He had just been shot in the thigh. The man was an outlaw from justice, who, having set out at nightfall to buy ammunition in the town, had fallen on the way into an ambuscade of Corsican gendarmes. After a vigorous defense, he had succeeded in making his escape, but the gendarmes had pursued him closely and fired at him from rock to rock. He had been just ahead of the soldiers, and his wound made it impossible for him to reach the *mâquis* without being captured.

He came up to Fortunato and asked:

"Are you Mateo Falcone's son?"

"Yes, I am."

"I'm Gianetto Sanpiero. The yellow necks are after me. Hide me, for I can go no farther."

"But what will my father say, if I hide you without his permission?"

"He will say that you did the right thing."

"How can I be sure of that?"

"Quick! Hide me! Here they come!"

"Wait till my father comes back."

"How the devil can I wait? They'll be here in five minutes. Come now, hide me, or I shall kill you."

Fortunato replied as cool as a cucumber:

"Your rifle is not loaded, and there are no cartridges in your pouch."

"I have my stiletto."

"But can you run as fast as I can?"

He bounded out of the man's reach.

"You are no son of Mateo Falcone. Will you let me be captured in front of his house?"

The child seemed touched.

"What will you give me if I hide you?" he said, coming nearer to him.

The fugitive felt in a leather wallet that hung from his belt, and took out a five-franc piece which he had been saving, no doubt, to buy powder. Fortunato smiled when he saw the piece of silver. He snatched it and said to Gianetto:

"Have no fear."

He made a large hole at once in a haystack beside the house. Gianetto huddled down in it, and the boy covered him up so as to leave a little breathing space, and yet so that no one could possibly suspect that a man was hidden there. He showed his ingenious wild cunning by another trick. He fetched a cat and her kittens and put them on top of the haystack, so that anyone who passed would think that it had not been disturbed for a long time. Then he noticed some bloodstains on the path in front of the house and covered them over carefully with dust. When he had finished, he lay down again in the sun looking as calm as ever.

A few minutes later, six men in brown uniforms with yellow collars, led by an adjutant, stopped in front of Mateo's door. The adjutant was a distant cousin of Falcone. (You know that degrees of kindred are traced farther in Corsica than anywhere else.) His name was Tiodoro Gamba. He was an energetic man, much feared by the outlaws, many of whom he had already hunted down.

"Good morning, little cousin," he said, accosting Fortunato. "How you have grown! Did you see a man go by just now?"

"Oh, I'm not as tall as you are yet, cousin," replied the child with an innocent smile.

"It won't take long. But, tell me, didn't you see a man go by?"

"Did I see a man go by?"

"Yes, a man with a black velvet peaked cap and a waistcoat embroidered in red and yellow?"

"A man with a black velvet peaked cap, and a waistcoat embroidered in red and yellow?"

"Yes. Hurry up and answer me, and don't keep repeating my questions."

"Monsieur the Curé went by this morning on his horse Pierrot. He enquired after papa's health, and I said to him that——"

"You are making a fool of me, you limb of the devil! Tell me at once which way Gianetto went. He's the man we're looking for, and I'm sure he went this way."

"How do you know?"

"How do I know? I know you've seen him."

"Can I see people pass by in my sleep?"

"You weren't asleep, you rascal. Our shots would wake you."

"So you think, cousin, that your rifles make all that hullaballoo? My father's rifle makes much more noise."

"The devil take you, you little scamp. I am positive that you have seen Gianetto. Maybe you've hidden him, in fact. Here, boys, search the house and see if our man isn't there. He could only walk on one foot, and he has too much sense, the rascal, to try and reach the *mâquis* limping. Besides, the trail of blood stops here."

"What will papa say?" asked Fortunato. "What will he say when he discovers that his house has been searched during his absence?"

"Do you realize that I can make you change your tune, you rogue?" cried the adjutant, as he pulled his ear. "Perhaps you will have something more to say when I have thrashed you with the flat of my sword."

Fortunato laughed in derision.

"My father is Mateo Falcone," he said meaningly.

"Do you realize, you rascal, that I can haul you off to Corte or to Bastia? I shall put you in a dungeon on straw, with your feet in irons, and I'll have your head chopped off unless you tell me where to find Gianetto Sanpiero."

The child laughed again derisively at this silly threat. He repeated:

"My father is Mateo Falcone."

"Adjutant, don't get us into trouble with Mateo," muttered one of the gendarmes.

You could see that Gamba was embarrassed. He whispered to his men, who had already searched the house thoroughly. This was not a lengthy matter, for a Corsican hut consists of one square room. There is no furniture other than a table, benches, chests, cooking utensils, and weapons. Meanwhile, little Fortunato was stroking the cat, and seemed to take a malicious satisfaction in the discomfiture of his cousin and the gendarmes.

One gendarme approached the haystack. He looked at the cat and carelessly stuck a bayonet into the hay, shrugging his shoulders as if he thought the precaution absurd. Nothing stirred, and the child's face remained perfectly calm.

The adjutant and his men were desperate. They looked seriously out across the plain, as if they were inclined to go back home, when their leader, satisfied that threats would make no impression on Falcone's son, decided to make a final attempt, and see what coaxing and gifts might do.

"Little cousin," said he, "I can see that your eyes are open. You'll get on in life. But you are playing a risky game with me, and, if it weren't for the trouble it would give my cousin Mateo, God help me if I wouldn't carry you off with me."

"Nonsense!"

"But, when my cousin returns, I am going to tell him all about it, and he'll horsewhip you till the blood comes because you've been telling me lies."

"How do you know?"

"You'll see! . . . But see here! Be a good boy, and I'll give you a present."

"I advise you to go and look for Gianetto in the *mâquis,* cousin. If you hang about here much longer, it will take a cleverer man than you to catch him." The adjutant took a silver watch worth ten dollars out of his pocket. He noticed that little Fortunato's eyes sparkled as he looked at it, and he dangled the watch out to him at the end of its steel chain as he said:

"You scamp, wouldn't you like to have a watch like this hanging round your neck, and to strut up and down the streets of Porto-Vecchio as proud as a peacock? Folk would ask you what time it was and you would say, 'Look at my watch!' "

"When I'm a big boy, my uncle, the magistrate, will give me a watch."

"Yes, but your uncle's son has one already—not as fine as this, to be sure—but he is younger than you are."

The boy sighed.

"Well, would you like this watch, little cousin?"

Fortunato kept eyeing the watch out of the corner of his eye, like a cat that has been given a whole chicken to play with. It does not dare to pounce upon it, because it is afraid folk are laughing at it, but it turns its eyes away now and then so as to avoid temptation, and keeps licking its lips, as much as to say to its master: "What a cruel trick to play on a cat!" And yet Gamba seemed to be really offering him the watch. Fortunato did not hold out his hand, but said with a bitter smile:

"Why are you mocking me?"

"I swear that I am not mocking you. Only tell me where Gianetto is, and the watch is yours."

Fortunato smiled incredulously and fixed his dark eyes on those of the adjutant, trying to read them to see if the man could be trusted.

"May I lose my epaulettes," cried the adjutant, "if I do not give you the watch on this one condition! My men are witnesses, and I cannot back out of it."

As he spoke, he held the watch nearer and nearer till it almost touched the pale cheek of the boy, whose face clearly showed the struggle going on in his heart between greed and the claims of hospitality. His bare breast heaved till he was almost suffocated. Meanwhile the watch dangled and twisted and even touched the tip of his nose. Little by little, his right hand rose toward it, the tips of his fingers touched it, and the whole weight of it rested on his hand, although the adjutant still had it by the chain. . . . The face of the watch was blue. . . . The case was newly burnished. . . . It flamed like fire in the sun. . . . The temptation was too great.

Fortunato raised his left hand and pointed with his thumb over his shoulder to the haystack on which he was leaning. The adjutant understood him at once and let go the end of the chain. Fortunato felt that he was now sole possessor of the watch. He leaped away like a deer, and paused ten paces from the haystack which the gendarmes began to tumble over at once.

It was not long before they saw the hay begin to stir and a bleeding man came out with a stiletto in his hand. But when he tried to rise to his feet, his congealed wound prevented him from standing. He fell down. The adjutant flung himself upon his prey and wrested the stiletto from his grasp. He was speedily trussed up, in spite of his resistance, bound securely, and flung on the ground like a bundle of sticks. He turned his head toward Fortunato who had drawn near again.

"Son of . . . !" he exclaimed, more in contempt than in anger.

The child threw him the piece of silver, realizing that he no longer deserved it, but the fugitive paid no attention to it. He merely said quietly to the adjutant:

"My dear Gamba, I cannot walk. You must carry me to town."

"You were running as fast as a kid just now," retorted his captor, roughly. "But don't worry! I'm so glad to have caught you that I could carry you a league on my own back without feeling it. Anyhow, my friend, we'll make a litter for you out of branches and your cloak. We'll find horses at the farm at Crespoli."

"Very well," said the prisoner. "I suppose you will put a little straw on the litter to make it easier for me."

While the gendarmes were busy, some making a crude litter of chestnut boughs, and others dressing Gianetto's wound, Mateo Falcone and his wife suddenly appeared at a turn of the path which led from the *mâquis*. His wife came first, bowed low beneath the weight of a huge sack of chestnuts, while her husband strolled along, carrying a gun in one hand, and another slung over his shoulder. It is beneath a man's dignity to carry any other burden than his weapons.

As soon as he saw the soldiers, Mateo's first thought was that they must have come to arrest him. But there was no reason for it. He had no quarrel with the forces of law and order. He had an excellent reputation. He was "well thought of," as they say, but he was a Corsican, and a mountaineer, and there are very few Corsican mountaineers who, if they search their past sufficiently, cannot find some peccadillo, a rifle shot or a thrust with a stiletto or some other trifle. Mateo had a clearer conscience than most of his friends, for it was at least ten years since he had pointed a rifle at a man; but all the same it behooved him to be cautious, and he prepared to put up a good defense, if necessary.

"Wife," he said, "put down your sack and be on your guard."

She obeyed at once. He gave her the gun from his shoulder belt, as it seemed likely that it might be in his way. He cocked the other rifle, and advanced in a leisurely manner toward the house, skirting the trees beside the path, and ready, at the least sign of hostility, to throw himself behind the largest trunk and fire from cover. His wife followed close behind him, holding her loaded rifle and his cartridges. It was a good wife's duty, in case of trouble, to reload her husband's arms.

The adjutant, on his side, was much troubled at seeing Mateo advance upon him so with measured steps, pointing his rifle, and keeping his finger on the trigger.

"If it should happen," thought he, "that Gianetto turns out to be Mateo's relative or friend, and he wishes to defend him, two of his bullets will reach us as sure as a letter goes by post, and if he aims at me, in spite of our kinship . . . !"

In his perplexity, he put the best face he could on the matter, and went forward by himself to meet Mateo and tell him all that had happened, greeting him like an old friend. But the short distance between him and Mateo seemed fearfully long.

"Hello, there, old comrade!" he cried out. "How are you? I'm your cousin Gamba."

Mateo stood still and said not a word. As the other man spoke, he slowly raised the barrel of his rifle so that, by

the time the adjutant came up to him, it was pointing to
the sky.

"Good-day, brother," said the adjutant, holding out his
hand. "It's an age since I've see you."

"Good-day, brother."

"I just stopped by to pass the time of day with you and
cousin Pepa. We've had a long march to-day, but we can't
complain, for we've made a famous haul. We've just
caught Gianetto Sanpiero."

"Heaven be praised!" exclaimed Giuseppa. "He stole
one of our milch goats a week ago."

Gamba was delighted at her words.

"Poor devil!" said Mateo, "he was hungry."

"The chap fought like a lion," pursued the adjutant,
somewhat annoyed. "He killed one of my men, and as if
that were not enough, broke Corporal Chardon's arm; not
that it matters, he's only a Frenchman. . . . Then he hid
himself so cleverly that the devil himself couldn't find
him. If it hadn't been for my little cousin Fortunato, I
should never have found him."

"Fortunato?" cried Mateo.

"Fortunato?" echoed Giuseppa.

"Yes! Gianetto was hidden in your haystack over there,
but my little cousin soon showed up his tricks. I shall tell
his uncle, the magistrate, and he'll send him a fine present
as a reward. And both his name and yours shall be in the
report that I'm sending to the Public Prosecutor."

"Damn you!" muttered Mateo under his breath.

They had now rejoined the gendarmes. Gianetto was
already laid on his litter, and they were all ready to start.
When he saw Mateo in Gamba's company, he smiled
oddly; then, turning toward the door of the house, he spat
at the threshold.

"The house of a traitor!"

It was asking for death to call Falcone a traitor. A quick
stiletto thrust, and no need of a second, would have instantly wiped out the insult. But Mateo's only movement
was to put his hand to his head as if he were stunned.

Fortunato had gone into the house when he saw his
father coming. Presently he reappeared with a bowl of
milk, which he offered with downcast eyes to Gianetto.

"Keep away from me!" thundered the outlaw.

Then, turning to one of the gendarmes, he said:

"Comrade, will you give me a drink?"

The gendarme put the flask in his hand, and the outlaw drank the water given him by the man with whom he had just been exchanging rifle shots. Then he requested that his hands might be tied crossed on his breast instead of behind his back.

"I would rather," he said, "lie comfortably."

They gratified his request. Then, at a sign from the adjutant, saying good-bye to Mateo, who vouchsafed no answer, they set off quickly toward the plain.

Ten minutes passed before Mateo opened his mouth. The child looked uneasily, first at his mother, then at his father, who was leaning on his gun and gazing at him with an expression of concentrated fury.

"You begin well," said Mateo at last, in a calm voice, terrifying enough to those who knew the man.

"Father!" cried the boy, with tears in his eyes, coming nearer as if to throw himself at his father's knee.

"Out of my sight!" Mateo shouted.

The child stopped short a few paces away from his father, and sobbed.

Giuseppa approached him. She had just noticed the watch-chain hanging out of his shirt.

"Who gave you that watch?" she asked sternly.

"My cousin, the adjutant."

Falcone snatched the watch and flung it against a stone with such violence that it was shattered into a thousand fragments.

"Woman," he said, "is this a child of mine?"

Giuseppa's brown cheeks flushed brick red.

"What are you saying, Mateo? Do you realize to whom you are speaking?"

"Yes, perfectly well. This child is the first traitor in my family."

Fortunato redoubled his sobs and choking, and Falcone kept watching him like a hawk. At last he struck the ground with the butt of his rifle, then flung it across his shoulder, returned to the path which led toward the *mâquis,* and commanded Fortunato to follow him. The child obeyed.

Giuseppa ran after Mateo and clutched his arm.

"He is your son," she said in a trembling voice, fixing her dark eyes on those of her husband, as if to read all that was passing in his soul.

"Leave me," replied Mateo. "I am his father."

Giuseppa kissed her son and went back weeping into the house. She flung herself on her knees before an image of the Blessed Virgin and prayed fervently. Falcone walked about two hundred paces along the path, and went down a little ravine where he stopped. He tested the ground with the butt of his rifle, and found it soft and easy to dig. The spot seemed suitable for his purpose.

"Fortunato, go over to that big rock."

The boy did as he was told. He knelt down.

"Father, Father, do not kill me!"

"Say your prayers!" shouted Mateo in a terrible voice.

The boy, stammering and sobbing, recited the Our Father and the Apostles' Creed. The father said "Amen!" in a firm voice at the end of each prayer.

"Are those all the prayers you know?"

"I know the Hail Mary, too, and the Litany my aunt taught me, Father."

"It is long, but never mind."

The boy finished the Litany in a stifled voice.

"Have you finished?"

"Oh, Father, forgive me! Forgive me! I'll never do it again. I'll beg my cousin, the magistrate, ever so hard to pardon Gianetto!"

He kept beseeching his father. Mateo loaded his gun and took aim.

"God forgive you!" he said.

The boy made a desperate effort to rise and clasp his father's knees, but he had no time. Mateo fired and Fortunato fell stone-dead.

Without glancing at the body, Mateo returned to the house to fetch a spade with which to dig his son's grave. He had only gone a few steps along the path when he met Giuseppa, running, for she had been alarmed by the rifle shot.

"What have you done?" she cried.

"Justice!"

"Where is he?"

"In the ravine. I am going to bury him. He died a Christian. I shall have a Mass said for him. Send word to my son-in-law, Tiodoro Bianchi, that he is to come and live with us."

His Excellency

INDRO MONTANELLI

"His Excellency" is a story of Italian prisoners of war
during the last days of World War II. The events of "His
Excellency" are few and are told with great simplicity.
Bertoni, an Italian cardsharp, pretending to be what he is
not, becomes the heroic figure he has never been. In the
end he faces a crucial challenge to the role he has created
for himself.

*INDRO MONTANELLI (1909–   ) is a well-known
Italian novelist and short story writer. "His Excellency"
was made into a distinguished and absorbing motion picture directed by Roberto Rossellini.*

His Excellency

Translated by Uguccione Ranieri

There it is, lined up with the other sixty-four coffins from
the Fossoli concentration camp, and the crowd has

45

sprinkled it, like the others, with flowers. Among all these people gathered here in the silence of the Milan cathedral, surely I am not the only one to know. Yet there has been no protest. Truly, men are as lenient to the dead as they are harsh with the living. The coffin will now pass like the others between the reverent throngs, like the others it will be buried and, on June 22 of each year, will receive its quota of rhetoric spilled over the common grave. Fair enough. . . . Who are we to judge?

His Excellency, General Della Rovere, army corps commander, intimate friend of Badoglio's and "technical adviser" to General Alexander, was locked up by the Germans in the San Vittore prison of Milan in the spring of 1944 when the Allied armies were still fighting their slow way up the Italian peninsula. He had been captured near Genoa while trying to land at night from an Allied submarine to take command of the resistance movement in the north. A soldier to his finger tips, he had impressed even Franz, the German warder, who would stand at attention when addressing him and had gone so far as to have a cot placed in his cell. So the Italian guard, Ceraso, informed me as he passed my spy hole with a rose in a glass, picked expressly for His Excellency. Later Ceraso returned to say that the General wished to see me, and, letting me out, escorted me to his cell.

"Cavalry officer" was written all over those arched legs, that slight build, and aristocratic profile. Tight-corseted, he wore a monocle and false teeth, and the thought struck me of how convincing, after all, is our racial destiny. What else could a man like that become if not a general? With steely grace he could give an order and make it sound like a plea, and even now, weeks after his capture, his cheeks were clean-shaven, his trousers miraculously pressed, while one could almost detect on his polished shoes a pair of invisible spurs.

"Montanelli, I presume?" he said with a slight drawl, polishing his monocle without giving me his hand. "I already knew of your presence here before landing. Badoglio in person had informed me. His Majesty's Government is following your case with the utmost sympathy. Let it be understood, however, that the day you face the firing squad you will have done no more than your duty.

Please stand at ease." Only at these last words did I realize that I was standing heels joined, thumbs touching the seams of my trousers just as the drill book says. "We are all on temporary duty here, right?" he continued, cleaning the nail of one little finger with the nail of the other. "An officer is at all times merely on temporary duty, he is a *novio de la muerte,* as the Spaniards say, a bridegroom of death." He smiled at me, paced leisurely up and down the cell flexing his slim, arched legs; then, stopping again before me, cleaned and replaced his monocle. "We two are very near our wedding day," he continued. "My sentence has already been pronounced. And yours?"

"Not yet, sir," I answered almost mortified.

"It will be," he went on. "You will have the honor of being shot in the chest, I hear. Splendid. There is no better proof of your conduct under interrogation. The Germans are rough in obtaining confessions but chivalrous toward those who abstain. Good. Your orders are to continue. In case of torture, if you feel you must utter a name—I cast no doubt on your spiritual endurance, but there is a limit to the physical—utter mine. I have nothing to lose. Actually, I had nothing to hide even from my old friend, Marshal Kesselring, when he questioned me. I did, however, explain that I hardly expected the British submarine captain to be such a fool as to answer the decoy signals of a German patrol boat. 'You trust the English?' Kesselring smiled. 'Why not? We even trusted the Germans once,' I smiled back. 'Sorry!' he said, 'I have no choice but to shoot you.' 'No hard feelings,' I concluded. But to come back to your case: when you are up for questioning again, stick to your line. After all, we have such a simple duty left: to die like gentlemen. What is your indictment?"

I explained my case fully. His Excellency listened with his eyes to the ground like a confessor, nodding approbation from time to time.

"A clear case," he concluded. "Captured in the performance of duty. It's a soldier's death. They absolutely *must* shoot you in the chest. It's strictly regulations. Let me know how things develop. You can go now."

That was the first day in all the six months since my

arrest that I did not think of my wife locked in her cell
in another wing of the building. Toward evening I begged
Ceraso to sign me up for the barber the next day and in
the meanwhile to bring me a comb. And that night,
braving the cold, I took my trousers off before lying on my
plank and hung them on the window bars hoping they
would regain their shape.

On the following days, through my spy hole, I was
able to observe His Excellency in his cell just across from
mine. One by one, all the prisoners were called to report to
him, and all came. In theory, our wing, the dreaded
Fifth, was for "solitaries" and so it had been up till that
time, but the prestige of His Excellency was obviously so
great that the Italian warders felt they could stretch a
point. On entering, his guests would stand at attention,
even the Communists, and bow stiffly. Later, on leaving,
they would walk with a prouder carriage. Number 215,
who so often sobbed for his wife and children, after talking
with the General fell silent, and even when caught smoking by Franz took his lashes without a whimper. Ceraso
told me that almost all, after their talk, had asked, like
me, for the barber, a comb, and a little soap. Even the
warders now wore their caps straight and tried to speak
correct Italian. The wing had never been so quiet, and
when Müller came on inspection he praised the new discipline. For the first time he omitted calling us "anti-
Fascist dogs" and "dirty Badoglian traitors," confining
himself to an allusion to the "felonious King," at which
we all looked at the ceiling pretending not to hear, while
His Excellency, who was standing a little forward as be-
fitted his rank, turned deliberately on his heels and re-
entered his cell. Müller snorted, but said nothing.

One morning Colonel P. and Colonel F. were taken.
Asked if they had a last wish, they mentioned the General,
who received them on his threshold, and that was the only
time I ever saw him shake hands. Then, caressing with a
slow gesture his silvery hair and adjusting his monocle,
he smiled and said something to the two officers—something cordial and tender, I am sure. Suddenly, snapping
to attention and fixing them coldly in the eyes, he gave
them the military salute. P. and F. were pale as chalk,
but smiling, and never had they looked so much like

colonels as when they moved off, erect, with firm step, between the S.S. men. We heard later that they had both cried, "Long live the King" as they fell.

That same afternoon I was taken down for questioning, and Müller warned me that this was my last chance and that if I did not speak up, etc. . . . But I hardly heard, nor, though I kept my eyes glued to his, saw him. All I could see were the two pale faces of P. and F. and the marblelike face of His Excellency, and all I could hear was his drawling soft voice . . . *"novio de la muerte* . . . performance of duty . . . death on the field. . . ." Müller gave me up without torture after two hours. Even if he had tortured me, I believe I would not have uttered a word, not even the name of His Excellency, in front of whose cell, on my return, I begged Ceraso to let me stop.

Della Rovere was sitting on the edge of his cot. Putting down his book, he stared at me at length while I stood at attention. Then he said slowly: "Yes, indeed. I expected as much of you," and dismissed me with a gesture. But on the threshold he called me back. "Just a second!" and he rose to his feet. "There is a thing I still wish to say. A—uhm—difficult thing. I am, I wish to say, extremely satisfied with your conduct, Captain Montanelli. And I wish this good warder to listen well, for he will be our only surviving witness. Very, very satisfied. . . . A jolly good show, sir!" And that night, for the first time, I felt alone in the world, joyously alone with my beautiful bride, Death, forgetful of my wife and my mother, and for once my Country seemed to me a real and an important thing.

I never saw him again, but after the liberation I gathered the details of his end from one of the survivors of Fossoli.

His Excellency appeared very put out when suddenly, together with a crowd of other San Vittore inmates, he was packed into a boxcar train and shipped to the Fossoli concentration camp. During the journey he sat on the kit packs which his fellow prisoners had laid down as a seat for him and refused to rise even when Schultze came in for inspection. Schultze struck him, shrieking: *"Du bist ein Schwein, Bertoni!"* But the General found it superfluous to explain that he was not Bertoni, but Della Rovere, a corps commander, friend of Badoglio's and technical adviser to Alexander. Without a twitch he picked up his monocle, luckily unbroken, replaced it, and remained seated. Schultze went out cursing.

At Fossoli, His Excellency no longer enjoyed the little favors he was used to. He was placed in a common shed and put to work. His companions took turns in sparing him the more humiliating tasks like latrine duty, but never, of his own initiative, did he shirk a job, even though manual labor weighed heavily on him, for he was no longer young. Digging, or carrying bricks, often with a grimace of pain, he would keep a sharp eye open to see that no one gave a poor show, and at day's end he would reprimand those who needed it. To him, they were all officers and gentlemen, and such did they continue to feel under the flash of his monocle and the lash of his words. Desperately, heroically, he struggled to keep his nails spotless and his cheeks shaven. He never complained.

Neither then, nor later, was the motive for the June 22 massacre ever made clear. The order came from Milan, some said as a reprisal for something which had happened in Genoa. Lieutenant Dickermann read out the sixty-five names drawn by lot from those of the four hundred inmates lined up in a square. Among the first was the name Bertoni. No one stepped forward. "Bertoni!" roared Dickermann. "Ber-to-ni!" and he stared at the point where Della Rovere stood. Did Dickermann understand, or did he merely choose to humor a dying man? *"Gut, gut,"* he chuckled. "Della Rovere, *wie Sie wollen. . . ."* All held their breath as they watched His Excellency slip his monocle into place and take three slow steps forward. *"General* Della Rovere, please!" he corrected, taking his place by the other doomed men. With the nail of his right forefinger he began to clean the nail of his left—both marvelously steady.

The sixty-five were manacled, blindfolded, and pushed against the wall. Only His Excellency refused to have his eyes covered and was humored. Then the machine guns were set. His Excellency took a step forward. "Hold it! Stop!" cried Dickermann reaching for his revolver. His Excellency took another step. "Gentlemen!" he cried with a voice like a bugle. "In this supreme moment let our thoughts rise . . ." But Dickermann's "Fire!" and the opening crash of the guns cut him short. They all went down. But the General was the only one who did not squirm on the ground, and his monocle remained miraculously in its place. It was still on when they dropped him into the common trench, and he is still wearing it, I assume, there in his coffin.

That coffin which today, June 22, anniversary of the massacre, stands before me in the Milan cathedral, does not contain the body of the imaginary General Della Rovere—true enough! Merely the remains of the former jailbird Bertoni, a Genoese, by profession cardsharp and thief, who, when arrested by the Germans for some petty crime, offered to spy for them in prison by impersonating a non-existent general, and succeeded only too well. . . .

Does it really matter? Surely the Cardinal Archbishop did no wrong in blessing this body together with the others?

For, after all, Bertoni, the cardsharp, the thief, the spy, was indeed a general at the hour of death, and undoubtedly he died convinced that he was the friend of Badoglio's and "technical adviser" to Alexander. But for him, I would never have felt a hero for one night in my cell. . . . And P. and F. would not have walked to the firing squad as colonels should. . . . Because of him, those who lacked courage found it, and Number 215 stopped whimpering for his wife and children. . . .

Peace to his twisted soul.

A Summer's Reading

BERNARD MALAMUD

George Stoyonovich, the central character in "A Summer's Reading," is a high-school dropout. Everyone worries about him. Most people don't really understand him. Mr. Malamud does.

Mr. Malamud's deep compassion for and sensitive understanding of those who are "dogged by grief" illuminates for us George's rootless life and his troubled longings for what he once thought he would be. Malamud's muted understated style is ideally suited to the grayness of the characters and their environment.

BERNARD MALAMUD (1914–   ) was born in Brooklyn, where he has spent most of his life. His father was a storekeeper, "a good man." His mother, who died young, came from a theatrical family. Malamud's Brooklyn childhood was filled with those familiar experiences which, on looking back, he says gave him a sense of adventure and a "sense that one was a boy."

Malamud started on his writing career early, while he was still a student at Erasmus Hall High School in Brooklyn; his compositions were published in the school magazine. He graduated from the City College of New York in 1936 and received his M.A. at Columbia University in 1942. From 1949 to 1961, he taught at Oregon State University. Since 1961, he has taught creative writing at Bennington College.

Mr. Malamud's works include the novels The Assistant *(1957),* A New Life *(1961), and* The Fixer *(1967). The* Magic Barrel *(1958), a collection of his short stories, won the National Book Award.* Idiots First, *another collection of short stories, was published in 1963.*

The leitmotif of Malamud's stories and novels is a profound compassion and concern for people, for the human condition, for what one critic has characterized as "the holiness of life." "To me," says Malamud, "writing must be true; it must have emotional depth; it must be imaginative." His writing has all of these qualities.

A Summer's Reading

George Stoyonovich was a neighborhood boy who had quit high school on an impulse when he was sixteen, run out of patience, and though he was ashamed everytime he went looking for a job, when people asked him if he had finished and he had to say no, he never went back to school. This summer was a hard time for jobs and he had none. Having so much time on his hands, George thought of going to summer school, but the kids in his classes would be too young. He also considered registering in a night high school, only he didn't like the idea of the teachers always telling him what to do. He felt they had not respected him. The result was he stayed off the streets and in his room most of the day. He was close to twenty and had needs with the neighborhood girls, but no money to spend, and he couldn't get more than an occasional few cents because his father was poor, and his sister Sophie, who resembled George, a tall bony girl of twenty-three, earned very little and what she had she kept for herself. Their mother was dead, and Sophie had to take care of the house.

Very early in the morning George's father got up to go

to work in a fish market. Sophie left at about eight for her long ride in the subway to a cafeteria in the Bronx. George had his coffee by himself, then hung around in the house. When the house, a five-room railroad flat above a butcher store, got on his nerves he cleaned it up—mopped the floors with a wet mop and put things away. But most of the time he sat in his room. In the afternoons he listened to the ball game. Otherwise he had a couple of old copies of the World Almanac he had bought long ago, and he liked to read in them and also the magazines and newspapers that Sophie brought home, that had been left on the tables in the cafeteria. They were mostly picture magazines about movie stars and sports figures, also usually the *News* and *Mirror*. Sophie herself read whatever fell into her hands, although she sometimes read good books.

She once asked George what he did in his room all day and he said he read a lot too.

"Of what besides what I bring home? Do you ever read any worthwhile books?"

"Some," George answered, although he really didn't. He had tried to read a book or two that Sophie had in the house but found he was in no mood for them. Lately he couldn't stand made-up stories, they got on his nerves. He wished he had some hobby to work at—as a kid he was good in carpentry, but where could he work at it? Sometimes during the day he went for walks, but mostly he did his walking after the hot sun had gone down and it was cooler in the streets.

In the evening after supper George left the house and wandered in the neighborhood. During the sultry days some of the storekeepers and their wives sat in chairs on the thick, broken sidewalks in front of their shops, fanning themselves, and George walked past them and the guys hanging out on the candy store corner. A couple of them he had known his whole life, but nobody recognized each other. He had no place special to go, but generally, saving it till the last, he left the neighborhood and walked for blocks till he came to a darkly lit little park with benches and trees and an iron railing, giving it a feeling of privacy. He sat on a bench here, watching the leafy trees and the flowers blooming on the inside of the railing, thinking of a better life for himself. He thought of the jobs he had had since he had quit school—delivery boy, stock clerk, runner, lately working in a factory— and he was dissatisfied with all of them. He felt he would someday like to have a good job and live in a private house with a porch, on a street with trees. He wanted to have some dough in his pocket to buy things with, and a girl to go with, so as not to be so lonely, especially on Saturday nights. He wanted people to like and respect him. He thought about these things often but mostly when he was alone at night. Around midnight he got up and drifted back to his hot and stony neighborhood.

One time while on his walk George met Mr. Cattanzara coming home very late from work. He wondered if he was drunk but then could tell he wasn't. Mr. Cattanzara, a stocky, bald-headed man who worked in a change booth on an IRT station, lived on the next block after George's, above a shoe repair store. Nights, during the hot weather, he sat on his stoop in an undershirt, reading the *New York Times* in the light of the shoemaker's window. He read it from the first page to the last, then went up to sleep. And all the time he was reading the paper, his wife, a fat woman with a white face, leaned out of the window, gazing into the street, her thick white arms folded under her loose breast, on the window ledge.

Once in a while Mr. Cattanzara came home drunk, but it was a quiet drunk. He never made any trouble, only walked stiffly up the street and slowly climbed the stairs into the hall. Though drunk, he looked the same as always, except for his tight walk, the quietness, and that his eyes were wet. George liked Mr. Cattanzara because he remembered him giving him nickels to buy lemon ice with when he was a squirt. Mr. Cattanzara was a different type than those in the neighborhood. He asked different questions than the others when he met you, and he seemed to know what went on in all the newspapers. He read them, as his fat sick wife watched from the window.

"What are you doing with yourself this summer, George?" Mr. Cattanzara asked. "I see you walkin' around at nights."

George felt embarrassed. "I like to walk."

"What are you doin' in the day now?"

"Nothing much just right now. I'm waiting for a job." Since it shamed him to admit he wasn't working, George said, "I'm staying home—but I'm reading a lot to pick up my education."

Mr. Cattanzara looked interested. He mopped his hot face with a red handkerchief.

"What are you readin'?"

George hesitated, then said, "I got a list of books in the library once, and now I'm gonna read them this summer." He felt strange and a little unhappy saying this, but he wanted Mr. Cattanzara to respect him.

"How many books are there on it?"

"I never counted them. Maybe around a hundred."

Mr. Cattanzara whistled through his teeth.

"I figure if I did that," George went on earnestly, "it would help me in my education. I don't mean the kind they give you in high school. I want to know different things than they learn there, if you know what I mean."

The change maker nodded. "Still and all, one hundred books is a pretty big load for one summer."

"It might take longer."

"After you're finished with some, maybe you and I can shoot the breeze about them?" said Mr. Cattanzara.

"When I'm finished," George answered.

Mr. Cattanzara went home and George continued on his walk. After that, though he had the urge to, George did nothing different from usual. He still took his walks at night, ending up in the little park. But one evening the shoemaker on the next block stopped George to say he was a good boy, and George figured that Mr. Cattanzara had told him all about the books he was reading. From the shoemaker it must have gone down the street, because George saw a couple of people smiling kindly at him, though nobody spoke to him personally. He felt a little better around the neighborhood and liked it more, though not so much he would want to live in it forever. He had never exactly disliked the people in it, yet he had never liked them very much either. It was the fault of the neighborhood. To his surprise, George found out that his father and Sophie knew about his reading too. His father was too shy to say anything about it—he was never much of a talker in his whole life—but Sophie was softer to George, and she showed him in other ways she was proud of him.

As the summer went on George felt in a good mood about things. He cleaned the house every day, as a favor to Sophie, and he enjoyed the ball games more. Sophie gave him a buck a week allowance, and though it still wasn't enough and he had to use it carefully, it was a helluva lot better than just having two bits now and then. What he bought with the money—cigarettes mostly, an occasional beer or movie ticket—he got a big kick out of. Life wasn't so bad if you knew how to appreciate it. Occasionally he bought a paperback book from the news-stand, but he never got around to reading it, though he was glad to have a couple of books in his room. But he read thoroughly Sophie's magazines and newspapers. And at night was the most enjoyable time, because when he passed the storekeepers sitting outside their stores, he could tell they regarded him highly. He walked erect, and though he did not say much to them, or they to him, he could feel approval on all sides. A couple of nights he felt so good that he skipped the park at the end of the evening.

He just wandered in the neighborhood, where people had known him from the time he was a kid playing punchball whenever there was a game of it going; he wandered there, then came home and got undressed for bed, feeling fine.

For a few weeks he had talked only once with Mr. Cattanzara, and though the change maker had said nothing more about the books, asked no questions, his silence made George a little uneasy. For a while George didn't pass in front of Mr. Cattanzara's house anymore, until one night, forgetting himself, he approached it from a different direction than he usually did when he did. It was already past midnight. The street, except for one or two people, was deserted, and George was surprised when he saw Mr. Cattanzara still reading his newspaper by the light of the street lamp overhead. His impulse was to stop at the stoop and talk to him. He wasn't sure what he wanted to say, though he felt the words would come when he began to talk; but the more he thought about it, the more the idea scared him, and he decided he'd better not. He even considered beating it home by another street, but he was too near Mr. Cattanzara, and the change maker might see him as he ran, and get annoyed. So George unobtrusively crossed the street, trying to make it seem as if he had to look in a store window on the other side, which he did, and then went on, uncomfortable at what he was doing. He feared Mr. Cattanzara would glance up from his paper and call him a dirty rat for walking on the other side of the street, but all he did was sit there, sweating through his undershirt, his bald head shining in the dim light as he read his *Times,* and upstairs his fat wife leaned out of the window, seeming to read the paper along with him. George thought she would spy him and yell out to Mr. Cattanzara, but she never moved her eyes off her husband.

George made up his mind to stay away from the change maker until he had got some of his softback books read, but when he started them and saw they were mostly story books, he lost his interest and didn't bother to finish them. He lost his interest in reading other things too. Sophie's magazines and newspapers went unread. She saw them piling up on a chair in his room and asked why he was no longer looking at them, and George told her it was because of all the other reading he had to do. Sophie said she had guessed that was it. So for most of the day, George had the radio on, turning to music when he was sick of the human voice. He kept the house fairly neat, and Sophie said nothing on the days when he neglected it. She was still kind and gave him his extra buck, though things weren't so good for him as they had been before.

But they were good enough, considering. Also his night walks invariably picked him up, no matter how bad the day was. Then one night George saw Mr. Cattanzara coming down the street toward him. George was about to turn and run but he recognized from Mr. Cattanzara's walk that he was drunk, and if so, probably he would not even bother to notice him. So George kept on walking straight ahead until he came abreast of Mr. Cattanzara and though he felt wound up enough to pop into the sky, he was not surprised when Mr. Cattanzara passed him without a word, walking slowly, his face and body stiff. George drew a breath in relief at his narrow escape, when he heard his name called, and there stood Mr. Cattanzara at his elbow, smelling like the inside of a beer barrel. His eyes were sad as he gazed at George, and George felt so intensely uncomfortable he was tempted to shove the drunk aside and continue on his walk.

But he couldn't act that way to him, and, besides, Mr. Cattanzara took a nickel out of his pants pocket and handed it to him.

"Go buy yourself a lemon ice, Georgie."

"It's not that time anymore, Mr. Cattanzara," George said, "I'm a big guy now."

"No, you ain't," said Mr. Cattanzara, to which George made no reply he could think of.

"How are all your books comin' along now?" Mr. Cattanzara asked. Though he tried to stand steady, he swayed a little.

"Fine, I guess," said George, feeling the red crawling up his face.

"You ain't sure?" The change maker smiled slyly, a way George had never seen him smile.

"Sure I'm sure. They're fine."

Though his head swayed in little arcs, Mr. Cattanzara's eyes were steady. He had small blue eyes which could hurt if you looked at them too long.

"George," he said, "name me one book on that list that you read this summer, and I will drink to your health."

"I don't want anybody drinking to me."

"Name me one so I can ask you a question on it. Who can tell, if it's a good book maybe I might wanna read it myself."

George knew he looked passable on the outside, but inside he was crumbling apart.

Unable to reply, he shut his eyes, but when—years later —he opened them, he saw that Mr. Cattanzara had, out of pity, gone away, but in his ears he still heard the words he had said when he left: "George, don't do what I did."

The next night he was afraid to leave his room, and

though Sophie argued with him he wouldn't open the door.

"What are you doing in there?" she asked.

"Nothing."

"Aren't you reading?"

"No."

She was silent a minute, then asked, "Where do you keep the books you read? I never see any in your room outside of a few cheap trashy ones."

He wouldn't tell her.

"In that case you're not worth a buck of my hard-earned money. Why should I break my back for you? Go on out, you bum, and get a job."

He stayed in his room for almost a week, except to sneak into the kitchen when nobody was home. Sophie railed at him, then begged him to come out, and his old father wept, but George wouldn't budge, though the weather was terrible and his small room stifling. He found it very hard to breathe, each breath was like drawing a flame into his lungs.

One night, unable to stand the heat anymore, he burst into the street at one A.M., a shadow of himself. He hoped to sneak to the park without being seen, but there were people all over the block, wilted and listless, waiting for a breeze. George lowered his eyes and walked, in disgrace, away from them, but before long he discovered they were still friendly to him. He figured Mr. Cattanzara hadn't told on him. Maybe when he woke up out of his drunk the next morning, he had forgotten all about meeting George. George felt his confidence slowly come back to him.

That same night a man on a street corner asked him if it was true that he had finished reading so many books, and George admitted he had. The man said it was a wonderful thing for a boy his age to read so much.

"Yeah," George said, but he felt relieved. He hoped nobody would mention the books anymore, and when, after a couple of days, he accidentally met Mr. Cattanzara again, *he* didn't, though George had the idea he was the one who had started the rumor that he had finished all the books.

One evening in the fall, George ran out of his house to

the library, where he hadn't been in years. There were books all over the place, wherever he looked, and though he was struggling to control an inward trembling, he easily counted off a hundred, then sat down at a table to read.

The Rocking-Horse Winner

D. H. LAWRENCE

On the first, obvious level, "The Rocking-Horse Winner" is a simple story about what people live for and by, what a son will do to win his mother's love and happiness, and what a self-centered unfeeling mother can drive her son into. But on a deeper, more fundamental level, "The Rocking-Horse Winner" is an angry, bitter parable for our times, a scathing attack on the way our materialistic society corrupts and ultimately dehumanizes the individual. In this story, D. H. Lawrence's indignation is directed, as always, at the social conventions and institutions that stifle man's free, full, natural development. Lawrence's penetrating psychological insights, the intensity of his feelings for the trapped innocent hurtling uncontrollably to his destiny, add a vibrant quality to the rich symbolism of "The Rocking-Horse Winner."

DAVID HERBERT LAWRENCE (1885–1930) was born in the mining village of Eastwood, Nottinghamshire. His father was a coal miner, his mother a teacher. Lawrence taught school for a short time. Ford Madox Ford first discovered Lawrence's gifts as a writer, and brought him to the attention of Edward Garnett, who helped him get his first novel, The White Peacock *(1911), published. Soon after the appearance of* The White Peacock, *Lawrence gave up teaching to devote his time to writing. He traveled widely through India, Australia, New Mexico, Mexico, and Europe. He died of tuberculosis in France at the age of forty-five.*

Lawrence was one of the most gifted of English prose writers—a magnificent stylist, a highly sensitive, perceptive writer, a man capable of almost extraordinary empathy for the world around him. His uncanny insight into men and women is revealed in his autobiographical novel, Sons and Lovers *(1913), and in* Women in Love *(1920) and* Lady Chatterley's Lover *(1928). Lawrence's mother, a possessive, domineering woman, exerted a profound and lasting influence over him; the story of this relationship is the theme of* Sons and Lovers. *Lawrence's passionate nature and his uncompromising handling of sexuality made him the center of violent controversy.*

The Rocking-Horse Winner

There was a woman who was beautiful, who started with all the advantages, yet she had no luck. She married for love, and the love turned to dust. She had bonny children, yet she felt they had been thrust upon her, and she could not love them. They looked at her coldly, as if they were finding fault with her. And hurriedly she felt she must cover up some fault in herself. Yet what it was that she must cover up she never knew. Nevertheless, when her children were present, she always felt the center of her heart go hard. This troubled her, and in her manner she was all the more gentle and anxious for her children, as if she loved them very much. Only she herself knew that at the center of her heart was a hard little place that could not feel love, no, not for anybody. Everybody else said of her: "She is such a good mother. She adores her children." Only she herself, and her children themselves, knew it was not so. They read it in each other's eyes.

There were a boy and two little girls. They lived in a

pleasant house, with a garden, and they had discreet servants, and felt themselves superior to anyone in the neighborhood.

Although they lived in style, they felt always an anxiety
in the house. There was never enough money. The mother
had a small income, and the father had a small income,
but not nearly enough for the social position which they
had to keep up. The father went in to town to some office.
But though he had good prospects, these prospects never
materialized. There was always the grinding sense of the
shortage of money, though the style was always kept up.

At last the mother said: "I will see if *I* can't make something." But she did not know where to begin. She racked
her brains, and tried this thing and the other, but could
not find anything successful. The failure made deep lines
come into her face. Her children were growing up, they
would have to go to school. There must be more money,
there must be more money. The father, who was always
very handsome and expensive in his tastes, seemed as if
he never *would* be able to do anything worth doing. And
the mother, who had a great belief in herself, did not
succeed any better, and her tastes were just as expensive.

And so the house came to be haunted by the unspoken
phrase: *There must be more money! There must be more
money!* The children could hear it all the time, though nobody said it aloud. They heard it at Christmas, when the
expensive and splendid toys filled the nursery. Behind the
shining modern rocking-horse, behind the smart doll's-
house, a voice would start whispering: "There *must* be
more money! There *must* be more money!" And the children would stop playing, to listen for a moment. They
would look into each other's eyes, to see if they had all
heard. And each one saw in the eyes of the other two that
they too had heard. "There *must* be more money! There
must be more money!"

It came whispering from the springs of the still-swaying
rocking-horse, and even the horse, bending his wooden,
champing head, heard it. The big doll, sitting so pink and
smirking in her new pram, could hear it quite plainly, and
seemed to be smirking all the more self-consciously because of it. The foolish puppy, too, that took the place of
the teddy-bear, he was looking so extraordinarily foolish

for no other reason but that he heard the secret whisper all over the house: "There *must* be more money!"

Yet nobody ever said it aloud. The whisper was everywhere, and therefore no one spoke it. Just as no one ever says: "We are breathing!" in spite of the fact that breath is coming and going all the time.

"Mother," said the boy Paul one day, "why don't we keep a car of our own? Why do we always use uncle's, or else a taxi?"

"Because we're the poor members of the family," said the mother.

"But why *are* we, mother?"

"Well—I suppose," she said slowly and bitterly, "it's because your father has no luck."

The boy was silent for some time.

"Is luck money, mother?" he asked, rather timidly.

"No, Paul. Not quite. It's what causes you to have money."

"Oh!" said Paul vaguely. "I thought when Uncle Oscar said *filthy lucker,* it meant money."

"*Filthy lucre* does mean money," said the mother. "But it's lucre, not luck."

"Oh!" said the boy. "Then what *is* luck, mother?"

"It's what causes you to have money. If you're lucky you have money. That's why it's better to be born lucky than rich. If you're rich, you may lose your money. But if you're lucky, you will always get more money."

"Oh! Will you? And is father not lucky?"

"Very unlucky, I should say," she said bitterly.

The boy watched her with unsure eyes.

"Why?" he asked.

"I don't know. Nobody ever knows why one person is lucky and another unlucky."

"Don't they? Nobody at all? Does *nobody* know?"

"Perhaps God. But He never tells."

"He ought to, then. And aren't you lucky either, mother?"

"I can't be, if I married an unlucky husband."

"But by yourself, aren't you?"

"I used to think I was, before I married. Now I think I am very unlucky indeed."

"Why?"

"Well—never mind! Perhaps I'm not really," she said.

The child looked at her, to see if she meant it. But he saw, by the lines of her mouth, that she was only trying to hide something from him.

"Well, anyhow," he said stoutly, "I'm a lucky person."

"Why?" said his mother, with a sudden laugh.

He stared at her. He didn't even know why he had said it.

"God told me," he asserted, brazening it out.

"I hope He did, dear!" she said, again with a laugh, but rather bitter.

"He did, mother!"

"Excellent!" said the mother, using one of her husband's exclamations.

The boy saw she did not believe him; or, rather, that she paid no attention to his assertion. This angered him somewhat, and made him want to compel her attention.

He went off by himself, vaguely, in a childish way, seeking for the clue to "luck." Absorbed, taking no heed of other people, he went about with a sort of stealth, seeking inwardly for luck. He wanted luck, he wanted it, he wanted it. When the two girls were playing dolls in the nursery, he would sit on his big rocking-horse, charging madly into space, with a frenzy that made the little girls peer at him uneasily. Wildly the horse careered, the waving dark hair of the boy tossed, his eyes had a strange glare in them. The little girls dared not speak to him.

When he had ridden to the end of his mad little journey, he climbed down and stood in front of his rocking-horse, staring fixedly into its lowered face. Its red mouth was slightly open, its big eye was wide and glassy-bright.

"Now!" he would silently command the snorting steed. "Now, take me to where there is luck! Now take me!"

And he would slash the horse on the neck with the little whip he had asked Uncle Oscar for. He *knew* the horse could take him to where there was luck, if only he forced it. So he would mount again, and start on his furious ride, hoping at last to get there. He knew he could get there.

"You'll break your horse, Paul!" said the nurse.

"He's always riding like that! I wish he'd leave off!" said his elder sister Joan.

But he only glared down on them in silence. Nurse gave

him up. She could make nothing of him. Anyhow he was growing beyond her.

One day his mother and his Uncle Oscar came in when he was on one of his furious rides. He did not speak to them.

"Hallo, you young jockey! Riding a winner?" said his uncle.

"Aren't you growing too big for a rocking-horse? You're not a very little boy any longer, you know," said his mother.

But Paul only gave a blue glare from his big, rather close-set eyes. He would speak to nobody when he was in full tilt. His mother watched him with an anxious expression on her face.

At last he suddenly stopped forcing his horse into the mechanical gallop, and slid down.

"Well, I got there!" he announced fiercely, his blue eyes still flaring, and his sturdy long legs straddling apart.

"Where did you get to?" asked his mother.

"Where I wanted to go," he flared back at her.

"That's right, son!" said Uncle Oscar. "Don't you stop till you get there. What's the horse's name?"

"He doesn't have a name," said the boy.

"Gets on without all right?" asked the uncle.

"Well, he has different names. He was called Sansovino last week."

"Sansovino, eh? Won the Ascot. How did you know his name?"

"He always talks about horse-races with Bassett," said Joan.

The uncle was delighted to find that his small nephew was posted with all the racing news. Bassett, the young gardener, who had been wounded in the left foot in the war and had got his present job through Oscar Cresswell, whose batman he had been, was a perfect blade of the "turf." He lived in the racing events, and the small boy lived with him.

Oscar Cresswell got it all from Bassett.

"Master Paul comes and asks me, so I can't do more than tell him, sir," said Bassett, his face terribly serious, as if he were speaking of religious matters.

"And does he ever put anything on a horse he fancies?"

"Well—I don't want to give him away—he's a young sport, a fine sport, sir. Would you mind asking him himself? He sort of takes a pleasure in it, and perhaps he'd feel I was giving him away, sir, if you don't mind."

Bassett was serious as a church.

The uncle went back to his nephew, and took him off for a ride in the car.

"Say, Paul, old man, do you ever put anything on a horse?" the uncle asked.

The boy watched the handsome man closely.

"Why, do you think I oughtn't to?" he parried.

"Not a bit of it! I thought perhaps you might give me a tip for the Lincoln."

The car sped on into the country, going down to Uncle Oscar's place in Hampshire.

"Honor bright?" said the nephew.

"Honor bright, son!" said the uncle.

"Well, then, Daffodil."

"Daffodil! I doubt it, sonny. What about Mirza?"

"I only know the winner," said the boy. "That's Daffodil."

"Daffodil, eh?"

There was a pause. Daffodil was an obscure horse comparatively.

"Uncle!"

"Yes, son?"

"You won't let it go any further, will you? I promised Bassett."

"Bassett be damned, old man! What's he got to do with it?"

"We're partners. We've been partners from the first. Uncle, he lent me my first five shillings, which I lost. I promised him, honor bright, it was only between me and him; only you gave me that ten-shilling note I started winning with, so I thought you were lucky. You won't let it go any further, will you?"

The boy gazed at his uncle from those big, hot, blue eyes, set rather close together. The uncle stirred and laughed uneasily.

"Right you are, son! I'll keep your tip private. Daffodil, eh? How much are you putting on him?"

"All except twenty pounds," said the boy. "I keep that in reserve."

The uncle thought it a good joke.

"You keep twenty pounds in reserve, do you, you young romancer? What are you betting, then?"

"I'm betting three hundred," said the boy gravely. "But it's between you and me, Uncle Oscar! Honor bright?"

The uncle burst into a roar of laughter.

"It's between you and me all right, you young Nat Gould," he said, laughingly. "But where's your three hundred?"

"Bassett keeps it for me. We're partners."

"You are, are you! And what is Bassett putting on Daffodil?"

"He won't go quite as high as I do, I expect. Perhaps he'll go a hundred and fifty."

"What, pennies?" laughed the uncle.

"Pounds," said the child, with a surprised look at his uncle. "Bassett keeps a bigger reserve than I do."

Between wonder and amusement Uncle Oscar was silent. He pursued the matter no further, but he determined to take his nephew with him to the Lincoln races.

"Now, son," he said, "I'm putting twenty on Mirza, and I'll put five for you on any horse you fancy. What's your pick?"

"Daffodil, uncle."

"No, not the fiver on Daffodil!"

"I should if it was my own fiver," said the child.

"Good! Good! Right you are! A fiver for me and a fiver for you on Daffodil."

The child had never been to a race-meeting before, and his eyes were blue fire. He pursed his mouth tight, and watched. A Frenchman just in front had put his money on Lancelot. Wild with excitement, he flayed his arms up and down, yelling *"Lancelot! Lancelot!"* in his French accent.

Daffodil came in first, Lancelot second, Mirza third. The child, flushed and with eyes blazing, was curiously serene. His uncle brought him four five-pound notes, four to one.

"What am I to do with these?" he cried, waving them before the boy's eyes.

"I suppose we'll talk to Bassett," said the boy. "I expect

I have fifteen hundred now; and twenty in reserve; and this twenty."

His uncle studied him for some moments.

"Look here, son!" he said. "You're not serious about Bassett and that fifteen hundred, are you?"

"Yes, I am. But it's between you and me, uncle. Honor bright!"

"Honor bright all right, son! But I must talk to Bassett."

"If you'd like to be a partner, uncle, with Bassett and me, we could all be partners. Only, you'd have to promise, honor bright, uncle, not to let it go beyond us three. Bassett and I are lucky, and you must be lucky, because it was your ten shillings I started winning with. . . ."

Uncle Oscar took both Bassett and Paul into Richmond Park for an afternoon, and there they talked.

"It's like this, you see, sir," Bassett said. "Master Paul would get me talking about racing events, spinning yarns, you know, sir. And he was always keen on knowing if I'd made or if I'd lost. It's about a year since, now, that I put five shillings on Blush of Dawn for him—and we lost. Then the luck turned, with that ten shillings he had from you, that we put on Singhalese. And since that time, it's been pretty steady, all things considering. What do you say, Master Paul?"

"We're all right when we're sure," said Paul. "It's when we're not quite sure that we go down."

"Oh, but we're careful then," said Bassett.

"But when are you *sure?*" smiled Uncle Oscar.

"It's Master Paul, sir," said Bassett, in a secret, religious voice. "It's as if he had it from heaven. Like Daffodil, now, for the Lincoln. That was as sure as eggs."

"Did you put anything on Daffodil?" asked Oscar Cresswell.

"Yes sir. I made my bit."

"And my nephew?"

Bassett was obstinately silent, looking at Paul.

"I made twelve hundred, didn't I, Bassett? I told uncle I was putting three hundred on Daffodil."

"That's right," said Bassett, nodding.

"But where's the money?" asked the uncle.

"I keep it safe locked up, sir. Master Paul he can have it any minute he likes to ask for it."

"What, fifteen hundred pounds?"

"And twenty! And *forty,* that is, with the twenty he made on the course."

"It's amazing!" said the uncle.

"If Master Paul offers you to be partners, sir, I would, if I were you; if you'll excuse me," said Bassett.

Oscar Cresswell thought about it.

"I'll see the money," he said.

They drove home again, and sure enough, Bassett came round to the garden-house with fifteen hundred pounds in notes. The twenty pounds reserve was left with Joe Glee, in the Turf Commission deposit.

"You see, it's all right, uncle, when I'm *sure!* Then we go strong, for all we're worth. Don't we, Bassett?"

"We do that, Master Paul."

"And when are you sure?" said the uncle, laughing.

"Oh, well, sometimes I'm *absolutely* sure, like about Daffodil," said the boy; "and sometimes I have an idea; and sometimes I haven't even an idea, have I, Bassett? Then we're careful, because we mostly go down."

"You do, do you! And when you're sure, like about Daffodil, what makes you sure, sonny?"

"Oh, well, I don't know," said the boy uneasily. "I'm sure, you know, uncle; that's all."

"It's as if he had it from heaven, sir," Bassett reiterated.

"I should say so!" said the uncle.

But he became a partner. And when the Leger was coming on, Paul was "sure" about Lively Spark, which was a quite inconsiderable horse. The boy insisted on putting a thousand on the horse, Basset went for five hundred, and Oscar Cresswell two hundred. Lively Spark came in first, and the betting had been ten to one against him. Paul had made ten thousand.

"You see," he said, "I was absolutely sure of him."

Even Oscar Cresswell had cleared two thousand.

"Look here, son," he said, "this sort of thing makes me nervous."

"It needn't, uncle! Perhaps I shan't be sure again for a long time."

"But what are you going to do with your money?" asked the uncle.

"Of course," said the boy, "I started it for mother. She

said she had no luck, because father is unlucky, so I thought if *I* was lucky, it might stop whispering."

"What might stop whispering?"

"Our house. I *hate* our house for whispering."

"What does it whisper?"

"Why—why"—the boy fidgeted—"why, I don't know. But it's always short of money, you know, uncle."

"I know it, son, I know it."

"You know people send mother writs, don't you, uncle?"

"I'm afraid I do," said the uncle.

"And then the house whispers, like people laughing at you behind your back. It's awful, that is! I thought if I was lucky . . ."

"You might stop it," added the uncle.

The boy watched him with big blue eyes, that had an uncanny cold fire in them, and he said never a word.

"Well, then!" said the uncle. "What are we doing?"

"I shouldn't like mother to know I was lucky," said the boy.

"Why not, son?"

"She'd stop me."

"I don't think she would."

"Oh!"—and the boy writhed in an odd way—"I *don't* want her to know, uncle."

"All right, son! We'll manage it without her knowing."

They managed it very easily. Paul, at the other's suggestion, handed over five thousand pounds to his uncle, who deposited it with the family lawyer, who was then to inform Paul's mother that a relative had put five thousand pounds into his hands, which sum was to be paid out a thousand pounds at a time, on the mother's birthday, for the next five years.

"So she'll have a birthday present of a thousand pounds for five successive years," said Uncle Oscar. "I hope it won't make it all the harder for her later."

Paul's mother had her birthday in November. The house had been "whispering" worse than ever lately, and, even in spite of his luck, Paul could not bear up against it. He was very anxious to see the effect of the birthday letter, telling his mother about the thousand pounds.

When there were no visitors, Paul now took his meals

with his parents, as he was beyond the nursery control. His mother went into town nearly every day. She had discovered that she had an odd knack of sketching furs and dress materials, so she worked secretly in the studio of a friend who was the chief "artist" for the leading drapers. She drew the figures of ladies in furs and ladies in silk and sequins for the newspaper advertisements. This young woman artist earned several thousand pounds a year, but Paul's mother only made several hundreds, and she was again dissatisfied. She so wanted to be first in something, and she did not succeed, even in making sketches for drapery advertisements.

She was down to breakfast on the morning of her birthday. Paul watched her face as she read her letters. He knew the lawyer's letter. As his mother read it, her face hardened and became more expressionless. Then a cold, determined look came on her mouth. She hid the letter under the pile of others, and said not a word about it.

"Didn't you have anything nice in the post for your birthday, mother?" said Paul.

"Quite moderately nice," she said, her voice cold and absent.

She went away to town without saying more.

But in the afternoon Uncle Oscar appeared. He said Paul's mother had had a long interview with the lawyer, asking if the whole five thousand could not be advanced at once, as she was in debt.

"What do you think, uncle?" said the boy.

"I leave it to you, son."

"Oh, let her have it, then! We can get some more with the other," said the boy.

"A bird in the hand is worth two in the bush, laddie!" said Uncle Oscar.

"But I'm sure to *know* for the Grand National; or the Lincolnshire; or else the Derby. I'm sure to know for *one* of them," said Paul.

So Uncle Oscar signed the agreement, and Paul's mother touched the whole five thousand. Then something very curious happened. The voices in the house suddenly went mad, like a chorus of frogs on a spring evening. There were certain new furnishings, and Paul had a tutor. He was *really* going to Eton, his father's school, in the following autumn. There were flowers in the winter, and a blossoming of the luxury Paul's mother had been used to. And yet the voices in the house, behind the sprays of mimosa and almond blossom, and from under the piles of iridescent cushions, simply trilled and screamed in a sort of ecstasy: "There *must* be more money! Oh-h-h; there *must* be more money. Oh, now, now-w! Now-w-w-w—there *must* be more money!—more than ever! More than ever!"

It frightened Paul terribly. He studied away at his Latin and Greek with his tutors. But his intense hours were spent with Bassett. The Grand National had gone by: he had not "known," and had lost a hundred pounds. Summer was at hand. He was in agony for the Lincoln. But even for the Lincoln he didn't "know," and he lost fifty pounds. He became wild-eyed and strange, as if something were going to explode in him.

"Let it alone, son! Don't you bother about it!" urged Uncle Oscar. But it was as if the boy couldn't really hear what his uncle was saying.

"I've got to know for the Derby! I've got to know for the Derby!" the child reiterated, his big blue eyes blazing with a sort of madness.

His mother noticed how overwrought he was.

"You'd better go to the seaside. Wouldn't you like to go now to the seaside, instead of waiting? I think you'd better," she said, looking down at him anxiously, her heart curiously heavy because of him.

But the child lifted his uncanny blue eyes.

"I couldn't possibly go before the Derby, mother!" he said. "I couldn't possibly!"

"Why not?" she said, her voice becoming heavy when she was opposed. "Why not? You can still go from the seaside to see the Derby with your Uncle Oscar, if that's what you wish. No need for you to wait here. Besides, I think you care too much about these races. It's a bad sign. My family has been a gambling family, and you won't know till you grow up how much damage it has done. But it has done damage. I shall have to send Bassett away, and ask Uncle Oscar not to talk racing to you, unless you promise to be reasonable about it; go away to the seaside and forget it. You're all nerves!"

"I'll do what you like, mother, so long as you don't send me away till after the Derby," the boy said.

"Send you away from where? Just from this house?"

"Yes," he said, gazing at her.

"Why, you curious child, what makes you care about this house so much, suddenly? I never knew you loved it."

He gazed at her without speaking. He had a secret within a secret, something he had not divulged, even to Bassett or to his Uncle Oscar.

But his mother, after standing undecided and a little bit sullen for some moments, said:

"Very well, then! Don't go to the seaside till after the Derby, if you don't wish it. But promise me you won't let your nerves go to pieces. Promise you won't think so much about horse-racing and *events,* as you call them!"

"Oh, no," said the boy casually. "I won't think much about them, mother. You needn't worry. I wouldn't worry, mother, if I were you."

"If you were me and I were you," said his mother, "I wonder what we *should* do!"

"But you know you needn't worry, mother, don't you?" the boy repeated.

"I should be awfully glad to know it," she said wearily.

"Oh, well, you *can,* you know. I mean, you *ought* to know you needn't worry," he insisted.

"Ought I? Then I'll see about it," she said.

Paul's secret of secrets was his wooden horse, that which had no name. Since he was emancipated from a nurse and a nursery-governess, he had had his rocking-horse removed to his own bedroom at the top of the house.

"Surely, you're too big for a rocking-horse!" his mother had remonstrated.

"Well, you see, mother, till I can have a *real* horse, I like to have *some* sort of animal about," had been his quaint answer.

"Do you feel he keeps you company?" she laughed.

"Oh, yes! He's very good, he always keeps me company, when I'm there," said Paul.

So the horse, rather shabby, stood in an arrested prance in the boy's bedroom.

The Derby was drawing near, and the boy grew more and more tense. He hardly heard what was spoken to him, he was very frail, and his eyes were really uncanny. His mother had sudden strange seizures of uneasiness about him. Sometimes, for half-an-hour, she would feel a sudden anxiety about him that was almost anguish. She wanted to rush to him at once, and know he was safe.

Two nights before the Derby, she was at a big party in town, when one of her rushes of anxiety about her boy, her first-born, gripped her heart till she could hardly speak. She fought with the feeling, might and main, for she believed in commonsense. But it was too strong. She had to leave the dance and go downstairs to telephone to the country. The children's nursery-governess was terribly surprised and startled at being rung up in the night.

"Are the children all right, Miss Wilmot?"

"Oh, yes, they are quite all right."

"Master Paul? Is he all right?"

"He went to bed as right as a trivet. Shall I run up and look at him?"

"No," said Paul's mother reluctantly. "No! Don't trouble. It's all right. Don't sit up. We shall be home fairly soon." She did not want her son's privacy intruded upon.

"Very good," said the governess.

It was about one o'clock when Paul's mother and father drove up to their house. All was still. Paul's mother went to her room and slipped off her white fur cloak. She had told her maid not to wait for her. She heard her husband downstairs, mixing a whisky-and-soda.

And then, because of the strange anxiety at her heart, she stole upstairs to her son's room. Noiselessly she went along the upper corridor. Was there a faint noise? What was it?

She stood, with arrested muscles, outside his door, listening. There was a strange, heavy, and yet not loud noise. Her heart stood still. It was a soundless noise, yet rushing and powerful. Something huge, in violent, hushed motion. What was it? What in God's name was it? She ought to know. She felt that she knew the noise. She knew what it was.

Yet she could not place it. She couldn't say what it was. And on and on it went, like a madness.

Softly, frozen with anxiety and fear, she turned the door-handle.

The room was dark. Yet in the space near the window, she heard and saw something plunging to and fro. She gazed in fear and amazement.

Then suddenly she switched on the light, and saw her son, in his green pyjamas, madly surging on the rocking-horse. The blaze of light suddenly lit him up, as he urged the wooden horse, and lit her up, as she stood, blonde, in her dress of pale green and crystal, in the doorway.

"Paul!" she cried. "Whatever are you doing?"

"It's Malabar!" he screamed, in a powerful, strange voice. "It's Malabar!"

His eyes blazed at her for one strange and senseless second, as he ceased urging his wooden horse. Then he fell with a crash to the ground, and she, all her tormented motherhood flooding upon her, rushed to gather him up.

But he was unconscious, and unconscious he remained, with some brain-fever. He talked and tossed, and his mother sat stonily by his side.

"Malabar! It's Malabar! Bassett, Bassett, I *know!* It's Malabar!"

So the child cried, trying to get up and urge the rocking-horse that gave him his inspiration.

"What does he mean by Malabar?" asked the heart-frozen mother.

"I don't know," said the father stonily.

"What does he mean by Malabar?" she asked her brother Oscar.

"It's one of the horses running for the Derby," was the answer.

And, in spite of himself, Oscar Cresswell spoke to Bassett, and himself put a thousand on Malabar: at fourteen to one.

The third day of the illness was critical; they were waiting for a change. The boy, with his rather long, curly hair, was tossing ceaselessly on the pillow. He neither slept nor regained consciousness, and his eyes were like blue stones. His mother sat, feeling her heart had gone, turned actually into a stone.

In the evening, Oscar Cresswell did not come, but Bassett sent a message, saying could he come up for one moment, just one moment? Paul's mother was very angry at the intrusion, but on second thought she agreed. The boy was the same. Perhaps Bassett might bring him to consciousness.

The gardener, a shortish fellow with a little brown moustache, and sharp little brown eyes, tiptoed into the room, touched his imaginary cap to Paul's mother, and stole to the bedside, staring with glittering, smallish eyes, at the tossing, dying child.

"Master Paul!" he whispered. "Master Paul! Malabar came in first all right, a clean win. I did as you told me. You've made over seventy thousand pounds, you have; you've got over eighty thousand. Malabar came in all right, Master Paul."

"Malabar! Malabar! Did I say Malabar, mother? Did I say Malabar? Do you think I'm lucky, mother? I knew Malabar, didn't I? Over eighty thousand pounds! I call that lucky, don't you, mother? Over eighty thousand pounds! I knew, didn't I know I knew? Malabar came in all right. If I ride my horse till I'm sure, then I tell you, Bassett, you can go as high as you like. Did you go for all you were worth, Bassett?"

"I went a thousand on it, Master Paul."

"I never told you, mother, that if I can ride my horse, and *get there,* then I'm absolutely sure—oh, absolutely! Mother, did I ever tell you? I *am* lucky!"

"No, you never did," said the mother.

But the boy died in the night.

And even as he lay dead, his mother heard her brother's voice saying to her: "My God, Hester, you're eighty-odd thousand to the good, and a poor devil of a son to the bad. But, poor devil, poor devil, he's best gone out of a life where he rides his rocking-horse to find a winner."

A Wreath for Miss Totten

HORTENSE CALISHER

"A Wreath for Miss Totten" is a story about a teacher
and her class. But it is far from being the run-of-the-mill,
specious, sentimental "school" story we are all familiar
with. Nor is Miss Totten a run-of-the-mill stereotype of
the teacher. She is a real and recognizable character with
depth, dimension, and dignity. Most of us remember
a teacher like Miss Totten, but, unlike the students in the
story, few of us ever got to know her.

In its quiet way, "A Wreath for Miss Totten" is a very
moving story. Like all of Miss Calisher's stories, it is
characterized by a meticulous attention to detail and a
remarkable feeling for the exact word to convey the exact
picture, the exact mood. It is written close to the bone,
deeply felt and sensitively realized.

*HORTENSE CALISHER (1911–   ) was born in Man-
hattan and educated at Hunter College and Barnard College. Following her graduation from college in 1932, she
tried her hand at various jobs: salesclerk, model, social
worker. She married in 1935, traveled a great deal with
her husband, and then settled down with their two young
children in the Hudson River Valley.*

While living in Nyack, Miss Calisher, always interested in becoming a writer, began to write again. She enrolled in a writing class and produced three short stories that were accepted by The New Yorker *in 1948. Since then, her work has been appearing regularly in the major magazines and in the annual anthologies of the short story "bests." The publication of her first collection of short stories,* In the Absence of Angels *(1951), immediately identified her as one of America's important short story writers. Her second collection,* Tale for the Mirror *(1962), added luster to her growing reputation. A* New York Herald-Tribune *reviewer said of her, "She has produced some of the most discomfortingly vivid writing of the decade."*

Miss Calisher has won two Guggenheim Fellowships and, in 1958, toured Southeast Asia under a State Department grant. She writes mostly about "the private tragedies, of loneliness and the dissolution of marriage." A persistent strain of melancholy runs through most of her stories. For her characters, Miss Calisher exhibits a "caustic, disciplined pity." Critics find in her style "an impeccable sense of the mot juste.*"*

A Wreath for Miss Totten

Children growing up in the country take their images of integrity from the land. The land with its changes is always about them, a pervasive truth, and their midget foregrounds are criss-crossed with minute dramas which are the animalcules of a larger vision. But children who grow in a city where there is nothing greater than the people brimming up out of subways, riveleting in the streets—these children must take their archetypes where and if they find them.

In P.S. 146, between periods, when the upper grades were shunted through the halls in that important procedure known as "departmental," most of the teachers stood about chatting relievedly in couples; Miss Totten, however, always stood at the door of her "home room," watching us straightforwardly, alone. As, straggling and muffled, we lined past the other teachers, we often caught snatches of upstairs gossip which we later perverted and enlarged; passing before Miss Totten we deflected only that austere look, bent solely on us.

Perhaps with the teachers, as with us, she was neither admired nor loathed but simply ignored. Certainly none of us ever fawned on her as we did on the harshly blonde and blue-eyed Miss Steele, who never wooed us with a smile but slanged us delightfully in the gym, giving out the exercises in a voice like scuffed gravel. Neither did she obsess us in the way of the Misses Comstock, two liverish, stunted women who could have had nothing so vivid about them as our hatred for them. And though all of us had a raffish hunger for metaphor, we never dubbed Miss Totten with a nickname.

Miss Totten's figure, as she sat tall at her desk or strode angularly in front of us rolling down the long maps over the blackboard, had that instantaneous clarity, one metallic step removed from the real, of the daguerreotype. Her clothes partook of this period too—long, saturnine waists and skirts of a stuff identical with that in a good family umbrella. There was one like it in the umbrella stand at home—a high black one with a seamed ivory head. The waists enclosed a vestee of dim but steadfast lace; the skirts grazed narrow boots of that etiolated black leather, venerable with creases, which I knew to be a sign of both respectability and foot trouble. But except for the vestee, all of Miss Totten, too, folded neatly to the dark point of her shoes, and separated from these by her truly extraordinary length, her face presided above, a lined, ocher ellipse. Sometimes, on drowsy afternoons, her face floated away altogether and came to rest on the stand at home. Perhaps it was because of this guilty image that I was the only one who noticed Miss Totten's strange preoccupation with Mooley Davis.

Most of us in Miss Totten's room had been together as a group since first grade, but we had not seen Mooley since down in second grade, under the elder and more frightening of the two Comstocks. I had forgotten Mooley completely but when she reappeared I remembered clearly the incident which had given her her name.

That morning, very early in the new term, back in Miss

Comstock's, we had lined up on two sides of the classroom
for a spelling bee. These were usually a relief to good
and bad spellers alike, since they were the only part of our
work which resembled a game, and even when one had to
miss and sit down there was a kind of dreamy catharsis
in watching the tenseness of those still standing. Miss
Comstock always rose for these occasions and came forward between the two lines, standing there in an oppressive close-up in which we could watch the terrifying
action of the cords in her spindling gray neck and her
slight smile as someone was spelled down. As the number
of those standing was reduced, the smile grew, exposing
the oversize slabs of her teeth, through which the words
issued in a voice increasingly unctuous and soft.

On this day the forty of us still shone with the first fall
neatness of new clothes, still basked in that delightful ano-
nymity in which neither our names nor our capacities were
already part of the dreary foreknowledge of the teacher.
The smart and quick had yet to assert themselves with
their flying, staccato hands; the uneasy dull, not yet
forced into recitations which would make their status
clear, still preserved in the small, sinking corners of their
hearts a lorn, factitious hope. Both teams were still intact
when the word "mule" fell to the lot of a thin colored girl
across the room from me, in clothes perky only with
starch, her rusty fuzz of hair drawn back in braids so tightly sectioned that her eyes seemed permanently widened.

"Mule," said Miss Comstock, giving out the word. The
ranks were still full. She had not yet begun to smile.

The girl looked back at Miss Comstock, soundlessly.
All her face seemed drawn backward from the silent,
working mouth, as if a strong, pulling hand had taken
hold of the braids.

My turn, I calculated, was next. The procedure was to
say the word, spell it out and say it again. I repeated it in
my mind: Mule. M-u-l-e. Mule.

Miss Comstock waited quite a long time. Then she
looked around the class, as if asking them to mark well
and early her handling of this first malfeasance.

"What's your name?" she said.

"Ul—ee." The word came out in a glottal, molasses
voice, hardly articulate, the *l*'s scarcely pronounced.

"Lilly?"

The girl nodded.

"Lilly what?"

"Duh—avis."

"Oh. Lilly Davis. Mmmm. Well, spell 'mule,' Lilly." Miss Comstock trilled out the name beautifully.

The tense brown bladder of the girl's face swelled desperately, then broke at the mouth. "Mool," she said, and stopped. "Mmm—ooo—"

The room tittered. Miss Comstock stepped closer.

"Mule!"

The girl struggled again. "Mool."

This time we were too near Miss Comstock to dare laughter.

Miss Comstock turned to our side. "Who's next?"

I half raised my hand.

"Go on." She wheeled around on Lilly, who was sinking into her seat. "No. Don't sit down."

I lowered my eyelids, hiding Lilly from my sight. "Mule," I said. "M-u-l-e. Mule."

The game continued, words crossing the room uneventfully. Some children survived. Others settled, abashed, into their seats, craning around to watch us. Again the turn came around to Lilly.

Miss Comstock cleared her throat. She had begun to smile.

"Spell it now, Lilly," she said. "Mule."

The long-chinned brown face swung from side to side in an odd writhing movement. Lilly's eyeballs rolled. Then the thick sound from her mouth was lost in the hooting, uncontrollable laughter of the whole class. For there was no doubt about it: the long, coffee-colored face, the whitish glint of the eyeballs, the bucking motion of the head suggested it to us all—a small brown quadruped, horse or mule, crazily stubborn or at bay.

"Quiet!" said Miss Comstock. And we hushed, although she had not spoken loudly. For the word had smirked out from a wide, flat smile and on the stringy neck beneath there was a creeping, pleasurable flush which made it pink as a young girl's.

That was how Mooley Davis got her name, although

we had a chance to use it for only a few weeks, in a taunt-
ing singsong when she hung up her coat in the morning
or as she flicked past the little dustbin of a store where we
shed our pennies for tasteless, mottoed hearts. For after
a few weeks, when it became clear that her cringing,
mucoused talk was getting worse, she was transferred to
the "ungraded" class. This group, made up of the mute,
the shambling and the oddly tall, some of whom were
delivered by bus, was housed in a basement, with a separate entrance which was forbidden us not only by rule but
by a lurking distaste of our own.

The year Mooley reappeared in Miss Totten's room, a
dispute in the school system had disbanded all the ungraded classes in the city. Here and there in the back seat
of a class now there would be some grown-size boy who
read haltingly from a primer, fingering the stubble on his
slack jaw. Down in 4-A there was a shiny, petted doll of
a girl, all crackling hair bow and nimble wheel chair, over
whom the teachers shook their heads feelingly, saying,
"Bright as a dollar! Imagine!" as if there were something
sinister in the fact that useless legs had not impaired the
musculature of a mind. And in our class, in harshly clean,
faded dresses which were always a little too infantile for
her, her spraying ginger hair cut short now and held by a
round comb which circled the back of her head like a
snaggle-toothed tiara which had slipped, there was this
bony, bug-eyed wraith of a girl who raised her hand instead of saying "Present!" when Miss Totten said "Lilly
Davis?" at roll call, and never spoke at all.

It was Juliet Hoffman who spoke Mooley's nickname
first. A jeweler's daughter, Juliet had achieved an emi-
nence even beyond that due her curly profile, embroidered dresses and prancing, leading-lady ways when,
the Christmas before, she had brought as her present to
teacher a real diamond ring. It had been a modest diamond, to be sure, but undoubtedly real, and set in real
gold. Juliet had heralded it for weeks before and we had
all seen it—it and the peculiar look on the face of the
teacher, a young substitute whom we hardly knew, when
she had lifted it from the pile of hankies and fancy note
paper on her desk. The teacher, over the syrupy protests

of Mrs. Hoffman, had returned the ring, but its sparkle lingered on, iridescent around Juliet's head.

On our way out at three o'clock that first day with Miss Totten, Juliet nudged at me to wait. Obediently, I waited behind her. Twiddling her bunny muff, she minced over to the clothes closet and confronted the new girl.

"I know you," she said. "Mooley Davis, that's who you are!" A couple of the other children hung back to watch. "Aren't you? Aren't you Mooley Davis?"

I remember just how Mooley stood there because of the coat she wore. She just stood there holding her coat against her stomach with both hands. It was a coat of some pale, vague tweed, cut the same length as mine. But it wrapped the wrong way over for a girl and the revers, wide ones, came all the way down and ended way below the pressing hands.

"Where you been?" Juliet flipped us all a knowing grin. "You been in ungraded?"

One of Mooley's shoulders inched up so that it almost touched her ear, but beyond that she did not seem able to move. Her eyes looked at us, wide and fixed. I had the feeling that all of her had retreated far, far back behind the eyes, which, large and light and purposefully empty, had been forced to stay.

My back was to the room but on the suddenly wooden faces of the others I saw Miss Totten's shadow. Then she loomed thinly over Juliet, her arms, which were crossed at her chest, hiding the one V of white in her garments so that she looked like an umbrella tightly furled.

"What's *your* name?" she asked, addressing not so much Juliet as the white muff, which, I noticed now, was slightly soiled.

"Jooly-ette."

"Hmm. Oh, yes. Juliet Hoffman."

"Jooly-ette, it is." She pouted creamily up at Miss Totten, her glance narrow with the assurance of finger rings to come.

Something flickered in the nexus of yellow wrinkles around Miss Totten's lips. Poking out a bony forefinger, she held it against the muff. "You tell your mother," she said slowly, "that the way she spells it, it's *Juliet*."

Then she dismissed the rest of us but put a delaying

hand on Mooley. Turning back to look, I saw that she had knelt down painfully, her skirt hem graying in the floor dust, and, staring absently over Mooley's head, she was buttoning up the wrongly shaped coat.

After a short, avid flurry of speculation we soon lost interest in Mooley and in the routine Miss Totten devised for her. At first, during any kind of oral work, Mooley took her place at the blackboard and wrote down her answers, but later Miss Totten sat her in the front row and gave her a small slate. She grew very quick at answering, particularly in "mental arithmetic" and in the card drills when Miss Totten held up large manila cards with significant locations and dates inscribed in her Palmer script, and we went down the rows, snapping back the answers.

Also, Mooley had acquired a protector in Ruby Green, the other Negro girl in the class—a huge, black girl with an arm-flailing, hee-haw way of talking and a rich contralto singing voice which we had often heard in solo at Assembly. Ruby, boasting of her singing in night clubs on Saturday nights, of a father who had done time, cowed us all with these pungent inklings of the world on the other side of the dividing line of Amsterdam Avenue, that deep, velvet murk of Harlem which she lit for us with the flash of razors, the honky-tonk beat of the "numbahs" and the plangent wails of the mugged. Once, hearing David Hecker, a doctor's son, declare, "Mooley has a cleft palate, that's what," Ruby wheeled and put a large hand on his shoulder in menacing caress.

"She ain' got no cleff palate, see? She talk sometime, roun' home." She glared at us each in turn with such a pug scowl that we flinched, thinking she was going to spit. Ruby giggled. "She got no cause to talk, roun' here. She just don' need to bother." She lifted her hand from David, spinning him backward, and joined arms with the silent Mooley. "Me neither!" she added, and walked Mooley away, flinging back at us her gaudy, syncopated laugh.

Then one day, lolloping home after three, I suddenly remembered my books and tam and above all my homework assignment, left in the pocket of my desk at school. I raced back there. The janitor, grumbling, unlocked the

side door at which he had been sweeping and let me in.
In the mauve, settling light the long maw of the gym
held a rank, uneasy stillness. I walked up the spiral metal
stairs feeling that I thieved on some part of the school's
existence not intended for me. Outside the ambushed
quiet of Miss Totten's room I stopped, gathering breath.
I heard voices, one surely Miss Totten's dark, firm tones,
the other no more than an arrested gurgle and pause.

I opened the door slowly. Miss Totten and Mooley
raised their heads. It was odd, but although Miss Totten
sat as usual at her desk, her hands clasped to one side of
her hat, lunch box and the crinkly boa she wore all spring,
and although Mooley was at her own desk in front of a
spread copy of our thick reader, I felt the distinct, startled
guilt of someone who interrupts an embrace.

"Yes?" said Miss Totten. Her eyes had the drugged look
of eyes raised suddenly from close work. I fancied that
she reddened slightly, like someone accused.

"I left my books."

Miss Totten nodded and sat waiting. I walked down the
row to my desk and bent over, fumbling for my things,
my haunches awkward under the watchfulness behind me.
At the door, with my arms full, I stopped, parroting the
formula of dismissal. "Good afternoon, Miss Totten."

"Good afternoon."

I walked home slowly. Miss Totten, when I spoke, had
seemed to be watching my mouth, almost with enmity.
And in front of Mooley there had been no slate.

In class the next morning, as I collected the homework
in my capacity as monitor, I lingered a minute at
Mooley's desk, expecting some change perhaps in her
notice of me, but there was none. Her paper was the same
as usual, written in a neat script quite legible in itself but
in a spidery backhand that just faintly silvered the page,
like a communiqué issued out of necessity but begrudged.

Once more I had a glimpse of Miss Totten and Mooley
together, on a day when I had joined the slangy, athletic
Miss Steele, who was striding capably along in her Ground
Grippers on the route I usually took home. Almost at
once I had known I was unwelcome, but I trotted desperately in her wake, not knowing how to relieve her of

my company. At last a stitch in my side forced me to stop, in front of a corner fishmonger's.

"Folks who want to walk home with me have to step on it!" said Miss Steele. She allotted me one measuring, stone blue glance and moved on.

Disposed on the bald white window stall of the fish store there was a rigidly mounted eel that looked as if only its stuffing prevented it from growing onward, sinuously, from either impersonal end. Beside it were several tawny shells. A finger would have to avoid the spines on them before being able to touch their rosy, pursed throats. As the pain in my side lessened, I raised my head and saw my own face in the window, egg-shaped and sad. I turned away. Miss Totten and Mooley stood on the corner, their backs to me, waiting to cross. A trolley clanged by, then the street was clear, and Miss Totten, looking down, nodded gently into the black boa and took Mooley by the hand. As they passed down the hill to St. Nicholas Avenue and disappeared, Mooley's face, smoothed out and grave, seemed to me, enviably, like the serene, guided faces of children seen walking securely under the restful duennaship of nuns.

Then came the first day of Visiting Week, during which, according to convention, the normal school day would be on display but for which we had actually been fortified with rapid-fire recitations which were supposed to erupt from us in sequence—like the somersaults which climax acrobatic acts. On this morning, just before we were called to order, Dr. Piatt, the principal, walked in. He was a gentle man, keeping to his office like a snail, and we had never succeeded in making a bogey of him, although we tried. Today he shepherded a group of mothers and two men, officiously dignified, all of whom he seated on some chairs up front at Miss Totten's left. Then he sat down too, looking upon us benignly, his head cocked a little to one side in a way he had, as if he hearkened to some unseen arbiter who whispered constantly to him of how bad children could be but he benevolently, insistently continued to disagree.

Miss Totten, alone among the teachers, was usually immune to visitors, but today she strode restlessly in front of us, and as she pulled down the maps one of them slipped

from her hand and snapped back up with a loud, flapping
roar. Fumbling for the roll book, she sat down and began
to call the roll, something she usually did without looking
at the book, favoring each of us with a warming nod instead.

"Arnold Ames?"

"Pres-unt!"

"Mary Bates?"

"Pres-unt!"

"Wanda Becovic?"

"Pres-unt!"

"Sidney Cohen?"

"Pres-unt!"

"L—Lilly Davis?"

It took us a minute to realize that Mooley had not raised
her hand. A light impatient groan rippled over the class.
But Mooley, her face uplifted in its blank, cataleptic stare,
was looking at Miss Totten. Miss Totten's own lips moved.
There seemed to be a cord between her lips and Mooley's.
Mooley's lips moved, opened.

"Pres-unt!" said Mooley.

The class caught its breath, then righted itself under the
sweet, absent smile of the visitors. With flushed, lowered
lids but in a rich, full voice, Miss Totten finished calling
the roll. Then she rose and came forward with the manila
cards. Each time, she held up the name of a State and we
answered with its capital city.

Pennsylvania.

"Harrisburg!" said Arnold Ames.

Illinois.

"Springfield!" said Mary Bates.

Arkansas.

"Little Rock!" said Wanda Becovic.

North Dakota.

"Bismarck!" said Sidney Cohen.

Idaho.

We were afraid to turn our heads.

"Buh . . . Boise!" said Mooley Davis.

After this we could hardly wait for the turn to come
around to Mooley again. When Miss Totten, using a
pointer against the map, indicated that Mooley was to
"bound" the State of North Carolina, we focused with

such attention that the visitors, grinning at each other, shook their heads at such zest. But Dr. Piatt was looking straight at Miss Totten, his lips parted, his head no longer to one side.

"N-North Cal . . . Callina." Just as the deaf gaze at the speaking, Mooley's eyes never left Miss Totten's. Her voice issued, burred here, choked there, but unmistakably a voice. "Bounded by Virginia on the north . . . Tennessee on the west . . . South Callina on the south . . . and on the east . . . and on the east . . ." She bent her head and gripped her desk with her hands. I gripped my own desk, until I saw that she suffered only from the common failing—she had forgotten. She raised her head.

"And on the east," she said joyously, "and on the east by the Atlannic Ocean."

Later that term Miss Totten died. She had been forty years in the school system, we heard in the eulogy at Assembly. There was no immediate family, and any of us who cared to might pay our respects at the chapel. After this, Mr. Moloney, who usually chose "Whispering" for the dismissal march, played something slow and thrumming which forced us to drag our feet until we reached the door.

Of course none of us went to the chapel, nor did we bother to wonder whether Mooley went. Probably she did not. For now that the girl withdrawn for so long behind those rigidly empty eyes had stepped forward into them, they flicked about quite normally, as captious as anyone's.

Once or twice in the days that followed we mentioned Miss Totten, but it was really death that we honored, clicking our tongues like our elders. Passing the umbrella stand at home I sometimes thought of Miss Totten, furled forever in her coffin. Then I forgot her too, along with the rest of the class. After all, this was only reasonable in a class which had achieved Miss Steele.

But memory, after a time, dispenses its own emphasis, making a feuilleton of what we once thought most ponderable, laying its wreath on what we never thought to recall. In the country, the children stumble upon the griffin mask of the mangled pheasant and they learn; they come upon the murderous love knot of the mantis and they surmise. But in the city, although no man looms very large against the sky, he is silhouetted all the more sharply against his fellows. And sometimes the children there, who know so little about the natural world, stumble upon that unsolicited good which is perhaps only a dislocation in the insensitive rhythm of the natural world. And if they are lucky, memory holds it in waiting. For what they have stumbled upon is their own humanity—their aberration and their glory. That is why I find myself wanting to say aloud to someone: "I remember . . . a Miss Elizabeth Totten."

Everything That Rises Must Converge

FLANNERY O'CONNOR

"Everything That Rises Must Converge" is a story about the basic relationships between a mother and son. It does not provide a final or definitive answer to the age-old problems that have plagued every mother and son, but it does pose them in a new and provocative context.

Written in Miss O'Connor's characteristically tight, spare, realistic style, informed with her uncompromising honesty and deep involvement in the social and personal mores of a decadent South, "Everything That Rises Must Converge" moves with a quiet inevitability to its crushing conclusion. Artfully woven into the fabric of the story are the cruel ambiguities and the corrosive white-black conflicts generated by the social patterns of the South. Few contemporary writers have Miss O'Connor's insight into the South, its people, its past and its present travails. Even fewer write about them with such honesty and intensity.

FLANNERY O'CONNOR (1925–1964) lived, died, and, except for a brief sojourn at the University of Iowa where she received her M.A., was educated in Georgia. In her tragically brief life, Miss O'Connor wrote two novels, Wise Blood *(1952) and* The Violent Bear It Away *(1960), and a number of brilliant short stories, many of which were brought together in her collection* A Good Man Is Hard to Find *(1955). All of her stories are set in the South and most of them in the Georgia backwoods.*

Measured against all standards, Miss O'Connor must be considered one of the important writers the South has produced in this century.

Everything That Rises Must Converge

Her doctor had told Julian's mother that she must lose twenty pounds on account of her blood pressure, so on Wednesday nights Julian had to take her downtown on the bus for a reducing class at the Y. The reducing class was designed for working girls over fifty, who weighed from 165 to 200 pounds. His mother was one of the slimmer ones, but she said ladies did not tell their age or weight. She would not ride the buses by herself at night since they had been integrated, and because the reducing class was one of her few pleasures, necessary for her health, and *free,* she said Julian could at least put himself out to take her, considering all she did for him. Julian did not like to consider all she did for him, but every Wednesday night he braced himself and took her.

She was almost ready to go, standing before the hall mirror, putting on her hat, while he, his hands behind him, appeared pinned to the door frame, waiting like Saint Sebastian for the arrows to begin piercing him. The hat was new and had cost her seven dollars and a half. She kept saying, "Maybe I shouldn't have paid that for it. No, I shouldn't have. I'll take it off and return it tomorrow. I shouldn't have bought it."

Julian raised his eyes to heaven. "Yes, you should have bought it," he said. "Put it on and let's go." It was a hideous hat. A purple velvet flap came down on one side of it and stood up on the other, the rest of it was green and looked like a cushion with the stuffing out. He de-

cided it was less comical than jaunty and pathetic. Everything that gave her pleasure was small and depressed him.

She lifted the hat one more time and set it down slowly
on top of her head. Two wings of gray hair protruded on
either side of her florid face, but her eyes, sky-blue, were
as innocent and untouched by experience as they must
have been when she was ten. Were it not that she was a
widow who had struggled fiercely to feed and clothe and
put him through school and who was supporting him still,
"until he got on his feet," she might have been a little
girl that he had to take to town.

"It's all right, it's all right," he said. "Let's go." He
opened the door himself and started down the walk to get
her going. The sky was a dying violet and the houses
stood out darkly against it, bulbous liver-colored mon-
strosities of a uniform ugliness though no two were alike.
Since this had been a fashionable neighborhood forty
years ago, his mother persisted in thinking they did well
to have an apartment in it. Each house had a narrow
collar of dirt around it in which sat, usually, a grubby
child. Julian walked with his hands in his pockets, his
head down and thrust forward and his eyes glazed with
the determination to make himself completely numb during the time he would be sacrificed to her pleasure.

The door closed and he turned to find the dumpy figure,
surmounted by the atrocious hat, coming toward him.
"Well," she said, "you only live once and paying a little
more for it, I at least won't meet myself coming and
going."

"Some day I'll start making money," Julian said
gloomily—he knew he never would—"and you can have
one of those jokes whenever you take the fit." But first
they would move. He visualized a place where the nearest
neighbors would be three miles away on either side.

"I think you're doing fine," she said, drawing on her
gloves. "You've only been out of school a year. Rome
wasn't built in a day."

She was one of the few members of the Y reducing class
who arrived in hat and gloves and who had a son who had
been to college. "It takes time," she said, "and the world
is in such a mess. This hat looked better on me than any
of the others, though when she brought it out I said, 'Take

that thing back. I wouldn't have it on my head,' and she said, 'Now wait till you see it on,' and when she put it on me, I said, 'We-ull,' and she said, 'If you ask me, that hat does something for you and you do something for the hat, and besides,' she said, 'with that hat, you won't meet yourself coming and going.' "

Julian thought he could have stood his lot better if she had been selfish, if she had been an old hag who drank and screamed at him. He walked along, saturated in depression, as if in the midst of his martyrdom he had lost his faith. Catching sight of his long, hopeless, irritated face, she stopped suddenly with a grief-stricken look, and pulled back on his arm. "Wait on me," she said. "I'm going back to the house and take this thing off and tomorrow I'm going to return it. I was out of my head. I can pay the gas bill with that seven-fifty."

He caught her arm in a vicious grip. "You are not going to take it back," he said. "I like it."

"Well," she said, "I don't think I ought . . ."

"Shut up and enjoy it," he muttered, more depressed than ever.

"With the world in the mess it's in," she said, "it's a wonder we can enjoy anything. I tell you, the bottom rail is on the top."

Julian sighed.

"Of course," she said, "if you know who you are, you can go anywhere." She said this every time he took her to the reducing class. "Most of them in it are not our kind of people," she said, "but I can be gracious to anybody. I know who I am."

"They don't give a damn for your graciousness," Julian said savagely. "Knowing who you are is good for one generation only. You haven't the foggiest idea where you stand now or who you are."

She stopped and allowed her eyes to flash at him. "I most certainly do know who I am," she said, "and if you don't know who you are, I'm ashamed of you."

"Oh hell," Julian said.

"Your great-grandfather was a former governor of this state," she said. "Your grandfather was a prosperous landowner. Your grandmother was a Godhigh."

"Will you look around you," he said tensely, "and see

where you are now?" and he swept his arm jerkily out to
indicate the neighborhood, which the growing darkness at
least made less dingy.

"You remain what you are," she said. "Your great-
grandfather had a plantation and two hundred slaves."

"There are no more slaves," he said irritably.

"They were better off when they were," she said. He
groaned to see that she was off on that topic. She rolled
onto it every few days like a train on an open track. He
knew every stop, every junction, every swamp along the
way, and knew the exact point at which her conclusion
would roll majestically into the station: "It's ridiculous. It's
simply not realistic. They should rise, yes, but on their
own side of the fence."

"Let's skip it," Julian said.

"The ones I feel sorry for," she said, "are the ones that
are half white. They're tragic."

"Will you skip it?"

"Suppose we were half white. We would certainly have
mixed feelings."

"I have mixed feelings now," he groaned.

"Well let's talk about something pleasant," she said. "I
remember going to Grandpa's when I was a little girl.
Then the house had double stairways that went up to what
was really the second floor—all the cooking was done on
the first. I used to like to stay down in the kitchen on
account of the way the walls smelled. I would sit with my
nose pressed against the plaster and take deep breaths.
Actually the place belonged to the Godhighs but your
grandfather Chestny paid the mortgage and saved it for
them. They were in reduced circumstances," she said, "but
reduced or not, they never forgot who they were."

"Doubtless that decayed mansion reminded them," Julian muttered. He never spoke of it without contempt or
thought of it without longing. He had seen it once when
he was a child before it had been sold. The double stairways had rotted and been torn down. Negroes were living
in it. But it remained in his mind as his mother had
known it. It appeared in his dreams regularly. He would
stand on the wide porch, listening to the rustle of oak
leaves, then wander through the high-ceilinged hall into
the parlor that opened onto it and gaze at the worn rugs

and faded draperies. It occurred to him that it was he, not she, who could have appreciated it. He preferred its threadbare elegance to anything he could name and it was because of it that all the neighborhoods they had lived in had been a torment to him—whereas she had hardly known the difference. She called her insensitivity "being adjustable."

"And I remember the old darky who was my nurse, Caroline. There was no better person in the world. I've always had a great respect for my colored friends," she said. "I'd do anything in the world for them and they'd . . ."

"Will you for God's sake get off that subject?" Julian said. When he got on a bus by himself, he made it a point to sit down beside a Negro, in reparation as it were for his mother's sins.

"You're mighty touchy tonight," she said. "Do you feel all right?"

"Yes I feel all right," he said. "Now lay off."

She pursed her lips. "Well, you certainly are in a vile humor," she observed. "I just won't speak to you at all."

They had reached the bus stop. There was no bus in sight and Julian, his hands still jammed in his pockets and his head thrust forward, scowled down the empty street. The frustration of having to wait on the bus as well as ride on it began to creep up his neck like a hot hand. The presence of his mother was borne in upon him as she gave a pained sigh. He looked at her bleakly. She was holding herself very erect under the preposterous hat, wearing it like a banner of her imaginary dignity. There was in him an evil urge to break her spirit. He suddenly unloosened his tie and pulled it off and put it in his pocket.

She stiffened. "Why must you look like *that* when you take me to town?" she said. "Why must you deliberately embarrass me?"

"If you'll never learn where you are," he said, "you can at least learn where I am."

"You look like a—thug," she said.

"Then I must be one," he murmured.

"I'll just go home," she said. "I will not bother you. If you can't do a little thing like that for me . . ."

Rolling his eyes upward, he put his tie back on. "Restored to my class," he muttered. He thrust his face toward her and hissed, "True culture is in the mind, the *mind*," he said, and tapped his head, "the mind."

"It's in the heart," she said, "and in how you do things and how you do things is because of who you *are*."

"Nobody in the damn bus cares who you are."

"I care who I am," she said icily.

The lighted bus appeared on top of the next hill and as it approached, they moved out into the street to meet it. He put his hand under her elbow and hoisted her up on the creaking step. She entered with a little smile, as if she were going into a drawing room where everyone had been waiting for her. While he put in the tokens, she sat down on one of the broad front seats for three which faced the aisle. A thin woman with protruding teeth and long yellow hair was sitting on the end of it. His mother moved up beside her and left room for Julian beside herself. He sat down and looked at the floor across the aisle where a pair of thin feet in red and white canvas sandals were planted.

His mother immediately began a general conversation meant to attract anyone who felt like talking. "Can it get any hotter?" she said and removed from her purse a folding fan, black with a Japanese scene on it, which she began to flutter before her.

"I reckon it might could," the woman with the protruding teeth said, "but I know for a fact my apartment couldn't get no hotter."

"It must get the afternoon sun," his mother said. She sat forward and looked up and down the bus. It was half filled. Everybody was white. "I see we have the bus to ourselves," she said. Julian cringed.

"For a change," said the woman across the aisle, the owner of the red and white canvas sandals. "I come on one the other day and they were thick as fleas—up front and all through."

"The world is in a mess everywhere," his mother said. "I don't know how we've let it get in this fix."

"What gets my goat is all those boys from good families stealing automobile tires," the woman with the protruding teeth said. "I told my boy, I said you may not be rich but you been raised right and if I ever catch you in any such mess, they can send you on to the reformatory. Be exactly where you belong."

"Training tells," his mother said. "Is your boy in high school?"

"Ninth grade," the woman said.

"My son just finished college last year. He wants to write but he's selling typewriters until he gets started," his mother said.

The woman leaned forward and peered at Julian. He threw her such a malevolent look that she subsided against the seat. On the floor across the aisle there was an abandoned newspaper. He got up and got it and opened it out in front of him. His mother discreetly continued the conversation in a lower tone but the woman across the aisle said in a loud voice, "Well that's nice. Selling typewriters is close to writing. He can go right from one to the other."

"I tell him," his mother said, "that Rome wasn't built in a day."

Behind the newspaper Julian was withdrawing into the inner compartment of his mind where he spent most of his time. This was a kind of mental bubble in which he established himself when he could not bear to be a part of what was going on around him. From it he could see out and judge but in it he was safe from any kind of penetration from without. It was the only place where he felt free of the general idiocy of his fellows. His mother had never entered it but from it he could see her with absolute clarity.

The old lady was clever enough and he thought that if she had started from any of the right premises, more might have been expected of her. She lived according to the laws of her own fantasy world, outside of which he had never seen her set foot. The law of it was to sacrifice herself for him after she had first created the necessity to do so by making a mess of things. If he had permitted her sacrifices, it was only because her lack of foresight had made them necessary. All of her life had been a struggle to act like a Chestny without the Chestny goods, and to give him everything she thought a Chestny ought to have; but since, said she, it was fun to struggle, why complain? And when you had won, as she had won, what fun to look back on the hard times! He could not forgive her that she had enjoyed the struggle and that she thought *she* had won.

What she meant when she said she had won was that she had brought him up successfully and had sent him to college and that he had turned out so well—good looking (her teeth had gone unfilled so that his could be straightened), intelligent (he realized he was too intelligent to be a success), and with a future ahead of him (there was of course no future ahead of him). She excused his gloominess on the grounds that he was still growing up and his radical ideas on his lack of practical experience. She said he didn't yet know a thing about "life," that he hadn't even entered the real world—when already he was as disenchanted with it as a man of fifty.

The further irony of all this was that in spite of her, he had turned out so well. In spite of going to only a third-rate college, he had, on his own initiative, come out with a first-rate education; in spite of growing up dominated by a small mind he had ended up with a large one; in spite of all her foolish views, he was free of prejudice and unafraid to face facts. Most miraculous of all, instead of being blinded by love for her as she was for him, he had cut himself emotionally free of her and could see her with complete objectivity. He was not dominated by his mother.

The bus stopped with a sudden jerk and shook him from his meditation. A woman from the back lurched forward with little steps and barely escaped falling in his newspaper as she righted herself. She got off and a large Negro got on. Julian kept his paper lowered to watch. It gave him a certain satisfaction to see injustice in daily operation. It confirmed his view that with a few exceptions there was no one worth knowing within a radius of three hundred miles. The Negro was well dressed and carried a briefcase. He looked around and then sat down on the other end of the seat where the woman with the red and white canvas sandals was sitting. He immediately unfolded a newspaper and obscured himself behind it. Julian's mother's elbow at once prodded insistently into his ribs. "Now you see why I won't ride on these buses by myself," she whispered.

The woman with the red and white canvas sandals had risen at the same time the Negro sat down and had gone further back in the bus and taken the seat of the woman who had got off. His mother leaned forward and cast her an approving look.

Julian rose, crossed the aisle, and sat down in the place of the woman with the canvas sandals. From this position, he looked serenely across at his mother. Her face had turned an angry red. He stared at her, making his eyes the eyes of a stranger. He felt his tension suddenly lift as if he had openly declared war on her.

He would have liked to get in conversation with the Negro and to talk with him about art or politics or any subject that would be above the comprehension of those around them, but the man remained entrenched behind his paper. He was either ignoring the change of seating or had never noticed it. There was no way for Julian to convey his sympathy.

His mother kept her eyes fixed reproachfully on his face. The woman with the protruding teeth was looking at him avidly as if he were a type of monster new to her.

"Do you have a light?" he asked the Negro.

Without looking away from his paper, the man reached in his pocket and handed him a packet of matches.

"Thanks," Julian said. For a moment he held the matches foolishly. A NO SMOKING sign looked down upon him from over the door. This alone would not have deterred him; he had no cigarettes. He had quit smoking some months before because he could not afford it. "Sorry," he muttered and handed back the matches. The Negro lowered the paper and gave him an annoyed look. He took the matches and raised the paper again.

His mother continued to gaze at him but she did not take advantage of his momentary discomfort. Her eyes retained their battered look. Her face seemed to be unnaturally red, as if her blood pressure had risen. Julian allowed no glimmer of sympathy to show on his face. Having got the advantage, he wanted desperately to keep it and carry it through. He would have liked to teach her a lesson that would last her a while, but there seemed no way to continue the point. The Negro refused to come out from behind his paper.

Julian folded his arms and looked stolidly before him, facing her but as if he did not see her, as if he had ceased to recognize her existence. He visualized a scene in which, the bus having reached their stop, he would remain in his seat and when she said, "Aren't you going to get off?" he would look at her as at a stranger who had rashly addressed him. The corner they got off on was usually deserted, but it was well lighted and it would not hurt her to walk by herself the four blocks to the Y. He decided to wait until the time came and then decide whether or not he would let her get off by herself. He would have to be at the Y at ten to bring her back, but he could leave her wondering if he was going to show up. There was no reason for her to think she could always depend on him.

He retired again into the high-ceilinged room sparsely settled with large pieces of antique furniture. His soul expanded momentarily but then he became aware of his mother across from him and the vision shriveled. He studied her coldly. Her feet in little pumps dangled like a child's and did not quite reach the floor. She was training on him an exaggerated look of reproach. He felt completely detached from her. At that moment he could with pleasure have slapped her as he would have slapped a particularly obnoxious child in his charge.

He began to imagine various unlikely ways by which he could teach her a lesson. He might make friends with some distinguished Negro professor or lawyer and bring him home to spend the evening. He would be entirely justified but her blood pressure would rise to 300. He could not push her to the extent of making her have a stroke, and moreover, he had never been successful at making any Negro friends. He had tried to strike up an acquaintance on the bus with some of the better types, with ones that looked like professors or ministers or lawyers. One morning he had sat down next to a distinguished-looking dark brown man who had answered his questions with a sonorous solemnity but who had turned out to be an undertaker. Another day he had sat down beside a cigar-smoking Negro with a diamond ring on his finger, but after a few stilted pleasantries, the Negro had rung the buzzer and risen, slipping two lottery tickets into Julian's hand as he climbed over him to leave.

He imagined his mother lying desperately ill and his being able to secure only a Negro doctor for her. He toyed with that idea for a few minutes and then dropped it for a momentary vision of himself participating as a sympathizer in a sit-in demonstration. This was possible but he did not linger with it. Instead, he approached the ultimate horror. He brought home a beautiful suspiciously Negroid woman. Prepare yourself, he said. There is nothing you can do about it. This is the woman I've chosen. She's intelligent, dignified, even good, and she's suffered and she hasn't thought it *fun*. Now persecute us, go ahead and persecute us. Drive her out of here, but remember, you're driving me too. His eyes were narrowed and through the indignation he had generated, he saw his mother across the aisle, purple-faced, shrunken to the dwarf-like proportions of her moral nature, sitting like a mummy beneath the ridiculous banner of her hat.

He was tilted out of his fantasy again as the bus stopped. The door opened with a sucking hiss and out of the dark a large, gaily dressed, sullen-looking colored woman got on with a little boy. The child, who might have been four, had on a short plaid suit and a Tyrolean hat with a blue feather in it. Julian hoped that he would sit down beside him and that the woman would push in beside his mother. He could think of no better arrangement.

As she waited for her tokens, the woman was surveying the seating possibilities—he hoped with the idea of sitting where she was least wanted. There was something familiar-looking about her but Julian could not place what it was. She was a giant of a woman. Her face was set not only to meet opposition but to seek it out. The downward tilt of her large lower lip was like a warning sign: DON'T TAMPER WITH ME. Her bulging figure was encased in a green crepe dress and her feet overflowed in red shoes. She had on a hideous hat. A purple velvet flap came down on one side of it and stood up on the other; the rest of it was green and looked like a cushion with the stuffing out. She carried a mammoth red pocketbook that bulged throughout as if it were stuffed with rocks.

To Julian's disappointment, the little boy climbed up on the empty seat beside his mother. His mother lumped all children, black and white, into the common category, "cute," and she thought little Negroes were on the whole cuter than little white children. She smiled at the little boy as he climbed on the seat.

Meanwhile the woman was bearing down upon the empty seat beside Julian. To his annoyance, she squeezed herself into it. He saw his mother's face change as the woman settled herself next to him and he realized with satisfaction that this was more objectionable to her than it was to him. Her face seemed almost gray and there was a look of dull recognition in her eyes, as if suddenly she had sickened at some awful confrontation. Julian saw that it was because she and the woman had, in a sense, swapped sons. Though his mother would not realize the symbolic significance of this, she would feel it. His amusement showed plainly on his face.

The woman next to him muttered something unintelligible to herself. He was conscious of a kind of bristling next to him, a muted growling like that of an angry cat. He could not see anything but the red pocketbook upright on the bulging green thighs. He visualized the woman as she had stood waiting for her tokens—the ponderous figure, rising from the red shoes upward over the solid hips, the mammoth bosom, the haughty face, to the green and purple hat.

His eyes widened.

The vision of the two hats, identical, broke upon him with the radiance of a brilliant sunrise. His face was suddenly lit with joy. He could not believe that Fate had thrust upon his mother such a lesson. He gave a loud chuckle so that she would look at him and see that he saw. She turned her eyes on him slowly. The blue in them seemed to have turned a bruised purple. For a moment he had an uncomfortable sense of her innocence, but it lasted only a second before principle rescued him. Justice entitled him to laugh. His grin hardened until it said to her as plainly as if he were saying aloud: Your punishment exactly fits your pettiness. This should teach you a permanent lesson.

Her eyes shifted to the woman. She seemed unable to bear looking at him and to find the woman preferable. He became conscious again of the bristling presence at his side. The woman was rumbling like a volcano about to become active. His mother's mouth began to twitch slightly at one corner. With a sinking heart, he saw incipient signs of recovery on her face and realized that this was going to strike her suddenly as funny and was going to be no lesson at all. She kept her eyes on the woman and an amused smile came over her face as if the woman were a monkey that had stolen her hat. The little Negro was looking up at her with large fascinated eyes. He had been trying to attract her attention for some time.

"Carver!" the woman said suddenly. "Come heah!"

When he saw that the spotlight was on him at last, Carver drew his feet up and turned himself toward Julian's mother and giggled.

"Carver!" the woman said. "You heah me? Come heah!"

Carver slid down from the seat but remained squatting with his back against the base of it, his head turned slyly around toward Julian's mother, who was smiling at him. The woman reached a hand across the aisle and snatched him to her. He righted himself and hung backwards on her knees, grinning at Julian's mother. "Isn't he cute?" Julian's mother said to the woman with the protruding teeth.

"I reckon he is," the woman said without conviction.

The Negress yanked him upright but he eased out of her grip and shot across the aisle and scrambled, giggling wildly, onto the seat beside his love.

"I think he likes me," Julian's mother said, and smiled at the woman. It was the smile she used when she was being particularly gracious to an inferior. Julian saw everything lost. The lesson had rolled off her like rain on a roof.

The woman stood up and yanked the little boy off the seat as if she were snatching him from contagion. Julian could feel the rage in her at having no weapon like his mother's smile. She gave the child a sharp slap across his leg. He howled once and then thrust his head into her stomach and kicked his feet against her shins. "Be-have," she said vehemently.

The bus stopped and the Negro who had been reading the newspaper got off. The woman moved over and set the little boy down with a thump between herself and Julian. She held him firmly by the knee. In a moment he put his hands in front of his face and peeped at Julian's mother through his fingers.

"I see yoooooooo!" she said and put her hand in front of her face and peeped at him.

The woman slapped his hand down. "Quit yo' foolishness," she said, "before I knock the living Jesus out of you!"

Julian was thankful that the next stop was theirs. He reached up and pulled the cord. The woman reached up and pulled it at the same time. Oh my God, he thought. He had the terrible intuition that when they got off the bus together, his mother would open her purse and give the little boy a nickel. The gesture would be as natural to her as breathing. The bus stopped and the woman got up and lunged to the front, dragging the child, who wished to stay on, after her. Julian and his mother got up and followed. As they neared the door, Julian tried to relieve her of her pocketbook.

"No," she murmured, "I want to give the little boy a nickel."

"No!" Julian hissed. "No!"

She smiled down at the child and opened her bag. The bus door opened and the woman picked him up by the arm and descended with him, hanging at her hip. Once in the street she set him down and shook him.

Julian's mother had to close her purse while she got down the bus step but as soon as her feet were on the ground, she opened it again and began to rummage inside. "I can't find but a penny," she whispered, "but it looks like a new one."

"Don't do it!" Julian said fiercely between his teeth. There was a streetlight on the corner and she hurried to get under it so that she could better see into her pocketbook. The woman was heading off rapidly down the street with the child still hanging backward on her hand.

"Oh little boy!" Julian's mother called and took a few quick steps and caught up with them just beyond the lamppost. "Here's a bright new penny for you," and she held out the coin, which shone bronze in the dim light.

The huge woman turned and for a moment stood, her shoulders lifted and her face frozen with frustrated rage, and stared at Julian's mother. Then all at once she seemed to explode like a piece of machinery that had been given one ounce of pressure too much. Julian saw the black fist swing out with the red pocketbook. He shut his eyes and cringed as he heard the woman shout, "He don't take nobody's pennies!" When he opened his eyes, the woman was disappearing down the street with the little boy staring wide-eyed over her shoulder. Julian's mother was sitting on the sidewalk.

"I told you not to do that," Julian said angrily. "I told you not to do that!"

He stood over her for a minute, gritting his teeth. Her legs were stretched out in front of her and her hat was on her lap. He squatted down and looked her in the face. It was totally expressionless. "You got exactly what you deserved," he said. "Now get up."

He picked up her pocketbook and put what had fallen out back in it. He picked the hat up off her lap. The penny caught his eye on the sidewalk and he picked that up and let it drop before her eyes into the purse. Then he stood up and leaned over and held his hands out to pull her up. She remained immobile. He sighed. Rising above them on either side were black apartment buildings, marked with irregular rectangles of light. At the end of the block a man came out of a door and walked off in the opposite direction. "All right," he said, "suppose somebody happens by and wants to know why you're sitting on the sidewalk?"

She took the hand and, breathing hard, pulled heavily up on it and then stood for a moment, swaying slightly as if the spots of light in the darkness were circling around her. Her eyes, shadowed and confused, finally settled on his face. He did not try to conceal his irritation. "I hope this teaches you a lesson," he said. She leaned forward and her eyes raked his face. She seemed trying to determine his identity. Then, as if she found nothing familiar about him, she started off with a headlong movement in the wrong direction.

"Aren't you going on to the Y?" he asked.

"Home," she muttered.

"Well, are we walking?"

For answer she kept going. Julian followed along, his hands behind him. He saw no reason to let the lesson she had had go without backing it up with an explanation of its meaning. She might as well be made to understand what had happened to her. "Don't think that was just an uppity Negro woman," he said. "That was the whole colored race which will no longer take your condescending pennies. That was your black double. She can wear the same hat as you, and to be sure," he added gratuitously (because he thought it was funny), "it looked better on her than it did on you. What all this means," he said, "is that the old world is gone. The old manners are obsolete and your graciousness is not worth a damn." He thought bitterly of the house that had been lost for him. "You aren't who you think you are," he said.

She continued to plow ahead, paying no attention to him. Her hair had come undone on one side. She dropped her pocketbook and took no notice. He stooped and picked it up and handed it to her but she did not take it.

"You needn't act as if the world had come to an end," he said, "because it hasn't. From now on you've got to live in a new world and face a few realities for a change. Buck up," he said, "it won't kill you."

She was breathing fast.

"Let's wait on the bus," he said.

"Home," she said thickly.

"I hate to see you behave like this," he said. "Just like a child. I should be able to expect more of you." He decided to stop where he was and make her stop and wait for a bus. "I'm not going any farther," he said, stopping. "We're going on the bus."

She continued to go on as if she had not heard him. He took a few steps and caught her arm and stopped her. He looked into her face and caught his breath. He was looking into a face he had never seen before. "Tell Grandpa to come get me," she said.

He stared, stricken.

"Tell Caroline to come get me," she said.

Stunned, he let her go and she lurched forward again, walking as if one leg were shorter than the other. A tide of darkness seemed to be sweeping her from him. "Mother!" he cried. "Darling, sweetheart, wait!" Crumpling, she fell to the pavement. He dashed forward and fell at her side, crying, "Mamma, Mamma!" He turned her over. Her face was fiercely distorted. One eye, large and staring, moved slightly to the left as if it had become unmoored. The other remained fixed on him, raked his face again, found nothing and closed.

"Wait here, wait here!" he cried and jumped up and began to run for help toward a cluster of lights he saw in the distance ahead of him. "Help, help!" he shouted, but his voice was thin, scarcely a thread of sound. The lights drifted farther away the faster he ran and his feet moved numbly as if they carried him nowhere. The tide of darkness seemed to sweep him back to her, postponing from moment to moment his entry into the world of guilt and sorrow.

The Waltz

DOROTHY PARKER

On the surface, "The Waltz" looks like a very simple story about what one girl thinks about (but doesn't tell) the man she is dancing with. Actually, she speaks for every girl who has ever danced with a man. Originally published in *The New Yorker* in 1933, "The Waltz" is probably Miss Parker's best known story—a merciless look at the painful hypocrisies that shape and direct our lives.

Miss Parker's work has an almost instantly recognizable quality: a unique amalgam of technical brilliance, an unerring ear for the characteristic nuances of speech, a devastating wit that probes deep into social pretensions and inequities. Yet very close to the surface of Miss Parker's stories lies a bitter-sweet compassion for the pathetic quality of the lives her characters lead, caught, as they are, in a mesh of indignities and futilities.

DOROTHY ROTHSCHILD PARKER (1893–1967) was born in West End, New Jersey. She is best known for her verse and her short stories. The best of her verses are preserved in the collections Enough Rope *(1927),* Death and Taxes *(1931), and* Not So Deep As a Well

(1936). As a short story writer she has few peers. In stories like "The Waltz" and "Big Blonde," something of the same disenchantment that pervades her verses comes through, but with considerably more compassion. Miss Parker's stories were published in Laments for the Living *(1930) and* Here Lies *(1939). Her* Collected Stories *appeared in 1942.*

Miss Parker also wrote drama criticism for Vanity Fair, *screenplays, and plays (*Close Harmony *with Elmer Rice and* The Coast of Illyria *with Ross Evans).*

The Waltz

Why, thank you so much, I'd adore to.

I don't want to dance with him. I don't want to dance with anybody. And even if I did, it wouldn't be him. He'd be well down among the last ten. I've seen the way he dances; it looks like something you do on Saint Walpurgis Night. Just think, not a quarter of an hour ago, here I was sitting, feeling so sorry for the poor girl he was dancing with. And now *I'm* going to be the poor girl. Well, well. Isn't it a small world?

And a peach of a world, too. A true little corker. Its events are so fascinatingly unpredictable, are not they? Here I was, minding my own business, not doing a stitch of harm to any living soul. And then he comes into my life, all smiles and city manners, to sue me for the favor of one memorable mazurka. Why, he scarcely knows my name, let alone what it stands for. It stands for Despair, Bewilderment, Futility, Degradation, and Premeditated Murder, but little does he wot. I don't wot his name, either; I haven't any idea what it is. Jukes, would be my guess from the look in his eyes. How do you do, Mr. Jukes? And how is that dear little brother of yours, with the two heads?

Ah, now why did he have to come around me, with his low requests? Why can't he let me lead my own life? I ask so little—just to be left alone in my quiet corner of the table, to do my evening brooding over all my sorrows. And he must come, with his bows and his scrapes and his may-I-have-this-ones. And I had to go and tell him that I'd adore to dance with him. I cannot understand why I wasn't struck right down dead. Yes, and being struck dead would look like a day in the country, compared to struggling out a dance with this boy. But what could I do? Everyone else at the table had got up to dance, except him and me. There was I, trapped. Trapped like a trap in a trap.

What can you say, when a man asks you to dance with him? I most certainly will *not* dance with you, I'll see you in hell first. Why, thank you, I'd like to awfully, but I'm having labor pains. Oh, yes, *do* let's dance together—it's so nice to meet a man who isn't a scaredy-cat about catching my beri-beri. No. There was nothing for me to do, but say I'd adore to. Well, we might as well get it over with. All right, Cannonball, let's run out on the field. You won the toss; you can lead.

Why, I think it's more of a waltz, really. Isn't it? We might just listen to the music a second. Shall we? Oh, yes, it's a waltz. Mind? Why, I'm simply thrilled. I'd love to waltz with you.

I'd love to waltz with you. I'd love to waltz with you. I'd love to have my tonsils out, I'd love to be in a midnight fire at sea. Well, it's too late now. We're getting under way. *Oh.* Oh, dear. Oh, dear, dear, dear. Oh, this is even worse than I thought it would be. I suppose that's the one dependable law of life—everything is always worse than you thought it was going to be. Oh, if I had any real grasp of what this dance would be like, I'd have held out for sitting it out. Well, it will probably amount to the same thing in the end. We'll be sitting it out on the floor in a minute, if he keeps this up.

I'm so glad I brought it to his attention that this is a waltz they're playing. Heaven knows what might have happened, if he had thought it was something fast; we'd have blown the sides right out of the building. Why does he always want to be somewhere that he isn't? Why can't we stay in one place just long enough to get acclimated? It's this constant rush, rush, rush, that's the curse of American life. That's the reason that we're all of us so—*Ow!* For God's sake, don't *kick,* you idiot; this is only second down. Oh, my shin. My poor, poor shin, that I've had ever since I was a little girl!

Oh, no, no, no. Goodness, no. It didn't hurt the least little bit. And anyway it was my fault. Really it was. Truly. Well, you're just being sweet, to say that. It really was all my fault.

I wonder what I'd better do—kill him this instant, with my naked hands, or wait and let him drop in his traces. Maybe it's best not to make a scene. I guess I'll just lie low, and watch the pace get him. He can't keep this up indefinitely—he's only flesh and blood. Die he must, and die he shall, for what he did to me. I don't want to be of the over-sensitive type, but you can't tell me that kick was unpremeditated. Freud says there are no accidents. I've led no cloistered life, I've known dancing partners who have spoiled my slippers and torn my dress; but when it comes to kicking, I am Outraged Womanhood. When you kick me in the shin, *smile.*

Maybe he didn't do it maliciously. Maybe it's just his way of showing his high spirits. I suppose I ought to be glad that one of us is having such a good time. I suppose I ought to think myself lucky if he brings me back alive. Maybe it's captious to demand of a practically strange man that he leave your shins as he found them. After all, the poor boy's doing the best he can. Probably he grew up in the hill country, and never had no larnin'. I bet they had to throw him on his back to get shoes on him.

Yes, it's lovely, isn't it? It's simply lovely. It's the loveliest waltz. Isn't it? Oh, I think it's lovely, too.

Why, I'm getting positively drawn to the Triple Threat here. He's my hero. He has the heart of a lion, and the sinews of a buffalo. Look at him—never a thought of the consequences, never afraid of his face, hurling himself into every scrimmage, eyes shining, cheeks ablaze. And shall it be said that I hung back? No, a thousand times no. What's it to me if I have to spend the next couple of years in a plaster cast? Come on, Butch, right through them! Who wants to live forever?

Oh. Oh, dear. Oh, he's all right, thank goodness. For a while I thought they'd have to carry him off the field. Ah, I couldn't bear to have anything happen to him. I love him. I love him better than anybody in the world. Look at the spirit he gets into a dreary, commonplace waltz; how effete the other dancers seem, beside him. He is youth and vigor and courage, he is strength and gaiety and—*Ow!* Get off my instep, you hulking peasant! What do you think I am, anyway—a gangplank? *Ow!*

No, of course it didn't hurt. Why, it didn't a bit. Honestly. And it was all my fault. You see, that little step of yours—well, it's perfectly lovely, but it's just a tiny bit tricky to follow at first. Oh, did you work it up yourself? You really did? Well, aren't you amazing! Oh, now I think I've got it. Oh, I think it's lovely. I was watching you do it when you were dancing before. It's awfully effective when you look at it.

It's awfully effective when you look at it. I bet I'm awfully effective when you look at me. My hair is hanging along my cheeks, my skirt is swaddling about me, I can feel the cold damp of my brow. I must look like something out of the "Fall of the House of Usher." This sort of thing takes a fearful toll of a woman my age. And he worked up his little step himself, he with his degenerate cunning. And it was just a tiny bit tricky at first, but now I think I've got it. Two stumbles, slip, and a twenty-yard dash; yes. I've got it. I've got several other things, too, including a split shin and a bitter heart. I hate this creature I'm chained to. I hated him the moment I saw his leering, bestial face. And here I've been locked in his noxious embrace for the thirty-five years this waltz has lasted. Is that orchestra never going to stop playing? Or must this obscene travesty of a dance go on until hell burns out?

Oh, they're going to play another encore. Oh, goody. Oh, that's lovely. Tired? I should say I'm not tired. I'd like to go on like this forever.

I should say I'm not tired. I'm dead, that's all I am. Dead, and in what a cause! And the music is never go-

ing to stop playing, and we're going on like this, Double-
Time Charlie and I, throughout eternity. I suppose I won't
care any more, after the first hundred thousand years. I
suppose nothing will matter then, not heat nor pain nor
broken heart nor cruel, aching weariness. Well. It can't
come too soon for me.

I wonder why I didn't tell him I was tired. I wonder
why I didn't suggest going back to the table. I could have
said let's just listen to the music. Yes, and if he would,
that would be the first bit of attention he has given it all
evening. George Jean Nathan said that the lovely rhythms
of the waltz should be listened to in stillness and not be
accompanied by strange gyrations of the human body. I
think that's what he said. I think it was George Jean
Nathan. Anyhow, whatever he said and whoever he was
and whatever he's doing now, he's better off than I am.
That's safe. Anybody who isn't waltzing with this Mrs.
O'Leary's cow I've got here is having a good time.

Still if we were back at the table, I'd probably have to
talk to him. Look at him—what could you say to a thing
like that! Did you go to the circus this year, what's your
favorite kind of ice cream, how do you spell cat? I guess
I'm as well off here. As well off as if I were in a cement
mixer in full action.

I'm past all feeling now. The only way I can tell when
he steps on me is that I can hear the splintering of bones.
And all the events of my life are passing before my
eyes. There was the time I was in a hurricane in the
West Indies, there was the day I got my head cut open
in the taxi smash, there was the night the drunken lady
threw a bronze ash-tray at her own true love and got
me instead, there was that summer that the sailboat kept
capsizing. Ah, what an easy, peaceful time was mine,
until I fell in with Swifty, here. I didn't know what
trouble was, before I got drawn into this *danse macabre*.
I think my mind is beginning to wander. It almost
seems to me as if the orchestra were stopping. It couldn't
be, of course; it could never, never be. And yet in my
ears there is a silence like the sound of angel voices. . . .

Oh, they've stopped, the mean things. They're not go-

ing to play any more. Oh, darn. Oh, do you think they would? Do you really think so, if you gave them twenty dollars? Oh, that would be lovely. And look, do tell them to play this same thing. I'd simply adore to go on waltzing.

University Days

JAMES THURBER

Most college students take their botany, economics, gymnasium, and military drill courses in stride—as learning experiences of varying interest and excitement, as hurdles to be surmounted, or just as something to be lived through. But not Mr. Thurber. In "University Days," he describes his extraordinary encounters with the commonplace, proving again that one man's meat is another man's—well, not exactly poison, but something pretty much like it.

Like all great humorists (and James Thurber is certainly one of the greatest America has produced), Mr. Thurber is essentially a critic. He sees man as a pathetic, timid, fumbling creature struggling feebly and ineffectually against what appears to him to be the world's organized confusion and mechanical, dehumanized stupidity. Every man's face and hand is set against him. Everything conspires to balk his futile efforts to make some sense and to extract a bit of joy out of the maddening perversities and inconsistencies that he encounters everywhere. Then, in his bemused, understated, deceptively simple way, Mr. Thurber makes amusing and bearable the tragic, the outrageous, the outré.

"University Days" reveals Mr. Thurber's wonderful gift for converting, by some inexplicable alchemy, his galling

117

frustrations into a high hilarity subtly shot through with
sharp commentary on human fallibility.

*JAMES THURBER (1894–1961), American humorist,
cartoonist, short story writer, and editor, was born and
grew up in Columbus, Ohio. A childhood eye injury led
to his later blindness. World War I interrupted his college
career, and during the war, he worked in Washington and
Paris as a code clerk in the State Department. He returned
to Ohio State University after the war and completed his
studies in 1919. Thurber wrote for several newspapers—
the* Columbus Dispatch, *the* Chicago Tribune, *and the*
New York Evening Post. *In 1925, through his friend E. B.
White, he joined the newly organized* New Yorker *magazine and became its managing editor. The executive suite,
Mr. Thurber found, was not to his liking. He withdrew,
but continued as one of the mainstays of* The New Yorker's *distinguished staff of contributors.*

*Until his eyesight failed, Thurber continued to draw
inimitable cartoons and illustrations for his own writing.
Among his works are* The Owl in the Attic and Other
Perplexities *(1931);* The Seal in the Bedroom and Other
Predicaments *(1932);* My Life and Hard Times *(1933);
and* The Male Animal *(1940), a play written in collaboration with Elliot Nugent.*

University Days

I passed all the other courses that I took at my University, but I could never pass botany. This was because all
botany students had to spend several hours a week in a
laboratory looking through a microscope at plant cells,
and I could never see through a microscope. I never
once saw a cell through a microscope. This used to en-
rage my instructor. He would wander around the laboratory pleased with the progress all the students were making in drawing the involved and, so I am told, interesting
structure of flower cells, until he came to me. I would

just be standing there. "I can't see anything," I would say. He would begin patiently enough, explaining how anybody can see through a microscope, but he would always end up in a fury, claiming that I could *too* see through a microscope but just pretended that I couldn't. "It takes away from the beauty of flowers anyway," I used to tell him. "We are not concerned with beauty in this course," he would say. "We are concerned solely with what I may call the *mechanics* of flars." "Well," I'd say, "I can't see anything." "Try it just once again," he'd say, and I would put my eye to the microscope and see nothing at all, except now and again a nebulous milky substance—a phenomenon of maladjustment. You were supposed to see a vivid, restless clockwork of sharply defined plant cells. "I see what looks like a lot of milk," I would tell him. This, he claimed, was the result of my not having adjusted the microscope properly, so he would readjust it for me, or rather, for himself. And I would look again and see milk.

I finally took a deferred pass, as they called it, and waited a year and tried again. (You had to pass one of the biological sciences or you couldn't graduate.) The professor had come back from vacation brown as a berry, bright-eyed, and eager to explain cell-structure again to his classes. "Well," he said to me, cheerily, when we met in the first laboratory hour of the semester, "we're going to see cells this time, aren't we?" "Yes, sir," I said. Students to right of me and to left of me and in front of me were seeing cells; what's more, they were quietly drawing pictures of them in their notebooks. Of course, I didn't see anything.

"We'll try it," the professor said to me, grimly, "with every adjustment of the microscope known to man. As God is my witness, I'll arrange this glass so that you see cells through it or I'll give up teaching. In twenty-two years of botany, I—" He cut off abruptly for he was beginning to quiver all over, like Lionel Barrymore, and he genuinely wished to hold onto his temper; his scenes with me had taken a great deal out of him.

So we tried it with every adjustment of the microscope known to man. With only one of them did I see anything but blackness or the familiar lacteal opacity, and that time I saw, to my pleasure and amazement, a variegated constellation of flecks, specks, and dots. These I hastily drew. The instructor, noting my activity, came back from an adjoining desk, a smile on his lips and his eyebrows high in hope. He looked at my cell drawing. "What's that?" he demanded, with a hint of a squeal in his voice. "That's what I saw," I said. "You didn't, you didn't, you *did*n't!" he screamed, losing control of his temper instantly, and he bent over and squinted into the microscope. His head snapped up. "That's your eye!" he shouted. "You've fixed the lens so that it reflects! You've drawn your eye!"

Another course that I didn't like, but somehow managed to pass, was economics. I went to that class straight from the botany class, which didn't help me any in understanding either subject. I used to get them mixed up. But not as mixed up as another student in my economics class who came there direct from a physics laboratory. He was a tackle on the football team, named Bolenciecwcz. At that time Ohio State University had one of the best football teams in the country, and Bolenciecwcz was one of its outstanding stars. In order to be eligible to play it was necessary for him to keep up in his studies, a very difficult matter, for while he was not dumber than an ox he was not any smarter. Most of his professors were lenient and helped him along. None gave him more hints, in answering questions, or asked him simpler ones than the economics professor, a thin, timid man named Bassum. One day when we were on the subject of transportation and distribution, it came Bolenciecwcz's turn to answer a question. "Name one means of transportation," the professor said to him. No light came into the big tackle's eyes. "Just any means of transportation," said the professor. Bolenciecwcz sat staring at him. "That is," pursued the professor, "any medium, agency, or method of going from one place to another." Bolenciecwcz had the look of a man who is being led into a trap. "You may choose among steam, horse-drawn, or electrically propelled vehicles," said the instructor. "I might suggest the one which we commonly take in making long journeys across land." There was a profound silence in which everybody stirred uneasily, including Bolenciecwcz and Mr. Bassum. Mr. Bassum abruptly broke this silence in an amazing manner. "Choo-choo-choo," he said, in a low voice, and turned instantly scarlet. He glanced appealingly around the room. All of us, of course, shared Mr. Bassum's desire that Bolenciecwcz should stay abreast of the class in economics, for the Illinois game, one of the hardest and most important of the season, was only a week off. "Toot, toot, too-toooooot!" some student with a deep voice moaned, and we all looked encouragingly at Bolenciecwcz. Somebody else gave a fine imitation of a locomotive letting off steam. Mr. Bassum himself rounded off the little show. "Ding, dong, ding, dong," he said, hopefully. Bolenciecwcz was staring at the floor now, trying to think, his great brow furrowed, his huge hands rubbing together, his face red.

"How did you come to college this year, Mr. Bolenciecwcz?" asked the professor. *"Chuf*fa, chuffa, *chuf*fa, chuffa."

"M'father sent me," said the football player.

"What on?" asked Bassum.

"I git an 'lowance," said the tackle, in a low, husky voice, obviously embarrassed.

"No, no," said Bassum. "Name a means of transportation. What did you *ride* here on?"

"Train," said Bolenciecwcz.

"Quite right," said the professor. "Now, Mr. Nugent, will you tell us—"

If I went through anguish in botany and economics—for different reasons—gymnasium work was even worse. I don't even like to think about it. They wouldn't let you play games or join in the exercises with your glasses on and I couldn't see with mine off. I bumped into professors, horizontal bars, agricultural students, and swinging iron rings. Not being able to see, I could take it but I couldn't dish it out. Also, in order to pass gymnasium (and you had to pass it to graduate) you had to learn to swim if you didn't know how. I didn't like the swimming pool, I didn't like swimming, and I didn't like the swimming instructor, and after all these years I still don't. I never swam but I passed my gym work anyway, by having another student give my gymnasium number (978) and swim across the pool in my place. He was a

quiet, amiable blonde youth, number 473, and he would
have seen through a microscope for me if we could have
got away with it, but we couldn't get away with it.
Another thing I didn't like about gymnasium work was
that they made you strip the day you registered. It is
impossible for me to be happy when I am stripped and
being asked a lot of questions. Still, I did better than a
lanky agricultural student who was cross-examined just
before I was. They asked each student what college he
was in—that is, whether Arts, Engineering, Commerce, or
Agriculture. "What college are you in?" the instructor
snapped at the youth in front of me. "Ohio State University," he said promptly.

It wasn't that agricultural student but it was another a
whole lot like him who decided to take up journalism,
possibly on the ground that when farming went to hell
he could fall back on newspaper work. He didn't realize,
of course, that that would be very much like falling back
full-length on a kit of carpenter's tools. Haskins didn't
seem cut out for journalism, being too embarrassed to
talk to anybody and unable to use a typewriter, but the
editor of the college paper assigned him to the cow barns,
the sheep house, the horse pavilion, and the animal husbandry department generally. This was a genuinely big
"beat," for it took up five times as much ground and got
ten times as great a legislative appropriation as the
College of Liberal Arts. The agricultural student knew
animals, but nevertheless his stories were dull and color-
lessly written. He took all afternoon on each of them, on
account of having to hunt for each letter on the typewriter. Once in a while he had to ask somebody to help
him hunt. "C" and "L," in particular, were hard letters
for him to find. His editor finally got pretty much annoyed at the farmer-journalist because his pieces were so
uninteresting. "See here, Haskins," he snapped at him one
day. "Why is it we never have anything hot from you on
the horse pavilion? Here we have two hundred head of
horses on this campus—more than any other university in
the Western Conference except Purdue—and yet you
never get any real low down on them. Now shoot over
to the horse barns and dig up something lively." Haskins
shambled out and came back in about an hour; he said

he had something. "Well, start it off snappily," said the editor. "Something people will read." Haskins set to work and in a couple of hours brought a sheet of typewritten paper to the desk; it was a two-hundred-word story about some disease that had broken out among the horses. Its opening sentence was simple but arresting. It read: "Who has noticed the sores on the tops of the horses in the animal husbandry building?"

Ohio State was a land grant university and therefore two years of military drill was compulsory. We drilled with old Springfield rifles and studied the tactics of the Civil War even though the World War was going on at the time. At 11 o'clock each morning thousands of freshmen and sophomores used to deploy over the campus, moodily creeping up on the old chemistry building. It was good training for the kind of warfare that was waged at Shiloh but it had no connection with what was going on in Europe. Some people used to think there was German money behind it, but they didn't dare say so or they would have been thrown in jail as German spies. It was a period of muddy thought and marked, I believe, the decline of higher education in the Middle West.

As a soldier I was never any good at all. Most of the cadets were glumly indifferent soldiers, but I was no good at all. Once General Littlefield, who was commandant of the cadet corps, popped up in front of me during regimental drill and snapped, "You are the main trouble with the university!" I think he meant that my type was the main trouble with the university but he may have meant me individually. I was mediocre at drill, certainly—that is, until my senior year. By that time I had drilled longer than anybody else in the Western Conference, having failed at military at the end of each preceding year so that I had to do it all over again. I was the only senior still in uniform. The uniform which, when new, had made me look like an interurban railway conductor, now that it had become faded and too tight made me look like Bert Williams in his bellboy act. This had a definitely bad effect on my morale. Even so, I had become by sheer practice little short of wonderful at squad maneuvers.

One day General Littlefield picked our company out of

the whole regiment and tried to get it mixed up by putting it through one movement after another as fast as we could execute them: squads right, squads left, squads on right into line, squads right about, squads left front into line, etc. In about three minutes one hundred and nine men were marching in one direction and I was marching away from them at an angle of forty degrees, all alone. "Company, halt!" shouted General Littlefield. "That man is the only man who has it right!" I was made a corporal for my achievement.

The next day General Littlefield summoned me to his office. He was swatting flies when I went in. I was silent and he was silent too, for a long time. I don't think he remembered me or why he had sent for me, but he didn't want to admit it. He swatted some more flies, keeping his eyes on them narrowly before he let go with the swatter. "Button up your coat!" he snapped. Looking back on it now I can see that he meant me although he was looking at a fly, but I just stood there. Another fly came to rest on a paper in front of the general and began rubbing its hind legs together. The general lifted the swatter cautiously. I moved restlessly and the fly flew away. "You startled him!" barked General Littlefield, looking at me severely. I said I was sorry. "That won't help the situation!" snapped the general, with cold military logic. I didn't see what I could do except offer to chase some more flies toward his desk, but I didn't say anything. He stared out the window at the faraway figures of co-eds crossing the campus toward the library. Finally, he told me I could go. So I went. He either didn't know which cadet I was or else he forgot what he wanted to see me about. It may have been that he wished to apologize for having called me the main trouble with the university; or maybe he had decided to compliment me on my brilliant drilling of the day before and then at the last minute decided not to. I don't know. I don't think about it much any more.

Silent Snow, Secret Snow

CONRAD AIKEN

For Paul the world finally became more than he could bear or understand. He took the only road that seemed to offer him the order and serenity he wanted. In this story Mr. Aiken takes us deep into Paul's troubled retreat from the world of his teachers, parents, and friends into the total peace of his own private world.

"Silent Snow, Secret Snow" clearly shows how deeply Conrad Aiken's writing and thinking have been influenced by Sigmund Freud and other psychoanalytic theoreticians. But Mr. Aiken's consummate artistry and creative imagination free the story of the disfiguring marks of the usual "case history" parading as literature. "Silent Snow, Secret Snow" is a brilliant example of the modern short story that derives its insights from psychoanalysis and yet remains a vibrant, unique, unforgettable work of art. Drawing upon his formidable poetic resources, Mr. Aiken, in powerful symbols and searing images, has created in Paul one of the most poignant and enduring fictional characters of our time.

CONRAD POTTER AIKEN (1899–) was born in Savannah, Georgia. He was graduated from Harvard Uni-

versity in 1912. A gifted poet, literary innovator, and ex-perimentalist, Aiken won the Pulitzer prize in 1930 for his Selected Poems. Although he is primarily a poet, Aiken has written some remarkable stories. His autobiography, Ushant, is one of the most interesting documents of its kind.

Silent Snow, Secret Snow

Just why it should have happened, or why it should have happened just when it did, he could not, of course, possibly have said; nor perhaps would it even have occurred to him to ask. The thing was above all a secret, something to be preciously concealed from Mother and Father; and to that very fact it owed an enormous part of its deliciousness. It was like a peculiarly beautiful trinket to be carried unmentioned in one's trouser pocket—a rare stamp, an old coin, a few tiny gold links found trodden out of shape on the path in the park, a pebble of carnelian, a seashell distinguishable from all others by an unusual spot or stripe—and, as if it were any one of these, he carried around with him everywhere a warm and persistent and increasingly beautiful sense of possession. Nor was it only a sense of possession—it was also a sense of protection. It was as if, in some delightful way, his secret gave him a fortress, a wall behind which he could retreat into heavenly seclusion. This was almost the first thing he had noticed about it—apart from the oddness of the thing itself—and it was this that now again, for the fiftieth time, occurred to him, as he sat in the little schoolroom. It was the half-hour for geography. Miss Buell was revolving with one finger, slowly, a huge terrestrial globe which had been placed on her desk. The green and yellow continents passed and repassed, questions were asked and answered, and now the little girl in front of him, Deirdre, who had a funny little constellation of freckles on the back of her neck, exactly like the Big Dipper, was standing up and telling Miss Buell that the equator was the line that ran round the middle.

Miss Buell's face, which was old and grayish and kindly, with gray stiff curls beside the cheeks, and eyes that swam very brightly, like little minnows, behind thick glasses, wrinkled itself into a complication of amusements.

"Ah! I see. The earth is wearing a belt, or a sash. Or someone drew a line round it!"

"Oh no—not that—I mean——"

In the general laughter, he did not share, or only a very little. He was thinking about the Arctic and Antarctic regions, which of course, on the globe, were white. Miss Buell was now telling them about the tropics, the jungles, the steamy heat of equatorial swamps, where the birds and butterflies, and even the snakes, were like living jewels. As he listened to these things, he was already, with a pleasant sense of half-effort, putting his secret between himself and the words. Was it really an effort at all? For effort implied something voluntary, and perhaps even something one did not especially want; whereas this was distinctly pleasant, and came almost of its own accord. All he needed to do was to think of that morning, the first one, and then of all the others——

But it was all so absurdly simple! It had amounted to so little. It was nothing, just an idea—and just why it should have become so wonderful, so permanent, was a mystery—a very pleasant one, to be sure, but also, in an amusing way, foolish. However, without ceasing to listen to Miss Buell, who had now moved up to the north temperate zones, he deliberately invited his memory of the first morning. It was only a moment or two after he had waked up—or perhaps the moment itself. But was there, to be exact, an exact moment? Was one awake all at once? or was it gradual? Anyway, it was after he had stretched a lazy hand up toward the headrail, and yawned, and then relaxed again among his warm covers, all the more grateful on a December morning, that the thing had happened. Suddenly, for no reason, he had thought of the postman, he remembered the postman. Perhaps there was nothing so odd in that. After all, he heard the postman almost every morning in his life—his heavy boots could be heard clumping round the corner at the top of the little cobbled hill-street, and then, progressively nearer, progressively louder, the double knock at each door, the crossings and recrossings of the street, till finally the clumsy steps came stumbling across to the very door, and the tremendous knock came which shook the house itself.

(Miss Buell was saying, "Vast wheat-growing areas in North America and Siberia."

Deirdre had for the moment placed her left hand across the back of her neck.)

But on this particular morning, the first morning, as he lay there with his eyes closed, he had for some reason *waited* for the postman. He wanted to hear him come round the corner. And that was precisely the joke—he never did. He never came. He never had come—*round the corner*—again. For when at last the steps *were* heard, they had already, he was quite sure, come a little down the hill, to the first house; and even so, the steps were curiously different—they were softer, they had a new secrecy about them, they were muffled and indistinct; and while the rhythm of them was the same, it now said a new thing—it said peace, it said remoteness, it said cold, it said sleep. And he had understood the situation at once —nothing could have seemed simpler—there had been snow in the night, such as all winter he had been longing for; and it was this which had rendered the postman's first footsteps inaudible, and the later ones faint. Of course! How lovely! And even now it must be snowing—it was going to be a snowy day—the long white ragged lines were drifting and sifting across the street, across the faces of the old houses, whispering and hushing, making little triangles of white in the corners between cobblestones, seething a little when the wind blew them over the ground to a drifted corner; and so it would be all day, getting deeper and deeper and silenter and silenter.

(Miss Buell was saying, "Land of perpetual snow.")

All this time, of course (while he lay in bed), he had kept his eyes closed, listening to the nearer progress of the postman, the muffled footsteps thumping and slipping on the snow-sheathed cobbles; and all the other sounds—the double knocks, a frosty far-off voice or two, a bell ringing thinly and softly as if under a sheet of ice—had the same slightly abstracted quality, as if removed by one degree from actuality—as if everything in the world had been insulated by snow. But when at last, pleased, he opened his eyes, and turned them toward the window, to see for himself this long-desired and now so clearly imagined miracle—what he saw instead was brilliant sunlight on a roof; and when, astonished, he jumped out of bed and stared down into the street, expecting to see the cobbles obliterated by the snow, he saw nothing but the bare bright cobbles themselves.

Queer, the effect this extraordinary surprise had had upon him—all the following morning he had kept with him a sense as of snow falling about him, a secret screen of new snow between himself and the world. If he had not dreamed such a thing—and how could he have dreamed it while awake?—how else could one explain it? In any case, the delusion had been so vivid as to affect his entire behavior. He could not now remember whether it was on the first or the second morning—or was it even the third?—that his mother had drawn attention to some oddness in his manner.

"But my darling"—she had said at the breakfast table —"what has come over you? You don't seem to be listening. . . ."

And how often that very thing had happened since!

(Miss Buell was now asking if anyone knew the difference between the North Pole and the Magnetic Pole. Deirdre was holding up her flickering brown hand, and he could see the four white dimples that marked the knuckles.)

Perhaps it hadn't been either the second or third morning—or even the fourth or fifth. How could he be sure? How could he be sure just when the delicious *progress* had become clear? Just when it had really *begun?* The intervals weren't very precise. . . . All he now knew was, that at some point or other—perhaps the second day, perhaps the sixth—he had noticed that the presence of the snow was a little more insistent, the sound of it clearer; and, conversely, the sound of the postman's footsteps more indistinct. Not only could he not hear the steps come round the corner, he could not even hear them at the first house. It was below the first house that he heard them; and then, a few days later, it was below the second house that he heard them; and a few days later again, below the third. Gradually, gradually, the snow was becoming heavier, the sound of its seething louder, the cobblestones more and more muffled. When he found, each morning, on going to the window, after the ritual of listening, that the roofs and cobbles were as bare as ever, it made no difference. This was, after all, only what he had expected. It was even what pleased him, what rewarded him: the thing was his own, belonged to no one else. No one else knew about it, not even his mother and father. There, outside, were the bare cobbles; and here, inside, was the snow. Snow growing heavier each day, muffling the world, hiding the ugly, and deadening increasingly—above all—the steps of the postman.

"But, my darling"—she said at the luncheon table—"what has come over you? You don't seem to listen when people speak to you. That's the third time I've asked you to pass your plate. . . ."

How was one to explain this to Mother? or to Father? There was, of course, nothing to be done about it: nothing. All one could do was to laugh embarrassedly, pretend to be a little ashamed, apologize, and take a sudden and somewhat disingenuous interest in what was being done or said. The cat had stayed out all night. He had a curious swelling on his left cheek—perhaps somebody had kicked him, or a stone had struck him. Mrs. Kempton was or was not coming to tea. The house was going to be housecleaned, or "turned out," on Wednesday instead of Friday. A new lamp was provided for his evening work—perhaps it was eyestrain which accounted for this new and so peculiar vagueness of his —Mother was looking at him with amusement as she said this, but with something else as well. A new lamp? A new lamp. Yes, Mother. No, Mother, Yes, Mother. School is going very well. The geometry is very easy. The history is very dull. The geography is very interesting—particularly when it takes one to the North Pole. Why the North Pole? Oh, well, it would be fun to be an explorer. Another Peary or Scott or Shackleton. And then abruptly he found his interest in the talk at an end, stared at the pudding on his plate, listened, waited, and began once more—ah, how heavenly, too, the first beginnings—

to hear or feel—for could he actually hear it?—the silent snow, the secret snow.

(Miss Buell was telling them about the search for the Northwest Passage, about Hendrik Hudson, the *Half Moon*.)

This had been, indeed, the only distressing feature of the new experience; the fact that it so increasingly had brought him into a kind of mute misunderstanding, or even conflict, with his father and mother. It was as if he were trying to lead a double life. On the one hand, he had to be Paul Hasleman, and keep up the appearance of being that person—dress, wash, and answer intelligently when spoken to—; on the other, he had to explore this new world which had been opened to him. Nor could there be the slightest doubt—not the slightest—that the new world was the profounder and more wonderful of the two. It was irresistible. It was miraculous. Its beauty was simply beyond anything—beyond speech as beyond thought—utterly incommunicable. But how then, between the two worlds, of which he was thus constantly aware, was he to keep a balance? One must get up, one must go to breakfast, one must talk with Mother, go to school, do one's lessons—and, in all this, try not to appear too much of a fool. But if all the while one was also trying to extract the full deliciousness of another and quite separate existence, one which could not easily (if at all) be spoken of—how was one to manage? How was one to explain? Would it be safe to explain? Would it be absurd? Would it merely mean that he would get into some obscure kind of trouble?

These thoughts came and went, came and went, as softly and secretly as the snow; they were not precisely a disturbance, perhaps they were even a pleasure; he liked to have them; their presence was something almost palpable, something he could stroke with his hand, without closing his eyes, and without ceasing to see Miss Buell and the schoolroom and the globe and the freckles on Deirdre's neck; nevertheless he did in a sense cease to see, or to see the obvious external world, and substituted for this vision the vision of snow, the sound of snow, and the slow, almost soundless, approach of the postman. Yesterday, it had been only at the sixth house that the postman had become audible; the snow was much deeper now, it was falling more swiftly and heavily, the sound of its seething was more distinct, more soothing, more persistent. And this morning, it had been—as nearly as he could figure—just above the seventh house—perhaps only a step or two above; at most, he had heard two or three foot-steps before the knock had sounded. . . . And with each such narrowing of the sphere, each nearer approach of the limit at which the postman was first audible, it was odd how sharply was increased the amount of illusion which had to be carried into the ordinary business of daily life. Each day, it was harder to get out of bed, to go to the window, to look out at the—as always—perfectly empty and snowless street. Each day it was more difficult to go through the perfunctory motions of greeting Mother and Father at breakfast, to reply to their questions, to put his books together and go to school. And at school, how extraordinarily hard to conduct with success simul-taneously the public life and the life that was secret! There were times when he longed—positively ached—to tell everyone about it—to burst out with it—only to be checked almost at once by a far-off feeling as of some faint absurdity which was inherent in it—but *was* it ab-surd?—and more importantly by a sense of mysterious power in his very secrecy. Yes; it must be kept secret. That, more and more, became clear. At whatever cost to himself, whatever pain to others—

(Miss Buell looked straight at him, smiling, and said, "Perhaps we'll ask Paul. I'm sure Paul will come out of his daydream long enough to be able to tell us. Won't you, Paul?" He rose slowly from his chair, resting one hand on the brightly varnished desk, and deliberately stared through the snow toward the blackboard. It was an effort, but it was amusing to make it. "Yes," he said slowly, "it was what we now call the Hudson River. This he thought to be the Northwest Passage. He was dis-appointed." He sat down again, and as he did so Deirdre half turned in her chair and gave him a shy smile, of ap-proval and admiration.)

At whatever pain to others.

This part of it was very puzzling, very puzzling. Moth-er was very nice, and so was Father. Yes, that was all true enough. He wanted to be nice to them, to tell them everything—and yet, was it really wrong of him to want to have a secret place of his own?

At bedtime, the night before, Mother had said, "If this goes on, my lad, we'll have to see a doctor, we will! We can't have our boy—" But what was it she had said? "Live in another world"? "Live so far away"? The word *far* had been in it, he was sure, and then Mother had taken up a magazine again and laughed a little, but with an expression which wasn't mirthful. He had felt sorry for her. . . .

The bell rang for dismissal. The sound came to him through long curved parallels of falling snow. He saw Deirdre rise, and had himself risen almost as soon—but not quite as soon—as she.

II

On the walk homeward, which was timeless, it pleased him to see through the accompaniment, or counterpoint, of snow, the items of mere externality on his way. There were many kinds of brick in the sidewalks, and laid in many kinds of pattern. The garden walls, too, were various, some of wooden palings, some of plaster, some of stone. Twigs of bushes leaned over the walls: the little hard green winter buds of lilac, on gray stems, sheathed and fat; other branches very thin and fine and black and desiccated. Dirty sparrows huddled in the bushes, as dull in color as dead fruit left in leafless trees. A single starling creaked on a weather vane. In the gutter, beside a drain, was a scrap of torn and dirty newspaper, caught in a little delta of filth, the word ECZEMA appeared in large capitals, and below it was a letter from Mrs. Amelia D. Cravath, 2100 Pine Street, Fort Worth, Texas, to the effect that being a sufferer for years she had been cured by Caley's Ointment. In the little delta, beside the fan-shaped and deeply runneled continent of brown mud, were lost twigs, descended from their parent trees, dead matches, a rusty horse-chestnut burr, a small concentration of eggshell, a streak of yellow sawdust which had been wet and now was dry and congealed, a brown pebble, and a broken feather. Farther on was a cement sidewalk, ruled into geometrical parallelograms, with a brass inlay at one end commemorating the contractors who had laid it, and, halfway across, an irregular and random series of dog tracks, immortalized in synthetic stone. He knew these well, and always stepped on them; to cover the little hollows with his own foot had always been a queer pleasure; today he did it once more, but perfunctorily and detachedly, all the while thinking of something else. That was a dog, a long time ago, who had made a mistake and walked on the cement while it was still wet. He had probably wagged his tail, but that hadn't been recorded. Now, Paul Hasleman, aged twelve, on his way home from school, crossed the same river, which in the meantime had frozen into rock. Homeward through the snow, the snow falling in bright sunshine. Homeward?

Then came the gateway with the two posts surmounted by egg-shaped stones which had been cunningly balanced on their ends, as if by Columbus, and mortared in the very act of balance; a source of perpetual wonder. On the brick wall just beyond, the letter *H* had been stenciled, presumably for some purpose. *H? H.*

The green hydrant, with a little green-painted chain attached to the brass screw-cap.

The elm tree, with the great gray wound in the bark, kidney-shaped, into which he always put his hand—to feel the cold but living wood. The injury, he had been sure, was due to the gnawings of a tethered horse. But now it deserved only a passing palm, a merely tolerant eye. There were more important things. Miracles. Beyond the thoughts of trees, mere elms. Beyond the thoughts of sidewalks, mere stone, mere brick, mere cement. Beyond the thoughts even of his own shoes, which trod these sidewalks obediently, bearing a burden—far above—of elaborate mystery. He watched them. They were not very well polished; he had neglected them, for a very good reason: they were one of the many parts of the increasing difficulty of the daily return to daily life, the morning struggle. To get up, having at last opened one's eyes, to go to the window, and discover no snow, to wash, to dress, to descend the curving stairs to breakfast—

At whatever pain to others, nevertheless, one must persevere in severance, since the incommunicability of the experience demanded it. It was desirable, of course, to be kind to Mother and Father, especially as they seemed to be worried, but it was also desirable to be resolute. If they should decide—as appeared likely—to consult the doctor, Doctor Howells, and have Paul inspected, his heart listened to through a kind of dictaphone, his lungs, his stomach—well, that was all right. He would go through with it. He would give them answer for question, too—perhaps such answers as they hadn't expected? No. That would never do. For the secret world must, at all costs, be preserved.

The birdhouse in the apple tree was empty—it was the wrong time of year for wrens. The little round black door had lost its pleasure. The wrens were enjoying other houses, other nests, remoter trees. But this too was a notion which he only vaguely and grazingly entertained— as if, for the moment, he merely touched an edge of it; there was something further on, which was already assuming a sharper importance; something which already teased at the corners of his eyes, teasing also at the corner of his mind. It was funny to think that he so wanted this, so awaited it—and yet found himself enjoying this momentary dalliance with the birdhouse, as if for a quite deliberate postponement and enhancement of the approaching pleasure. He was aware of his delay, of his smiling and detached and now almost uncomprehending gaze at the little birdhouse; he knew what he was going to look at next: it was his own little cobbled hill-street, his own house, the little river at the bottom of the hill, the grocer's shop with the cardboard man in the window —and now, thinking of all this, he turned his head, still smiling, and looking quickly right and left through the snow-laden sunlight.

And the mist of snow, as he had foreseen, was still on it—a ghost of snow falling in the bright sunlight, softly and steadily floating and turning and pausing, soundlessly meeting the snow that covered, as with a transparent mirage, the bare bright cobbles. He loved it—he stood still and loved it. Its beauty was paralyzing—beyond all words, all experience, all dream. No fairy story he had ever read could be compared with it—none had ever given him this extraordinary combination of ethereal loveliness with a something else, unnameable, which was just faintly and deliciously terrifying. What was this thing? As he thought of it, he looked upward toward his own bedroom window, which was open—and it was as if he looked straight into the room and saw himself lying half awake in his bed. There he was—at this very instant he was still perhaps actually there—more truly there than standing here at the edge of the cobbled hill-street, with one hand lifted to shade his eyes against the snow-sun. Had he indeed ever left his room, in all this time? since that very first morning? Was the whole progress still being enacted there, was it still the same morning, and himself not yet wholly awake? And even now, had the postman not yet come round the corner? . . .

This idea amused him, and automatically, as he thought of it, he turned his head and looked toward the top of the hill. There was, of course, nothing there—nothing and no one. The street was empty and quiet. And all the more because of its emptiness it occurred to him to count the houses—a thing which, oddly enough, he hadn't before thought of doing. Of course, he had known there weren't many—many, that is, on his own side of the street, which were the ones that figured in the postman's progress—but nevertheless it came as something of a shock to find that there were precisely *six,* above his own house—his own house was the seventh.

Six!

Astonished, he looked at his own house—looked at the door, on which was the number thirteen—and then realized that the whole thing was exactly and logically and absurdly what he ought to have known. Just the same, the realization gave him abruptly, and even a little frighteningly, a sense of hurry. He was being hurried— he was being rushed. For—he knit his brow—he couldn't be mistaken—it was just above the *seventh* house, his *own* house, that the postman had first been audible this very morning. But in that case—in that case—did it mean that tomorrow he would hear nothing? The knock he had heard must have been the knock of their own door. Did it mean—and this was an idea which gave

him a really extraordinary feeling of surprise—that he
would never hear the postman again?—that tomorrow
morning the postman would already have passed the
house, in a snow so deep as to render his footsteps completely inaudible? That he would have made his approach
down the snow-filled street so soundlessly, so secretly,
that he, Paul Hasleman, there lying in bed, would not
have waked in time, or waking, would have heard nothing?

But how could that be? Unless even the knocker should
be muffled in the snow—frozen tight, perhaps? . . . But
in that case—

A vague feeling of disappointment came over him; a
vague sadness as if he felt himself deprived of something
which he had long looked forward to, something much
prized. After all this, all this beautiful progress, the slow
delicious advance of the postman through the silent and
secret snow, the knock creeping closer each day, and the
footsteps nearer, the audible compass of the world thus
daily narrowed, narrowed, narrowed, as the snow sooth-
ingly and beautifully encroached and deepened, after all
this, was he to be defrauded of the one thing he had so
wanted—to be able to count, as it were, the last two
or three solemn footsteps, as they finally approached his
own door? Was it all going to happen, at the end, so
suddenly? or indeed, had it already happened? with
no slow and subtle gradations of menace, in which he
could luxuriate?

He gazed upward again, toward his own window which
flashed in the sun; and this time almost with a feeling
that it would be better if he *were* still in bed, in that
room; for in that case this must still be the first morning,
and there would be six more mornings to come—or, for
that matter, seven or eight or nine—how could he be
sure?—or even more.

III

After supper, the inquisition began. He stood before
the doctor, under the lamp, and submitted silently to the
usual thumpings and tappings.

"Now will you please say 'Ah!'?"

"Ah!"

"Now again, please, if you don't mind."

"Ah."

"Say it slowly, and hold it if you can——"

"Ah-h-h-h-h-h—"

"Good."

How silly all this was. As if it had anything to do with his throat! Or his heart, or lungs!

Relaxing his mouth, of which the corners, after all this absurd stretching, felt uncomfortable, he avoided the doctor's eyes, and stared toward the fireplace, past his mother's feet (in gray slippers) which projected from the green chair, and his father's feet (in brown slippers) which stood neatly side by side on the hearth rug.

"Hm. There is certainly nothing wrong there . . . ?"

He felt the doctor's eyes fixed upon him, and, as if merely to be polite, returned the look, but with a feeling of justifiable evasiveness.

"Now, young man, tell me—do you feel all right?"

"Yes, sir, quite all right."

"No headaches? no dizziness?"

"No, I don't think so."

"Let me see. Let's get a book, if you don't mind—yes, thank you, that will do splendidly—and now, Paul, if you'll just read it, holding it as you would normally hold it—"

He took the book and read:

"And another praise have I to tell for this city our mother, the gift of a great god, a glory of the land most high; the might of horses, the might of young horses, the might of the sea. . . . For thou, son of Cronus, our lord Poseidon, hath throned herein this pride, since in these roads first thou didst show forth the curb that cures the rage of steeds. And the shapely oar, apt to men's hands, hath a wondrous speed on the brine, following the hundred-footed Nereids. . . . O land that art praised above all lands, now is it for thee to make those bright praises seen in deeds."

He stopped, tentatively, and lowered the heavy book.

"No—as I thought—there is certainly no superficial sign of eyestrain."

Silence thronged the room, and he was aware of the

focused scrutiny of the three people who confronted him. . . .

"We could have his eyes examined—but I believe it is something else."

"What could it be?" That was his father's voice.

"It's only this curious absent-mindedness—" This was his mother's voice.

In the presence of the doctor, they both seemed irritatingly apologetic.

"I believe it is something else. Now Paul—I would like very much to ask you a question or two. You will answer them, won't you—you know I'm an old, old friend of yours, eh? That's right! . . ."

His back was thumped twice by the doctor's fat fist—then the doctor was grinning at him with false amiability, while with one fingernail he was scratching the top button of his waistcoat. Beyond the doctor's shoulder was the fire, the fingers of flame making light prestidigitation against the sooty fireback, the soft sound of their random flutter the only sound.

"I would like to know—is there anything that worries you?"

The doctor was again smiling, his eyelids low against the little black pupils, in each of which was a tiny white bead of light. Why answer him? why answer him at all? "At whatever pain to others"—but it was all a nuisance, this necessity for resistance, this necessity for attention; it was as if one had been stood up on a brilliantly lighted stage, under a great round blaze of spotlight; as if one were merely a trained seal, or a performing dog, or a fish, dipped out of an aquarium and held up by the tail. It would serve them right if he were merely to bark or growl. And meanwhile, to miss these last few precious hours, these hours of which each minute was more beautiful than the last, more menacing—! He still looked, as if from a great distance, at the beads of light in the doctor's eyes, at the fixed false smile, and then, beyond, once more at his mother's slippers, his father's slippers, the soft flutter of the fire. Even here, even amongst these hostile presences, and in this arranged light, he could see the snow, he could hear it—it was in the corners of the room, where the shadow was deepest, under the sofa, behind the half-opened door which led to the dining room. It was gentler here, softer, its seethe the quietest of whispers, as if, in deference to a drawing room, it had quite deliberately put on its "manners"; it kept itself out of sight, obliterated itself, but distinctly with an air of saying, "Ah, but just wait! Wait till we are alone together! Then I will begin to tell you something new! Something white! something cold! something sleepy! something of cease, and peace, and the long bright curve of space! Tell them to go away. Banish them. Refuse to speak. Leave them, go upstairs to your room, turn out the light and get into bed—I will go with you. I will be waiting for you, I will tell you a better story than Little Kay of the Skates, or The Snow Ghost—I will surround your bed. I will close the windows, pile a deep drift against the door, so that none will ever again be able to enter. Speak to them! . . ." It seemed as if the little hissing voice came from a slow white spiral of falling flakes in the corner by the front window—but he could not be sure. He felt himself smiling, then, and said to the doctor, but without looking at him, looking beyond him still—

"Oh no, I think not—"

"But are you sure, my boy?"

His father's voice came softly and coldly then—the familiar voice of silken warning.

"You needn't answer at once, Paul—remember we're trying to help you—think it over and be quite sure, won't you?"

He felt himself smiling again, at the notion of being quite sure. What a joke. As if he weren't so sure that assurance was no longer necessary, and all this cross-examination a ridiculous farce, a grotesque parody! What could they know about it? these gross intelligences, these humdrum minds so bound to the usual, the ordinary? Impossible to tell them about it! Why, even now, even now, with the proof so abundant, so formidable, so imminent, so appallingly present here in this very room, could they believe it?—could even his mother believe it? No—it was only too plain that if anything were said about it, the merest hint given, they would be incredulous—they would laugh—they would say "Absurd!"—think things about him which weren't true. . . .

"Why no, I'm not worried—why should I be?"

He looked then straight at the doctor's low-lidded eyes, looked from one of them to the other, from one bead of light to the other, and gave a little laugh.

The doctor seemed to be disconcerted by this. He drew back in his chair, resting a fat white hand on either knee. The smile faded slowly from his face.

"Well, Paul!" he said, and paused gravely, "I'm afraid you don't take this quite seriously enough. I think you perhaps don't quite realize—don't quite realize—" He took a deep quick breath, and turned, as if helplessly, at a loss for words, to the others. But Mother and Father were both silent—no help was forthcoming.

"You must surely know, be aware, that you have not been quite yourself, of late. Don't you know that? . . ."

It was amusing to watch the doctor's renewed attempt at a smile, a queer disorganized look, as of confidential embarrassment.

"I feel all right, sir," he said, and again gave the little laugh.

"And we're trying to help you." The doctor's tone sharpened.

"Yes, sir, I know. But why? I'm all right. I'm just *thinking,* that's all."

His mother made a quick movement forward, resting a hand on the back of the doctor's chair.

"Thinking?" she said. "But my dear, about what?"

This was a direct challenge—and would have to be directly met. But before he met it, he looked again into the corner by the door, as if for reassurance. He smiled again at what he saw, at what he heard. The little spiral was still there, still softly whirling, like the ghost of a white kitten chasing the ghost of a white tail, and making as it did so the faintest of whispers. It was all right! If only he could remain firm, everything was going to be all right.

"Oh, about anything, about nothing—*you* know the way you do!"

"You mean—daydreaming?"

"Oh, no—thinking!"

"But thinking about *what?*"

"Anything."

He laughed a third time—but this time, happening to glance upward toward his mother's face, he was appalled

at the effect his laughter seemed to have upon her. Her
mouth had opened in an expression of horror. . . . This
was too bad! Unfortunate! He had known it would cause
pain, of course—but he hadn't expected it to be quite so
bad as this. Perhaps—perhaps if he just gave them a tiny
gleaming hint—?

"About the snow," he said.

"What on earth?" This was his father's voice. The brown
slippers came a step nearer on the hearthrug.

"But my dear, what do you mean?" This was his
mother's voice.

The doctor merely stared.

"Just *snow,* that's all. I like to think about it."

"Tell us about it, my boy."

"But that's all it is. There's nothing to tell. *You* know
what snow is."

This he said almost angrily, for he felt that they were
trying to corner him. He turned sideways so as no longer
to face the doctor, and the better to see the inch of blackness between the window sill and the lowered curtain—
the cold inch of beckoning and delicious night. At once
he felt better, more assured.

"Mother—can I go to bed, now, please? I've got a
headache."

"But I thought you said—"

"It's just come. It's all these questions—! Can I,
Mother?"

"You can go as soon as the doctor has finished."

"Don't you think this thing ought to be gone into thoroughly, and *now?*" This was Father's voice. The brown
slippers again came a step nearer, the voice was the well-
known "punishment" voice, resonant and cruel.

"Oh, what's the use, Norman—"

Quite suddenly, everyone was silent. And without precisely facing them, nevertheless he was aware that all
three of them were watching him with an extraordinary
intensity—staring hard at him—as if he had done something monstrous, or was himself some kind of monster.
He could hear the soft irregular flutter of the flames; the
cluck-click-cluck-click of the clock; far and faint, two sudden spurts of laughter from the kitchen, as quickly cut off
as begun; a murmur of water in the pipes; and then, the

silence seemed to deepen, to spread out, to become world-long and world-wide, to become timeless and shapeless, and to center inevitably and rightly, with a slow and sleepy but enormous concentration of all power, on the beginning of a new sound. What this new sound was going to be, he knew perfectly well. It might begin with a hiss, but it would end with a roar—there was no time to lose—he must escape. It mustn't happen here—

Without another word, he turned and ran up the stairs.

IV

Not a moment too soon. The darkness was coming in long white waves. A prolonged sibilance filled the night —a great seamless seethe of wild influence went abruptly across it—a cold low humming shook the windows. He shut the door and flung off his clothes in the dark. The bare black floor was like a little raft tossed in waves of snow, almost overwhelmed, washed under whitely, up again, smothered in curled billows of feather. The snow was laughing; it spoke from all sides at once; it pressed closer to him as he ran and jumped exulting into his bed.

"Listen to us!" it said. "Listen! We have come to tell you the story we told you about. You remember? Lie down. Shut your eyes, now—you will no longer see much —in this white darkness who could see, or want to see? We will take the place of everything. . . . Listen—"

A beautiful varying dance of snow began at the front of the room, came forward and then retreated, flattened out toward the floor, then rose fountainlike to the ceiling, swayed, recruited itself from a new stream of flakes which poured laughing in through the humming window, advanced again, lifted long white arms. It said peace, it said remoteness, it said cold—it said—

But then a gash of horrible light fell brutally across the room from the opening door—the snow drew back hissing—something alien had come into the room—something hostile. This thing rushed at him, clutched at him, shook him—and he was not merely horrified, he was filled with such a loathing as he had never known. What was this? this cruel disturbance? this act of anger and hate? It was as if he had to reach up a hand toward another world for any understanding of it—an effort of which he was only barely capable. But of that other world he still remembered just enough to know the exorcising words. They tore themselves from his other life suddenly—

"Mother! Mother! Go away! I hate you!"

And with that effort, everything was solved, everything became all right: the seamless hiss advanced once more, the long white wavering lines rose and fell like enormous whispering seawaves, the whisper becoming louder, the laughter more numerous.

"Listen!" it said. "We'll tell you the last, the most beautiful and secret story—shut your eyes—it is a very small story—a story that gets smaller and smaller—it comes inward instead of opening like a flower—it is a flower becoming a seed—a little cold seed—do you hear? we are leaning closer to you—"

The hiss was now becoming a roar—the whole world was a vast moving screen of snow—but even now it said peace, it said remoteness, it said cold, it said sleep.

Paul's Case

WILLA CATHER

Paul lived in a world he never made, a hostile world he didn't understand or care about. It didn't understand or care about him either.

What does a boy do in the face of the insufferable? Rebel? Run away? Give in? Paul had an answer to these questions.

"Paul's Case" is suffused with Willa Cather's encompassing sympathy for the hurt ones, the different ones, the weak and the rebellious ones. In Paul's problem and his solution Miss Cather touches upon a theme central to her work and outlook—the perennial struggle of the sensitive, beleaguered human heart against the world's crassness, materialism, and uncomprehending indifference. "Paul's Case" is written with Miss Cather's characteristic simplicity and clarity.

WILLA SIBERT CATHER (1876–1947) was born in Virginia. When she was five years old, her parents moved to Red Cloud, Nebraska, where she witnessed the struggles of the immigrant homesteaders against the pitiless forces of nature and economics. In her later writing she was to draw on these childhood observations. After gradu-

ating from the University of Nebraska, she worked as reporter, editor, and high-school teacher.

Three of Miss Cather's novels deal memorably with the lives of the settlers as she knew them: O Pioneers! *(1913),* The Song of the Lark *(1915), and* My Antonia *(1918).* Death Comes for the Archbishop *(1927) reveals Miss Cather's growing interest in Catholicism and the Southwest. In 1922, Miss Cather was awarded the Pulitzer prize for* One of Ours—*not one of her best novels.*

Miss Cather's deep affection and respect for the courage, dignity, and honesty of the pioneers turned in time into a profound dislike of the modern world. Maxwell Geismar has called her "a defender of spiritual grace in the midst of an increasingly materialistic culture."

Paul's Case

It was Paul's afternoon to appear before the faculty of the Pittsburgh High School to account for his various misdemeanors. He had been suspended a week ago, and his father had called at the Principal's office and confessed his perplexity about his son. Paul entered the faculty room suave and smiling. His clothes were a trifle outgrown, and the tan velvet on the collar of his open overcoat was frayed and worn; but for all that there was something of the dandy about him, and he wore an opal pin in his neatly knotted black four-in-hand, and a red carnation in his buttonhole. This latter adornment the faculty somehow felt was not properly significant of the contrite spirit befitting a boy under the ban of suspension.

Paul was tall for his age and very thin, with high, cramped shoulders and a narrow chest. His eyes were remarkable for a certain hysterical brilliancy, and he continually used them in a conscious, theatrical sort of way, peculiarly offensive in a boy. The pupils were abnormally large, as though he were addicted to belladonna, but there was a glassy glitter about them which that drug does not produce.

When questioned by the Principal as to why he was

there, Paul stated, politely enough, that he wanted to come back to school. This was a lie, but Paul was quite accustomed to lying; found it, indeed, indispensable for overcoming friction. His teachers were asked to state their respective charges against him, which they did with such a rancor and aggrievedness as evinced that this was not a usual case. Disorder and impertinence were among the offenses named, yet each of his instructors felt that it was scarcely possible to put into words the real cause of the trouble, which lay in a sort of hysterically defiant manner of the boy's; in the contempt which they all knew he felt for them, and which he seemingly made not the least effort to conceal. Once, when he had been making a synopsis of a paragraph at the blackboard, his English teacher had stepped to his side and attempted to guide his hand. Paul had started back with a shudder and thrust his hands violently behind him. The astonished woman could scarcely have been more hurt and embarrassed had he struck at her. The insult was so involuntary and definitely personal as to be unforgettable. In one way and another, he had made all his teachers, men and women alike, conscious of the same feeling of physical aversion. In one class he habitually sat with his hand shading his eyes; in another he always looked out of the window during the recitation; in another he made a running commentary on the lecture, with humorous intent.

His teachers felt this afternoon that his whole attitude was symbolized by his shrug and his flippantly red carnation flower, and they fell upon him without mercy, his English teacher leading the pack. He stood through it smiling, his pale lips parted over his white teeth. (His lips were continually twitching, and he had a habit of raising his eyebrows that was contemptuous and irritating to the last degree.) Older boys than Paul had broken down and shed tears under the ordeal, but his set smile did not once desert him, and his only sign of discomfort was the nervous trembling of the fingers that toyed with the buttons of his overcoat, and an occasional jerking of the other hand which held his hat. Paul was always smiling, always glancing about him, seeming to feel that people might be watching him and trying to detect something. This conscious expression, since it was as far as possible from boyish mirthfulness, was usually attributed to insolence or "smartness."

As the inquisition proceeded, one of his instructors repeated an impertinent remark of the boy's, and the Principal asked him whether he thought that a courteous speech to make to a woman. Paul shrugged his shoulder slightly and his eyebrows twitched.

"I don't know," he replied. "I didn't mean to be polite or impolite, either. I guess it's a sort of way I have, of saying things regardless."

The Principal asked him whether he didn't think that a way it would be well to get rid of. Paul grinned and said he guessed so. When he was told that he could go, he bowed gracefully and went out. His bow was like a repetition of the scandalous red carnation.

His teachers were in despair, and his drawing master voiced the feeling of them all when he declared there was something about the boy which none of them understood. He added: "I don't really believe that smile of his comes altogether from insolence; there's something sort of haunted about it. The boy is not strong, for one thing. There is something wrong about the fellow."

The drawing master had come to realize that, in looking at Paul, one saw only his white teeth and the forced animation of his eyes. One warm afternoon the boy had gone to sleep at his drawing board, and his master had noted with amazement what a white, blue-veined face it was; drawn and wrinkled like an old man's about the eyes, the lips twitching even in his sleep.

His teachers left the building dissatisfied and unhappy, humiliated to have felt so vindictive toward a mere boy, to have uttered this feeling in cutting terms, and to have set each other on, as it were, in the gruesome game of intemperate reproach. One of them remembered having seen a miserable street cat set at bay by a ring of tormentors.

As for Paul, he ran down the hill whistling the Soldiers' Chorus from *Faust*, looking wildly behind him now and then to see whether some of his teachers were not there to witness his light-heartedness. As it was now late in the afternoon and Paul was on duty that evening as usher at

Carnegie Hall, he decided that he would not go home to supper.

When he reached the concert hall the doors were not yet open. It was chilly outside, and he decided to go up into the picture gallery—always deserted at this hour—where there were some of Raffelli's gay studies of Paris streets and an airy blue Venetian scene or two that always exhilarated him. He was delighted to find no one in the gallery but the old guard, who sat in the corner, a newspaper on his knee, a black patch over one eye and the other closed. Paul possessed himself of the place and walked confidently up and down, whistling under his breath. After a while he sat down before a blue Rico and lost himself. When he bethought him to look at his watch, it was after seven o'clock, and he rose with a start and ran downstairs, making a face at Augustus Caesar, peering out from the cast-room, and an evil gesture at the Venus of Milo as he passed her on the stairway.

When Paul reached the ushers' dressing-room half a dozen boys were there already, and he began excitedly to tumble into his uniform. It was one of the few that at all approached fitting, and Paul thought it very becoming—though he knew the tight, straight coat accentuated his narrow chest, about which he was exceedingly sensitive. He was always excited while he dressed, twangling all over to the tuning of the strings and the preliminary flourishes of the horns in the music-room; but tonight he seemed quite beside himself, and he teased and plagued the boys until, telling him that he was crazy, they put him down on the floor and sat on him.

Somewhat calmed by his suppression, Paul dashed out to the front of the house to seat the early comers. He was a model usher. Gracious and smiling he ran up and down the aisles. Nothing was too much trouble for him; he carried messages and brought programs as though it were his greatest pleasure in life, and all the people in his section thought him a charming boy, feeling that he remembered and admired them. As the house filled, he grew more and more vivacious and animated, and the color came to his cheeks and lips. It was very much as though this were a great reception and Paul were the host. Just as the musicians came out to take their places, his English

teacher arrived with checks for the seats which a promi-
nent manufacturer had taken for the season. She betrayed
some embarrassment when she handed Paul the tickets,
and a *hauteur* which subsequently made her feel very
foolish. Paul was startled for a moment, and had the
feeling of wanting to put her out; what business had she
here among all these fine people and gay colors? He looked
her over and decided that she was not appropriately
dressed and must be a fool to sit downstairs in such togs.
The tickets had probably been sent her out of kindness,
he reflected, as he put down a seat for her, and she had
about as much right to sit there as he had.

When the symphony began Paul sank into one of the
rear seats with a long sigh of relief, and lost himself as he
had done before the Rico. It was not that symphonies, as
such, meant anything in particular to Paul, but the first
sigh of the instruments seemed to free some hilarious spirit
within him; something that struggled there like the Genius
in the bottle found by the Arab fisherman. He felt a sudden zest of life; the lights danced before his eyes and the
concert hall blazed into unimaginable splendor. When the
soprano soloist came on, Paul forgot even the nastiness of
his teacher's being there, and gave himself up to the peculiar intoxication such personages always had for him.
The soloist chanced to be a German woman, by no means
in her first youth, and the mother of many children; but
she wore a satin gown and a tiara, and she had that in-
definable air of achievement, that world-shine upon her,
which always blinded Paul to any possible defects.

After a concert was over, Paul was often irritable and
wretched until he got to sleep—and tonight he was even
more than usually restless. He had the feeling of not being
able to let down; of its being impossible to give up this
delicious excitement which was the only thing that could
be called living at all. During the last number he withdrew and, after hastily changing his clothes in the dressing-room, slipped out to the side door where the singer's
carriage stood. Here he began pacing rapidly up and
down the walk, waiting to see her come out.

Over yonder the Schenley, in its vacant stretch, loomed
big and square through the fine rain, the windows of its
twelve stories glowing like those of a lighted cardboard

house under a Christmas tree. All the actors and singers
of any importance stayed there when they were in the city,
and a number of the big manufacturers of the place lived
there in the winter. Paul had often hung about the hotel,
watching the people go in and out, longing to enter and
leave schoolmasters and dull care behind him forever.

At last the singer came out, accompanied by the conductor, who helped her into her carriage and closed
the door with a cordial *auf wiedersehen*—which set
Paul to wondering whether she were not an old sweetheart of his. Paul followed the carriage over to the hotel,
walking so rapidly as not to be far from the entrance
when the singer alighted and disappeared behind the
swinging glass doors which were opened by a Negro in a
tall hat and a long coat. In the moment that the door was
ajar, it seemed to Paul that he, too, entered. He seemed to
feel himself go after her up the steps, into the warm,
lighted building, into an exotic, a tropical world of shiny,
glistening surfaces and basking ease. He reflected upon
the mysterious dishes that were brought into the dining
room, the green bottles in buckets of ice, as he had seen
them in the supper party pictures of the Sunday supple-
ment. A quick gust of wind brought the rain down with
sudden vehemence, and Paul was startled to find that
he was still outside in the slush of the gravel driveway;
that his boots were letting in the water and his scanty
overcoat was clinging wet about him; that the lights in
front of the concert hall were out, and that the rain was
driving in sheets between him and the orange glow of the
windows above him. There it was, what he wanted—tan-
gibly before him, like the fairy world of a Christmas pantomime; as the rain beat in his face, Paul wondered
whether he were destined always to shiver in the black
night outside, looking up at it.

He turned and walked reluctantly toward the car tracks.
The end had to come some time; his father in his night-
clothes at the top of the stairs, explanations that did not
explain, hastily improvised fictions that were forever trip-
ping him up, his upstairs room and its horrible yellow
wallpaper, the creaking bureau with the greasy plush col-
larbox, and over his painted wooden bed the pictures of
George Washington and John Calvin, and the framed

motto, "Feed my Lambs," which had been worked in red worsted by his mother, whom Paul could not remember.

Half an hour later, Paul alighted from the Negley Avenue car and went slowly down one of the side streets off the main thoroughfare. It was a highly respectable street, where all the houses were exactly alike, and where business men of moderate means begot and reared large families of children, all of whom went to Sabbath-school and learned the shorter catechism, and were interested in arithmetic; all of whom were as exactly alike as their homes, and of a piece with the monotony in which they lived. Paul never went up Cordelia Street without a shudder of loathing. His home was next to the house of the Cumberland minister. He approached it tonight with the nerveless sense of defeat, the hopeless feeling of sinking back forever into ugliness and commonness that he had always had when he came home. The moment he turned into Cordelia Street he felt the waters close above his head. After each of these orgies of living, he experienced all the physical depression which follows a debauch; the loathing of respectable beds, of common food, of a house permeated by kitchen odors; a shuddering repulsion for the flavorless, colorless mass of everyday existence; a morbid desire for cool things and soft lights and fresh flowers.

The nearer he approached the house, the more absolutely unequal Paul felt to the sight of it all; his ugly sleeping chamber; the cold bathroom with the grimy zinc tub, the cracked mirror, the dripping spigots; his father, at the top of the stairs, his hairy legs sticking out from his nightshirt, his feet thrust into carpet slippers. He was so much later than usual that there would certainly be inquiries and reproaches. Paul stopped short before the door. He felt that he could not be accosted by his father tonight; that he could not toss again on that miserable bed. He would not go in. He would tell his father that he had no carfare, and it was raining so hard he had gone home with one of the boys and stayed all night.

Meanwhile, he was wet and cold. He went around to the back of the house and tried one of the basement windows, found it open, raised it cautiously, and scrambled down the cellar wall to the floor. There he stood, holding his breath, terrified by the noise he had made; but the floor above him was silent, and there was no creak on the stairs. He found a soap-box, and carried it over to the soft ring of light that streamed from the furnace door, and sat down. He was horribly afraid of rats, so he did not try to sleep, but sat looking distrustfully at the dark, still terrified lest he might have awakened his father. In such reactions, after one of the experiences which made days and nights out of the dreary blanks of the calendar, when his senses were deadened, Paul's head was always singularly clear. Suppose his father had heard him getting in at the window and had come down and shot him for a burglar? Then, again, suppose his father had come down, pistol in hand, and he had cried out in time to save himself, and his father had been horrified to think how nearly he had killed him? Then, again, suppose a day should come when his father would remember that night, and wish there had been no warning cry to stay his hand? With this last supposition Paul entertained himself until daybreak.

The following Sunday was fine; the sodden November chill was broken by the last flash of autumnal summer. In the morning Paul had to go to church and Sabbath-school, as always. On seasonable Sunday afternoons the burghers of Cordelia Street usually sat out on their front "stoops," and talked to their neighbors on the next stoop, or called to those across the street in neighborly fashion. The men sat placidly on gay cushions placed upon the steps that led down to the sidewalk, while the women, in their Sunday "waists," sat in rockers on the cramped porches, pretending to be greatly at their ease. The children played in the streets; there were so many of them that the place resembled the recreation grounds of a kindergarten. The men on the steps—all in their shirt sleeves, their vests unbuttoned—sat with their legs well apart, their stomachs comfortably protruding, and talked of the prices of things, or told anecdotes of the sagacity of their various chiefs and overlords. They occasionally looked over the multitude of squabbling children, listened affectionately to their high-pitched, nasal voices, smiling to see their own proclivities reproduced in their offspring, and interspersed their legends of the iron kings with remarks about their sons' progress at school, their grades in arithmetic, and the amounts they had saved in their toy banks. On this last Sunday of November, Paul sat all the afternoon on the lowest step of his "stoop," staring into the street, while his sisters, in their rockers, were talking to the minister's daughters next door about how many shirtwaists they had made in the last week, and how many waffles someone had eaten at the last church supper. When the weather was warm, and his father was in a particularly jovial frame of mind, the girls made lemonade, which was always brought out in a red-glass pitcher, ornamented with forget-me-nots in blue enamel. This the girls thought very fine, and the neighbors joked about the suspicious color of the pitcher.

Today Paul's father, on the top step, was talking to a young man who shifted a restless baby from knee to knee. He happened to be the young man who was daily held up to Paul as a model, and after whom it was his father's dearest hope that he would pattern. This young man was of a ruddy complexion, with a compressed, red mouth, and faded near-sighted eyes, over which he wore thick spectacles, with gold bows that curved about his ears. He was clerk to one of the magnates of a great steel corporation, and was looked upon in Cordelia Street as a young man with a future. There was a story that, some five years ago—he was now barely twenty-six—he had been a trifle "dissipated," but in order to curb his appetites and save the loss of time and strength that a sowing of wild oats might have entailed, he had taken his chief's advice, oft reiterated to his employees, and at twenty-one had married the first woman whom he could persuade to share his fortunes. She happened to be an angular school mistress, much older than he, who also wore thick glasses, and who had now borne him four children, all near-sighted, like herself.

The young man was relating how his chief, now cruising in the Mediterranean, kept in touch with all the details of the business, arranging his office hours on his yacht just as though he were at home, and "knocking off work enough to keep two stenographers busy." His father told, in turn, the plan his corporation was considering, of putting in an electric railway plant at Cairo. Paul snapped his teeth; he had an awful apprehension that they might spoil it all before he got there. Yet he rather liked to hear these legends of the iron kings, that were told and retold on Sundays and holidays; these stories of palaces in Venice, yachts on the Mediterranean, and high play at Monte Carlo appealed to his fancy, and he was interested in the triumphs of cash boys who had become famous, though he had no mind for the cash-boy stage.

After supper was over, and he had helped to dry the dishes, Paul nervously asked his father whether he could go to George's to get some help in his geometry, and still more nervously asked for carfare. This latter request he had to repeat, as his father, on principle, did not like to hear requests for money, whether much or little. He asked Paul whether he could not go to some boy who lived nearer, and told him that he ought not to leave his school work until Sunday; but he gave him the dime. He was not a poor man, but he had a worthy ambition to come up in the world. His only reason for allowing Paul to usher was that he thought a boy ought to be earning a little.

Paul bounded upstairs, scrubbed the greasy odor of the dishwater from his hands with the ill-smelling soap he hated, and then shook over his fingers a few drops of violet water from the bottle he kept hidden in his drawer. He left the house with his geometry conspicuously under his arm, and the moment he got out of Cordelia Street and boarded a downtown car, he shook off the lethargy of two deadening days, and began to live again.

The leading juvenile of the permanent stock company which played at one of the downtown theaters was an acquaintance of Paul's, and the boy had been invited to drop in at the Sunday night rehearsals whenever he could. For more than a year Paul had spent every available moment loitering about Charley Edwards's dressing-room. He had won a place among Edwards's following not only because the young actor, who could not afford to employ a dresser, often found him useful, but because he recognized in Paul something akin to what churchmen termed "vocation."

It was at the theater and at Carnegie Hall that Paul really lived; the rest was but a sleep and a forgetting. This was Paul's fairy tale, and it had for him all the allurement of a secret love. The moment he inhaled the gassy, painty, dusty odor behind the scenes, he breathed like a prisoner set free, and felt within him the possibility of doing or saying splendid, brilliant things. The moment the cracked orchestra beat out the overture from *Martha,* or jerked at the serenade from *Rigoletto,* all stupid and ugly things slid from him, and his senses were deliciously, yet delicately fired.

Perhaps it was because, in Paul's world, the natural nearly always wore the guise of ugliness, that a certain element of artificiality seemed to him necessary in beauty. Perhaps it was because his experience of life elsewhere was so full of Sabbath-school picnics, petty economies, wholesome advice as to how to succeed in life, and the unescapable odors of cooking, that he found this existence so alluring, these smartly-clad men and women so attractive, that he was so moved by these starry apple orchards that bloomed perennially under the limelight.

It would be difficult to put it strongly enough how convincingly the stage entrance of that theater was for Paul the actual portal of Romance. Certainly none of the company ever suspected it, least of all Charley Edwards. It was very like the old stories that used to float about London of fabulously rich Jews, who had subterranean halls, with palms, and fountains, and soft lamps and richly apparelled women who never saw the disenchanting light of London day. So, in the midst of that smoke-palled city, enamored of figures and grimy toil, Paul had his secret temple, his wishing-carpet, his bit of blue-and-white Mediterranean shore bathed in perpetual sunshine.

Several of Paul's teachers had a theory that his imagination had been perverted by garish fiction; but the truth was, he scarcely ever read at all. The books at home were not such as would either tempt or corrupt a youthful mind, and as for reading the novels that some of his friends urged upon him—well, he got what he wanted much more quickly from music; any sort of music, from an orchestra to a barrel organ. He needed only the spark, the indescribable thrill that made his imagination master of his senses, and he could make plots and pictures enough of his own. It was equally true that he was not stage-struck—not, at any rate, in the usual acceptation of that expression. He had no desire to become an actor,

any more than he had to become a musician. He felt no
necessity to do any of these things; what he wanted was to
see, to be in the atmosphere, float on the wave of it, to be
carried out, blue league after blue league, away from
everything.

After a night behind the scenes, Paul found the schoolroom more than ever repulsive; the bare floors and naked
walls; the prosy men who never wore frock coats, or violets in their buttonholes; the women with their dull gowns,
shrill voices, and pitiful seriousness about prepositions
that govern the dative. He could not bear to have the
other pupils think, for a moment, that he took these people seriously; he must convey to them that he considered
it all trivial, and was there only by way of a joke, anyway.
He had autograph pictures of all the members of the stock
company which he showed his classmates, telling them
the most incredible stories of his familiarity with these
people, of his acquaintance with the soloists who came to
Carnegie Hall, his suppers with them and the flowers he
sent them. When these stories lost their effect, and his
audience grew listless, he would bid all the boys good-by,
announcing that he was going to travel for a while; going
to Naples, to California, to Egypt. Then, next Monday,
he would slip back, self-conscious and nervously smiling,
his sister was ill, and he would have to defer his voyage
until spring.

Matters went steadily worse with Paul at school. In the
itch to let his instructors know how heartily he despised
them, and how thoroughly he was appreciated elsewhere,
he mentioned once or twice that he had no time to fool
with theorems; adding—with a twitch of the eyebrows and
a touch of that nervous bravado which so perplexed them
—that he was helping the people down at the stock company; they were old friends of his.

The upshot of the matter was that the Principal went to
Paul's father, and Paul was taken out of school and put to
work. The manager at Carnegie Hall was told to get another usher in his stead; the door-keeper at the theater
was warned not to admit him to the house; and Charley
Edwards remorsefully promised the boy's father not to see
him again.

The members of the stock company were vastly amused

when some of Paul's stories reached them—especially the
women. They were hard-working women, most of them
supporting indolent husbands or brothers, and they
laughed rather bitterly at having stirred the boy to such
fervid and florid inventions. They agreed with the faculty
and with his father, that Paul's was a bad case.

The east-bound train was plowing through a January
snowstorm; the dull dawn was beginning to show gray
when the engine whistled a mile out of Newark. Paul
started up from the seat where he had lain curled in uneasy slumber, rubbed the breath-misted window glass with
his hand, and peered out. The snow was whirling in curl-
ing eddies above the white bottom lands, and the drifts
lay already deep in the fields and along the fences, while
here and there the long dead grass and dried weed stalks
protruded black above it. Lights shone from the scattered
houses, and a gang of laborers who stood beside the track
waved their lanterns.

Paul had slept very little, and he felt grimy and uncomfortable. He had made the all-night journey in a day
coach because he was afraid if he took a Pullman he
might be seen by some Pittsburgh business man who had
noticed him in Denny & Carson's office. When the whistle
woke him, he clutched quickly at his breast pocket, glancing about him with an uncertain smile. But the little, clay-
bespattered Italians were still sleeping, the slatternly
women across the aisle were in open-mouthed oblivion,
and even the crumby, crying babies were for the nonce
stilled. Paul settled back to struggle with his impatience
as best he could.

When he arrived at the Jersey City station, he hurried
through his breakfast, manifestly ill at ease and keeping
a sharp eye about him. After he reached the Twenty-
third Street station, he consulted a cabman, and had himself driven to a men's furnishing establishment which was
just opening for the day. He spent upward of two hours
there, buying with endless reconsidering and great care.
His new street suit he put on in the fitting-room; the frock
coat and dress clothes he had bundled into the cab with
his new shirts. Then he drove to a hatter's and a shoe
house. His next errand was at Tiffany's, where he selected
silver-mounted brushes and a scarf-pin. He would not

wait to have his silver marked, he said. Lastly, he stopped at a trunk shop on Broadway, and had his purchases packed into various traveling bags.

It was a little after one o'clock when he drove up to the Waldorf, and, after settling with the cabman, went into the office. He registered from Washington; said his mother and father had been abroad, and that he had come down to await the arrival of their steamer. He told his story plausibly and had no trouble, since he offered to pay for them in advance, in engaging his rooms; a sleeping-room, sitting room and bath.

Not once, but a hundred times Paul had planned this entry into New York. He had gone over every detail of it with Charley Edwards, and in his scrap book at home there were pages of description about New York hotels, cut from the Sunday papers.

When he was shown to his sitting room on the eighth floor, he saw at a glance that everything was as it should be; there was but one detail in his mental picture that the place did not realize, so he rang for the bell boy and sent him down for flowers. He moved about nervously until the boy returned, putting away his new linen and fingering it delightedly as he did so. When the flowers came, he put them hastily into water, and then tumbled into a hot bath. Presently he came out of his white bathroom, resplendent in his new silk underwear, and playing with the tassels of his red robe. The snow was whirling so fiercely outside his windows that he could scarcely see across the street; but within, the air was deliciously soft and fragrant. He put the violets and jonquils on the tabouret beside the couch, and threw himself down with a long sigh, covering himself with a Roman blanket. He was thoroughly tired; he had been in such haste, he had stood up to such a strain, covered so much ground in the last twenty-four hours, that he wanted to think how it had all come about. Lulled by the sound of the wind, the warm air, and the cool fragrance of the flowers, he sank into deep, drowsy retrospection.

It had been wonderfully simple; when they had shut him out of the theater and concert hall, when they had taken away his bone, the whole thing was virtually determined. The rest was a mere matter of opportunity. The

only thing that at all surprised him was his own courage
—for he realized well enough that he had always been
tormented by fear, a sort of apprehensive dread that, of
late years, as the meshes of the lies he had told closed
about him, had been pulling the muscles of his body
tighter and tighter. Until now, he could not remember a
time when he had not been dreading something. Even
when he was a little boy, it was always there—behind him,
or before, or on either side. There had always been the
shadowed corner, the dark place into which he dared not
look, but from which something seemed always to be
watching him—and Paul had done things that were not
pretty to watch, he knew.

But now he had a curious sense of relief, as though he
had at last thrown down the gauntlet to the thing in the
corner.

Yet it was but a day since he had been sulking in the
traces; but yesterday afternoon that he had been sent to
the bank with Denny & Carson's deposit, as usual—
but this time he was instructed to leave the book to be
balanced. There was above two thousand dollars in
checks, and nearly a thousand in the bank notes which he
had taken from the book and quietly transferred to his
pocket. At the bank he had made out a new deposit slip.
His nerves had been steady enough to permit of his returning to the office, where he had finished his work and
asked for a full day's holiday tomorrow, Saturday, giving
a perfectly reasonable pretext. The bank book, he knew,
would not be returned before Monday or Tuesday, and his
father would be out of town for the next week. From the
time he slipped the bank notes into his pocket until he
boarded the night train for New York, he had not known
a moment's hesitation.

How astonishingly easy it had all been; here he was,
the thing done; and this time there would be no awakening, no figure at the top of the stairs. He watched the
snowflakes whirling by his window until he fell asleep.

When he awoke, it was four o'clock in the afternoon.
He bounded up with a start; one of his precious days gone
already! He spent nearly an hour in dressing, watching
every stage of his toilet carefully in the mirror. Every-

thing was quite perfect; he was exactly the kind of boy he had always wanted to be.

When he went downstairs, Paul took a carriage and drove up Fifth Avenue toward the Park. The snow had somewhat abated; carriages and tradesmen's wagons were hurrying soundlessly to and fro in the winter twilight; boys in woolen mufflers were shoveling off the doorsteps; the avenue stages made fine spots of color against the white street. Here and there on the corners whole flower gardens blooming behind glass windows, against which the snowflakes stuck and melted; violets, roses, carnations, lilies of the valley—somehow vastly more lovely and alluring that they blossomed thus unnaturally in the snow. The Park itself was a wonderful stage winter-piece.

When he returned, the pause of the twilight had ceased, and the tune of the streets had changed. The snow was falling faster, lights streamed from the hotels that reared their many stories fearlessly up into the storm, defying the raging Atlantic winds. A long, black stream of carriages poured down the avenue, intersected here and there by other streams, tending horizontally. There were a score of cabs about the entrance of his hotel, and his driver had to wait. Boys in livery were running in and out of the awning stretched across the sidewalk, up and down the red velvet carpet laid from the door to the street. Above, about, within it all, was the rumble and roar, the hurry and toss of thousands of human beings as hot for pleasure as himself, and on every side of him towered the glaring affirmation of the omnipotence of wealth.

The boy set his teeth and drew his shoulders together in a spasm of realization; the plot of all dramas, the text of all romances, the nerve-stuff of all sensations was whirling about him like the snowflakes. He burnt like a faggot in a tempest.

When Paul came down to dinner, the music of the orchestra floated up the elevator shaft to greet him. As he stepped into the thronged corridor, he sank back into one of the chairs against the wall to get his breath. The lights, the chatter, the perfumes, the bewildering medley of color —he had, for a moment, the feeling of not being able to stand it. But only for a moment; these were his own people, he told himself. He went slowly about the corridors, through the writing-rooms, smoking-rooms, reception-rooms, as though he were exploring the chambers of an enchanted palace, built and peopled for him alone.

When he reached the dining room he sat down at a table near a window. The flowers, the white linen, the many-colored wine glasses, the gay toilettes of the women, the low popping of corks, the undulating repetitions of the *Blue Danube* from the orchestra, all flooded Paul's dream with bewildering radiance. When the roseate tinge of his champagne was added—that cold, precious, bubbling stuff that creamed and foamed in his glass—Paul wondered that there were honest men in the world at all. This was what all the world was fighting for, he reflected; this was what all the struggle was about. He doubted the reality of his past. Had he ever known a place called Cordelia Street, a place where fagged-looking business men boarded the early car? Mere rivets in a machine they seemed to Paul—sickening men, with combings of children's hair always hanging to their coats, and the smell of cooking in their clothes. Cordelia Street—Ah, that belonged to another time and country! Had he not always been thus, had he not sat here night after night, from as far back as he could remember, looking pensively over just such shimmering textures, and slowly twirling the stem of a glass like this one between his thumb and middle finger? He rather thought he had.

He was not in the least abashed or lonely. He had no especial desire to meet or to know any of these people; all he demanded was the right to look on and conjecture, to watch the pageant. The mere stage properties were all he contended for. Nor was he lonely later in the evening, in his loge at the Opera. He was entirely rid of his nervous misgivings, of his forced aggressiveness, of the imperative desire to show himself different from his surroundings. He felt now that his surroundings explained him. Nobody questioned the purple; he had only to wear it passively. He had only to glance down at his dress coat to reassure himself that here it would be impossible for anyone to humiliate him.

He found it hard to leave his beautiful sitting room to go to bed that night, and sat long watching the raging storm from his turret window. When he went to sleep, it was with the lights turned on in his bedroom; partly because of his old timidity, and partly so that, if he should wake in the night, there would be no wretched moment of doubt, no horrible suspicion of yellow wallpaper, or of Washington and Calvin above his bed.

On Sunday morning the city was practically snowbound. Paul breakfasted late, and in the afternoon he fell in with a wild San Francisco boy, a freshman at Yale, who said he had run down for a "little flyer" over Sunday. The young man offered to show Paul the night side of the town, and the two boys went off together after dinner, not returning to the hotel until seven o'clock the next morning. They had started out in the confiding warmth of a champagne friendship, but their parting in the elevator was singularly cool. The freshman pulled himself together to make his train, and Paul went to bed. He awoke at two o'clock in the afternoon, very thirsty and dizzy, and rang for ice water, coffee and the Pittsburgh papers.

On the part of the hotel management, Paul excited no suspicion. There was this to be said for him, that he wore his spoils with dignity and in no way made himself conspicuous. His chief greediness lay in his ears and eyes, and his excesses were not offensive ones. His dearest pleasures were the gray winter twilights in his sitting room; his quiet enjoyment of his flowers, his clothes, his wide divan, his cigarette and his sense of power. He could not remember a time when he had felt so at peace with himself. The mere release from the necessity of petty lying, lying every day and every day, restored his self-respect. He had never lied for pleasure, even at school; but to make himself noticed and admired, to assert his difference from other Cordelia Street boys; and he felt a good deal more manly, more honest, even, now that he had no need for boastful pretensions, now that he could, as his actor friends used to say, "dress the part." It was characteristic that remorse did not occur to him. His golden days went by without a shadow, and he made each as perfect as he could.

On the eighth day after his arrival in New York, he found the whole affair exploited in the Pittsburgh papers, exploited with a wealth of detail which indicated that local news of a sensational nature was at a low ebb. The firm of Denny & Carson announced that the boy's father had refunded the full amount of his theft, and that they had no intention of prosecuting. The Cumberland minister had been interviewed, and expressed his hope of yet reclaiming the motherless lad, and Paul's Sabbath-school teacher declared that she would spare no effort to that end. The rumor had reached Pittsburgh that the boy had been seen in a New York hotel, and his father had gone East to find him and bring him home.

Paul had just come in to dress for dinner; he sank into a chair, weak in the knees, and clasped his head in his hands. It was to be worse than jail, even; the tepid waters of Cordelia Street were to close over him finally and forever. The gray monotony stretched before him in hopeless, unrelieved years; Sabbath-school, Young People's Meeting, the yellow-papered room, the damp dish-towels; it all rushed back upon him with sickening vividness. He had the old feeling that the orchestra had suddenly stopped, the sinking sensation that the play was over. The sweat broke out on his face, and he sprang to his feet, looked about him with his white, conscious smile, and winked at himself in the mirror. With something of the childish belief in miracles with which he had so often gone to class, all his lessons unlearned, Paul dressed and dashed whistling down the corridor to the elevator.

He had no sooner entered the dining room and caught the measure of the music, than his remembrance was lightened by his old elastic power of claiming the moment, mounting with it, and finding it all sufficient. The glare and glitter about him, the mere scenic accessories had again, and for the last time, their old potency. He would show himself that he was game, he would finish the thing splendidly. He doubted, more than ever, the existence of Cordelia Street, and for the first time he drank his wine recklessly. Was he not, after all, one of these fortunate beings? Was he not still himself, and in his own place? He drummed a nervous accompaniment to the music and looked about him, telling himself over and over that it had paid.

He reflected drowsily, to the swell of the violin and the chill sweetness of his wine, that he might have done it more wisely. He might have caught an outbound steamer

and been well out of their clutches before now. But the
other side of the world had seemed too far away and too
uncertain then; he could not have waited for it; his need
had been too sharp. If he had to choose over again, he
would do the same thing tomorrow. He looked affectionately about the dining room, now gilded with a soft mist.
Ah, it had paid indeed!

Paul was awakened next morning by a painful throbbing
in his head and feet. He had thrown himself across the
bed without undressing, and had slept with his shoes on.
His limbs and hands were lead heavy, and his tongue and
throat were parched. There came upon him one of those
fateful attacks of clear-headedness that never occurred except when he was physically exhausted and his nerves
hung loose. He lay still and closed his eyes and let the
tide of realities wash over him.

His father was in New York; "stopping at some joint or
other," he told himself. The memory of successive sum-
mers on the front stoop fell upon him like a weight of
black water. He had not a hundred dollars left; and he
knew now, more than ever, that money was everything,
the wall that stood between all he loathed and all he
wanted. The thing was winding itself up; he had thought
of that on his first glorious day in New York, and had
even provided a way to snap the thread. It lay on his
dressing-table now; he had got it out last night when he
came blindly up from dinner—but the shiny metal hurt
his eyes, and he disliked the look of it, anyway.

He rose and moved about with a painful effort, suc-
cumbing now and again to attacks of nausea. It was the
old depression exaggerated; all the world had become
Cordelia Street. Yet somehow he was not afraid of anything, was absolutely calm; perhaps because he had
looked into the dark corner at last, and knew. It
was bad enough, what he saw there; but somehow not so
bad as his long fear of it had been. He saw everything
clearly now. He had a feeling that he had made the best of
it, that he had lived the sort of life he was meant to live,
and for half an hour he sat staring at the revolver point.
But he told himself that was not the way, so he went
downstairs and took a cab to the ferry.

When Paul arrived at Newark, he got off the train and

took another cab, directing the driver to follow the Pennsylvania tracks out of the town. The snow lay heavy on the roadways and had drifted deep in the open fields. Only here and there the dead grass or dried weed stalks projected, singularly black, above it. Once well into the country, Paul dismissed the carriage and walked, floundering along the tracks, his mind a medley of irrelevant things. He seemed to hold in his brain an actual picture of everything he had seen that morning. He remembered every feature of both his drivers, the toothless old woman from whom he had bought the red flowers in his coat, the agent from whom he had got his ticket, and all of his fellow-passengers on the ferry. His mind, unable to cope with vital matters near at hand, worked feverishly and deftly at sorting and grouping these images. They made for him a part of the ugliness of the world, of the ache in his head, and the bitter burning on his tongue. He stooped and put a handful of snow into his mouth as he walked, but that, too, seemed hot. When he reached a little hillside, where the tracks ran through a cut some twenty feet below him, he stopped and sat down.

The carnations in his coat were drooping with the cold, he noticed; all their red glory over. It occurred to him that all the flowers he had seen in the show windows that first night must have gone the same way, long before this. It was only one splendid breath they had, in spite of their brave mockery at the winter outside the glass. It was a losing game in the end, it seemed, this revolt against the homilies by which the world is run. Paul took one of the blossoms carefully from his coat and scooped a little hole in the snow, where he covered it up. Then he dozed a while, from his weak condition, seeming insensible to the cold.

The sound of an approaching train woke him, and he started to his feet, remembering only his resolution, and afraid lest he should be too late. He stood watching the approaching locomotive, his teeth chattering, his lips drawn away from them in a frightened smile; once or twice he glanced nervously sidewise, as though he were being watched. When the right moment came, he jumped. As he fell, the folly of his haste occurred to him with merciless clearness, the vastness of what he had left undone.

There flashed through his brain, clearer than ever before, the blue of Adriatic water, the yellow of Algerian sands.

He felt something strike his chest—his body was being thrown swiftly through the air, on and on, immeasurably far and fast, while his limbs gently relaxed. Then, because the picture-making mechanism was crushed, the disturbing visions flashed into black, and Paul dropped back into the immense design of things.

The Bet

ANTON CHEKHOV

Some people will bet only on a "sure thing." Others are exhilarated when their money is riding on the "long shot." But the strangest, and also the most famous, bettors in fiction are the central characters in Anton Chekhov's "The Bet." Ever since this story was published in the late 1880's, readers have been arguing about who really wins. A convincing case has been made for the lawyer, and an equally strong one for the financier—and some have persuasively contended that, paradoxical as it may seem, both of them win!

While the highly structured plot of "The Bet" is not typical of Chekhov's narrative technique, this story dramatically underscores the author's concern for the human condition and the individual's sense of futility and isolation.

ANTON PAVLOVICH CHEKHOV (1860–1904) was born in Taganrog in southern Russia into a family of liberated serfs whose freedom had been purchased by Chekhov's grandfather. Anton graduated from the University of Moscow in 1884, qualified to practice medicine. He soon found, however, that he preferred to write. With

He recollected further what happened after the evening party. It was decided that the lawyer must undergo his imprisonment under the strictest observation, in a garden wing of the banker's house. It was agreed that during the period he would be deprived of the right to cross the threshold, to see living people, to hear human voices, and to receive letters and newspapers. He was permitted to have a musical instrument, to read books, to write letters, to drink wine and smoke tobacco. By the agreement he could communicate, but only in silence, with the outside world through a little window specially constructed for this purpose. Everything necessary, books, music, wine, he could receive in any quantity by sending a note through the window. The agreement provided for all the minutest details, which made the confinement strictly solitary, and it obliged the lawyer to remain exactly fifteen years from twelve o'clock of November 14th, 1870, to twelve o'clock of November 14th, 1885. The least attempt on his part to violate the conditions, to escape if only for two minutes before the time, freed the banker from the obligation to pay him the two millions.

During the first year of imprisonment, the lawyer, as far as it was possible to judge from his short notes, suffered terribly from loneliness and boredom. From his wing day and night came the sound of the piano. He rejected wine and tobacco. "Wine," he wrote, "excites desires, and desires are the chief foes of a prisoner; besides, nothing is more boring than to drink good wine alone, and tobacco spoils the air in his room." During the first year the lawyer was sent books of a light character; novels with a complicated love interest, stories of crime and fantasy, comedies, and so on.

In the second year the piano was heard no longer and the lawyer asked only for classics. In the fifth year, music was heard again, and the prisoner asked for wine. Those who watched him said that during the whole of that year he was only eating, drinking, and lying on his bed. He yawned often and talked angrily to himself. Books he did not read. Sometimes at nights he would sit down to write. He would write for a long time and tear it all up in the morning. More than once he was heard to weep.

In the second half of the sixth year, the prisoner began

zealously to study languages, philosophy, and history. He fell on these subjects so hungrily that the banker hardly had time to get books enough for him. In the space of four years about six hundred volumes were bought at his request. It was while that passion lasted that the banker received the following letter from the prisoner: "My dear gaoler, I am writing these lines in six languages. Show them to experts. Let them read them. If they do not find one single mistake, I beg you to give orders to have a gun fired off in the garden. By the noise I shall know that my efforts have not been in vain. The geniuses of all ages and countries speak in different languages; but in them all burns the same flame. Oh, if you knew my heavenly happiness now that I can understand them!" The prisoner's desire was fulfilled. Two shots were fired in the garden by the banker's order.

Later on, after the tenth year, the lawyer sat immovable before his table and read only the New Testament. The banker found it strange that a man who in four years had mastered six hundred erudite volumes, should have spent nearly a year in reading one book, easy to understand and by no means thick. The New Testament was then replaced by the history of religions and theology.

During the last two years of his confinement the prisoner read an extraordinary amount, quite haphazard. Now he would apply himself to the natural sciences, then he would read Byron or Shakespeare. Notes used to come from him in which he asked to be sent at the same time a book on chemistry, a textbook of medicine, a novel, and some treatise on philosophy or theology. He read as though he were swimming in the sea among broken pieces of wreckage, and in his desire to save his life was eagerly grasping one piece after another.

II

The banker recalled all this, and thought:

"Tomorrow at twelve o'clock he receives his freedom. Under the agreement, I shall have to pay him two millions. If I pay, it's all over with me. I am ruined forever . . ."

Fifteen years before he had too many millions to count, but now he was afraid to ask himself which he had more of, money or debts. Gambling on the Stock-Exchange, risky speculation, and the recklessness of which he could not rid himself even in old age, had gradually brought his business to decay; and the fearless, self-confident, proud man of business had become an ordinary banker, trembling at every rise and fall in the market.

"That cursed bet," murmured the old man clutching his head in despair. . . . "Why didn't the man die? He's only forty years old. He will take away my last farthing, marry, enjoy life, gamble on the Exchange, and I will look on like an envious beggar and hear the same words from him every day: 'I'm obliged to you for the happiness of my life. Let me help you.' No, it's too much! The only escape from bankruptcy and disgrace—is that the man should die."

The clock had just struck three. The banker was listening. In the house every one was asleep, and one could hear only the frozen trees whining outside the windows. Trying to make no sound, he took out of his safe the key of the door which had not been opened for fifteen years, put on his overcoat, and went out of the house. The garden was dark and cold. It was raining. A damp, penetrating wind howled in the garden and gave the trees no rest. Though he strained his eyes, the banker could see neither the ground, nor the white statues, nor the garden wing, nor the trees. Approaching the garden wing, he called the watchman twice. There was no answer. Evidently the watchman had taken shelter from the bad weather and was now asleep somewhere in the kitchen or the greenhouse.

"If I have the courage to fulfill my intention," thought the old man, "the suspicion will fall on the watchman first of all."

In the darkness he groped for the steps and the door and entered the hall of the garden-wing, then poked his way into a narrow passage and struck a match. Not a soul was there. Some one's bed, with no bedclothes on it, stood there, and an iron stove loomed dark in the corner. The seals on the door that led into the prisoner's room were unbroken.

When the match went out, the old man, trembling from agitation, peeped into the little window.

In the prisoner's room a candle was burning dimly. The prisoner himself sat by the table. Only his back, the hair on his head and his hands were visible. Open books were strewn about on the table, the two chairs, and on the carpet near the table.

Five minutes passed and the prisoner never once stirred. Fifteen years' confinement had taught him to sit motionless. The banker tapped on the window with his finger, but the prisoner made no movement in reply. Then the banker cautiously tore the seals from the door and put the key into the lock. The rusty lock gave a hoarse groan and the door creaked. The banker expected instantly to hear a cry of surprise and the sound of steps. Three minutes passed and it was as quiet as it had been before. He made up his mind to enter.

Before the table sat a man, unlike an ordinary human being. It was a skeleton, with tight-drawn skin, with long curly hair like a woman's, and a shaggy beard. The color of his face was yellow, of an earthy shade; the cheeks were sunken, the back long and narrow, and the hand upon which he leaned his hairy head was so lean and skinny that it was painful to look upon. His hair was already silvering with gray, and no one who glanced at the senile emaciation of the face would have believed that he was only forty years old. On the table, before his bended head, lay a sheet of paper on which something was written in a tiny hand.

"Poor devil," thought the banker, "he's asleep and probably seeing millions in his dreams. I have only to take and throw this half-dead thing on the bed, smother him a moment with the pillow, and the most careful examination will find no trace of unnatural death. But, first, let us read what he has written here."

The banker took the sheet from the table and read:

"Tomorrow at twelve o'clock midnight, I shall obtain my freedom and the right to mix with people. But before I leave this room and see the sun I think it necessary to say a few words to you. On my own clear conscience and before God who sees me I declare to you that I despise freedom, life, health, and all that your books call the blessings of the world.

"For fifteen years I have diligently studied earthly life.

True, I saw neither the earth nor the people, but in your books I drank fragrant wine, sang songs, hunted deer and wild boar in the forests, loved women. . . . And beautiful women, like clouds ethereal, created by the magic of your poets' genius, visited me by night and whispered to me wonderful tales, which made my head drunken. In your books I climbed the summits of Elburz and Mont Blanc and saw from there how the sun rose in the morning, and in the evening suffused the sky, the ocean, and the mountain ridges with a purple gold. I saw from there how above me lightnings glimmered cleaving the clouds; I saw green forests, fields, rivers, lakes, cities; I heard sirens singing, and the playing of the pipes of Pan; I touched the wings of beautiful devils who came flying to me to speak of God. . . . In your books I cast myself into bottomless abysses, worked miracles, burned cities to the ground, preached new religions, conquered whole countries. . . .

"Your books gave me wisdom. All that unwearying human thought created in the centuries is compressed to a little lump in my skull. I know that I am cleverer than you all.

"And I despise your books, despise all worldly blessings and wisdom. Everything is void, frail, visionary and delusive as a mirage. Though you be proud and wise and beautiful, yet will death wipe you from the face of the earth like the mice underground; and your posterity, your history, and the immortality of your men of genius will be as frozen slag, burnt down together with the terrestrial globe.

"You are mad, and gone the wrong way. You take falsehood for truth and ugliness for beauty. You would marvel if suddenly apple and orange trees should bear frogs and lizards instead of fruit, and if roses should begin to breathe the odor of a sweating horse. So do I marvel at you, who have bartered heaven for earth. I do not want to understand you.

"That I may show you in deed my contempt for that by which you live, I waive the two millions of which I once dreamed as of paradise, and which I now despise. That I may deprive myself of my right to them, I shall come out from here five minutes before the stipulated term, and thus shall violate the agreement."

When he had read, the banker put the sheet on the table, kissed the head of the strange man, and began to weep. He went out of the wing. Never at any other time, not even after his terrible losses on the Exchange, had he felt such contempt for himself as now. Coming home, he lay down on his bed, but agitation and tears kept him a long time from sleeping. . . .

The next morning the poor watchman came running to him and told him that they had seen the man who lived in the wing climb through the window into the garden. He had gone to the gate and disappeared. The banker instantly went with his servants to the wing and established the escape of his prisoner. To avoid unnecessary rumors he took the paper with the renunciation from the table and, on his return, locked it in his safe.

The Jilting of
Granny Weatherall

KATHERINE ANNE PORTER

It happened sixty years ago. Most girls would have been crushed by the experience, but not Granny Weatherall. And now, before the light goes out, she is still struggling to communicate to those around her the ultimate worth of living, loving, and creating life.

Katherine Anne Porter is one of the most talented of living American writers. She is a superior literary craftsman with a style, voice, and point of view all her own. In the direct line of Hawthorne, Flaubert, and James, she writes with a straightforward, quiet, patient elegance and precision. Out of her sure and sensitive insight into the sources of human feeling and behavior, she has created a gallery of richly unique characters.

KATHERINE ANNE PORTER (1894–   ) was born in Indian Creek, a small town in Texas. She has confined most of her energies to short story writing and has published only four volumes of short stories: Flowering Judas *(1930),* Noon Wine *(1937),* Pale Horse, Pale Rider *(1939), and* The Leaning Tower *(1944). The purity of her style, her mastery of form, and the depth and variety of her perceptions have established her as one of the contempo-*

*rary masters of the short story. Miss Porter has also
written a novel,* Ship of Fools, *which was made into a
movie. She has been actively engaged in university teaching and lecturing both here and abroad.*

The Jilting of Granny Weatherall

She flicked her wrist neatly out of Doctor Harry's pudgy
careful fingers and pulled the sheet up to her chin. The
brat ought to be in knee breeches. Doctoring around the
country with spectacles on his nose! "Get along now, take
your schoolbooks and go. There's nothing wrong with
me."

Doctor Harry spread a warm paw like a cushion on
her forehead where the forked green vein danced and
made her eyelids twitch. "Now, now, be a good girl, and
we'll have you up in no time."

"That's no way to speak to a woman nearly eighty years
old just because she's down. I'd have you respect your
elders, young man."

"Well, Missy, excuse me." Doctor Harry patted her
cheek. "But I've got to warn you, haven't I? You're a
marvel, but you must be careful or you're going to be
good and sorry."

"Don't tell me what I'm going to be. I'm on my feet
now, morally speaking. It's Cornelia. I had to go to bed
to get rid of her."

Her bones felt loose, and floated around in her skin,
and Doctor Harry floated like a balloon around the foot
of the bed. He floated and pulled down his waistcoat
and swung his glasses on a cord. "Well, stay where you
are, it certainly can't hurt you."

"Get along and doctor your sick," said Granny
Weatherall. "Leave a well woman alone. I'll call for you
when I want you. . . . Where were you forty years ago
when I pulled through milkleg and double pneumonia?
You weren't even born. Don't let Cornelia lead you on,"
she shouted, because Doctor Harry appeared to float up

to the ceiling and out. "I pay my own bills, and I don't throw my money away on nonsense!"

She meant to wave goodby, but it was too much trouble. Her eyes closed of themselves, it was like a dark curtain drawn around the bed. The pillow rose and floated under her, pleasant as a hammock in a light wind. She listened to the leaves rustling outside the window. No, somebody was swishing newspapers: no, Cornelia and Doctor Harry were whispering together. She leaped broad awake, thinking they whispered in her ear.

"She was never like this, *never* like this!" "Well, what can we expect?" "Yes, eighty years old. . . ."

Well, and what if she was? She still had ears. It was like Cornelia to whisper around doors. She always kept things secret in such a public way. She was always being tactful and kind. Cornelia was dutiful; that was the trouble with her. Dutiful and good: "So good and dutiful," said Granny, "that I'd like to spank her." She saw herself spanking Cornelia and making a fine job of it.

"What'd you say, Mother?"

Granny felt her face tying up in hard knots.

"Can't a body think, I'd like to know?"

"I thought you might want something."

"I do. I want a lot of things. First off, go away and don't whisper."

She lay and drowsed, hoping in her sleep that the children would keep out and let her rest a minute. It had been a long day. Not that she was tired. It was always pleasant to snatch a minute now and then. There was always so much to be done, let me see: tomorrow.

Tomorrow was far away and there was nothing to trouble about. Things were finished somehow when the time came; thank God there was always a little margin over for peace: then a person could spread out the plan of life and tuck in the edges orderly. It was good to have everything clean and folded away, with the hair brushes and tonic bottles sitting straight on the white embroidered linen: the day started without fuss and the pantry shelves laid out with rows of jelly glasses and brown jugs and white stone-china jars with blue whirligigs and words painted on them: coffee, tea, sugar, ginger, cinnamon, all-spice: and the bronze clock with the lion on top nicely dusted off. The dust that lion could collect in twenty-four hours! The box in the attic with all those letters tied up, well, she'd have to go through that tomorrow. All those letters—George's letters and John's letters and her letters to them both—lying around for the children to find afterward made her uneasy. Yes, that would be tomorrow's business. No use to let them know how silly she had been once.

While she was rummaging around she found death in her mind and it felt clammy and unfamiliar. She had spent so much time preparing for death there was no need for bringing it up again. Let it take care of itself now. When she was sixty she had felt very old, finished, and went around making farewell trips to see her children and grandchildren, with a secret in her mind: This is the very last of your mother, children! Then she made her will and came down with a long fever. That was all just a notion like a lot of other things, but it was lucky too, for she had once and for all got over the idea of dying for a long time. Now she couldn't be worried. She hoped she had better sense now. Her father had lived to be one hundred and two years old and had drunk a noggin of strong hot toddy on his last birthday. He told the reporters it was his daily habit, and he owed his long life to that. He had made quite a scandal and was very pleased about it. She believed she'd just plague Cornelia a little.

"Cornelia! Cornelia!" No footsteps, but a sudden hand on her cheek. "Bless you, where have you been?"

"Here, Mother."

"Well, Cornelia, I want a noggin of hot toddy."

"Are you cold, darling?"

"I'm chilly, Cornelia. Lying in bed stops the circulation. I must have told you that a thousand times."

Well, she could just hear Cornelia telling her husband that Mother was getting a little childish and they'd have to humor her. The thing that most annoyed her was that Cornelia thought she was deaf, dumb, and blind. Little hasty glances and tiny gestures tossed around her and over her head saying, "Don't cross her, let her have her way, she's eighty years old," and she sitting there as if she lived in a thin glass cage. Sometimes Granny almost made up her mind to pack up and move back to her own house where nobody could remind her every minute that she was old. Wait, wait, Cornelia, till your own children whisper behind your back!

In her day she had kept a better house and had got more work done. She wasn't too old yet for Lydia to be driving eighty miles for advice when one of the children jumped the track, and Jimmy still dropped in and talked things over: "Now, Mammy, you've a good business head, I want to know what you think of this? . . ." Old. Cornelia couldn't change the furniture around without asking. Little things, little things! They had been so sweet when they were little. Granny wished the old days were back again with the children young and everything to be done over. It had been a hard pull, but not too much for her. When she thought of all the food she had cooked, and all the clothes she had cut and sewed, and all the gardens she had made—well, the children showed it. There they were, made out of her, and they couldn't get away from that. Sometimes she wanted to see John again and point to them and say, Well, I didn't do so badly, did I? But that would have to wait. That was for tomorrow. She used to think of him as a man, but now all the children were older than their father, and he would be a child beside her if she saw him now. It seemed strange and there was something wrong in the idea. Why, he couldn't possibly recognize her. She had fenced in a hundred acres once, digging the postholes herself and clamping the wires with just a Negro boy to help. That changed a woman. John would be looking for a young woman with the peaked Spanish comb in her hair and the painted fan. Digging postholes changed a woman. Riding country roads in the winter when women had their babies was another thing: sitting up nights with sick horses and sick Negroes and sick children and hardly ever losing one. John, I hardly ever lost one of them! John would see that in a minute, that would be something he could understand, she wouldn't have to explain anything!

It made her feel like rolling up her sleeves and putting the whole place to rights again. No matter if Cornelia was determined to be everywhere at once, there were a great many things left undone on this place. She would start tomorrow and do them. It was good to be strong enough for everything, even if all you made melted and changed and slipped under your hands, so that by the time you finished you almost forgot what you were working for. What was it I set out to do? she asked herself intently, but she could not remember. A fog rose over the valley, she saw it marching across the creek swallowing the trees and moving up the hill like an army of ghosts. Soon it would be at the near edge of the orchard, and then it was time to go in and light the lamps. Come in, children, don't stay out in the night air.

Lighting the lamps had been beautiful. The children huddled up to her and breathed like little calves waiting at the bars in the twilight. Their eyes followed the match and watched the flame rise and settle in a blue curve, then they moved away from her. The lamp was lit, they didn't have to be scared and hang on to mother any more. Never, never, never more. God, for all my life I thank Thee. Without Thee, my God, I could never have done it. Hail, Mary, full of grace.

I want you to pick all the fruit this year and see that nothing is wasted. There's always someone who can use it. Don't let good things rot for want of using. You waste life when you waste good food. Don't let things get lost. It's bitter to lose things. Now, don't let me get to thinking, not when I am tired and taking a little nap before supper. . . .

The pillow rose about her shoulders and pressed against her heart and the memory was being squeezed out of it: oh, push down the pillow, somebody: it would smother her if she tried to hold it. Such a fresh breeze blowing and such a green day with no threats in it. But he had not come, just the same. What does a woman do when she has put on the white veil and set out the white cake for a man and he doesn't come? She tried to remember. No, I swear he never harmed me but in that. He never harmed me but in that . . . and what if he did? There was the day, the day, but a whirl of dark smoke rose and covered it, crept up and over into the bright field where everything was planted so carefully in orderly rows. That was hell, she knew hell when she saw it. For sixty years she had prayed against remembering him and against losing her soul in the deep pit of hell, and now the two things were mingled in one and the thought of him was a smoky cloud from hell that moved and crept in her head when she had just got rid of Doctor Harry and was trying to rest a minute. Wounded vanity, Ellen, said a sharp voice in the top of her mind. Don't let your wounded vanity get the upper hand of you. Plenty of girls get jilted. You were jilted, weren't you? Then stand up to it. Her eyelids wavered and let in streamers of blue-gray light like tissue paper over her eyes. She must get up and pull the shades down or she'd never sleep. She was in bed again and the shades were not down. How could that happen? Better turn over, hide from the light, sleeping in the light gave you nightmares. "Mother, how do you feel now?" and a stinging wetness on her forehead. But I don't like having my face washed in cold water!

Hapsy? George? Lydia? Jimmy? No, Cornelia, and her features were swollen and full of little puddles. "They're coming, darling, they'll all be here soon." Go wash your face, child, you look funny.

Instead of obeying, Cornelia knelt down and put her head on the pillow. She seemed to be talking but there was no sound. "Well, are you tongue-tied? Whose birthday is it? Are you going to give a party?"

Cornelia's mouth moved urgently in strange shapes. "Don't do that, you bother me, daughter."

"Oh, no, Mother. Oh, no. . . ."

Nonsense. It was strange about children. They disputed your every word. "No what, Cornelia?"

"Here's Doctor Harry."

"I won't see that boy again. He just left five minutes ago."

"That was this morning, Mother. It's night now. Here's the nurse."

"This is Doctor Harry, Mrs. Weatherall. I never saw you look so young and happy!"

"Ah, I'll never be young again—but I'd be happy if they'd let me lie in peace and get rested."

She thought she spoke up loudly, but no one answered. A warm weight on her forehead, a warm bracelet on her wrist, and a breeze went on whispering, trying to tell her something. A shuffle of leaves in the everlasting hand of

God, He blew on them and they danced and rattled. "Mother, don't mind, we're going to give you a little hypodermic." "Look here, daughter, how do ants get in this bed? I saw sugar ants yesterday." Did you send for Hapsy too?

It was Hapsy she really wanted. She had to go a long way back through a great many rooms to find Hapsy standing with a baby on her arm. She seemed to herself to be Hapsy also, and the baby on Hapsy's arm was Hapsy and himself and herself, all at once, and there was no surprise in the meeting. Then Hapsy melted from within and turned flimsy as gray gauze and the baby was a gauzy shadow, and Hapsy came up close and said, "I thought you'd never come," and looked at her very searchingly and said, "You haven't changed a bit!" They leaned forward to kiss, when Cornelia began whispering from a long way off, "Oh, is there anything you want to tell me? Is there anything I can do for you?"

Yes, she had changed her mind after sixty years and she would like to see George. I want you to find George. Find him and be sure to tell him I forgot him. I want him to know I had my husband just the same and my children and my house like any other woman. A good house too and a good husband that I loved and fine children out of him. Better than I hoped for even. Tell him I was given back everything he took away and more. Oh, no, oh, God, no, there was something else besides the house and the man and the children. Oh, surely they were not all? What was it? Something not given back. . . . Her breath crowded down under her ribs and grew into a monstrous frightening shape with cutting edges; it bored up into her head, and the agony was unbelievable: Yes, John, get the Doctor now, no more talk, my time has come.

When this one was born it should be the last. The last. It should have been born first, for it was the one she had truly wanted. Everything came in good time. Nothing left out, left over. She was strong, in three days she would be as well as ever. Better. A woman needed milk in her to have her full health.

"Mother, do you hear me?"

"I've been telling you—"

"Mother, Father Connolly's here."

"I went to Holy Communion only last week. Tell him I'm not so sinful as all that."

"Father just wants to speak to you."

He could speak as much as he pleased. It was like him to drop in and inquire about her soul as if it were a teething baby, and then stay on for a cup of tea and a round of cards and gossip. He always had a funny story of some sort, usually about an Irishman who made his little mistakes and confessed them, and the point lay in some absurd thing he would blurt out in the confessional showing his struggles between native piety and original sin. Granny felt easy about her soul. Cornelia, where are your manners? Give Father Connolly a chair. She had her secret comfortable understanding with a few favorite saints who cleared a straight road to God for her. All as surely signed and sealed as the papers for the new Forty Acres. Forever . . . heirs and assigns forever. Since the day the wedding cake was not cut, but thrown out and wasted. The whole bottom dropped out of the world, and there she was blind and sweating with nothing under her feet and the walls falling away. His hand had caught her under the breast, she had not fallen, there was the freshly polished floor with the green rug on it, just as before. He had cursed like a sailor's parrot and said, "I'll kill him for you." Don't lay a hand on him, for my sake leave something to God. "Now, Ellen, you must believe what I tell you. . . ."

So there was nothing, nothing to worry about any more, except sometimes in the night one of the children screamed in a nightmare, and they both hustled out shaking and hunting for the matches and calling, "There, wait a minute, here we are!" John, get the doctor now, Hapsy's time has come. But there was Hapsy standing by the bed in a white cap. "Cornelia, tell Hapsy to take off her cap. I can't see her plain."

Her eyes opened very wide and the room stood out like a picture she had seen somewhere. Dark colors with the shadows rising toward the ceiling in long angles. The tall black dresser gleamed with nothing on it but John's picture, enlarged from a little one, with John's eyes very black when they should have been blue. You never saw him, so how do you know how he looked? But the man insisted the copy was perfect, it was very rich and handsome. For a picture, yes, but it's not my husband. The table by the bed had a linen cover and a candle and a crucifix. The light was blue from Cornelia's silk lampshades. No sort of light at all, just frippery. You had to live forty years with kerosene lamps to appreciate honest electricity. She felt very strong and she saw Doctor Harry with a rosy nimbus around him.

"You look like a saint, Doctor Harry, and I vow that's as near as you'll ever come to it."

"She's saying something."

"I heard you, Cornelia. What's all this carrying-on?"

"Father Connolly's saying—"

Cornelia's voice staggered and bumped like a cart in a bad road. It rounded corners and turned back again and arrived nowhere. Granny stepped up in the cart very lightly and reached for the reins, but a man sat beside her and she knew him by his hands, driving the cart. She did not look in his face, for she knew without seeing, but looked instead down the road where the trees leaned over and bowed to each other and a thousand birds were singing a Mass. She felt like singing too, but she put her hand in the bosom of her dress and pulled out a rosary, and Father Connolly murmured Latin in a very solemn voice and tickled her feet. My God, will you stop that nonsense? I'm a married woman. What if he did run away and leave me to face the priest by myself? I found another a whole world better. I wouldn't have exchanged my husband for anybody except St. Michael himself, and you may tell him that for me with a thank you in the bargain.

Light flashed on her closed eyelids, and a deep roaring shook her. Cornelia, is that lightning? I hear thunder. There's going to be a storm. Close all the windows. Call the children in. . . . "Mother, here we are, all of us." "Is that you, Hapsy?" "Oh, no, I'm Lydia. We drove as fast as we could." Their faces drifted above her, drifted away. The rosary fell out of her hands and Lydia put it back. Jimmy tried to help, their hands fumbled together, and Granny closed two fingers around Jimmy's thumb. Beads wouldn't do; it must be something alive. She was so amazed her thoughts ran round and round.

So, my dear Lord, this is my death and I wasn't even thinking about it. My children have come to see me die. But I can't, it's not time. Oh, I always hated surprises. I wanted to give Cornelia the amethyst set—Cornelia, you're to have the amethyst set, but Hapsy's to wear it when she wants, and, Doctor Harry, do shut up. Nobody sent for you. Oh, my dear Lord, do wait a minute. I meant to do something about the Forty Acres, Jimmy doesn't need it and Lydia will later on, with that worthless husband of hers. I meant to finish the altar cloth and send six bottles of wine to Sister Borgia for her dyspepsia. I want to send six bottles of wine to Sister Borgia, Father Connolly, now don't let me forget.

Cornelia's voice made short turns and tilted over and crashed. "Oh, Mother, oh, Mother, oh, Mother. . . ."

"I'm not going, Cornelia. I'm taken by surprise. I can't go."

You'll see Hapsy again. What about her? "I thought you'd never come." Granny made a long journey outward, looking for Hapsy. What if I don't find her? What then? Her heart sank down and down, there was no bottom to death, she couldn't come to the end of it. The blue light from Cornelia's lampshade drew into a tiny point in the center of her brain, it flickered and winked like an eye, quietly it fluttered and dwindled. Granny lay curled down within herself, amazed and watchful, staring at the point of light that was herself; her body was now only a deeper mass of shadow in an endless darkness and this darkness would curl around the light and swallow it up. God, give a sign!

For the second time there was no sign. Again no bridegroom and the priest in the house. She could not remember any other sorrow because this grief wiped them all away. Oh, no, there's nothing more cruel than this— I'll never forgive it. She stretched herself with a deep breath and blew out the light.

The Story of My Dovecot

ISAAC BABEL

All that he and his parents wanted was for him to go to high school. But in Czarist Russia in 1905 it wasn't easy. The doors that were open to his fellow-students were closed to the young narrator of "The Story of My Dovecot."

In this poignant drama, injustice and discrimination come between a boy and his hunger to know. Its humble characters are caught in the pogroms of 1905 and 1906, in which more than a thousand of them were systematically slaughtered and thousands of others wounded and maimed.

"The Story of My Dovecot," seen through the bright, innocent eyes of childhood, details with shattering simplicity man's continuing inhumanity to man. Because Mr. Babel lived through the tragic horrors of the pogrom, his writing in "The Story of My Dovecot" has an authentic, eye-witness reality. But the author is no mere recorder of local events, nor is his narrative just an exercise recalling in tranquillity his turbulent, anxiety-ridden childhood. In "The Story of My Dovecot" he has, in the lives of his "little" people, projected a universal symbol of unquenchable longings and indomitable courage.

*ISAAC EMMANUELOVICH BABEL (1894–1939(?)),
born in Odessa of Jewish parents, is considered by most
critics to be the finest modern Russian short story writer.
During the Russian Revolution and in the Civil War that
followed, Babel rode as a war correspondent with Buden-
ny's Cossacks. His Odessa and military experiences form
the basis for his two collections of stories,* Odessa Tales
(1923) and Red Cavalry *(1926).*

*Babel was last heard from in 1936. He is said to have
died in a concentration camp in 1939.*

The Story of My Dovecot

When I was a kid I longed for a dovecot. Never in all
my life have I wanted a thing more. But not till I was
nine did father promise the wherewithal to buy the wood
to make one and three pairs of pigeons to stock it with.
It was then 1904, and I was studying for the entrance
exam to the preparatory class of the secondary school
at Nikolayev in the Province of Kherson, where my people were at that time living. This province of course
no longer exists, and our town has been incorporated in
the Odessa Region.

I was only nine, and I was scared stiff of the exams.
In both subjects, Russian language and arithmetic, I
couldn't afford to get less than top marks. At our secondary school the *numerus clausus* was stiff: a mere five
percent. So that out of forty boys only two that were
Jews could get into the preparatory class. The teachers
used to put cunning questions to Jewish boys; no one
else was asked such devilish questions. So when father
promised to buy the pigeons he demanded top marks with
distinction in both subjects. He absolutely tortured me to
death. I fell into a state of permanent daydream, into an
endless, despairing childish reverie. I went to the exam
deep in this dream, and nevertheless did better than
everybody else.

I had a knack for book-learning. Even though they

asked cunning questions, the teachers could not rob me
of my intelligence and my avid memory. I was good at
learning, and got top marks in both subjects. But then
everything went wrong. Khariton Efrussi, the corn-dealer
who exported wheat to Marseille, slipped someone a 500-
rouble bribe. My mark was changed from A to A—, and
Efrussi Junior went to the secondary school instead of me.
Father took it very badly. From the time I was six he
had been cramming me with every scrap of learning he
could, and that A— drove him to despair. He wanted to
beat Efrussi up, or at least bribe two longshoremen to
beat Efrussi up, but mother talked him out of the idea,
and I started studying for the second exam the following
year, the one for the lowest class. Behind my back my
people got the teacher to take me in one year through
the preparatory and first-year courses simultaneously, and
conscious of the family's despair, I got three whole books
by heart. These were Smirnovsky's *Russian Grammar*,
Yevtushevsky's *Problems*, and Putsykovich's *Manual of
Early Russian History*. Children no longer cram from
these books, but I learned them by heart line upon line,
and the following year in the Russian exam Karavayev
gave me an unrivaled A+.

This Karavayev was a red-faced, irritable fellow, a
graduate of Moscow University. He was hardly more than
thirty. Crimson glowed in his manly cheeks as it does in
the cheeks of peasant children. A wart sat perched on
one cheek, and from it there sprouted a tuft of ash-
colored cat's whiskers. At the exam, besides Karavayev,
there was the Assistant Curator Pyatnitsky, who was
reckoned a big noise in the school and throughout the
province. When the Assistant Curator asked me about
Peter the Great a feeling of complete oblivion came over
me, an awareness that the end was near: an abyss seemed
to yawn before me, an arid abyss lined with exultation
and despair.

About Peter the Great I knew things by heart from
Putsykovich's book and Pushkin's verses. Sobbing, I recited these verses, while the faces before me suddenly
turned upside down, were shuffled as a pack of cards is
shuffled. This card-shuffling went on, and meanwhile,
shivering, jerking my back straight, galloping headlong,

I was shouting Pushkin's stanzas at the top of my voice. On and on I yelled them, and no one broke into my crazy mouthings. Through a crimson blindness, through the sense of absolute freedom that had filled me, I was aware of nothing but Pyatnitsky's old face with its silver-touched beard bent toward me. He didn't interrupt me, and merely said to Karavayev, who was rejoicing for my sake and Pushkin's:

"What a people," the old man whispered, "those little Jews of yours! There's a devil in them!"

And when at last I could shout no more, he said:

"Very well, run along, my little friend."

I went out from the classroom into the corridor, and there, leaning against a wall that needed a coat of whitewash, I began to awake from my trance. About me Russian boys were playing, the school bell hung not far away above the stairs, the caretaker was snoozing on a chair with a broken seat. I looked at the caretaker, and gradually woke up. Boys were creeping toward me from all sides. They wanted to give me a jab, or perhaps just have a game, but Pyatnitsky suddenly loomed up in the corridor. As he passed me he halted for a moment, the frock coat flowing down his back in a slow heavy wave. I discerned embarrassment in that large, fleshy, upper-class back, and got closer to the old man.

"Children," he said to the boys, "don't touch this lad." And he laid a fat hand tenderly on my shoulder.

"My little friend," he went on, turning me toward him, "tell your father that you are admitted to the first class."

On his chest a great star flashed, and decorations jingled in his lapel. His great black-uniformed body started to move away on its stiff legs. Hemmed in by the shadowy walls, moving between them as a barge moves through a deep canal, it disappeared in the doorway of the headmaster's study. The little servingman took in a tray of tea, clinking solemnly, and I ran home to the shop.

In the shop a peasant customer, tortured by doubt, sat scratching himself. When he saw me my father stopped trying to help the peasant make up his mind, and without a moment's hesitation believed everything I had to say. Calling to the assistant to start shutting up shop, he dashed out into Cathedral Street to buy me a school cap

with a badge on it. My poor mother had her work cut
out getting me away from the crazy fellow. She was pale
at that moment, she was experiencing destiny. She kept
smoothing me, and pushing me away as though she hated
me. She said there was always a notice in the paper about
those who had been admitted to the school, and that
God would punish us, and that folk would laugh at us
if we bought a school cap too soon. My mother was pale;
she was experiencing destiny through my eyes. She looked
at me with bitter compassion as one might look at a
little cripple boy, because she alone knew what a family
ours was for misfortunes.

All the men in our family were trusting by nature,
and quick to ill-considered actions. We were unlucky in
everything we undertook. My grandfather had been a
rabbi somewhere in the Belaya Tserkov region. He had
been thrown out for blasphemy, and for another forty
years he lived noisily and sparsely, teaching foreign languages. In his eightieth year he started going off his head.
My Uncle Leo, my father's brother, had studied at the
Talmudic Academy in Volozhin. In 1892 he ran away
to avoid doing military service, eloping with the daughter
of someone serving in the commissariat in the Kiev military district. Uncle Leo took this woman to California,
to Los Angeles, and there he abandoned her, and died
in a house of ill fame among Negroes and Malays. After
his death the American police sent us a heritage from
Los Angeles, a large trunk bound with brown iron hoops.
In this trunk there were dumbbells, locks of women's
hair, uncle's talith, horsewhips with gilt handles, scented
tea in boxes trimmed with imitation pearls. Of all the family there remained only crazy Uncle Simon-Wolf, who
lived in Odessa, my father, and I. But my father had
faith in people, and he used to put them off with the
transports of first love. People could not forgive him for
this, and used to play him false. So my father believed
that his life was guided by an evil fate, an inexplicable
being that pursued him, a being in every respect unlike
him. And so I alone of all our family was left to my
mother. Like all Jews I was short, weakly, and had headaches from studying. My mother saw all this. She had
never been dazzled by her husband's pauper pride, by

his incomprehensible belief that our family would one day be richer and more powerful than all others on earth. She desired no success for us, was scared of buying a school jacket too soon, and all she would consent to was that I should have my photo taken.

On September 20, 1905, a list of those admitted to the first class was hung up at the school. In the list my name figured too. All our kith and kin kept going to look at this paper, and even Shoyl, my granduncle, went along. I loved that boastful old man, for he sold fish at the market. His fat hands were moist, covered with fish-scales, and smelt of worlds chill and beautiful. Shoyl also differed from ordinary folk in the lying stories he used to tell about the Polish Rising of 1861. Years ago Shoyl had been a tavern-keeper at Skvira. He had seen Nicholas I's soldiers shooting Count Godlevski and other Polish insurgents. But perhaps he hadn't. *Now* I know that Shoyl was just an old ignoramus and a simple-minded liar, but his cock-and-bull stories I have never forgotten: they were good stories. Well now, even silly old Shoyl went along to the school to read the list with my name on it, and that evening he danced and pranced at our pauper ball.

My father got up the ball to celebrate my success, and asked all his pals—grain-dealers, real-estate brokers, and the traveling salesmen who sold agricultural machinery in our parts. These salesmen would sell a machine to anyone. Peasants and landowners went in fear of them: you couldn't break loose without buying something or other. Of all Jews, salesmen are the widest-awake and the jolliest. At our party they sang Hasidic songs consisting of three words only but which took an awful long time to sing, songs performed with endless comical intonations. The beauty of these intonations may only be recognized by those who have had the good fortune to spend Passover with the Hasidim or who have visited their noisy Volhynian synagogues. Besides the salesmen, old Lieberman who had taught me the Torah and ancient Hebrew honored us with his presence. In our circle he was known as Monsieur Lieberman. He drank more Bessarabian wine than he should have. The ends of the traditional silk tassels poked out from beneath his waistcoat, and in ancient Hebrew he proposed my health. In this toast the old man

congratulated my parents and said that I had vanquished
all my foes in single combat: I had vanquished the Russian boys with their fat cheeks, and I had vanquished
the sons of our own vulgar parvenus. So too in ancient
times David King of Judah had overcome Goliath, and just
as I had triumphed over Goliath, so too would our people
by the strength of their intellect conquer the foes who
had encircled us and were thirsting for our blood. Monsieur Lieberman started to weep as he said this, drank
more wine as he wept, and shouted *"Vivat!"* The guests
formed a circle and danced an old-fashioned quadrille
with him in the middle, just as at a wedding in a little
Jewish town. Everyone was happy at our ball. Even
mother took a sip of vodka, though she neither liked the
stuff nor understood how anyone else could—because of
this she considered all Russians cracked, and just couldn't
imagine how women managed with Russian husbands.

But our happy days came later. For mother they came
when of a morning, before I set off for school, she would
start making me sandwiches; when we went shopping to
buy my school things—pencil box, money box, satchel,
new books in cardboard bindings, and exercise books in
shiny covers. No one in the world has a keener feeling
for new things than children have. Children shudder at
the smell of newness as a dog does when it scents a hare,
experiencing the madness which later, when we grow up,
is called inspiration. And mother acquired this pure and
childish sense of the ownership of new things. It took us
a whole month to get used to the pencil box, to the
morning twilight as I drank my tea on the corner of the
large, brightly lit table and packed my books in my
satchel. It took us a month to grow accustomed to our
happiness, and it was only after the first half-term that I
remembered about the pigeons.

I had everything ready for them: one rouble fifty and
a dovecot made from a box by Grandfather Shoyl, as we
called him. The dovecot was painted brown. It had nests
for twelve pairs of pigeons, carved strips on the roof,
and a special grating that I had devised to facilitate the
capture of strange birds. All was in readiness. On Sunday,
October 20, I set out for the bird market, but unexpected obstacles arose in my path.

The events I am relating, that is to say my admission to the first class at the secondary school, occurred in the autumn of 1905. The Emperor Nicholas was then bestowing a constitution on the Russian people. Orators in shabby overcoats were clambering onto tall curbstones and haranguing the people. At night shots had been heard in the streets, and so mother didn't want me to go to the bird market. From early morning on October 20 the boys next door were flying a kite right by the police station, and our water carrier, abandoning all his buckets, was walking about the streets with a red face and brilliantined hair. Then we saw baker Kalistov's sons drag a leather vaulting-horse out into the street and start doing gym in the middle of the roadway. No one tried to stop them: Semernikov the policeman even kept inciting them to jump higher. Sermernikov was girt with a silk belt his wife had made him, and his boots had been polished that day as they had never been polished before. Out of his customary uniform, the policeman frightened my mother more than anything else. Because of him she didn't want me to go out, but I sneaked out by the back way and ran to the bird market, which in our town was behind the station.

At the bird market Ivan Nikodimych, the pigeon-fancier, sat in his customary place. Apart from pigeons, he had rabbits for sale, too, and a peacock. The peacock, spreading its tail, sat on a perch moving a passionless head from side to side. To its paw was tied a twisted cord, and the other end of the cord was caught beneath one leg of Ivan Nikodimych's wicker chair. The moment I got there I bought from the old man a pair of cherry-colored pigeons with luscious tousled tails, and a pair of crowned pigeons, and put them away in a bag on my chest under my shirt. After these purchases I had only forty copecks left, and for this price the old man was not prepared to let me have a male and female pigeon of the Kryukov breed. What I liked about Kryukov pigeons was their short, knobbly, good-natured beaks. Forty copecks was the proper price, but the fancier insisted on haggling, averting from me a yellow face scorched by the unsociable passions of bird-snarers. At the end of our bargaining, seeing that there were no other customers,

Ivan Nikodimych beckoned me closer. All went as I wished, and all went badly.

Toward twelve o'clock, or perhaps a bit later, a man in felt boots passed across the square. He was stepping lightly on swollen feet, and in his worn-out face lively eyes glittered.

"Ivan Nikodimych," he said as he walked past the bird-fancier, "pack up your gear. In town the Jerusalem aristocrats are being granted a constitution. On Fish Street Grandfather Babel has been constitutioned to death."

He said this and walked lightly on between the cages like a barefoot ploughman walking along the edge of a field.

"They shouldn't," murmured Ivan Nikodimych in his wake. "They shouldn't!" he cried more sternly. He started collecting his rabbits and his peacock, and shoved the Kryukov pigeons at me for forty copecks. I hid them in my bosom and watched the people running away from the bird market. The peacock on Ivan Nikodimych's shoulder was last of all to depart. It sat there like the sun in a raw autumnal sky; it sat as July sits on a pink riverbank, a white-hot July in the long cool grass. No one was left in the market, and not far off shots were rattling. Then I ran to the station, cut across a square that had gone topsy-turvy, and flew down an empty lane of trampled yellow earth. At the end of the lane, in a little wheeled armchair, sat the legless Makarenko, who rode about town in his wheel-chair selling cigarettes from a tray. The boys in our street used to buy smokes from him, children loved him, I dashed toward him down the lane.

"Makarenko," I gasped, panting from my run, and I stroked the legless one's shoulder, "have you seen Shoyl?"

The cripple did not reply. A light seemed to be shining through his coarse face built up of red fat, clenched fists, chunks of iron. He was fidgeting on his chair in his excitement, while his wife Kate, presenting a wadded behind, was sorting out some things scattered on the ground.

"How far have you counted?" asked the legless man, and moved his whole bulk away from the woman, as though aware in advance that her answer would be unbearable.

"Fourteen pair of leggings," said Kate, still bending over, "six undersheets. Now I'm a-counting the bonnets."

"Bonnets!" cried Makarenko, with a choking sound like a sob, "it's clear, Catherine, that God has picked on me, that I must answer for all. People are carting off whole rolls of cloth, people have everything they should, and we're stuck with bonnets."

And indeed a woman with a beautiful burning face ran past us down the lane. She was clutching an armful of fezzes in one arm and a piece of cloth in the other, and in a voice of joyful despair she was yelling for her children, who had strayed. A silk dress and a blue blouse fluttered after her as she flew, and she paid no attention to Makarenko, who was rolling his chair in pursuit of her. The legless man couldn't catch up. His wheels clattered as he turned the handles for all he was worth.

"Little lady," he cried in a deafening voice, "where did you get that striped stuff?"

But the woman with the fluttering dress was gone. Round the corner to meet her leaped a rickety cart in which a peasant lad stood upright.

"Where've they all run to?" asked the lad, raising a red rein above the nags jerking in their collars.

"Everybody's on Cathedral Street," said Makarenko pleadingly, "everybody's there, sonny. Anything you happen to pick up, bring it along to me. I'll give you a good price."

The lad bent down over the front of the cart and whipped up his piebald nags. Tossing their filthy croups like calves, the horses shot off at a gallop. The yellow lane was once more yellow and empty. Then the legless man turned his quenched eyes upon me.

"God's picked on me, I reckon," he said lifelessly, "I'm a son of man, I reckon."

And he stretched a hand spotted with leprosy toward me.

"What's that you've got in your sack?" he demanded, and took the bag that had been warming my heart.

With his fat hand the cripple fumbled among the tumbler pigeons and dragged to light a cherry-colored she-bird. Jerking back its feet, the bird lay still on his palm.

"Pigeons," said Makarenko, and squeaking his wheels

he rode right up to me. "Damned pigeons," he repeated, and struck me on the cheek.

He dealt me a flying blow with the hand that was clutching the bird. Kate's wadded back seemed to turn upside down, and I fell to the ground in my new overcoat.

"Their spawn must be wiped out," said Kate, straightening up over the bonnets. "I can't a-bear their spawn, nor their stinking menfolk."

She said more things about our spawn, but I heard nothing of it. I lay on the ground, and the guts of the crushed bird trickled down from my temple. They flowed down my cheek, winding this way and that, splashing, blinding me. The tender pigeon-guts slid down over my forehead, and I closed my solitary unstopped-up eye so as not to see the world that spread out before me. This world was tiny, and it was awful. A stone lay just before my eyes, a little stone so chipped as to resemble the face of an old woman with a large jaw. A piece of string lay not far away, and a bunch of feathers that still breathed. My world was tiny, and it was awful. I closed my eyes so as not to see it, and pressed myself tight into the ground that lay beneath me in soothing dumbness. This trampled earth in no way resembled real life, waiting for exams in real life. Somewhere far away Woe rode across it on a great steed, but the noise of the hoofbeats grew weaker and died away, and silence, the bitter silence that sometimes overwhelms children in their sorrow, suddenly deleted the boundary between my body and the earth that was moving nowhither. The earth smelled of raw depths, of the tomb, of flowers. I smelled its smell and started crying, unafraid. I was walking along an unknown street set on either side with white boxes, walking in a getup of bloodstained feathers, alone between the pavements swept clean as on Sunday, weeping bitterly, fully and happily as I never wept again in all my life. Wires that had grown white hummed above my head, a watchdog trotted on in front, in the lane on one side a young peasant in a waistcoat was smashing a window frame in the house of Khariton Efrussi. He was smashing it with a wooden mallet, striking out with his whole body. Sighing, he smiled all around with the amiable grin of drunkenness, sweat, and spiritual power. The whole street was filled with a splitting, a snapping, the song of flying wood. The peasant's whole existence consisted in bending over, sweating, shouting queer words in some unknown, non-Russian language. He shouted the words and sang, shot out his blue eyes; till in the street there appeared a procession bearing the Cross and moving from the Municipal Building. Old men bore aloft the portrait of the neatly combed Tsar, banners with graveyard saints swayed above their heads, inflamed old women flew on in front. Seeing the procession, the peasant pressed his mallet to his chest and dashed off in pursuit of the banners, while I, waiting till the tail-end of the procession had passed, made my furtive way home. The house was empty. Its white doors were open, the grass by the dovecot had been trampled down. Only Kuzma was still in the yard. Kuzma the yardman was sitting in the shed laying out the dead Shoyl.

"The wind bears you about like an evil wood-chip," said the old man when he saw me. "You've been away ages. And now look what they've done to granddad."

Kuzma wheezed, turned away from me, and started pulling a fish out of a rent in grandfather's trousers. Two pike perch had been stuck into grandfather: one into the rent in his trousers, the other into his mouth. And while grandfather was dead, one of the fish was still alive, and struggling.

"They've done grandfather in, but nobody else," said Kuzma, tossing the fish to the cat. "He cursed them all good and proper, a wonderful damning and blasting it was. You might fetch a couple of pennies to put on his eyes."

But then, at ten years of age, I didn't know what need the dead had of pennies.

"Kuzma," I whispered, "save us."

And I went over to the yardman, hugged his crooked old back with its one shoulder higher than the other, and over this back I saw grandfather. Shoyl lay in the sawdust, his chest squashed in, his beard twisted upwards, battered shoes on his bare feet. His feet, thrown wide apart, were dirty, lilac-colored, dead. Kuzma was fussing over him. He tied the dead man's jaws and kept glancing

over the body to see what else he could do. He fussed
as though over a newly purchased garment, and only
cooled down when he had given the dead man's beard
a good combing.

"He cursed the lot of 'em right and left," he said,
smiling, and cast a loving look over the corpse. "If Tartars
had crossed his path he'd have sent them packing, but
Russians came, and their women with them, Rooski
women. Russians just can't bring themselves to forgive, I
know what Rooskis are."

The yardman spread some more sawdust beneath the
body, threw off his carpenter's apron, and took me by
the hand.

"Let's go to father," he mumbled, squeezing my hand
tighter and tighter. "Your father has been searching for
you since morning, sure as fate you was dead."

And so with Kuzma I went to the house of the tax-
inspector, where my parents, escaping the pogrom, had
sought refuge.

By the Waters
of Babylon

STEPHEN VINCENT BENÉT

Ours is a haunted civilization living in daily fear that we can—and may yet—destroy ourselves in a nuclear war that nobody wants and nobody will be able to stop.

Written in 1933 (twelve years before the explosion of the first atomic bomb), "By the Waters of Babylon" projects a prophetic answer to the chilling questions of our times, and probes the appalling choices that man's nature and accomplishments have opened up to him.

"By the Waters of Babylon" is, in a sense, science fiction, but with a significant difference and dimension. Running through this vividly conceived dissolution of a world is Mr. Benét's deep conviction that ultimately man will master the machine, himself, and his destiny.

STEPHEN VINCENT BENÉT (1898–1943) was born in Bethlehem, Pennsylvania, and attended school in Georgia and California. By the time he had enrolled at Yale University in 1915, he had published some of his poems in St. Nicholas *and other magazines. In his senior year at Yale, he became editor of the Yale literary magazine. That same year saw the publication of his second book of verse.* John Brown's Body, *a poem about the Civil War, brought Benét fame and the Pulitzer prize for the best volume of poetry written in 1928.*

All his life, Benét was a prolific writer of poems and stories. His zesty and vigorous exploitation of American themes—and the American past—brought him wide and appreciative recognition. Among his most successful and popular poetic works are John Brown's Body *(1928) and* Western Star *(1943), which was posthumously awarded the Pulitzer pride in 1944. In his last years, Benét wrote patriotic plays for radio passionately attacking tyranny and dictatorship.*

Most of Benét's short stories have been collected in The Barefoot Saint *(1929),* The Devil and Daniel Webster *(1937), and* Johnny Pye and the Fool Killer *(1938). "The Devil and Daniel Webster" was eventually turned into a one-act play, a radio play, a motion picture, and an opera.*

In spite of some unevenness in his writing, Benét at his best added something vital and fresh to "the small body of great American writing about America."

By the Waters of Babylon

The north and the west and the south are good hunting ground, but it is forbidden to go east. It is forbidden to go to any of the Dead Places except to search for metal and then he who touches the metal must be a priest or the son of a priest. Afterwards, both the man and the metal must be purified. These are the rules and the laws; they are well made. It is forbidden to cross the great river and look upon the place that was the Place of the Gods—this is most strictly forbidden. We do not even say its name though we know its name. It is there that spirits live, and demons—it is there that there are the ashes of the Great Burning. These things are forbidden—they have been forbidden since the beginning of time.

My father is a priest; I am the son of a priest. I have been in the Dead Places near us, with my father—at first, I was afraid. When my father went into the house to search for the metal, I stood by the door and my heart felt small and weak. It was a dead man's house, a spirit house. It did not have the smell of man, though there were old bones in a corner. But it is not fitting that a priest's son should show fear. I looked at the bones in the shadow and kept my voice still.

Then my father came out with the metal—a good, strong piece. He looked at me with both eyes but I had not run away. He gave me the metal to hold—I took it and did not die. So he knew that I was truly his son and would be a priest in my time. That was when I was very young—nevertheless, my brothers would not have done it, though they are good hunters. After that, they gave me the good piece of meat and the warm corner by the fire. My father watched over me—he was glad that I should be a priest. But when I boasted or wept without a reason, he punished me more strictly than my brothers. That was right.

After a time, I myself was allowed to go into the dead houses and search for metal. So I learned the ways of those houses—and if I saw bones, I was no longer afraid. The bones are light and old—sometimes they will fall into dust if you touch them. But that is a great sin.

I was taught the chants and the spells—I was taught how to stop the running of blood from a wound and many secrets. A priest must know many secrets—that was what my father said. If the hunters think we do all things by chants and spells, they may believe so—it does not hurt them. I was taught how to read in the old books and how to make the old writings—that was hard and took a long time. My knowledge made me happy—it was like a fire in my heart. Most of all, I liked to hear of the Old Days and the stories of the gods. I asked myself many questions that I could not answer, but it was good to ask them. At night, I would lie awake and listen to the wind—it seemed to me that it was the voice of the gods as they flew through the air.

We are not ignorant like the Forest People—our women spin wool on the wheel, our priests wear a white robe. We do not eat grubs from the tree, we have not forgotten the old writings, although they are hard to understand. Nevertheless, my knowledge and my lack of knowledge burned in me—I wished to know more. When I was a man at last, I came to my father and said, "It is time for me to go on my journey. Give me your leave."

He looked at me for a long time, stroking his beard, then he said at last, "Yes. It is time." That night, in the house of the priesthood, I asked for and received purification. My body hurt but my spirit was a cool stone. It was my father himself who questioned me about my dreams.

He bade me look into the smoke of the fire and see—I saw and told what I saw. It was what I have always seen—a river, and, beyond it, a great Dead Place and in it the gods walking. I have always thought about that. His eyes were stern when I told him—he was no longer my father but a priest. He said, "This is a strong dream."

"It is mine," I said, while the smoke waved and my head felt light. They were singing the Star song in the outer chamber and it was like the buzzing of bees in my head.

He asked me how the gods were dressed and I told him how they were dressed. We know how they were dressed from the book, but I saw them as if they were before me. When I had finished, he threw the sticks three times and studied them as they fell.

"This is a very strong dream," he said. "It may eat you up."

"I am not afraid," I said and looked at him with both eyes. My voice sounded thin in my ears but that was because of the smoke.

He touched me on the breast and the forehead. He gave me the bow and the three arrows.

"Take them," he said. "It is forbidden to travel east. It is forbidden to cross the river. It is forbidden to go to the Place of the Gods. All these things are forbidden."

"All these things are forbidden," I said, but it was my voice that spoke and not my spirit. He looked at me again.

"My son," he said. "Once I had young dreams. If your dreams do not eat you up, you may be a great priest. If they eat you, you are still my son. Now go on your journey."

I went fasting, as is the law. My body hurt but not

my heart. When the dawn came, I was out of sight of the village. I prayed and purified myself, waiting for a sign. The sign was an eagle. It flew east.

Sometimes signs are sent by bad spirits. I waited again on the flat rock, fasting, taking no food. I was very still— I could feel the sky above me and the earth beneath. I waited till the sun was beginning to sink. Then three deer passed in the valley, going east—they did not wind me or see me. There was a white fawn with them—a very great sign.

I followed them, at a distance, waiting for what would happen. My heart was troubled about going east, yet I knew that I must go. My head hummed with my fasting —I did not even see the panther spring upon the white fawn. But, before I knew it, the bow was in my hand. I shouted and the panther lifted his head from the fawn. It is not easy to kill a panther with one arrow but the arrow went through his eye and into his brain. He died as he tried to spring—he rolled over, tearing at the ground. Then I knew I was meant to go east—I knew that was my journey. When the night came, I made my fire and roasted meat.

It is eight suns' journey to the east and a man passes by many Dead Places. The Forest People are afraid of them but I am not. Once I made my fire on the edge of a Dead Place at night and, next morning, in the dead house, I found a good knife, little rusted. That was small to what came afterward but it made my heart feel big. Always when I looked for game, it was in front of my arrow, and twice I passed hunting parties of the Forest People without their knowing. So I knew my magic was strong and my journey clean, in spite of the law.

Toward the setting of the eighth sun, I came to the banks of the great river. It was half-a-day's journey after I had left the god-road—we do not use the god-roads now for they are falling apart into great blocks of stone, and the forest is safer going. A long way off, I had seen the water through trees but the trees were thick. At last, I came out upon an open place at the top of a cliff. There was the great river below, like a giant in the sun. It is very long, very wide. It could eat all the streams we know and still be thirsty. Its name is Ou-dis-sun, the Sacred, the

Long. No man of my tribe had seen it, not even my father, the priest. It was magic and I prayed.

Then I raised my eyes and looked south. It was there, the Place of the Gods.

How can I tell what it was like—you do not know. It was there, in the red light, and they were too big to be houses. It was there with the red light upon it, mighty and ruined. I knew that in another moment the gods would see me. I covered my eyes with my hands and crept back into the forest.

Surely, that was enough to do, and live. Surely it was enough to spend the night upon the cliff. The Forest People themselves do not come near. Yet, all through the night, I knew that I should have to cross the river and walk in the places of the gods, although the gods ate me up. My magic did not help me at all and yet there was a fire in my bowels, a fire in my mind. When the sun rose, I thought, "My journey has been clean. Now I will go home from my journey." But, even as I thought so, I knew I could not. If I went to the Place of the Gods, I would surely die, but, if I did not go, I could never be at peace with my spirit again. It is better to lose one's life than one's spirit, if one is a priest and the son of a priest.

Nevertheless, as I made the raft, the tears ran out of my eyes. The Forest People could have killed me without fight, if they had come upon me then, but they did not come. When the raft was made, I said the sayings for the dead and painted myself for death. My heart was cold as a frog and my knees like water, but the burning in my mind would not let me have peace. As I pushed the raft from the shore, I began my death song—I had the right. It was a fine song.

"I am John, son of John," I sang. "My people are the Hill People. They are the men.
I go into the Dead Places but I am not slain.
I take the metal from the Dead Places but I am not blasted.
I travel upon the god-roads and am not afraid. E-yah!
I have killed the panther, I have killed the fawn!

E-yah! I have come to the great river. No man has come
there before.

It is forbidden to go east, but I have gone, forbidden
to go on the great river, but I am there.

Open your hearts, you spirits, and hear my song.

Now I go to the Place of the Gods, I shall not return.

My body is painted for death and my limbs weak, but
my heart is big as I go to the Place of the Gods!"

All the same, when I came to the Place of the Gods,
I was afraid, afraid. The current of the great river is
very strong—it gripped my raft with its hands. That was
magic, for the river itself is wide and calm. I could feel
evil spirits about me, in the bright morning; I could feel
their breath on my neck as I was swept down the stream.
Never have I been so much alone—I tried to think of my
knowledge, but it was a squirrel's heap of winter nuts.
There was no strength in my knowledge any more and
I felt small and naked as a new-hatched bird—alone upon
the great river, the servant of the gods.

Yet, after a while, my eyes were opened and I saw. I
saw both banks of the river—I saw that once there had
been god-roads across it, though now they were broken
and fallen like broken vines. Very great they were, and
wonderful and broken—broken in the time of the Great
Burning when the fire fell out of the sky. And always
the current took me nearer to the Place of the Gods, and
the huge ruins rose before my eyes.

I do not know the customs of rivers—we are the People
of the Hills. I tried to guide my raft with the pole but
it spun around. I thought the river meant to take me past
the Place of the Gods and out into the Bitter Water of
the legends. I grew angry then—my heart felt strong. I
said aloud, "I am a priest and the son of a priest!" The
gods heard me—they showed me how to paddle with the
pole on one side of the raft. The current changed itself—
I drew near to the Place of the Gods.

When I was very near, my raft struck and turned over.
I can swim in our lakes—I swam to the shore. There was
a great spike of rusted metal sticking out into the river
—I hauled myself up upon it and sat there, panting. I
had saved my bow and two arrows and the knife I found

in the Dead Place but that was all. My raft went whirling downstream toward the Bitter Water. I looked after it,
and thought if it had trod me under, at least I would
be safely dead. Nevertheless, when I had dried my bow-
string and re-strung it, I walked forward to the Place of
the Gods.

It felt like ground underfoot; it did not burn me. It
is not true what some of the tales say, that the ground
there burns forever, for I have been there. Here and
there were the marks and stains of the Great Burning,
on the ruins, that is true. But they were old marks and
old stains. It is not true either, what some of our priests
say, that it is an island covered with fogs and enchant-
ments. It is not. It is a great Dead Place—greater than any
Dead Place we know. Everywhere in it there are god-
roads, though most are cracked and broken. Everywhere
there are the ruins of the high towers of the gods.

How shall I tell what I saw? I went carefully, my strung
bow in my hand, my skin ready for danger. There should
have been the wailings of spirits and the shrieks of demons, but there were not. It was very silent and sunny
where I had landed—the wind and the rain and the birds
that drop seeds had done their work—the grass grew
in the cracks of the broken stone. It is a fair island—
no wonder the gods built there. If I had come there, a
god, I also would have built.

How shall I tell what I saw? The towers are not all
broken—here and there one still stands, like a great tree
in a forest, and the birds nest high. But the towers themselves look blind, for the gods are gone. I saw a fish-
hawk, catching fish in the river. I saw a little dance of
white butterflies over a great heap of broken stones and
columns. I went there and looked about me—there was
a carved stone with cut-letters, broken in half. I can read
letters but I could not understand these. They said
UBTREAS. There was also the shattered image of a man
or a god. It had been made of white stone and he wore
his hair tied back like a woman's. His name was ASH-
ING, as I read on the cracked half of a stone, I thought
it wise to pray to ASHING, though I do not know that
god.

How shall I tell what I saw? There was no smell of

man left, on stone or metal. Nor were there many trees in that wilderness of stone. There are many pigeons, nesting and dropping in the towers—the gods must have loved them, or, perhaps, they used them for sacrifices. There are wild cats that roam the god-roads, green-eyed, unafraid of man. At night they wail like demons but they are not demons. The wild dogs are more dangerous, for they hunt in a pack, but them I did not meet till later. Everywhere there are the carved stones, carved with magical numbers or words.

I went north—I did not try to hide myself. When a god or a demon saw me, then I would die, but meanwhile I was no longer afraid. My hunger for knowledge burned in me—there was so much that I could not understand. After awhile, I knew that my belly was hungry. I could have hunted for my meat, but I did not hunt. It is known that the gods did not hunt as we do—they got their food from enchanted boxes and jars. Sometimes these are still found in the Dead Places—once, when I was a child and foolish, I opened such a jar and tasted it and found the food sweet. But my father found out and punished me for it strictly, for, often, that food is death. Now, though, I had long gone past what was forbidden, and I entered the likeliest towers, looking for the food of the gods.

I found it at last in the ruins of a great temple in the mid-city. A mighty temple it must have been, for the roof was painted like the sky at night with its stars—that much I could see, though the colors were faint and dim. It went down into great caves and tunnels—perhaps they kept their slaves there. But when I started to climb down, I heard the squeaking of rats, so I did not go—rats are unclean, and there must have been many tribes of them, from the squeaking. But near there, I found food, in the heart of a ruin, behind a door that still opened. I ate only the fruits from the jars—they had a very sweet taste. There was drink, too, in bottles of glass—the drink of the gods was strong and made my head swim. After I had eaten and drunk, I slept on the top of a stone, my bow at my side.

When I woke, the sun was low. Looking down from where I lay, I saw a dog sitting on his haunches. His tongue was hanging out of his mouth; he looked as if he were laughing. He was a big dog, with a gray-brown coat, as big as a wolf. I sprang up and shouted at him but he did not move—he just sat there as if he were laughing. I did not like that. When I reached for a stone to throw, he moved swiftly out of the way of the stone. He was not afraid of me; he looked at me as if I were meat. No doubt I could have killed him with an arrow, but I did not know if there were others. Moreover, night was falling.

I looked about me—not far away there was a great, broken god-road, leading north. The towers were high enough, but not so high, and while many of the dead-houses were wrecked, there were some that stood. I went toward this god-road, keeping to the heights of the ruins, while the dog followed. When I had reached the god-road, I saw that there were others behind him. If I had slept later, they would have come upon me asleep and torn out my throat. As it was, they were sure enough of me; they did not hurry. When I went into the dead-house, they kept watch at the entrance—doubtless they thought they would have a fine hunt. But a dog cannot open a door and I knew, from the books, that the gods did not like to live on the ground but on high.

I had just found a door I could open when the dogs decided to rush. Ha! They were surprised when I shut the door in their faces—it was a good door, of strong metal. I could hear their foolish baying beyond it but I did not stop to answer them. I was in darkness—I found stairs and climbed. There were many stairs, turning around till my head was dizzy. At the top was another door—I found the knob and opened it. I was in a long small chamber—on one side of it was a bronze door that could not be opened, for it had no handle. Perhaps there was a magic word to open it but I did not have the word. I turned to the door in the opposite side of the wall. The lock of it was broken and I opened it and went in.

Within, there was a place of great riches. The god who lived there must have been a powerful god. The first room was a small anteroom—I waited there for some time, telling the spirits of the place that I came in peace and not as a robber. When it seemed to me that they had had time to hear me, I went on. Ah, what riches! Few, even, of the windows had been broken—it was all as it had been. The great windows that looked over the city had not been broken at all though they were dusty and streaked with many years. There were coverings on the floors, the colors not greatly faded, and the chairs were soft and deep. There were pictures upon the walls, very strange, very wonderful—I remember one of a bunch of flowers in a jar—if you came close to it, you could see nothing but bits of color, but if you stood away from it, the flowers might have been picked yesterday. It made my heart feel strange to look at this picture—and to look at the figure of a bird, in some hard clay, on a table and see it so like our birds. Everywhere there were books and writings, many in tongues that I could not read. The god who lived there must have been a wise god and full of knowledge. I felt I had right there, as I sought knowledge also.

Nevertheless, it was strange. There was a washing-place but no water—perhaps the gods washed in air. There was a cooking-place but no wood, and though there was a machine to cook food, there was no place to put fire in it. Nor were there candles or lamps—there were things that looked like lamps but they had neither oil nor wick. All these things were magic, but I touched them and lived—the magic had gone out of them. Let me tell one thing to show. In the washing-place, a thing said "Hot" but it was not hot to the touch—another thing said "Cold" but it was not cold. This must have been a strong magic but the magic was gone. I do not understand—they had ways—I wish that I knew.

It was close and dry and dusty in their house of the gods. I have said the magic was gone but that is not true—it had gone from the magic things but it had not gone from the place. I felt the spirits about me, weighing upon me. Nor had I ever slept in a Dead Place before—and yet, tonight, I must sleep there. When I thought of it, my tongue felt dry in my throat, in spite of my wish for knowledge. Almost I would have gone down again and faced the dogs, but I did not.

I had not gone through all the rooms when the darkness fell. When it fell, I went back to the big room looking over the city and made fire. There was a place to make fire and a box with wood in it, though I do not think they cooked there. I wrapped myself in a floor-covering and slept in front of the fire—I was very tired.

Now I tell what is very strong magic. I woke in the midst of the night. When I woke, the fire had gone out and I was cold. It seemed to me that all around me there were whisperings and voices. I closed my eyes to shut them out. Some will say that I slept again, but I do not think that I slept. I could feel the spirits drawing my spirit out of my body as a fish is drawn on a line.

Why should I lie about it? I am a priest and the son of a priest. If there are spirits, as they say, in the small Dead Places near us, what spirits must there not be in that great Place of the Gods? And would not they wish to speak? After such long years? I know that I felt myself drawn as a fish is drawn on a line. I had stepped out of my body—I could see my body asleep in front of the cold fire, but it was not I. I was drawn to look out upon the city of the gods.

It should have been dark, for it was night, but it was not dark. Everywhere there were lights—lines of light—circles and blurs of light—ten thousand torches would not have been the same. The sky itself was alight—you could barely see the stars for the glow in the sky. I thought to myself "This is strong magic" and trembled. There was a roaring in my ears like the rushing of rivers. Then my eyes grew used to the light and my ears to the sound. I knew that I was seeing the city as it had been when the gods were alive.

That was a sight indeed—yes, that was a sight: I could not have seen it in the body—my body would have died. Everywhere went the gods, on foot and in chariots—there were gods beyond number and counting and their chariots blocked the streets. They had turned night to day for their pleasure—they did not sleep with the sun. The noise of their coming and going was the noise of many waters. It was magic what they could do—it was magic what they did.

I looked out of another window—the great vines of their bridges were mended and the god-roads went east and west. Restless, restless, were the gods and always in motion! They burrowed tunnels under rivers—they flew in the air. With unbelievable tools they did giant works— no part of the earth was safe from them, for, if they wished for a thing, they summoned it from the other side of the world. And always, as they labored and rested, as they feasted and made love, there was a drum in their ears—the pulse of the giant city, beating and beating like a man's heart.

Were they happy? What is happiness to the gods? They were great, they were mighty, they were wonderful and terrible. As I looked upon them and their magic, I felt like a child—but a little more, it seemed to me, and they would pull down the moon from the sky. I saw them with wisdom beyond wisdom and knowledge beyond knowledge. And yet not all they did was well done— even I could see that—and yet their wisdom could not but grow until all was peace.

Then I saw their fate come upon them and that was terrible past speech. It came upon them as they walked the streets of their city. I have been in the fights with the Forest People—I have seen men die. But this was not like that. When gods war with gods, they use weapons we do not know. It was fire falling out of the sky and a mist that poisoned. It was the time of the Great Burning and the Destruction. They ran about like ants in the streets of their city—poor gods, poor gods! Then the towers began to fall. A few escaped—yes, a few. The legends tell it. But, even after the city had become a Dead Place, for many years the poison was still in the ground. I saw it happen, I saw the last of them die. It was darkness over the broken city and I wept.

All this, I saw. I saw it as I have told it, though not in the body. When I woke in the morning, I was hungry, but I did not think first of my hunger for my heart was perplexed and confused. I knew the reason for the Dead Places but I did not see why it had happened. It seemed to me it should not have happened, with all the magic they had. I went through the house looking for an answer. There was so much in the house I could not understand—and yet I am a priest and the son of a priest. It was like being on one side of the great river, at night, with no light to show the way.

Then I saw the dead god. He was sitting in his chair, by the window, in a room I had not entered before and, for the first moment, I thought that he was alive. Then I saw the skin on the back of his hand—it was like dry leather. The room was shut, hot and dry—no doubt that had kept him as he was. At first I was afraid to approach him—then the fear left me. He was sitting looking out over the city—he was dressed in the clothes of the gods. His age was neither young nor old—I could not tell his age. But there was wisdom in his face and great sadness. You could see that he would have not run away. He had sat at his window, watching his city die—then he himself had died. But it is better to lose one's life than one's spirit—and you could see from the face that his spirit had not been lost. I knew that, if I touched him, he would fall into dust—and yet, there was something unconquered in the face.

That is all of my story, for then I knew he was a man—I knew then that they had been men, neither gods nor demons. It is a great knowledge, hard to tell and believe. They were men—they went a dark road, but they were men. I had no fear after that—I had no fear going home, though twice I fought off the dogs and once I was hunted for two days by the Forest People. When I saw my father again, I prayed and was purified. He touched my lips and my breast, he said, "You went away a boy. You come back a man and a priest." I said, "Father, they were men! I have been in the Place of the Gods and seen it! Now slay me, if it is the law—but still I know they were men."

He looked at me out of both eyes. He said, "The law is not always the same shape—you have done what you have done. I could not have done it in my time, but you come after me. Tell!"

I told and he listened. After that, I wished to tell all the people but he showed me otherwise. He said, "Truth is a hard deer to hunt. If you eat too much truth at once, you may die of the truth. It was not idly that our fathers forbade the Dead Places." He was right—it is better the truth should come little by little. I have learned that, being a priest. Perhaps, in the old days, they ate knowledge too fast.

Nevertheless, we make a beginning. It is not for the metal alone we go to the Dead Places now—there are the books and the writings. They are hard to learn. And the magic tools are broken—but we can look at them and wonder. At least, we make a beginning. And, when I am chief priest we shall go beyond the great river. We shall go to the Place of the Gods—the place newyork—not one man but a company. We shall look for the images of the gods and find the god ASHING and the others—the gods Lincoln and Baltimore and Moses. But they were men who built the city, not gods or demons. They were men. I remember the dead man's face. They were men who were here before us. We must build again.

The Open Boat

STEPHEN CRANE

In 1896, Stephen Crane sailed to Cuba to cover a political campaign for the New York *Journal*. On the way his ship, the S.S. *Commodore,* was wrecked, and Crane spent four days in a small open boat before he and his companions were rescued. "The Open Boat" draws upon those harrowing, storm-tossed days.

"The Open Boat" is the age-old story of men against the sea—the story of raw courage and faith triumphing over the monstrous savagery and indifference of the sea.

With its very first and now famous sentence, "None of them knew the color of the sky," "The Open Boat" seizes the reader and rivets him to the epic drama being played out against the monumental, impersonal anger of the sea. There is no escaping the tremendous power of Crane's writing. It takes possession of the reader's mind and senses at once, makes him part of everything that is happening to every one of the boat's occupants.

"The Open Boat" is more than just a vivid tale. Touched with Crane's acute sensibilities, his uncanny ability to create in the reader the illusion of reality, his feeling for and mastery of literary form, "The Open Boat" is heavily freighted with Crane's deeply pessimistic view of a meaningless universe governed by a divine indifference to man's fate.

STEPHEN TOWNLEY CRANE (1871–1900) was born in Newark, New Jersey, the last child in a family of fourteen. After a year each at Lafayette College and Syracuse University, he abandoned formal schooling and turned his talents to journalism and literature. Unable to find a publisher for Maggie: A Girl of the Streets *(1893), he published it at his own expense, borrowing seven hundred dollars from his brother.* Maggie *sold one hundred copies, but it attracted the respectful attention of Hamlin Garland and William Dean Howells. The publication of* The Red Badge of Courage *(1895), a remarkable account of soldiers under fire in the American Civil War, brought Crane international recognition and fame. In 1898, Crane married Cora Taylor. On June 5, 1900, he died at Badenweiler in the Black Forest.*

"The Open Boat" is thought by some critics to be the finest story in the language. Among the distinguished stories of his later years are "The Bride Comes to Yellow Sky" and "The Blue Hotel." Largely ignored by the public and the critics immediately following his death, Crane has now come into his own as a writer of undisputed importance.

The Open Boat

A Tale intended to be after the fact. Being the Experience of Four Men from the Sunk Steamer "Commodore."

I

None of them knew the color of the sky. Their eyes glanced level, and were fastened upon the waves that swept toward them. These waves were of the hue of slate, save for the tops, which were of foaming white, and all of the men knew the colors of the sea. The horizon narrowed and widened, and dipped and rose, and at all times its edge was jagged with waves that seemed thrust up in points like rocks.

Many a man ought to have a bath-tub larger than the boat which here rode upon the sea. These waves were most wrongfully and barbarously abrupt and tall, and each froth-top was a problem in small boat navigation.

The cook squatted in the bottom and looked with both eyes at the six inches of gunwale which separated him from the ocean. His sleeves were rolled over his fat forearms, and the two flaps of his unbuttoned vest dangled as he bent to bail out the boat. Often he said: "Gawd! That was a narrow clip." As he remarked it he invariably gazed eastward over the broken sea.

The oiler, steering with one of the two oars in the boat, sometimes raised himself suddenly to keep clear of water that swirled in over the stern. It was a thin little oar and it seemed often ready to snap.

The correspondent, pulling at the other oar, watched the waves and wondered why he was there.

The injured captain, lying in the bow, was at this time buried in that profound dejection and indifference which comes, temporarily at least, to even the bravest and most enduring when, willy nilly, the firm fails, the army loses, the ship goes down. The mind of the master of a vessel is rooted deep in the timbers of her, though he command for a day or a decade, and this captain had on him the stern impression of a scene in the grays of dawn of seven turned faces, and later a stump of a top-mast with a white ball on it that slashed to and fro at the waves, went low and lower, and down. Thereafter there was something strange in his voice. Although steady, it was deep with mourning, and of a quality beyond oration or tears.

"Keep 'er a little more south, Billie," said he.

" 'A little more south,' sir," said the oiler in the stern.

A seat in this boat was not unlike a seat upon a bucking bronco, and, by the same token, a bronco is not much smaller. The craft pranced and reared, and plunged like an animal. As each wave came, and she rose for it, she seemed like a horse making at a fence outrageously high.

The manner of her scramble over these walls of water is a mystic thing, and, moreover, at the top of them were ordinarily these problems in white water, the foam racing down from the summit of each wave, requiring a new leap, and a leap from the air. Then, after scornfully bumping a crest, she would slide, and race, and splash down a long incline, and arrive bobbing and nodding in front of the next menace.

A singular disadvantage of the sea lies in the fact that after successfully surmounting one wave you discover that there is another behind it just as important and just as nervously anxious to do something effective in the way of swamping boats. In a ten-foot dingey one can get an idea of the resources of the sea in the line of waves that is not probable to the average experience which is never at sea in a dingey. As each slaty wall of water approached, it shut all else from the view of the men in the boat, and it was not difficult to imagine that this particular wave was the final outburst of the ocean, the last effort of the grim water. There was a terrible grace in the move of the waves, and they came in silence, save for the snarling of the crests.

In the wan light, the faces of the men must have been gray. Their eyes must have glinted in strange ways as they gazed steadily astern. Viewed from a balcony, the whole thing would doubtless have been weirdly picturesque. But the men in the boat had no time to see it, and if they had had leisure there were other things to occupy their minds. The sun swung steadily up the sky, and they knew it was broad day because the color of the sea changed from slate to emerald-green, streaked with amber lights, and the foam was like tumbling snow. The process of the breaking day was unknown to them. They were aware only of this effect upon the color of the waves that rolled toward them.

In disjointed sentences the cook and the correspondent argued as to the difference between a life-saving station and a house of refuge. The cook had said: "There's a house of refuge just north of the Mosquito Inlet Light, and as soon as they see us, they'll come off in their boat and pick us up."

"As soon as who see us?" said the correspondent.

"The crew," said the cook.

"Houses of refuge don't have crews," said the correspondent. "As I understand them, they are only places where clothes and grub are stored for the benefit of shipwrecked people. They don't carry crews."

"Oh, yes, they do," said the cook.

"No, they don't," said the correspondent.

"Well, we're not there yet, anyhow," said the oiler, in the stern.

"Well," said the cook, "perhaps it's not a house of refuge that I'm thinking of as being near Mosquito Inlet Light. Perhaps it's a life-saving station."

"We're not there yet," said the oiler, in the stern.

II

As the boat bounced from the top of each wave, the wind tore through the hair of the hatless men, and as the craft plopped her stern down again the spray slashed past them. The crest of each of these waves was a hill, from the top of which the men surveyed, for a moment, a broad tumultuous expanse, shining and wind-riven. It was probably splendid. It was probably glorious, this play of the free sea, wild with lights of emerald and white and amber.

"Bully good thing it's an on-shore wind," said the cook. "If not, where would we be? Wouldn't have a show."

"That's right," said the correspondent.

The busy oiler nodded his assent.

Then the captain, in the bow, chuckled in a way that expressed humor, contempt, tragedy, all in one. "Do you think we've got much of a show now, boys?" said he.

Whereupon the three were silent, save for a trifle of hemming and hawing. To express any particular optimism at this time they felt to be childish and stupid, but they all doubtless possessed this sense of the situation in their mind. A young man thinks doggedly at such times. On the other hand, the ethics of their condition was decidedly against any open suggestion of hopelessness. So they were silent.

"Oh, well," said the captain, soothing his children, "we'll get ashore all right."

But there was that in his tone which made them think, so the oiler quoth: "Yes! If this wind holds!"

The cook was bailing: "Yes! If we don't catch hell in the surf."

Canton flannel gulls flew near and far. Sometimes they sat down on the sea, near patches of brown seaweed that rolled over the waves with a movement like carpets on a line in a gale. The birds sat comfortably in groups, and they were envied by some in the dingey, for the wrath of the sea was no more to them than it was to a covey of prairie chickens a thousand miles inland. Often they came very close and stared at the men with black bead-like eyes. At these times they were uncanny and sinister in their unblinking scrutiny, and the men hooted angrily at them, telling them to be gone. One came, and evidently decided to alight on the top of the captain's head. The bird flew parallel to the boat and did not circle, but made short sidelong jumps in the air in chicken-fashion. His black eyes were wistfully fixed upon the captain's head. "Ugly brute," said the oiler to the bird. "You look as if you were made with a jack-knife." The cook and the correspondent swore darkly at the creature. The captain naturally wished to knock it away with the end of the heavy painter; but he did not dare do it, because anything resembling an emphatic gesture would have capsized this freighted boat, and so with his open hand, the captain gently and carefully waved the gull away. After it had been discouraged from the pursuit the captain breathed easier on account of his hair, and others breathed easier because the bird struck their minds at this time as being somehow gruesome and ominous.

In the meantime the oiler and the correspondent rowed. And also they rowed.

They sat together in the same seat, and each rowed an oar. Then the oiler took both oars; then the correspondent took both oars; then the oiler; then the correspondent. They rowed and they rowed. The very ticklish part of the business was when the time came for the reclining one in the stern to take his turn at the oars. By the very last star of truth, it is easier to steal eggs from under a hen than it was to change seats in the dingey. First the man in the stern slid his hand along the thwart and moved with care, as if he were of Sèvres. Then the man in the rowing seat slid his hand along the other thwart. It was all done with the most extraordinary care. As the two sidled past each other, the whole party kept watchful eyes on the coming wave, and the captain cried: "Look out now! Steady there!"

The brown mats of seaweed that appeared from time to time were like islands, bits of earth. They were travelling, apparently, neither one way nor the other. They were, to all intents, stationary. They informed the men in the boat that it was making progress slowly toward the land.

The captain, rearing cautiously in the bow, after the dingey soared on a great swell, said that he had seen the lighthouse at Mosquito Inlet. Presently the cook remarked that he had seen it. The correspondent was at the oars then, and for some reason he too wished to look at the lighthouse, but his back was toward the far shore and the waves were important, and for some time he could not seize an opportunity to turn his head. But at last there came a wave more gentle than the others, and when at the crest of it he swiftly scoured the western horizon.

"See it?" said the captain.

"No," said the correspondent slowly. "I didn't see anything."

"Look again," said the captain. He pointed. "It's exactly in that direction."

At the top of another wave, the correspondent did as he was bid, and this time his eyes chanced on a small still thing on the edge of the swaying horizon. It was precisely like the point of a pin. It took an anxious eye to find a lighthouse so tiny.

"Think we'll make it, captain?"

"If this wind holds and the boat don't swamp, we can't do much else," said the captain.

The little boat, lifted by each towering sea, and splashed viciously by the crests, made progress that in the absence of seaweed was not apparent to those in her. She seemed just a wee thing wallowing, miraculously top up, at the mercy of five oceans. Occasionally, a great spread of water, like white flames, swarmed into her.

"Bail her, cook," said the captain serenely.

"All right, captain," said the cheerful cook.

III

It would be difficult to describe the subtle brotherhood of men that was here established on the seas. No one said that it was so. No one mentioned it. But it dwelt in the boat, and each man felt it warm him. They were a captain, an oiler, a cook, and a correspondent, and they were friends, friends in a more curiously iron-bound degree than may be common. The hurt captain, lying against the water-jar in the bow, spoke always in a low voice and calmly, but he could never command a more ready and swiftly obedient crew than the motley three of the dingey. It was more than a mere recognition of what was best for the common safety. There was surely in it a quality that was personal and heartfelt. And after this devotion to the commander of the boat there was this comradeship that the correspondent, for instance, who had been taught to be cynical of men, knew even at the time was the best experience of his life. But no one said that it was so. No one mentioned it.

"I wish we had a sail," remarked the captain. "We might try my overcoat on the end of an oar and give you two boys a chance to rest." So the cook and the correspondent held the mast and spread wide the overcoat. The oiler steered, and the little boat made good way with her new rig. Sometimes the oiler had to scull sharply to keep a sea from breaking into the boat, but otherwise sailing was a success.

Meanwhile the lighthouse had been growing slowly larger. It had now almost assumed color, and appeared like a little gray shadow on the sky. The man at the oars could not be prevented from turning his head rather often to try for a glimpse of this little gray shadow.

At last, from the top of each wave the men in the tossing boat could see land. Even as the lighthouse was an upright shadow on the sky, this land seemed but a long black shadow on the sea. It certainly was thinner than paper. "We must be about opposite New Smyrna," said the cook, who had coasted this shore often in schooners. "Captain, by the way, I believe they abandoned that life-saving station there about a year ago."

"Did they?" said the captain.

The wind slowly died away. The cook and the correspondent were not now obliged to slave in order to hold high the oar. But the waves continued their old impetuous swooping at the dingey, and the little craft, no longer under way, struggled woundily over them. The oiler or the correspondent took the oars again.

Shipwrecks are apropos of nothing. If men could only train for them and have them occur when the men had reached pink condition, there would be less drowning at sea. Of the four in the dingey none had slept any time worth mentioning for two days and two nights previous to embarking in the dingey, and in the excitement of clambering about the deck of a foundering ship they had also forgotten to eat heartily.

For these reasons, and for others, neither the oiler nor the correspondent was fond of rowing at this time. The correspondent wondered ingenuously how in the name of all that was sane could there be people who thought it amusing to row a boat. It was not an amusement; it was a diabolical punishment, and even a genius of mental aberrations could never conclude that it was anything but a horror to the muscles and a crime against the back. He mentioned to the boat in general how the amusement of rowing struck him, and the weary-faced oiler smiled in full sympathy. Previously to the foundering, by the way, the oiler had worked double-watch in the engine-room of the ship.

"Take her easy, now, boys," said the captain. "Don't spend yourselves. If we have to run a surf you'll need all your strength, because we'll sure have to swim for it. Take your time."

Slowly the land arose from the sea. From a black line it became a line of black and a line of white, trees and sand. Finally, the captain said that he could make out a house on the shore. "That's the house of refuge, sure," said the cook. "They'll see us before long, and come out after us."

The distant lighthouse reared high. "The keeper ought to be able to make us out now, if he's looking through a glass," said the captain. "He'll notify the life-saving people."

"None of those other boats could have got ashore to give word of the wreck," said the oiler, in a low voice. "Else the life-boat would be out hunting us."

Slowly and beautifully the land loomed out of the sea. The wind came again. It had veered from the north-east to the south-east. Finally, a new sound struck the ears of the men in the boat. It was the low thunder of the surf on the shore. "We'll never be able to make the lighthouse now," said the captain. "Swing her head a little more north, Billie."

" 'A little more north,' sir," said the oiler.

Whereupon the little boat turned her nose once more down the wind, and all but the oarsman watched the shore grow. Under the influence of this expansion doubt and direful apprehension was leaving the minds of the men. The management of the boat was still most absorbing, but it could not prevent a quiet cheerfulness. In an hour, perhaps, they would be ashore.

Their backbones had become thoroughly used to balancing in the boat, and they now rode this wild colt of a dingey like circus men. The correspondent thought that he had been drenched to the skin, but happening to feel in the top pocket of his coat, he found therein eight cigars. Four of them were soaked with seawater; four were perfectly scatheless. After a search, somebody produced three dry matches, and thereupon the four waifs rode in their little boat, and with an assurance of an impending rescue shining in their eyes, puffed at the big cigars and judged well and ill of all men. Everybody took a drink of water.

IV

"Cook," remarked the captain, "there don't seem to be any signs of life about your house of refuge."

"No," replied the cook. "Funny they don't see us!"

A broad stretch of lowly coast lay before the eyes of the men. It was of low dunes topped with dark vegetation. The roar of the surf was plain, and sometimes they could see the white lip of a wave as it spun up the beach. A

tiny house was blocked out black upon the sky. Southward, the slim lighthouse lifted its little gray length.

Tide, wind, and waves were swinging the dingey northward. "Funny they don't see us," said the men.

The surf's roar was here dulled, but its tone was, nevertheless, thunderous and mighty. As the boat swam over
the great rollers, the men sat listening to this roar. "We'll
swamp sure," said everybody.

It is fair to say here that there was not a life-saving
station within twenty miles in either direction, but the
men did not know this fact, and in consequence they made
dark and opprobrious remarks concerning the eyesight of
the nation's life-savers. Four scowling men sat in the
dingey and surpassed records in the invention of epithets.

"Funny they don't see us."

The light-heartedness of a former time had completely
faded. To their sharpened minds it was easy to conjure
pictures of all kinds of incompetency and blindness and,
indeed, cowardice. There was the shore of the populous
land, and it was bitter and bitter to them that from it
came no sign.

"Well," said the captain, ultimately, "I suppose we'll
have to make a try for ourselves. If we stay out here
too long, we'll none of us have strength left to swim after
the boat swamps."

And so the oiler, who was at the oars, turned the boat
straight for the shore. There was a sudden tightening of
muscles. There was some thinking.

"If we don't all get ashore——" said the captain. "If we
don't all get ashore, I suppose you fellows know where
to send news of my finish?"

They then briefly exchanged some addresses and ad-
monitions. As for the reflections of the men, there was a
great deal of rage in them. Perchance they might be for-
mulated thus: "If I am going to be drowned—if I am going
to be drowned—if I am going to be drowned, why, in
the name of the seven mad gods who rule the sea, was
I allowed to come thus far and contemplate sand and
trees? Was I brought here merely to have my nose
dragged away as I was about to nibble the sacred cheese
of life? It is preposterous. If this old ninny-woman, Fate,
cannot do better than this, she should be deprived of the

management of men's fortunes. She is an old hen who knows not her intention. If she has decided to drown me, why did she not do it in the beginning and save me all this trouble? The whole affair is absurd. ... But no, she cannot mean to drown me. She dare not drown me. She cannot drown me. Not after all this work." Afterward the man might have had an impulse to shake his fist at the clouds: "Just you drown me, now, and then hear what I call you!"

The billows that came at this time were more formidable. They seemed always just about to break and roll over the little boat in a turmoil of foam. There was a preparatory and long growl in the speech of them. No mind unused to the sea would have concluded that the dingey could ascend these sheer heights in time. The shore was still afar. The oiler was a wily surfman. "Boys," he said swiftly, "she won't live three minutes more, and we're too far out to swim. Shall I take her to sea again, captain?"

"Yes! Go ahead!" said the captain.

This oiler, by a series of quick miracles, and fast and steady oarsmanship, turned the boat in the middle of the surf and took her safely to sea again.

There was a considerable silence as the boat bumped over the furrowed sea to deeper water. Then somebody in gloom spoke. "Well, anyhow, they must have seen us from the shore by now."

The gulls went in slanting flight up the wind toward the gray desolate east. A squall, marked by dingy clouds, and clouds brick-red, like smoke from a burning building, appeared from the south-east.

"What do you think of those life-saving people? Ain't they peaches?"

"Funny they haven't seen us."

"Maybe they think we're out here for sport! Maybe they think we're fishin'. Maybe they think we're damned fools."

It was a long afternoon. A changed tide tried to force them southward, but wind and wave said northward. Far ahead, where coastline, sea, and sky formed their mighty angle, there were little dots which seemed to indicate a city on the shore.

"St. Augustine?"

The captain shook his head. "Too near Mosquito Inlet."

And the oiler rowed, and then the correspondent rowed. Then the oiler rowed. It was a weary business. The human back can become the seat of more aches and pains than are registered in books for the composite anatomy of a regiment. It is a limited area, but it can become the theater of innumerable muscular conflicts, tangles, wrenches, knots, and other comforts.

"Did you ever like to row, Billie?" asked the correspondent.

"No," said the oiler. "Hang it!"

When one exchanged the rowing-seat for a place in the bottom of the boat, he suffered a bodily depression that caused him to be careless of everything save an obligation to wiggle one finger. There was cold sea-water swashing to and fro in the boat, and he lay in it. His head, pillowed on a thwart, was within an inch of the swirl of a wave crest, and sometimes a particularly obstreperous sea came in-board and drenched him once more. But these matters did not annoy him. It is almost certain that if the boat had capsized he would have tumbled comfortably out upon the ocean as if he felt sure that it was a great soft mattress.

"Look! There's a man on the shore!"

"Where?"

"There! See 'im? See 'im?"

"Yes, sure! He's walking along."

"Now he's stopped. Look! He's facing us!"

"He's waving at us!"

"So he is! By thunder!"

"Ah, now we're all right! Now we're all right! There'll be a boat out here for us in half an hour."

"He's going on. He's running. He's going up to that house there."

The remote beach seemed lower than the sea, and it required a searching glance to discern the little black figure. The captain saw a floating stick and they rowed to it. A bath-towel was by some weird chance in the boat, and tying this on the stick, the captain waved it. The oarsman did not dare turn his head, so he was obliged to ask questions.

"What's he doing now?"

"He's standing still again. He's looking. I think. . . . There he goes again. Toward the house. . . . Now he's stopped again."

"Is he waving at us?"

"No, not now! He was, though."

"Look! There comes another man!"

"He's running."

"Look at him go, would you."

"Why, he's on a bicycle. Now he's met the other man. They're both waving at us. Look!"

"There comes something up the beach."

"What the devil is that thing?"

"Why, it looks like a boat."

"Why, certainly it's a boat."

"No, it's on wheels."

"Yes, so it is. Well, that must be the life-boat. They drag them along shore on a wagon."

"That's the life-boat, sure."

"No, by—, it's—it's an omnibus."

"I tell you it's a life-boat."

"It is not! It's an omnibus. I can see it plain. See? One of these big hotel omnibuses."

"By thunder, you're right. It's an omnibus, sure as fate. What do you suppose they are doing with an omnibus? Maybe they are going around collecting the life-crew, hey?"

"That's it, likely. Look! There's a fellow waving a little black flag. He's standing on the steps of the omnibus. There come those other two fellows. Now they're all talking together. Look at the fellow with the flag. Maybe he ain't waving it."

"That ain't a flag, is it? That's his coat. Why, certainly, that's his coat."

"So it is. It's his coat. He's taken it off and is waving it around his head. But would you look at him swing it."

"Oh, say, there isn't any life-saving station there. That's just a winter resort hotel omnibus that has brought over some of the boarders to see us drown."

"What's that idiot with the coat mean? What's he signaling, anyhow?"

"It looks as if he were trying to tell us to go north. There must be a life-saving station up there."

"No! He thinks we're fishing. Just giving us a merry hand. See? Ah, there, Willie."

"Well, I wish I could make something out of those signals. What do you suppose he means?"

"He don't mean anything. He's just playing."

"Well, if he'd just signal us to try the surf again, or to go to sea and wait, or go north, or go south, or go to hell—there would be some reason in it. But look at him. He just stands there and keeps his coat revolving like a wheel. The ass!"

"There come more people."

"Now there's quite a mob. Look! Isn't that a boat?"

"Where? Oh, I see where you mean. No, that's no boat."

"That fellow is still waving his coat."

"He must think we like to see him do that. Why don't he quit it? It don't mean anything."

"I don't know. I think he is trying to make us go north. It must be that there's a life-saving station there somewhere."

"Say, he ain't tired yet. Look at 'im wave."

"Wonder how long he can keep that up. He's been revolving his coat ever since he caught sight of us. He's an idiot. Why aren't they getting men to bring a boat out? A fishing boat—one of those big yawls—could come out here all right. Why don't he do something?"

"Oh, it's all right, now."

"They'll have a boat out here for us in less than no time, now that they've seen us."

A faint yellow tone came into the sky over the low land. The shadows on the sea slowly deepened. The wind bore coldness with it, and the men began to shiver.

"Holy smoke!" said one, allowing his voice to express his impious mood, "if we keep on monkeying out here! If we've got to flounder out here all night!"

"Oh, we'll never have to stay here all night! Don't you worry. They've seen us now, and it won't be long before they'll come chasing out after us."

The shore grew dusky. The man waving a coat blended

gradually into this gloom, and it swallowed in the same manner the omnibus and the group of people. The spray, when it dashed uproariously over the side, made the voyagers shrink and swear like men who were being branded.

"I'd like to catch the chump who waved the coat. I feel like soaking him one, just for luck."

"Why? What did he do?"

"Oh, nothing, but then he seemed so damned cheerful."

In the meantime the oiler rowed, and then the correspondent rowed, and then the oiler rowed. Gray-faced and bowed forward, they mechanically, turn by turn, plied the leaden oars. The form of the lighthouse had vanished from the southern horizon, but finally a pale star appeared, just lifting from the sea. The streaked saffron in the west passed before the all-merging darkness, and the sea to the east was black. The land had vanished, and was expressed only by the low and drear thunder of the surf.

"If I am going to be drowned—if I am going to be drowned—if I am going to be drowned, why, in the name of the seven mad gods who rule the sea, was I allowed to come thus far and contemplate sand and trees? Was I brought here merely to have my nose dragged away as I was about to nibble the sacred cheese of life?"

The patient captain, drooped over the water-jar, was sometimes obliged to speak to the oarsman.

"Keep her head up! Keep her head up!"

" 'Keep her head up,' sir." The voices were weary and low.

This was surely a quiet evening. All save the oarsman lay heavily and listlessly in the boat's bottom. As for him, his eyes were just capable of noting the tall black waves that swept forward in a most sinister silence, save for an occasional subdued growl of a crest.

The cook's head was on a thwart, and he looked without interest at the water under his nose. He was deep in other scenes. Finally he spoke. "Billie," he murmured, dreamfully, "what kind of pie do you like best?"

V

"Pie," said the oiler and the correspondent, agitatedly. "Don't talk about those things, blast you!"

"Well," said the cook, "I was just thinking about ham sandwiches, and——"

A night on the sea in an open boat is a long night. As darkness settled finally, the shine of the light, lifting from the sea in the south, changed to full gold. On the northern horizon a new light appeared, a small bluish gleam on the edge of the waters. These two lights were the furniture of the world. Otherwise there was nothing but waves.

Two men huddled in the stern, and distances were so magnificent in the dingey that the rower was enabled to keep his feet partly warmed by thrusting them under his companions. Their legs indeed extended far under the rowing-seat until they touched the feet of the captain forward. Sometimes, despite the efforts of the tired oarsman, a wave came piling into the boat, an icy wave of the night, and the chilling water soaked them anew. They would twist their bodies for a moment and groan, and sleep the dead sleep once more, while the water in the boat gurgled about them as the craft rocked.

The plan of the oiler and the correspondent was for one to row until he lost the ability, and then arouse the other from his sea-water couch in the bottom of the boat.

The oiler plied the oars until his head drooped forward, and the overpowering sleep blinded him. And he rowed yet afterward. Then he touched a man in the bottom of the boat, and called his name. "Will you spell me for a little while?" he said, meekly.

"Sure, Billie," said the correspondent, awakening and dragging himself to a sitting position. They exchanged places carefully, and the oiler, cuddling down in the sea-water at the cook's side, seemed to go to sleep instantly.

The particular violence of the sea had ceased. The waves came without snarling. The obligation of the man at the oars was to keep the boat headed so that the tilt of the rollers would not capsize her, and to preserve her from filling when the crests rushed past. The black waves were silent and hard to be seen in the darkness. Often one was almost upon the boat before the oarsman was aware.

In a low voice the correspondent addressed the captain. He was not sure that the captain was awake, although this iron man seemed to be always awake. "Captain, shall I keep her making for that light north, sir?"

The same steady voice answered him. "Yes. Keep it about two points off the port bow."

The cook had tied a life-belt around himself in order to get even the warmth which this clumsy cork contrivance could donate, and he seemed almost stove-like when a rower, whose teeth invariably chattered wildly as soon as he ceased his labor, dropped down to sleep.

The correspondent, as he rowed, looked down at the two men sleeping underfoot. The cook's arm was around the oiler's shoulders, and, with their fragmentary clothing and haggard faces, they were the babes of the sea, a grotesque rendering of the old babes in the wood.

Later he must have grown stupid at his work, for suddenly there was a growling of water, and a crest came with a roar and a swash into the boat, and it was a wonder that it did not set the cook afloat in his life-belt. The cook continued to sleep, but the oiler sat up, blinking his eyes and shaking with the new cold.

"Oh, I'm awful sorry, Billie," said the correspondent, contritely.

"That's all right, old boy," said the oiler, and lay down again and was asleep.

Presently it seemed that even the captain dozed, and the correspondent thought that he was the one man afloat on all the oceans. The wind had a voice as it came over the waves, and it was sadder than the end.

There was a long, loud swishing astern of the boat, and a gleaming trail of phosphorescence, like blue flame, was furrowed on the black waters. It might have been made by a monstrous knife.

Then there came a stillness, while the correspondent breathed with the open mouth and looked at the sea.

Suddenly there was another swish and another long flash of bluish light, and this time it was alongside the boat, and might almost have been reached with an oar. The correspondent saw an enormous fin speed like a shadow through the water, hurling the crystalline spray and leaving the long glowing trail.

The correspondent looked over his shoulder at the captain. His face was hidden, and he seemed to be asleep. He looked at the babes of the sea. They certainly were asleep. So, being bereft of sympathy, he leaned a little way to one side and swore softly into the sea.

But the thing did not then leave the vicinity of the boat. Ahead or astern, on one side or the other, at intervals long or short, fled the long sparkling streak, and there was to be heard the whiroo of the dark fin. The speed and power of the thing was greatly to be admired. It cut the water like a gigantic and keen projectile.

The presence of this biding thing did not affect the man with the same horror that it would if he had been a picnicker. He simply looked at the sea dully and swore in an undertone.

Nevertheless, it is true that he did not wish to be alone. He wished one of his companions to awaken by chance and keep him company with it. But the captain hung motionless over the water-jar, and the oiler and the cook in the bottom of the boat were plunged in slumber.

VI

"If I am going to be drowned—if I am going to be drowned—if I am going to be drowned, why, in the name of the seven mad gods who rule the sea, was I allowed to come thus far and contemplate sand and trees?"

During this dismal night, it may be remarked that a man would conclude that it was really the intention of the seven mad gods to drown him, despite the abominable injustice of it. For it was certainly an abominable injustice to drown a man who had worked so hard, so hard. The man felt it would be a crime most unnatural. Other people had drowned at sea since galleys swarmed with painted sails, but still—

When it occurs to a man that nature does not regard him as important, and that she feels she would not maim the universe by disposing of him, he at first wishes to throw bricks at the temple, and he hates deeply the fact that there are no bricks and no temples. Any visible expression of nature would surely be pelleted with his jeers.

Then, if there be no tangible thing to hoot he feels, perhaps, the desire to confront a personification and indulge in pleas, bowed to one knee, and with hands supplicant, saying: "Yes, but I love myself."

A high cold star on a winter's night is the word he feels that she says to him. Thereafter he knows the pathos of his situation.

The men in the dingey had not discussed these matters, but each had, no doubt, reflected upon them in silence and according to his mind. There was seldom any expression upon their faces save the general one of complete weariness. Speech was devoted to the business of the boat.

To chime the notes of his emotion, a verse mysteriously entered the correspondent's head. He had even forgotten that he had forgotten this verse, but it suddenly was in his mind.

"A soldier of the Legion lay dying in Algiers,
There was lack of woman's nursing, there was dearth of woman's tears;
But a comrade stood beside him, and he took that comrade's hand,
And he said: 'I shall never see my own, my native land.' "

In his childhood, the correspondent had been made acquainted with the fact that a soldier of the Legion lay dying in Algiers, but he had never regarded the fact as important. Myriads of his school-fellows had informed him of the soldier's plight, but the dinning had naturally ended by making him perfectly indifferent. He had never considered it his affair that a soldier of the Legion lay dying in Algiers, nor had it appeared to him as a matter for sorrow. It was less to him than the breaking of a pencil's point.

Now, however, it quaintly came to him as a human, living thing. It was no longer merely a picture of a few throes in the breast of a poet, meanwhile drinking tea and warming his feet at the grate; it was an actuality—stern, mournful, and fine.

The correspondent plainly saw the soldier. He lay on the sand with his feet out straight and still. While his pale left hand was upon his chest in an attempt to thwart the going of his life, the blood came between his fingers. In the far Algerian distance, a city of low square forms was set against a sky that was faint with the last sunset hues. The correspondent, plying the oars and dreaming of the slow and slower movements of the lips of the soldier, was moved by a profound and perfectly impersonal comprehension. He was sorry for the soldier of the Legion who lay dying in Algiers.

The thing which had followed the boat and waited had evidently grown bored at the delay. There was no longer to be heard the slash of the cut water, and there was no longer the flame of the long trail. The light in the north still glimmered, but it was apparently no nearer to the boat. Sometimes the boom of the surf rang in the correspondent's ears, and he turned the craft seaward then and rowed harder. Southward, someone had evidently built a watch-fire on the beach. It was too low and too far to be seen, but it made a shimmering, roseate reflection upon the bluff back of it, and this could be discerned from the boat. The wind came stronger and sometimes a wave suddenly raged out like a mountain-cat, and there was to be seen the sheen and sparkle of a broken crest.

The captain, in the bow, moved on his water-jar and sat erect. "Pretty long night," he observed to the correspondent. He looked at the shore. "Those life-saving people take their time."

"Did you see that shark playing around?"

"Yes, I saw him. He was a big fellow, all right."

"Wish I had known you were awake."

Later the correspondent spoke into the bottom of the boat.

"Billie!" There was a slow and gradual disentanglement. "Billie, will you spell me?"

"Sure," said the oiler.

As soon as the correspondent touched the cold comfortable sea-water in the bottom of the boat, and had huddled close to the cook's life-belt he was deep in sleep, despite the fact that his teeth played all the popular airs. This sleep was so good to him that it was but a moment before he heard a voice call his name in a tone that demonstrated the last stages of exhaustion. "Will you spell me?"

"Sure, Billie."

The light in the north had mysteriously vanished, but the correspondent took his course from the wide-awake captain.

Later in the night they took the boat farther out to sea, and the captain directed the cook to take one oar at the stern and keep the boat facing the seas. He was to call out if he should hear the thunder of the surf. This plan enabled the oiler and the correspondent to get respite together. "We'll give those boys a chance to get into shape again," said the captain. They curled down and, after a few preliminary chatterings and trembles, slept once more the dead sleep. Neither knew they had bequeathed to the cook the company of another shark, or perhaps the same shark.

As the boat caroused on the waves, spray occasionally bumped over the side and gave them a fresh soaking, but this had no power to break their repose. The ominous slash of the wind and the water affected them as it would have affected mummies.

"Boys," said the cook, with the notes of every reluctance in his voice, "she's drifted in pretty close. I guess one of you had better take her to sea again." The correspondent, aroused, heard the crash of the toppled crests.

As he was rowing, the captain gave him some whisky-and-water, and this steadied the chills out of him. "If I ever get ashore and anybody shows me even a photograph of an oar—"

At last there was a short conversation.

"Billie . . . Billie, will you spell me?"

"Sure," said the oiler.

VII

When the correspondent again opened his eyes, the sea and the sky were each of the gray hue of the dawning. Later, carmine and gold was painted upon the waters. The morning appeared finally, in its splendor, with a sky of pure blue, and the sunlight flamed on the tips of the waves.

On the distant dunes were set many little black cottages, and a tall white windmill reared above them. No man, nor dog, nor bicycle appeared on the beach. The cottages might have formed a deserted village.

The voyagers scanned the shore. A conference was held in the boat. "Well," said the captain, "if no help is coming, we might better try a run through the surf right away. If we stay out here much longer we will be too weak to do anything for ourselves at all." The others silently acquiesced in this reasoning. The boat was headed for the beach. The correspondent wondered if none ever ascended the tall wind-tower, and if then they never looked seaward. This tower was a giant, standing with its back to the plight of the ants. It represented in a degree, to the correspondent, the serenity of nature amid the struggles of the individual—nature in the wind, and nature in the vision of men. She did not seem cruel to him then, nor beneficent, nor treacherous, nor wise. But she was indifferent, flatly indifferent. It is, perhaps, plausible that a man in this situation, impressed with the unconcern of the universe, should see the innumerable flaws of his life, and have them taste wickedly in his mind and wish for another chance. A distinction between right and wrong seems absurdly clear to him, then, in this new ignorance of the grave-edge, and he understands that if he were given another opportunity he would mend his conduct and his words, and be better and brighter during an introduction or at a tea.

"Now, boys," said the captain, "she is going to swamp sure. All we can do is to work her in as far as possible, and then when she swamps, pile out and scramble for the beach. Keep cool now, and don't jump until she swamps sure."

The oiler took the oars. Over his shoulders he scanned the surf. "Captain," he said, "I think I'd better bring her about, and keep her head-on to the seas and back her in."

"All right, Billie," said the captain. "Back her in." The oiler swung the boat then and, seated in the stern, the cook and the correspondent were obliged to look over their shoulders to contemplate the lonely and indifferent shore.

The monstrous in-shore rollers heaved the boat high until the men were again enabled to see the white sheets of water scudding up the slanted beach. "We won't get in very close," said the captain. Each time a man could wrest his attention from the rollers, he turned his glance toward the shore, and in the expression of the eyes during this contemplation there was a singular quality. The correspondent, observing the others, knew that they were not afraid, but the full meaning of their glances was shrouded.

As for himself, he was too tired to grapple fundamentally with the fact. He tried to coerce his mind into thinking of it, but the mind was dominated at this time by the muscles, and the muscles said they did not care. It merely occurred to him that if he should drown it would be a shame.

There were no hurried words, no pallor, no plain agitation. The men simply looked at the shore. "Now, remember to get well clear of the boat when you jump," said the captain.

Seaward the crest of a roller suddenly fell with a thunderous crash, and the long white comber came roaring down upon the boat.

"Steady now," said the captain. The men were silent. They turned their eyes from the shore to the comber and waited. The boat slid up the incline, leaped at the furious top, bounced over it, and swung down the long back of the waves. Some water had been shipped and the cook bailed it out.

But the next crest crashed also. The tumbling, boiling flood of white water caught the boat and whirled it almost perpendicular. Water swarmed in from all sides. The correspondent had his hands on the gunwale at this time, and when the water entered at that place he swiftly withdrew his fingers, as if he objected to wetting them.

The little boat, drunken with this weight of water, reeled and snuggled deeper into the sea.

"Bail her out, cook! Bail her out," said the captain.

"All right, captain," said the cook.

"Now, boys, the next one will do for us, sure," said the oiler. "Mind to jump clear of the boat."

The third wave moved forward, huge, furious, implacable. It fairly swallowed the dingey, and almost simultaneously the men tumbled into the sea. A piece of life-belt had lain in the bottom of the boat, and as the correspondent went overboard he held this to his chest with his left hand.

The January water was icy, and he reflected immediately that it was colder than he had expected to find it off the coast of Florida. This appeared to his dazed mind as a fact important enough to be noted at the time. The coldness of the water was sad; it was tragic. This fact was somehow so mixed and confused with his opinion of his own situation that it seemed almost a proper reason for tears. The water was cold.

When he came to the surface he was conscious of little but the noisy water. Afterward he saw his companions in the sea. The oiler was ahead in the race. He was swimming strongly and rapidly. Off to the correspondent's left, the cook's great white and corked back bulged out of the water, and in the rear the captain was hanging with his one good hand to the keel of the overturned dingey.

There is a certain immovable quality to a shore, and the correspondent wondered at it amid the confusion of the sea.

It seemed also very attractive, but the correspondent knew that it was a long journey, and he paddled leisurely. The piece of life-preserver lay under him, and sometimes he whirled down the incline of a wave as if he were on a hand-sled.

But finally he arrived at a place in the sea where travel was beset with difficulty. He did not pause swimming to inquire what manner of current had caught him, but there his progress ceased. The shore was set before him like a bit of scenery on a stage, and he looked at it and understood with his eyes each detail of it.

As the cook passed, much farther to the left, the captain was calling to him, "Turn over on your back, cook! Turn over on your back and use the oar."

"All right, sir." The cook turned on his back, and, paddling with an oar, went ahead as if he were a canoe.

Presently the boat also passed to the left of the correspondent with the captain clinging with one hand to the keel. He would have appeared like a man raising himself to look over a board fence, if it were not for the extraordinary gymnastics of the boat. The correspondent marvelled that the captain could still hold to it.

They passed on, nearer to shore—the oiler, the cook, the captain—and following them went the water-jar, bouncing gaily over the seas.

The correspondent remained in the grip of this strange new enemy—a current. The shore, with its white slope of sand and its green bluff, topped with little silent cottages, was spread like a picture before him. It was very near to him then, but he was impressed as one who in a gallery looks at a scene from Brittany or Algiers.

He thought: "I am going to drown? Can it be possible? Can it be possible? Can it be possible?" Perhaps an individual must consider his own death to be the final phenomenon of nature.

But later a wave perhaps whirled him out of this small deadly current, for he found suddenly that he could again make progress toward the shore. Later still, he was aware that the captain, clinging with one hand to the keel of the dingey, had his face turned away from the shore and toward him, and was calling his name. "Come to the boat! Come to the boat!"

In his struggle to reach the captain and the boat, he reflected that when one gets properly wearied, drowning must really be a comfortable arrangement, a cessation of hostilities accompanied by a large degree of relief, and he was glad of it, for the main thing in his mind for some moments had been horror of the temporary agony. He did not wish to be hurt.

Presently he saw a man running along the shore. He was undressing with most remarkable speed. Coat, trousers, shirt, everything flew magically off him.

"Come to the boat," called the captain.

"All right, captain." As the correspondent paddled, he saw the captain let himself down to bottom and leave the boat. Then the correspondent performed his one little marvel of the voyage. A large wave caught him and flung him with ease and supreme speed completely over the boat and far beyond it. It struck him even then as an event in gymnastics, and a true miracle of the sea. An overturned boat in the surf is not a plaything to a swimming man.

The correspondent arrived in water that reached only to his waist, but his condition did not enable him to stand for more than a moment. Each wave knocked him into a heap, and the under-tow pulled at him.

Then he saw the man who had been running and undressing, and undressing and running, come bounding into the water. He dragged ashore the cook, and then waded toward the captain, but the captain waved him away, and sent him to the correspondent. He was naked, naked as a tree in winter, but a halo was about his head, and he shone like a saint. He gave a strong pull, and a long drag, and a bully heave at the correspondent's hand. The correspondent, schooled in the minor formulae, said: "Thanks, old man." But suddenly the man cried: "What's that?" He pointed a swift finger. The correspondent said: "Go."

In the shallows, face downward, lay the oiler. His forehead touched sand that was periodically, between each wave, clear of the sea.

The correspondent did not know all that transpired afterward. When he achieved safe ground he fell, striking the sand with each particular part of his body. It was as if he had dropped from a roof, but the thud was grateful to him.

It seemed that instantly the beach was populated with men, with blankets, clothes, and flasks, and women with coffee-pots and all the remedies sacred to their minds. The welcome of the land to the men from the sea was warm and generous, but a still and dripping shape was carried slowly up the beach, and the land's welcome for it could only be the different and sinister hospitality of the grave.

When it came night, the white waves paced to and fro in the moonlight, and the wind brought the sound of the great sea's voice to the men on shore, and they felt that they could then be interpreters.

Act of Faith

IRWIN SHAW

"Act of Faith" is a twentieth-century story. It couldn't have been written at any other time, for it grows out of the harrowing experience of being Jewish in a world bent on destroying the Jew. Only in our century has man's massive inhumanity to man become possible. It is this that forms the appalling backdrop for Seeger's act of faith, a testament to hope.

In "Act of Faith" Mr. Shaw is a "spokesman for his generation," saying essentially what he has said elsewhere in his work and saying it just as trenchantly and as memorably: war is a ghastly waste, a deep perversion of all our values; simple human decency and the desire for justice will survive the horrors and miseries of war. Shaw's "rightness of feeling," his warmth and humanity, his apt, earthy humor, his flair for the topical, the acuity of his observations and perceptions—they are all here communicated in a style that is bright, sharp, felicitous.

IRWIN SHAW (1913–   ). Born and educated in Brooklyn, Mr. Shaw has led a varied and active life as playwright, novelist, and short story writer. His first short stories were published while he was still in college, but he

first achieved critical recognition with the Broadway per-
formance of his passionate antiwar play, Bury the Dead
(1936). During World War II Shaw served with the
United States Army in Europe, and out of his wartime
experiences, he wrote his provocative, widely acclaimed
The Young Lions. *The setting of "Act of Faith" is a U.S.*
army base in Europe.

   Shaw has written four novels, but none of them has the
power, drive, and sense of reality of his short stories.
Here his brilliant craftsmanship and the broad range of his
sympathies find their most eloquent expression. The best
of Shaw's stories are in the following collections: Sailor
off the Bremen *(1937),* Welcome to the City *(1942), and*
Tip on a Dead Jockey *(1957).*

Act of Faith

"Present it in a pitiful light," Olson was saying, as they
picked their way through the mud toward the orderly
room tent. "Three combat-scarred veterans, who fought
their way from Omaha Beach to—what was the name of
the town we fought our way to?"

   "Konigstein," Seeger said.

   "Konigstein." Olson lifted his right foot heavily out of
a puddle and stared admiringly at the three pounds of
mud clinging to his overshoe. "The backbone of the army.
The noncommissioned officer. We deserve better of our
country. Mention our decorations in passing."

   "What decorations should I mention?" Seeger asked.
"The marksman's medal?"

   "Never quite made it," Olson said. "I had a cross-eyed
scorer at the butts. Mention the Bronze Star, the Silver
Star, the Croix de Guerre, with palms, the unit citation,
the Congressional Medal of Honor."

   "I'll mention them all." Seeger grinned. "You don't
think the CO'll notice that we haven't won most of them,
do you?"

   "Gad, sir," Olson said with dignity, "do you think that

one southern military gentleman will dare doubt the word of another southern military gentleman in the hour of victory?"

"I come from Ohio," Seeger said.

"Welch comes from Kansas," Olson said, coolly staring down a second lieutenant who was passing. The lieutenant made a nervous little jerk with his hand as though he expected a salute, then kept it rigid, as a slight superior smile of scorn twisted at the corner of Olson's mouth. The lieutenant dropped his eyes and splashed on through the mud. "You've heard of Kansas," Olson said. "Magnolia-scented Kansas."

"Of course," said Seeger. "I'm no fool."

"Do your duty by your men, Sergeant." Olson stopped to wipe the rain off his face and lectured him. "Highest ranking noncom present took the initiative and saved his comrades, at great personal risk, above and beyond the call of you-know-what, in the best traditions of the American army."

"I will throw myself in the breach," Seeger said.

"Welch and I can't ask more," said Olson, approvingly.

They walked heavily through the mud on the streets between the rows of tents. The camp stretched drearily over the Rheims plain, with the rain beating on the sagging tents. The division had been there over three weeks by now, waiting to be shipped home, and all the meager diversions of the neighborhood had been sampled and exhausted, and there was an air of watchful suspicion and impatience with the military life hanging over the camp now, and there was even reputed to be a staff sergeant in C Company who was laying odds they would not get back to America before July Fourth.

"I'm redeployable," Olson sang. "It's so enjoyable . . ." It was a jingle he had composed to no recognizable melody in the early days after the victory in Europe, when he had added up his points and found they only came to 63. "Tokyo, wait for me. . ."

They were going to be discharged as soon as they got back to the States, but Olson persisted in singing the song, occasionally adding a mournful stanza about dengue fever and brown girls with venereal disease. He was a short, round boy who had been flunked out of air cadets' school and transferred to the infantry, but whose spirits had not been damaged in the process. He had a high, childish voice and a pretty baby face. He was very good-natured, and had a girl waiting for him at the University of California, where he intended to finish his course at government expense when he got out of the army, and he was just the type who is killed off early and predictably and sadly in motion pictures about the war, but he had gone through four campaigns and six major battles without a scratch.

Seeger was a large lanky boy, with a big nose, who had been wounded at Saint Lô, but had come back to his outfit, in the Siegried Line, quite unchanged. He was cheerful and dependable, and he knew his business and had broken in five or six second lieutenants who had been killed or wounded and the CO had tried to get him commissioned in the field, but the war had ended while the paperwork was being fumbled over at headquarters.

They reached the door of the orderly tent and stopped. "Be brave, Sergeant," Olson said. "Welch and I are depending on you."

"O.K.," Seeger said, and went in.

The tent had the dank, army-canvas smell that had been so much a part of Seeger's life in the past three years. The company clerk was reading a July, 1945, issue of the *Buffalo Courier-Express,* which had just reached him, and Captain Taney, the company CO, was seated at a sawbuck table he used as a desk, writing a letter to his wife, his lips pursed with effort. He was a small, fussy man, with sandy hair that was falling out. While the fighting had been going on, he had been lean and tense and his small voice had been cold and full of authority. But now he had relaxed, and a little pot belly was creeping up under his belt and he kept the top button of his trousers open when he could do it without too public loss of dignity. During the war Seeger had thought of him as a natural soldier, tireless, fanatic about detail, aggressive, severely anxious to kill Germans. But in the past few months Seeger had seen him relapsing gradually and pleasantly into a small-town wholesale hardware merchant, which he had been before the war, sedentary and a little shy, and, as he had once told Seeger, worried, here in the bleak champagne fields of France, about his daughter, who had just turned

twelve and had a tendency to go after the boys and had
been caught by her mother kissing a fifteen-year-old
neighbor in the hammock after school.

"Hello, Seeger," he said, returning the salute in a mild,
offhand gesture. "What's on your mind?"

"Am I disturbing you, sir?"

"Oh, no. Just writing a letter to my wife. You married,
Seeger?" He peered at the tall boy standing before him.

"No, sir."

"It's very difficult," Taney sighed, pushing dissatisfiedly
at the letter before him. "My wife complains I don't tell
her I love her often enough. Been married fifteen years.
You'd think she'd know by now." He smiled at Seeger. "I
thought you were going to Paris," he said. "I signed the
passes yesterday."

"That's what I came to see you about, sir."

"I suppose something's wrong with the passes." Taney
spoke resignedly, like a man who has never quite got the
hang of army regulations and has had requisitions, fur-
loughs, requests for court-martial returned for correction
in a baffling flood.

"No, sir," Seeger said. "The passes're fine. They start tomorrow. Well, it's just . . ." He looked around at the company clerk, who was on the sports page.

"This confidential?" Taney asked.

"If you don't mind, sir."

"Johnny," Taney said to the clerk, "go stand in the
rain some place."

"Yes, sir," the clerk said, and slowly got up and walked
out.

Taney looked shrewdly at Seeger, spoke in a secret
whisper. "You pick up anything?" he asked.

Seeger grinned. "No, sir, haven't had my hands on a
girl since Strasbourg."

"Ah, that's good." Taney leaned back, relieved, happy
he didn't have to cope with the disapproval of the Medical
Corps.

"It's—well," said Seeger, embarrassed, "it's hard to say
—but it's money."

Taney shook his head sadly. "I know."

"We haven't been paid for three months, sir, and . . ."

"Damn it!" Taney stood up and shouted furiously. "I

would like to take every bloody chair-warming old lady in the Finance Department and wring their necks."

The clerk stuck his head into the tent. "Anything wrong? You call for me, sir?"

"No," Taney shouted. "Get out of here."

The clerk ducked out.

Taney sat down again. "I suppose," he said, in a more normal voice, "they have their problems. Outfits being broken up, being moved all over the place. But it is rugged."

"It wouldn't be so bad," Seeger said. "But we're going to Paris tomorrow, Olson, Welch and myself. And you need money in Paris."

"Don't I know it." Taney wagged his head. "Do you know what I paid for a bottle of champagne on the Place Pigalle in September . . . ?" He paused significantly. "I won't tell you. You won't have any respect for me the rest of your life."

Seeger laughed. "Hanging," he said, "is too good for the guy who thought up the rate of exchange."

"I don't care if I never see another franc as long as I live." Taney waved his letter in the air, although it had been dry for a long time.

There was silence in the tent and Seeger swallowed a little embarrassedly, watching the CO wave the flimsy sheet of paper in regular sweeping movements. "Sir," he said, "the truth is, I've come to borrow some money for Welch, Olson and myself. We'll pay it back out of the first pay we get, and that can't be too long from now. If you don't want to give it to us, just tell me and I'll understand and get the hell out of here. We don't like to ask, but you might just as well be dead as be in Paris broke."

Taney stopped waving his letter and put it down thoughtfully. He peered at it, wrinkling his brow, looking like an aged bookkeeper in the single gloomy light that hung in the middle of the tent.

"Just say the word, Captain," Seeger said, "and I'll blow . . ."

"Stay where you are, son," said Taney. He dug in his shirt pocket and took out a worn, sweat-stained wallet. He looked at it for a moment. "Alligator," he said, with automatic, absent pride. "My wife sent it to me when we

were in England. Pounds don't fit in it. However . . ."
He opened it and took out all the contents. There was a
small pile of francs on the table in front of him.
He counted them. "Four hundred francs," he said. "Eight
bucks."

"Excuse me," Seeger said humbly. "I shouldn't have
asked."

"Delighted," Taney said vigorously. "Absolutely delighted." He started dividing the francs into two piles.
"Truth is, Seeger, most of my money goes home in allot-
ments. And the truth is, I lost eleven hundred francs in a
poker game three nights ago, and I ought to be ashamed
of myself. Here . . ." He shoved one pile toward Seeger.
"Two hundred francs."

Seeger looked down at the frayed, meretricious paper,
which always seemed to him like stage money, anyway.
"No, sir," he said, "I can't take it."

"Take it," Taney said. "That's a direct order."

Seeger slowly picked up the money, not looking at
Taney. "Some time, sir," he said, "after we get out, you
have to come over to my house and you and my father
and my brother and I'll go on a real drunk."

"I regard that," Taney said, gravely, "as a solemn com-
mitment."

They smiled at each other and Seeger started out.

"Have a drink for me," said Taney, "at the Café de la
Paix. A small drink." He was sitting down to write his
wife he loved her when Seeger went out of the tent.

Olson fell into step with Seeger and they walked silently
through the mud between the tents.

"Well, *mon vieux?*" Olson said finally.

"Two hundred francs," said Seeger.

Olson groaned. "Two hundred francs! That miserable,
penny-loving Yankee!"

"He only had four hundred," Seeger said.

"I revise my opinion," said Olson.

They walked disconsolately and heavily back toward
their tent.

Olson spoke only once before they got there. "These
raincoats," he said, patting his. "Most ingenious invention
of the war. Highest saturation point of any modern fabric.

Collect more water per square inch, and hold it, than any material known to man. All hail the quartermaster!"

Welch was waiting at the entrance of their tent. He was standing there peering excitedly and short-sightedly out at the rain through his glasses, looking angry and tough, like a big-city hack driver, individual and incorruptible even in the ten-million colored uniform. Every time Seeger came upon Welch unexpectedly, he couldn't help smiling at the belligerent stance, the harsh stare through the steel-rimmed GI glasses, which had nothing at all to do with the way Welch really was. "It's a family inheritance," Welch had once explained. "My whole family stands as though we were getting ready to rap a drunk with a beer glass. Even my old lady." Welch had six brothers, all devout, according to Welch, and Seeger from time to time idly pictured them standing in a row, on Sunday mornings in church, seemingly on the verge of general violence, amid the hushed Latin and Sabbath millinery.

"How much?" Welch asked loudly.

"Don't make us laugh," Olson said, pushing past him into the tent.

"What do you think I could get from the French for my combat jacket?" Seeger said. He went into the tent and lay down on his cot.

Welch followed them in and stood between the two of them, a superior smile on his face. "Boys," he said, "on a man's errand."

"I can just see us now," Olson murmured, lying on his cot with his hands clasped behind his head, "painting Montmartre red. Please bring on the naked dancing girls. Four bucks worth."

"I am not worried," Welch announced.

"Get out of here." Olson turned over on his stomach.

"I know where we can put our hands on sixty-five bucks." Welch looked triumphantly first at Olson, then at Seeger.

Olson turned over slowly and sat up. "I'll kill you," he said, "if you're kidding."

"While you guys are wasting your time," Welch said, "fooling around with the infantry, I used my head. I went into Reems and used my head."

"Rance," Olson said automatically. He had had two

years of French in college and he felt, now that the war was over, that he had to introduce his friends to some of his culture.

"I got to talking to a captain in the air force," Welch said eagerly. "A little fat old paddle-footed captain that never got higher off the ground than the second floor of the Com Z headquarters, and he told me that what he would admire to do more than anything else is to take home a nice shiny German Luger pistol with him to show to the boys back in Pacific Grove, California."

Silence fell on the tent and Welch and Olson looked tentatively at Seeger.

"Sixty-five bucks for a Luger, these days," Olson said, "is a very good figure."

"They've been sellin' for as low as thirty-five," said Welch hesitantly. "I'll bet," he said to Seeger, "you could sell yours now and buy another one back when you get some dough, and make a clear twenty-five on the deal."

Seeger didn't say anything. He had killed the owner of the Luger, an enormous SS major, in Coblenz, behind some paper bales in a warehouse, and the major had fired at Seeger three times with it, once knicking his helmet, before Seeger hit him in the face at twenty feet. Seeger had kept the Luger, a long, heavy, well-balanced gun, very carefully since then, lugging it with him, hiding it at the bottom of his bedroll, oiling it three times a week, avoiding all opportunities of selling it, although he had been offered as much as a hundred dollars for it and several times eighty and ninety, while the war was still on, before German weapons became a glut on the market.

"Well," said Welch, "there's no hurry. I told the captain I'd see him tonight around 8 o'clock in front of the Lion d'Or Hotel. You got five hours to make up your mind. Plenty of time."

"Me," said Olson, after a pause. "I won't say anything."

Seeger looked reflectively at his feet and the other two men avoided looking at him. Welch dug in his pocket. "I forgot," he said. "I picked up a letter for you." He handed it to Seeger.

"Thanks," Seeger said. He opened it absently, thinking about the Luger.

"Me," said Olson, "I won't say a bloody word. I'm just

going to lie here and think about that nice fat air force captain."

Seeger grinned a little at him and went to the tent opening to read the letter in the light. The letter was from his father, and even from one glance at the handwriting, scrawly and hurried and spotted, so different from his father's usual steady, handsome, professorial script, he knew that something was wrong.

"Dear Norman," it read, "sometime in the future, you must forgive me for writing this letter. But I have been holding this in so long, and there is no one here I can talk to, and because of your brother's condition I must pretend to be cheerful and optimistic all the time at home, both with him and your mother, who has never been the same since Leonard was killed. You're the oldest now, and although I know we've never talked very seriously about anything before, you have been through a great deal by now, and I imagine you must have matured considerably, and you've seen so many different places and people. . . . Norman, I need help. While the war was on and you were fighting, I kept this to myself. It wouldn't have been fair to burden you with this. But now the war is over, and I no longer feel I can stand up under this alone. And you will have to face it some time when you get home, if you haven't faced it already, and perhaps we can help each other by facing it together. . . ."

"I'm redeployable," Olson was singing softly, on his cot. "It's so enjoyable, In the Pelilu mud, With the tropical crud . . ." He fell silent after his burst of song.

Seeger blinked his eyes, at the entrance of the tent, in the wan rainy light, and went on reading his father's letter, on the stiff white stationery with the University letterhead in polite engraving at the top of each page.

"I've been feeling this coming on for a long time," the letter continued, "but it wasn't until last Sunday morning that something happened to make me feel it in its full force. I don't know how much you've guessed about the reason for Jacob's discharge from the army. It's true he was pretty badly wounded in the leg at Metz, but I've asked around, and I know that men with worse wounds were returned to duty after hospitalization. Jacob got a medical discharge, but I don't think it was for the shrapnel wound in his thigh. He is suffering now from what I suppose you call combat fatigue, and he is subject to fits of depression and hallucinations. Your mother and I thought that as time went by and the war and the army receded, he would grow better. Instead, he is growing worse. Last Sunday morning when I came down into the living room from upstairs he was crouched in his old uniform, next to the window, peering out . . ."

"What the hell," Olson was saying, "if we don't get the sixty-five bucks we can always go to the Louvre. I understand the Mona Lisa is back."

"I asked Jacob what he was doing," the letter went on. "He didn't turn around. 'I'm observing,' he said. 'V-1's and V-2's. Buzz-bombs and rockets. They're coming in by the hundreds.' I tried to reason with him and he told me to crouch and save myself from flying glass. To humor him I got down on the floor beside him and tried to tell him the war was over, that we were in Ohio, 4,000 miles away from the nearest spot where bombs had fallen, that America had never been touched. He wouldn't listen. 'These're the new rocket bombs,' he said, 'for the Jews.' "

"Did you ever hear of the Pantheon?" Olson asked loudly.

"No," said Welch.

"It's free."

"I'll go," said Welch.

Seeger shook his head a little and blinked his eyes before he went back to the letter.

"After that," his father went on, "Jacob seemed to forget about the bombs from time to time, but he kept saying that the mobs were coming up the street armed with bazookas and Browning automatic rifles. He mumbled incoherently a good deal of the time and kept walking back and forth saying, 'What's the situation? Do you know what the situation is?' And he told me he wasn't worried about himself, he was a soldier and he expected to be killed, but he was worried about Mother and myself and Leonard and you. He seemed to forget that Leonard was dead. I tried to calm him and get him back to bed before your mother came down, but he refused and wanted to set out immediately to rejoin his division. It was all terribly disjointed and at one time he took the

ribbon he got for winning the Bronze Star and threw it in
the fireplace, then he got down on his hands and knees
and picked it out of the ashes and made me pin it on him
again, and he kept repeating, 'This is when they are coming for the Jews.' "

"The next war I'm in," said Olson, "they don't get me
under the rank of colonel."

It had stopped raining by now and Seeger folded the un-
finished letter and went outside. He walked slowly down
to the end of the company street, and facing out across
the empty, soaked French fields, scarred and neglected
by various armies, he stopped and opened the letter
again.

"I don't know what Jacob went through in the army,"
his father wrote, "that has done this to him. He never
talks to me about the war and he refuses to go to a
psychoanalyst, and from time to time he is his own bouncing, cheerful self, playing in tennis tournaments, and going around with a large group of girls. But he has devoured all the concentration camp reports, and I have
found him weeping when the newspapers reported that a
hundred Jews were killed in Tripoli some time ago.

"The terrible thing is, Norman, that I find myself coming to believe that it is not neurotic for a Jew to behave
like this today. Perhaps Jacob is the normal one, and I,
going about my business, teaching economics in a quiet
classroom, pretending to understand that the world is
comprehensible and orderly, am really the mad one. I
ask you once more to forgive me for writing you a letter
like this, so different from any letter or any conversation
I've ever had with you. But it is crowding me, too. I do
not see rockets and bombs, but I see other things.

"Wherever you go these days—restaurants, hotels,
clubs, trains—you seem to hear talk about the Jews,
mean, hateful, murderous talk. Whatever page you turn
to in the newspapers you seem to find an article about
Jews being killed somewhere on the face of the globe.
And there are large, influential newspapers and well-
known columnists who each day are growing more and
more outspoken and more popular. The day that Roosevelt
died I heard a drunken man yelling outside a bar,
'Finally, they got the Jew out of the White House.' And

some of the people who heard him merely laughed and nobody stopped him. And on V-E Day, in celebration, hoodlums in Los Angeles savagely beat a Jewish writer. It's difficult to know what to do, whom to fight, where to look for allies.

"Three months ago, for example, I stopped my Thursday night poker game, after playing with the same men for over ten years. John Reilly happened to say that the Jews were getting rich out of this war, and when I demanded an apology, he refused, and when I looked around at the faces of the men who had been my friends for so long, I could see they were not with me. And when I left the house no one said good night to me. I know the poison was spreading from Germany before the war and during it, but I had not realized it had come so close.

"And in my economics class, I find myself idiotically hedging in my lectures. I discover that I am loath to praise any liberal writer or any liberal act and find myself somehow annoyed and frightened to see an article of criticism of existing abuses signed by a Jewish name. And I hate to see Jewish names on important committees, and hate to read of Jews fighting for the poor, the oppressed, the cheated and hungry. Somehow, even in a country where my family has lived a hundred years, the enemy has won this subtle victory over me—he has made me disfranchise myself from honest causes by calling them foreign, Communist, using Jewish names connected with them as ammunition against them.

"And, most hateful of all, I find myself looking for Jewish names in the casualty lists and secretly being glad when I discover them there, to prove that there at least, among the dead and wounded, we belong. Three times, thanks to you and your brothers, I have found our name there, and, may God forgive me, at the expense of your blood and your brother's life, through my tears, I have felt that same twitch of satisfaction. . . .

"When I read the newspapers and see another story that Jews are still being killed in Poland, or Jews are requesting that they be given back their homes in France, or that they be allowed to enter some country where they will not be murdered, I am annoyed with them, I feel they are boring the rest of the world with their problems, they

are making demands upon the rest of the world by being
killed, they are disturbing everyone by being hungry and
asking for the return of their property. If we could all
fall through the crust of the earth and vanish in one hour,
with our heroes and poets and prophets and martyrs, perhaps we would be doing the memory of the Jewish race
a service. . . .

"This is how I feel today, son. I need some help. You've
been to the war, you've fought and killed men, you've
seen the people of other countries. Maybe you understand
things that I don't understand. Maybe you see some hope
somewhere. Help me. Your loving father."

Seeger folded the letter slowly, not seeing what he was
doing because the tears were burning his eyes. He walked
slowly and aimlessly across the dead autumn grass of the
empty field, away from the camp.

He tried to wipe away his tears, because with his eyes
full and dark, he kept seeing his father and brother
crouched in the old-fashioned living room in Ohio and
hearing his brother, dressed in the old, discarded uniform,
saying, "These're the new rocket bombs. For the Jews."

He sighed, looking out over the bleak, wasted land.
Now, he thought, now I have to think about it. He felt a
slight, unreasonable twinge of anger at his father for presenting him with the necessity of thinking about it. The
army was good about serious problems. While you were
fighting, you were too busy and frightened and weary to
think about anything, and at other times you were relaxing, putting your brain on a shelf, postponing everything
to that impossible time of clarity and beauty after the war.
Well, now, here was the impossible, clear, beautiful time,
and here was his father, demanding that he think. There
are all sorts of Jews, he thought, there are the sort whose
every waking moment is ridden by the knowledge of Jew-
ishness, who see signs against the Jew in every smile on a
streetcar, every whisper, who see pogroms in every newspaper article, threats in every change of the weather, scorn
in every handshake, death behind each closed door. He
had not been like that. He was young, he was big and
healthy and easy-going and people of all kinds had
seemed to like him all his life, in the army and out. In
America, especially, what was going on in Europe had

seemed remote, unreal, unrelated to him. The chanting, bearded old men burning in the Nazi furnaces, and the dark-eyed women screaming prayers in Polish and Russian and German as they were pushed naked into the gas chambers had seemed as shadowy and almost as unrelated to him as he trotted out onto the Stadium field for a football game, as they must have been to the men named O'Dwyer and Wickersham and Poole who played in the line beside him.

They had seemed more related in Europe. Again and again in the towns that had been taken back from the Germans, gaunt, gray-faced men had stopped him humbly, looking searchingly at him, and had asked, peering at his long, lined, grimy face, under the anonymous helmet, "Are you a Jew?" Sometimes they asked it in English, sometimes French, or Yiddish. He didn't know French or Yiddish, but he learned to recognize the phrase. He had never understood exactly why they had asked the question, since they never demanded anything from him, rarely even could speak to him, until, one day in Strasbourg, a little bent old man and a small, shapeless woman had stopped him, and asked, in English, if he was Jewish.

"Yes," he said, smiling at them.

The two old people had smiled widely, like children. "Look," the old man had said to his wife. "A young American soldier. A Jew. And so large and strong." He had touched Seeger's arm reverently with the tips of his fingers, then had touched the Garand he was carrying. "And such a beautiful rifle . . ."

And there, for a moment, although he was not particularly sensitive, Seeger got an inkling of why he had been stopped and questioned by so many before. Here, to these bent, exhausted old people, ravaged of their families, familiar with flight and death for so many years, was a symbol of continuing life. A large young man in the uniform of the liberator, blood, as they thought, of their blood, but not in hiding, not quivering in fear and helplessness, but striding secure and victorious down the street, armed and capable of inflicting terrible destruction on his enemies.

Seeger had kissed the old lady on the cheek and she had wept and the old man had scolded her for it, while shaking

Seeger's hand fervently and thankfully before saying goodby.

And, thinking back on it, it was silly to pretend that, even before his father's letter, he had been like any other American soldier going through the war. When he had stood over the huge dead SS major with the face blown in by his bullets in the warehouse in Coblenz, and had taken the pistol from the dead hand, he had tasted a strange little extra flavor of triumph. How many Jews, he'd thought, has this man killed, how fitting it is that I've killed him. Neither Olson nor Welch, who were like his brothers, would have felt that in picking up the Luger, its barrel still hot from the last shots its owner had fired before dying. And he had resolved that he was going to make sure to take his gun back with him to America, and plug it and keep it on his desk at home, as a kind of vague, half-understood sign to himself that justice had once been done and he had been its instrument.

Maybe, he thought, maybe I'd better take it back with me, but not as a memento. Not plugged, but loaded. America by now was a strange country for him. He had been away a long time and he wasn't sure what was waiting for him when he got home. If the mobs were coming down the street toward his house, he was not going to die singing and praying.

When he was taking basic training he'd heard a scrawny, clerk-like-looking soldier from Boston talking at the other end of the PX bar, over the watered beer. "The boys at the office," the scratchy voice was saying, "gave me a party before I left. And they told me one thing. 'Charlie,' they said, 'hold onto your bayonet. We're going to be able to use it when you get back. On the Yids.'"

He hadn't said anything then, because he'd felt it was neither possible nor desirable to fight against every random overheard voice raised against the Jews from one end of the world to another. But again and again, at odd moments, lying on a barracks cot, or stretched out trying to sleep on the floor of a ruined French farmhouse, he had heard that voice, harsh, satisfied, heavy with hate and ignorance, saying above the beery grumble of apprentice soldiers at the bar, "Hold onto your bayonet. . . ."

And the other stories—Jews collected stories of hatred

and injustice and inklings of doom like a special, lunatic kind of miser. The story of the naval officer, commander of a small vessel off the Aleutians, who, in the officers' wardroom, had complained that he hated the Jews because it was the Jews who had demanded that the Germans be beaten first and the forces in the Pacific had been starved in consequence. And when one of his junior officers, who had just come aboard, had objected and told the commander that he was a Jew, the commander had risen from the table and said, "Mister, the Constitution of the United States says I have to serve in the same navy with Jews, but it doesn't say I have to eat at the same table with them." In the fogs and the cold, swelling Arctic seas off the Aleutians, in a small boat, subject to sudden, mortal attack at any moment . . .

And the two young combat engineers in an attached company on D Day, when they were lying off the coast right before climbing down into the landing barges. "There's France," one of them had said.

"What's it like?" the second one had asked, peering out across the miles of water toward the smoking coast.

"Like every place else," the first one had answered. "The Jews've made all the dough during the war."

"Shut up!" Seeger had said, helplessly thinking of the dead, destroyed, wandering, starving Jews of France. The engineers had shut up, and they'd climbed down together into the heaving boat, and gone into the beach together.

And the million other stories. Jews, even the most normal and best adjusted of them, became living treasuries of them, scraps of malice and bloodthirstiness, clever and confusing and cunningly twisted so that every act by every Jew became suspect and blameworthy and hateful. Seeger had heard the stories, and had made an almost conscious effort to forget them. Now, holding his father's letter in his hand, he remembered them all.

He stared unseeingly out in front of him. Maybe, he thought, maybe it would've been better to have been killed in the war, like Leonard. Simpler. Leonard would never have to face a crowd coming for his mother and father. Leonard would not have to listen and collect these hideous, fascinating little stories that made of every Jew a stranger in any town, on any field, on the face of the earth. He had come so close to being killed so many times, it would have been so easy, so neat and final.

Seeger shook his head. It was ridiculous to feel like that, and he was ashamed of himself for the weak moment. At the age of twenty-one, death was not an answer.

"Seeger!" It was Olson's voice. He and Welch had sloshed silently up behind Seeger, standing in the open field. "Seeger, *mon vieux,* what're you doing—grazing?"

Seeger turned slowly to them. "I wanted to read my letter," he said.

Olson looked closely at him. They had been together so long, through so many things, that flickers and hints of expression on each other's faces were recognized and acted upon. "Anything wrong?" Olson asked.

"No," said Seeger. "Nothing much."

"Norman," Welch said, his voice young and solemn. "Norman, we've been talking, Olson and me. We decided—you're pretty attached to that Luger, and maybe —if you—well . . ."

"What he's trying to say," said Olson, "is we withdraw the request. If you want to sell it, O.K. If you don't, don't do it for our sake. Honest."

Seeger looked at them, standing there, disreputable and tough and familiar. "I haven't made up my mind yet," he said.

"Anything you decide," Welch said oratorically, "is perfectly all right with us. Perfectly."

They walked aimlessly and silently across the field, away from camp. As they walked, their shoes making a wet, sliding sound in the damp, dead grass, Seeger thought of the time Olson had covered him in the little town outside Cherbourg, when Seeger had been caught going down the side of a street by four Germans with a machine gun on the second story of a house on the corner and Olson had had to stand out in the middle of the street with no cover at all for more than a minute, firing continuously, so that Seeger could get away alive. And he thought of the time outside Saint Lô when he had been wounded and had lain in a mine field for three hours and Welch and Captain Taney had come looking for him in the darkness and had found him and picked him up and run for it, all of them expecting to get blown up any second.

And he thought of all the drinks they'd had together and the long marches and the cold winter together, and all the girls they'd gone out with together, and he thought of his father and brother crouching behind the window in Ohio waiting for the rockets and the crowds armed with Browning automatic rifles.

"Say," he stopped and stood facing them. "Say, what do you guys think of the Jews?"

Welch and Olson looked at each other, and Olson glanced down at the letter in Seeger's hand.

"Jews?" Olson said finally. "What're they? Welch, you ever hear of the Jews?"

Welch looked thoughtfully at the gray sky. "No," he said. "But remember, I'm an uneducated fellow."

"Sorry, Bud," Olson said, turning to Seeger. "We can't help you. Ask us another question. Maybe we'll do better."

Seeger peered at the faces of his friends. He would have to rely upon them, later on, out of uniform, on their native streets, more than he had ever relied on them on the bullet-swept street and in the dark mine field in France. Welch and Olson stared back at him, troubled, their faces candid and tough and dependable.

"What time," Seeger asked, "did you tell that captain you'd meet him?"

"Eight o'clock," Welch said. "But we don't have to go. If you have any feeling about that gun . . ."

"We'll meet him," Seeger said. "We can use that sixty-five bucks."

"Listen," Olson said, "I know how much you like that gun and I'll feel like a heel if you sell it."

"Forget it," Seeger said, starting to walk again. "What could I use it for in America?"

A Worn Path

EUDORA WELTY

Phoenix Jackson was old and tired. Natchez was a long way off. The sun was hot, the road treacherous. But she had to make the journey. There were some things that had to be done, simply because not to do them would be wrong, unthinkable.

At the end of "A Worn Path," Phoenix Jackson stands as an eloquent testament to the dignity and durability of the human spirit. Miss Welty has profound compassion for her small-town Southern characters, but there is nothing condescending in her treatment of them. Because she knows them so well and respects them so deeply, she writes about them with an understanding touched with genuine tenderness and humor.

EUDORA WELTY (1909–   ) was born and raised in Jackson, Mississippi, a city in which she continues to live and which provides, along with the surrounding country-side and neighboring cities of Natchez and Vicksburg, the setting for most of her fiction. A resourceful and accomplished craftsman, Miss Welty has received numerous awards for her literary achievements. She enjoys a substantial reputation as a creative artist. She is the author of three novels, including The Ponder Heart *(1954), for which she won the Howells medal awarded every five years for "the most distinguished work in American fiction." But it is as a short story writer that Miss Welty has created her most memorable fiction. Her six volumes of short stories constitute a significant achievement in American letters. Like William Faulkner, Eudora Welty is fascinated by the people of Mississippi. The depth of her insight and feeling gives a universal dimension to their daily lives.*

A Worn Path

It was December—a bright frozen day in the early morning. Far out in the country there was an old Negro woman with her head tied in a red rag, coming along a path through the pinewoods. Her name was Phoenix Jackson. She was very old and small and she walked slowly in the dark pine shadows, moving a little from side to side in her steps, with the balanced heaviness and lightness of a pendulum in a grandfather clock. She carried a thin, small cane made from an umbrella, and with this she kept tapping the frozen earth in front of her. This made a grave and persistent noise in the still air, that seemed meditative like the chirping of a solitary little bird.

She wore a dark striped dress reaching down to her shoe tops, and an equally long apron of bleached sugar sacks, with a full pocket: all neat and tidy, but every time she took a step she might have fallen over her shoelaces, which dragged from her unlaced shoes. She looked straight ahead. Her eyes were blue with age. Her skin had a pattern all its own of numberless branching wrinkles as though a whole little tree stood in the middle of her forehead, but a golden color ran underneath, and the two knobs of her cheeks were illumined by a yellow burning under the dark. Under the red rag her hair came down on her neck in the frailest of ringlets, still black, and with an odor like copper.

Now and then there was a quivering in the thicket. Old

Phoenix said, "Out of my way, all you foxes, owls, beetles, jack rabbits, coons, and wild animals! . . . Keep out from under these feet, little bob-whites. . . . Keep the big wild hogs out of my path. Don't let none of those come running my direction. I got a long way." Under her small black-freckled hand her cane, limber as a buggy whip, would switch at the brush as if to rouse up any hiding things.

On she went. The woods were deep and still. The sun made the pine needles almost too bright to look at, up where the wind rocked. The cones dropped as light as feathers. Down in the hollow was the mourning dove—it was not too late for him.

The path ran up a hill. "Seem like there is chains about my feet, time I get this far," she said, in the voice of argument old people keep to use with themselves. "Something always take a hold of me on this hill—pleads I should stay."

After she got to the top she turned and gave a full, severe look behind her where she had come. "Up through pines," she said at length. "Now down through oaks."

Her eyes opened their widest, and she started down gently. But before she got to the bottom of the hill a bush caught her dress.

Her fingers were busy and intent, but her skirts were full and long, so that before she could pull them free in one place they were caught in another. It was not possible to allow the dress to tear. "I in the thorny bush," she said. "Thorns, you doing your appointed work. Never want to let folks pass, no sir. Old eyes thought you was a pretty little *green* bush."

Finally, trembling all over, she stood free, and after a moment dared to stoop for her cane.

"Sun so high!" she cried, leaning back and looking, while the thick tears went over her eyes. "The time getting all gone here."

At the foot of this hill was a place where a log was laid across the creek.

"Now comes the trial," said Phoenix.

Putting her right foot out, she mounted the log and shut her eyes. Lifting her skirt, leveling her cane fiercely before her, like a festival figure in some parade, she began to march across. Then she opened her eyes and she was safe on the other side.

"I wasn't as old as I thought," she said.

But she sat down to rest. She spread her skirts on the bank around her and folded her hands over her knees. Up above her was a tree in a pearly cloud of mistletoe. She did not dare to close her eyes, and when a little boy brought her a plate with a slice of marble-cake on it she spoke to him. "That would be acceptable," she said. But when she went to take it there was just her own hand in the air.

So she left that tree, and had to go through a barbed-wire fence. There she had to creep and crawl, spreading her knees and stretching her fingers like a baby trying to climb the steps. But she talked loudly to herself: she could not let her dress be torn now, so late in the day, and she could not pay for having her arm or leg sawed off if she got caught fast where she was.

At last she was safe through the fence and risen up out in the clearing. Big dead trees, like black men with one arm, were standing in the purple stalks of the withered cotton field. There sat a buzzard.

"Who you watching?"

In the furrow she made her way along.

"Glad this not the season for bulls," she said, looking sideways, "and the good Lord made his snakes to curl up and sleep in the winter. A pleasure I don't see no two-headed snake coming around that tree, where it come once. It took a while to get by him, back in the summer."

She passed through the old cotton and went into a field of dead corn. It whispered and shook and was taller than her head. "Through the maze now," she said, for there was no path.

Then there was something tall, black, and skinny there, moving before her.

At first she took it for a man. It could have been a man dancing in the field. But she stood still and listened, and it did not make a sound. It was as silent as a ghost.

"Ghost," she said sharply, "who be you the ghost of? For I have heard of nary death close by."

But there was no answer—only the ragged dancing in the wind.

She shut her eyes, reached out her hand, and touched a sleeve. She found a coat and inside that an emptiness, cold as ice.

"You scarecrow," she said. Her face lighted. "I ought to be shut up for good," she said with laughter. "My senses is gone. I too old. I the oldest people I ever know. Dance, old scarecrow," she said, "while I dancing with you."

She kicked her foot over the furrow, and with mouth drawn down, shook her head once or twice in a little strutting way. Some husks blew down and whirled in streamers about her skirts.

Then she went on, parting her way from side to side with the cane, through the whispering field. At last she came to the end, to a wagon track where the silver grass blew between the red ruts. The quail were walking around like pullets, seeming all dainty and unseen.

"Walk pretty," she said. "This the easy place. This the easy going."

She followed the track, swaying through the quiet bare fields, through the little strings of trees silver in their dead leaves, past cabins silver from weather, with the doors and windows boarded shut, all like old women under a spell sitting there. "I walking in their sleep," she said, nodding her head vigorously.

In a ravine she went where a spring was silently flowing through a hollow log. Old Phoenix bent and drank. "Sweet-gum makes the water sweet," she said, and drank more. "Nobody know who made this well, for it was here when I was born."

The track crossed a swampy part where the moss hung as white as lace from every limb. "Sleep on, alligators, and blow your bubbles." Then the track went into the road.

Deep, deep the road went down between the high green-colored banks. Overhead the live-oaks met, and it was as dark as a cave.

A black dog with a lolling tongue came up out of the weeds by the ditch. She was meditating, and not ready, and when he came at her she only hit him a little with her cane. Over she went in the ditch, like a little puff of milkweed.

Down there, her senses drifted away. A dream visited

her, and she reached her hand up, but nothing reached down and gave her a pull. So she lay there and presently went to talking. "Old woman," she said to herself, "that black dog come up out of the weeds to stall you off, and now there he sitting on his fine tail, smiling at you."

A white man finally came along and found her—a hunter, a young man, with his dog on a chain.

"Well, Granny!" he laughed. "What are you doing there?"

"Lying on my back like a June-bug waiting to be turned over, mister," she said, reaching up her hand.

He lifted her up, gave her a swing in the air, and set her down. "Anything broken, Granny?"

"No sir, them old dead weeds is springy enough," said Phoenix, when she had got her breath. "I thank you for your trouble."

"Where do you live, Granny?" he asked, while the two dogs were growling at each other.

"Away back yonder, sir, behind the ridge. You can't even see it from here."

"On your way home?"

"No sir, I going to town."

"Why, that's too far! That's as far as I walk when I come out myself, and I get something for my trouble." He patted the stuffed bag he carried, and there hung down a little closed claw. It was one of the bob-whites, with its beak hooked bitterly to show it was dead. "Now you go on home, Granny!"

"I bound to go to town, mister," said Phoenix. "The time come around."

He gave another laugh, filling the whole landscape. "I know you old colored people! Wouldn't miss going to town to see Santa Claus!"

But something held old Phoenix very still. The deep lines in her face went into a fierce and different radiation. Without warning, she had seen with her own eyes a flashing nickel fall out of the man's pocket onto the ground.

"How old are you, Granny?" he was saying.

"There is no telling, mister," she said, "no telling."

Then she gave a little cry and clapped her hands and said, "Git on away from here, dog! Look! Look at that dog!" She laughed as if in admiration. "He ain't scared of nobody. He a big black dog." She whispered, "Sic him!"

"Watch me get rid of that cur," said the man. "Sic him, Pete! Sic him!"

Phoenix heard the dogs fighting and heard the man running and throwing sticks. She even heard a gunshot. But she was slowly bending forward by that time, further and further forward, the lids stretched down over her eyes, as if she were doing this in her sleep. Her chin was lowered almost to her knees. The yellow palm of her hand came out from the fold of her apron. Her fingers slid down and along the ground under the piece of money with the grace and care they would have in lifting an egg from under a setting hen. Then she slowly straightened up, she stood erect, and the nickel was in her apron pocket. A bird flew by. Her lips moved. "God watching me the whole time. I come to stealing."

The man came back, and his own dog panted about them. "Well, I scared him off that time," he said, and then he laughed and lifted his gun and pointed it at Phoenix.

She stood straight and faced him.

"Doesn't the gun scare you?" he said, still pointing it.

"No, sir, I seen plenty go off closer by, in my day, and for less than what I done," she said, holding utterly still.

He smiled, and shouldered the gun. "Well, Granny," he said, "you must be a hundred years old, and scared of nothing. I'd give you a dime if I had any money with me. But you take my advice and stay home, and nothing will happen to you."

"I bound to go on my way, mister," said Phoenix. She inclined her head in the red rag. Then they went in different directions, but she could hear the gun shooting again and again over the hill.

She walked on. The shadows hung from the oak trees to the road like curtains. Then she smelled wood-smoke, and smelled the river, and she saw a steeple and the cabins on their steep steps. Dozens of little black children whirled around her. There ahead was Natchez shining. Bells were ringing. She walked on.

In the paved city it was Christmas time. There were red and green electric lights strung and crisscrossed everywhere, and all turned on in the daytime. Old Phoenix would have been lost if she had not distrusted her eyesight and depended on her feet to know where to take her.

She paused quietly on the sidewalk where people were passing by. A lady came along in the crowd, carrying an armful of red-, green- and silver-wrapped presents; she gave off perfume like the red roses in hot summer, and Phoenix stopped her.

"Please, missy, will you lace up my shoe?" She held up her foot.

"What do you want, Grandma?"

"See my shoe," said Phoenix. "Do all right for out in the country, but wouldn't look right to go in a big building."

"Stand still then, Grandma," said the lady. She put her packages down on the sidewalk beside her and laced and tied both shoes tightly.

"Can't lace 'em with a cane," said Phoenix. "Thank you, missy. I doesn't mind asking a nice lady to tie up my shoe, when I gets out on the street."

Moving slowly and from side to side, she went into the big building, and into a tower of steps, where she walked up and around and around until her feet knew to stop.

She entered a door, and there she saw nailed up on the wall the document that had been stamped with the gold seal and framed in the gold frame, which matched the dream that was hung up in her head.

"Here I be," she said. There was a fixed and ceremonial stiffness over her body.

"A charity case, I suppose," said an attendant who sat at the desk before her.

But Phoenix only looked above her head. There was sweat on her face, the wrinkles in her skin shone like a bright net.

"Speak up, Grandma," the woman said. "What's your name? We must have your history, you know. Have you been here before? What seems to be the trouble with you?"

Old Phoenix only gave a twitch to her face as if a fly were bothering her.

"Are you deaf?" cried the attendant.

But then the nurse came in.

"Oh, that's just old Aunt Phoenix," she said. "She doesn't come for herself—she has a little grandson. She lives away back off the Old Natchez Trace." She bent down. "Well, Aunt Phoenix, why don't you just take a seat? We won't keep you standing after your long trip." She pointed.

The old woman sat down, bolt upright in the chair.

"Now, how is the boy?" asked the nurse.

Old Phoenix did not speak.

"I said, how is the boy?"

But Phoenix only waited and stared straight ahead, her face very solemn and withdrawn into rigidity.

"Is his throat any better?" asked the nurse. "Aunt Phoenix, don't you hear me? Is your grandson's throat any better since the last time you came for the medicine?"

With her hands on her knees, the old woman waited, silent, erect and motionless, just as if she were in armor.

"You mustn't take up our time this way, Aunt Phoenix," the nurse said. "Tell us quickly about your grandson, and get it over. He isn't dead, is he?"

At last there came a flicker and then a flame of comprehension across her face, and she spoke.

"My grandson. It was my memory had left me. There I sat and forgot why I made my long trip."

"Forgot?" The nurse frowned. "After you came so far?"

Then Phoenix was like an old woman begging a dignified forgiveness for waking up frightened in the night. "I never did go to school, I was too old at the Surrender," she said in a soft voice. "I'm an old woman without an education. It was my memory fail me. My little grandson, he is just the same, and I forgot it in the coming."

"Throat never heals, does it?" said the nurse, speaking in a loud, sure voice to old Phoenix. By now she had a card with something written on it, a little list. "Yes. Swallowed lye. When was it?—January—two-three years ago—"

Phoenix spoke unasked now. "No, missy, he not dead, he just the same. Every little while his throat begin to close up again, and he not able to swallow. He not get his breath. He not able to help himself. So the time come around, and I go on another trip for the soothing medicine."

"All right. The doctor said as long as you came to get it,

you could have it," said the nurse. "But it's an obstinate case."

"My little grandson, he sit up there in the house all wrapped up, waiting by himself," Phoenix went on. "We is the only two left in the world. He suffer and it don't seem to put him back at all. He got a sweet look. He going to last. He wear a little patch quilt and peep out holding his mouth open like a little bird. I remembers so plain now. I not going to forget him again, no, the whole enduring time. I could tell him from all the others in creation."

"All right." The nurse was trying to hush her now. She brought her a bottle of medicine. "Charity," she said, making a check mark in a book.

Old Phoenix held the bottle close to her eyes, and then carefully put it into her pocket.

"I thank you," she said.

"It's Christmas time, Grandma," said the attendant. "Could I give you a few pennies out of my purse?"

"Five pennies is a nickel," said Phoenix stiffly.

"Here's a nickel," said the attendant.

Phoenix rose carefully and held out her hand. She received the nickel and then fished the other nickel out of her pocket and laid it beside the new one. She stared at her palm closely, with her head on one side.

Then she gave a tap with her cane on the floor.

"This is what come to me to do," she said. "I going to the store and buy my child a little windmill they sells, made out of paper. He going to find it hard to believe there such a thing in the world. I'll march myself back where he waiting, holding it straight up in this hand."

She lifted her free hand, gave a little nod, turned around, and walked out of the doctor's office. Then her slow step began on the stairs, going down.

Tomorrow and Tomorrow and So Forth

JOHN UPDIKE

"Tomorrow and Tomorrow and So Forth" deals with the daily relationships in which teachers and students are caught up. Here are all the familiar tensions and conflicts, the common experiences, the deep human involvements that make the American classroom a uniquely trying yet satisfying experience. Sometime in high school every student has met a teacher like Mark Prosser. And sometime in his teaching career every teacher has met a class like Mark Prosser's.

Beneath Mr. Updike's apparently light, witty, almost wry treatment of the young people in "Tomorrow and Tomorrow and So Forth," there is a deeply serious and concerned intelligence at work. Mr. Updike understands adolescents intuitively. Because he remembers his own youth so clearly and so well, he is not put off by the superficial and frequently exasperating postures adolescents assume. He knows what they are really like.

His sensitivity to people, the precision of his language and imagery, his stylistic virtuosity, stamp him as one of the most original and compelling young American writers.

JOHN HOYER UPDIKE (1932–   ), American poet, novelist, and short story writer, was born and went to

*school in Pennsylvania. He attended Harvard University
and spent a year studying art at Oxford. From 1955 to
1957 he worked for* The New Yorker *magazine, where his
fresh and original verse, essays, parodies, and stories were
welcomed. In 1959, Updike published his first collection
of stories,* The Same Door, *followed in 1962 by another
collection,* Pigeon Feathers. *His first novel,* The Poor-
house Fair *(1959), received wide and favorable acclaim,
as did his later novel* Rabbit, Run *(1960).*

Tomorrow and Tomorrow
and So Forth

Whirling, talking, 11D began to enter Room 109. From
the quality of the class's excitement Mark Prosser guessed
it would rain. He had been teaching high school for three
years, yet his students still impressed him; they were such
sensitive animals. They reacted so infallibly to merely
barometric pressure.

In the doorway, Brute Young paused while little Barry
Snyder giggled at his elbow. Barry's stagy laugh rose and
fell, dipping down toward some vile secret that had to be
tasted and retasted, then soaring like a rocket to proclaim
that he, little Barry, shared such a secret with the school's
fullback. Being Brute's stooge was precious to Barry. The
fullback paid no attention to him; he twisted his neck to
stare at something not yet coming through the door. He
yielded heavily to the procession pressing him forward.

Right under Prosser's eyes, like a murder suddenly appearing in an annalistic frieze of kings and queens, someone stabbed a girl in the back with a pencil. She ignored
the assault saucily. Another hand yanked out Geoffrey
Langer's shirt-tail. Geoffrey, a bright student, was uncertain whether to laugh it off or defend himself with anger,
and made a weak, half-turning gesture of compromise,
wearing an expression of distant arrogance that Prosser
instantly coördinated with baffled feelings he used to have.

All along the line, in the glitter of key chains and the acute angles of turned-back shirt cuffs, an electricity was expressed which simple weather couldn't generate.

Mark wondered if today Gloria Angstrom wore that sweater, an ember-pink angora, with very brief sleeves. The virtual sleevelessness was the disturbing factor: the exposure of those two serene arms to the air, white as thighs against the delicate wool.

His guess was correct. A vivid pink patch flashed through the jiggle of arms and shoulders as the final knot of youngsters entered the room.

"Take your seats," Mr. Prosser said. "Come on. Let's go."

Most obeyed, but Peter Forrester, who had been at the center of the group around Gloria, still lingered in the doorway with her, finishing some story, apparently determined to make her laugh or gasp. When she did gasp, he tossed his head with satisfaction. His orange hair, preened into a kind of floating bang, bobbed. Mark had always disliked redheaded males, with their white eyelashes and puffy faces and thyroid eyes, and absurdly self-confident mouths. A race of bluffers. His own hair was brown.

When Gloria, moving in a considered, stately way, had taken her seat, and Peter had swerved into his, Mr. Prosser said, "Peter Forrester."

"Yes?" Peter rose, scrabbling through his book for the right place.

"Kindly tell the class the exact meaning of the words 'Tomorrow, and tomorrow, and tomorrow/Creeps in this petty pace from day to day.' "

Peter glanced down at the high-school edition of *Macbeth* lying open on his desk. One of the duller girls tittered expectantly from the back of the room. Peter was popular with the girls; girls that age had minds like moths.

"Peter. With your book shut. We have all memorized this passage for today. Remember?" The girl in the back of the room squealed in delight. Gloria laid her own book face-open on her desk, where Peter could see it.

Peter shut his book with a bang and stared into Gloria's. "Why," he said at last, "I think it means pretty much what it says."

"Which is?"

"Why, that tomorrow is something we often think about. It creeps into our conversation all the time. We couldn't make any plans without thinking about tomorrow."

"I see. Then you would say that Macbeth is here referring to the, the date-book aspect of life?"

Geoffrey Langer laughed, no doubt to please Mr. Prosser. For a moment, he *was* pleased. Then he realized he had been playing for laughs at a student's expense.

His paraphrase had made Peter's reading of the lines seem more ridiculous than it was. He began to retract. "I admit—"

But Peter was going on; redheads never know when to quit. "Macbeth means that if we quit worrying about tomorrow, and just live for today, we could appreciate all the wonderful things that are going on under our noses."

Mark considered this a moment before he spoke. He would not be sarcastic. "Uh, without denying that there is truth in what you say, Peter, do you think it likely that Macbeth, in his situation, would be expressing such"—he couldn't help himself—"such sunny sentiments?"

Geoffrey laughed again. Peter's neck reddened; he studied the floor. Gloria glared at Mr. Prosser, the indignation in her face clearly meant for him to see.

Mark hurried to undo his mistake. "Don't misunderstand me, please," he told Peter. "I don't have all the answers myself. But it seems to me the whole speech, down to 'Signifying nothing,' is saying that life is—well, a *fraud*. Nothing wonderful about it."

"Did Shakespeare really think that?" Geoffrey Langer asked, a nervous quickness pitching his voice high.

Mark read into Geoffrey's question his own adolescent premonitions of the terrible truth. The attempt he must make was plain. He told Peter he could sit down and looked through the window toward the steadying sky. The clouds were gaining intensity. "There is," Mr. Prosser slowly began, "much darkness in Shakespeare's work, and no play is darker than 'Macbeth.' The atmosphere is poisonous, oppressive. One critic has said that in this play, humanity suffocates." He felt himself in danger of suffocating, and cleared his throat.

"In the middle of his career, Shakespeare wrote plays

about men like Hamlet and Othello and Macbeth—men who aren't allowed by their society, or bad luck, or some minor flaw in themselves, to become the great men they might have been. Even Shakespeare's comedies of this period deal with a world gone sour. It is as if he had seen through the bright, bold surface of his earlier comedies and histories and had looked upon something terrible. It frightened him, just as some day it may frighten some of you." In his determination to find the right words, he had been staring at Gloria, without meaning to. Embarrassed, she nodded, and, realizing what had happened, he smiled at her.

He tried to make his remarks gentler, even diffident. "But then I think Shakespeare sensed a redeeming truth. His last plays are serene and symbolical, as if he had pierced through the ugly facts and reached a realm where the facts are again beautiful. In this way, Shakespeare's total work is a more complete image of life than that of any other writer, except perhaps for Dante, an Italian poet who wrote several centuries earlier." He had been taken far from the Macbeth soliloquy. Other teachers had been happy to tell him how the kids made a game of getting him talking. He looked toward Geoffrey. The boy was doodling on his tablet, indifferent. Mr. Prosser concluded, "The last play Shakespeare wrote is an extraordinary poem called 'The Tempest.' Some of you may want to read it for your next book reports—the ones due May 10th. It's a short play."

The class had been taking a holiday. Barry Snyder was snicking BBs off the blackboard and glancing over at Brute Young to see if he noticed. "Once more, Barry," Mr. Prosser said, "and out you go." Barry blushed, and grinned to cover the blush, his eyeballs sliding toward Brute. The dull girl in the rear of the room was putting on lipstick. "Put that away, Alice," Prosser said. "This isn't a beauty parlor." Sejak, the Polish boy who worked nights, was asleep at his desk, his cheek white with pressure against the varnished wood, his mouth sagging sidewise. Mr. Prosser had an impulse to let him sleep. But the impulse might not be true kindness, but just the self-congratulatory, kindly pose in which he sometimes discovered himself. Besides, one breach of discipline encouraged others. He strode down the aisle and squeezed Sejak's shoulder; the boy awoke. A mumble was growing at the front of the room.

Peter Forrester was whispering to Gloria, trying to make her laugh. The girl's face, though, was cool and solemn, as if a thought had been provoked in her head— as if there lingered there something of what Mr. Prosser had been saying. With a bracing sense of chivalrous intercession, Mark said, "Peter. I gather from this noise that you have something to add to your theories."

Peter responded courteously. "No, sir. I honestly don't understand the speech. Please, sir, what *does* it mean?"

This candid admission and odd request stunned the class. Every white, round face, eager, for once, to learn, turned toward Mark. He said, "I don't know. I was hoping *you* would tell *me*."

In college, when a professor made such a remark, it was with grand effect. The professor's humility, the necessity for creative interplay between teacher and student were dramatically impressed upon the group. But to 11D, ignorance in an instructor was as wrong as a hole in a roof. It was as if Mark had held forty strings pulling forty faces taut toward him and then had slashed the strings. Heads waggled, eyes dropped, voices buzzed. Some of the discipline problems, like Peter Forrester, smirked signals to one another.

"Quiet!" Mr. Prosser shouted. "All of you. Poetry isn't arithmetic. There's no single right answer. I don't want to force my own impression on you; that's not why I'm here." The silent question, *Why are you here?* seemed to steady the air with suspense. "I'm here," he said, "to let you teach yourselves."

Whether or not they believed him, they subsided, somewhat. Mark judged he could safely reassume his human-among-humans pose. He perched on the edge of the desk, informal, friendly, and frankly beseeching. "Now, honestly. Don't any of you have some personal feeling about the lines that you would like to share with the class and me?"

One hand, with a flowered handkerchief balled in it, unsteadily rose. "Go ahead, Teresa," Mr. Prosser said.

She was a timid, sniffly girl whose mother was a Jehovah's Witness.

"It makes me think of cloud shadows," Teresa said.

Geoffrey Langer laughed. "Don't be rude, Geoff," Mr. Prosser said sideways, softly, before throwing his voice forward: "Thank you, Teresa. I think that's an interesting and valid impression. Cloud movement has something in it of the slow, monotonous rhythm one feels in the line 'Tomorrow, and tomorrow, and tomorrow.' It's a very gray line, isn't it, class?" No one agreed or disagreed.

Beyond the windows actual clouds were bunching rapidly, and erratic sections of sunlight slid around the room. Gloria's arm, crooked gracefully above her head, turned gold. "Gloria?" Mr. Prosser asked.

She looked up from something on her desk with a face of sullen radiance. "I think what Teresa said was very good," she said, glaring in the direction of Geoffrey Langer. Geoffrey snickered defiantly. "And I have a question. What does 'petty pace' mean?"

"It means the trivial day-to-day sort of life that say, a bookkeeper or a bank clerk leads. Or a schoolteacher," he added, smiling.

She did not smile back. Thought wrinkles irritated her perfect brow. "But Macbeth has been fighting wars, and killing kings, and being a king himself, and all," she pointed out.

"Yes, but it's just these acts Macbeth is condemning as 'nothing.' Can you see that?"

Gloria shook her head. "Another thing I worry about— isn't it silly for Macbeth to be talking to himself right in the middle of this war, with his wife just dead, and all?"

"I don't think so, Gloria. No matter how fast events happen, thought is faster."

His answer was weak; everyone knew it, even if Gloria hadn't mused, supposedly to herself, but in a voice the entire class could hear, "It seems so *stupid*."

Mark winced, pierced by the awful clarity with which his students saw him. Through their eyes, how queer he looked, with his chalky hands, and his horn-rimmed glasses, and his hair never slicked down, all wrapped up in "literature," where, when things get rough, the king mumbles a poem nobody understands. He was suddenly conscious of a terrible tenderness in the young, a frightening patience and faith. It was so good of them not to laugh him out of the room. He looked down and rubbed his fingertips together, trying to erase the chalk dust. The class noise sifted into unnatural quiet. "It's getting late," he said finally. "Let's start the recitations of the memorized passage. Bernard Amilson, you begin."

Bernard had trouble enunciating, and his rendition began " 'T'mau 'n' t'mau 'n' t'mau.' " It was reassuring, the extent to which the class tried to repress its laughter. Mr. Prosser wrote "A" in his marking book opposite Bernard's name. He always gave Bernard A on recitations, despite the school nurse, who claimed there was nothing organically wrong with the boy's mouth.

It was the custom, cruel but traditional, to deliver recitations from the front of the room. Alice, when her turn came, was reduced to a helpless state by the first funny face Peter Forrester made at her. Mark let her hang up there a good minute while her face ripened to cherry redness, and at last relented. "Alice, you may try it later." Many of the class knew the passage gratifyingly well, though there was a tendency to leave out the line "To the last syllable of recorded time" and to turn "struts and frets" into "frets and struts" or simply "struts and struts." Even Sejak, who couldn't have looked at the passage before he came to class, got through it as far as "And then is heard no more."

Geoffrey Langer showed off, as he always did, by interrupting his own recitation with bright questions. " 'Tomorrow, and tomorrow, and tomorrow,' " he said, " 'creeps in'—shouldn't that be 'creep in,' Mr. Prosser?"

"It is 'creeps.' The trio is in effect singular. Go on. Without the footnotes." Mr. Prosser was tired of coddling Langer. The boy's black hair, short and stiff, seemed deliberately ratlike.

" 'Creepsss in this petty pace from day to day, to the last syllable of recorded time, and all our yesterdays have lighted fools the way to dusty death. Out, out—' "

"No, no!" Mr. Prosser jumped out of his chair. "This is poetry. Don't mushmouth it! Pause a little after 'fools.' " Geoffrey looked genuinely startled this time, and Mark himself did not quite understand his annoyance and, men-

tally turning to see what was behind him, seemed to
glimpse in the humid undergrowth the two stern eyes of
the indignant look Gloria had thrown Geoffrey. He
glimpsed himself in the absurd position of acting as
Gloria's champion in her private war with this intelligent
boy. He sighed apologetically. "Poetry is made up of
lines," he began, turning to the class. Gloria was passing a
note to Peter Forrester.

The rudeness of it! To pass notes during a scolding that
she herself had caused! Mark caged in his hand the girl's
frail wrist and ripped the note from her fingers. He read
it to himself, letting the class see he was reading it, though
he despised such methods of discipline. The note went:

> Pete—I think you're *wrong* about Mr. Prosser. I think
> he's wonderful and I get a lot out of his class. He's
> heavenly with poetry. I think I love him. I really do
> *love* him. So there.

Mr. Prosser folded the note once and slipped it into his
side coat pocket. "See me after class, Gloria," he said.
Then, to Geoffrey, "Let's try it again. Begin at the beginning."

While the boy was reciting the passage, the buzzer
sounded the end of the period. It was the last class of the
day. The room quickly emptied, except for Gloria. The
noise of lockers slamming open and books being thrown
against metal and shouts drifted in.

"Who has a car?"

"Lend me a cig, pig."

"We can't have practice in this slop."

Mark hadn't noticed exactly when the rain started, but
it was coming down hard now. He moved around the
room with the window pole, closing windows and pulling
down shades. Spray bounced in on his hands. He began to
talk to Gloria in a crisp voice that, like his device of
shutting the windows, was intended to protect them both
from embarrassment.

"About note passing." She sat motionless at her desk in
the front of the room, her short, brushed-up hair like a
cool torch. From the way she sat, her naked arms folded
at her breasts and her shoulders hunched, he felt she was

chilly. "It is not only rude to scribble when a teacher is talking, it is stupid to put one's words down on paper, where they look much more foolish than they might have sounded if spoken." He leaned the window pole in its corner and walked toward his desk.

"And about love. 'Love' is one of those words that illustrate what happens to an old, overworked language. These days, with movie stars and crooners and preachers and psychiatrists all pronouncing the word, it's come to mean nothing but a vague fondness for something. In this sense, I love the rain, this blackboard, these desks, you. It means nothing, you see, whereas once the word signified a quite explicit thing—a desire to share all you own and are with someone else. It is time we coined a new word to mean that, and when you think up the word *you* want to use, I suggest that you be economical with it. Treat it as something you can spend only once—if not for your own sake, for the good of the language." He walked over to his own desk and dropped two pencils on it, as if to say, "That's all."

"I'm sorry," Gloria said.

Rather surprised, Mr. Prosser said, "Don't be."

"But you don't understand."

"Of course I don't. I probably never did. At your age, I was like Geoffrey Langer."

"I bet you weren't." The girl was almost crying; he was sure of that.

"Come on, Gloria. Run along. Forget it." She slowly cradled her books between her bare arm and her sweater, and left the room with that melancholy shuffling teen-age gait, so that her body above her thighs seemed to float over the desktops.

What was it, Mark asked himself, these kids were after? What did they want? Glide, he decided, the quality of glide. To slip along, always in rhythm, always cool, the little wheels humming under you, going nowhere special. If Heaven existed, that's the way it would be there. *He's heavenly with poetry.* They loved the word. Heaven was in half their songs.

"Christ, he's humming." Strunk, the physical ed teacher,

had come into the room without Mark's noticing. Gloria had left the door ajar.

"Ah," Mark said, "a fallen angel, full of grit."

"What the hell makes you so happy?"

"I'm not happy, I'm just heavenly. I don't know why you don't appreciate me."

"Say." Strunk came up an aisle with a disagreeably effeminate waddle, pregnant with gossip. "Did you hear about Murchison?"

"No." Mark mimicked Strunk's whisper.

"He got the pants kidded off him today."

"Oh dear."

Strunk started to laugh, as he always did before beginning a story. "You know what a goddam lady's man he thinks he is?"

"You bet," Mark said, although Strunk said that about every male member of the faculty.

"You have Gloria Angstrom, don't you?"

"You bet."

"Well, this morning Murky intercepts a note she was writing, and the note says what a damn neat guy she thinks Murchison is and how she *loves* him!" Strunk waited for Mark to say something, and then, when he didn't, continued, "You could see he was tickled pink. But—get this—it turns out at lunch that the same damn thing happened to Fryeburg in history yesterday!" Strunk laughed and cracked his knuckles viciously. "The girl's too dumb to have thought it up herself. We all think it was Peter Forrester's idea."

"Probably was," Mark agreed. Strunk followed him out to his locker, describing Murchison's expression when Fryeburg (in all innocence, mind you) told what had happened to him.

Mark turned the combination of his locker, 18—24—3. "Would you excuse me, Dave?" he said. "My wife's in town waiting."

Strunk was too thick to catch Mark's anger. "I got to get over to the gym. Can't take the little darlings outside in the rain; their mommies'll write notes to teacher." He waddled down the hall and wheeled at the far end, shouting, "Now don't tell You-know-who!"

Mr. Prosser took his coat from the locker and shrugged

it on. He placed his hat upon his head. He fitted his rubbers over his shoes, pinching his fingers painfully, and lifted his umbrella off the hook. He thought of opening it right there in the vacant hall, as a kind of joke, and decided not to. The girl had been almost crying; he was sure of that.

The Fifty-first Dragon

HEYWOOD BROUN

"The Fifty-first Dragon" is a delicious satire on knighthood, a delightful parody of Arthurian legends and knightly dragon slayers learning their ancient craft at a strangely conceived university. But there is a serious underlying point to this parable. Simply and skillfully it raises and answers the question, "What should a man believe in?"

Mr. Broun's puckish humor, his sharp yet kindly eye for human weakness and pretension, his abiding interest in people, his easy, disarming style have endowed "The Fifty-first Dragon" with contemporary and continuing relevance.

HEYWOOD BROUN (1888–1939) was born in Brooklyn and educated at Horace Mann High School and Harvard University. During World War I, he served as a war correspondent overseas. When he returned to New York, he worked as a sports reporter, then as a widely syndicated columnist for various newspapers. He ran unsuccessfully for Congress in 1930. He was a founder and president of the New York Newspaper Guild.

A skillful humorist, satirist, and commentator, Broun grew increasingly concerned over the social injustices that scarred the lives of so many Americans. He was active in many causes, always championing the underdog.

The Fifty-first Dragon

Of all the pupils at the knight school Gawaine le Coeur-Hardy was among the least promising. He was tall and sturdy, but his instructors soon discovered that he lacked spirit. He would hide in the woods when the jousting class was called, although his companions and members of the faculty sought to appeal to his better nature by shouting to him to come out and break his neck like a man. Even when they told him that the lances were padded, the horses no more than ponies, and the field unusually soft for late autumn, Gawaine refused to grow enthusiastic. The Headmaster and the Assistant Professor of Pleasaunce were discussing the case one spring afternoon, and the Assistant Professor could see no remedy but expulsion.

"No," said the Headmaster, as he looked out at the purple hills which ringed the school, "I think I'll train him to slay dragons."

"He might be killed," objected the Assistant Professor.

"So he might," replied the Headmaster brightly; "but," he added more soberly, "we must consider the greater good. We are responsible for the formation of this lad's character."

"Are the dragons particularly bad this year?" interrupted the Assistant Professor. This was characteristic. He always seemed restive when the head of the school began to talk ethics and the ideals of the institution.

"I've never known them worse," replied the Headmaster. "Up in the hills to the south last week they killed a number of peasants, two cows, and a prize pig. And if this dry spell holds there's no telling when they may start a forest fire simply by breathing around indiscriminately."

"Would any refund on the tuition fee be necessary in case of an accident to young Coeur-Hardy?"

"No," the principal answered judicially; "that's all covered in the contract. But as a matter of fact he won't be killed. Before I send him up in the hills I'm going to give him a magic word."

"That's a good idea," said the Professor. "Sometimes they work wonders."

From that day on Gawaine specialized in dragons. His course included both theory and practice. In the morning there were long lectures on the history, anatomy, manners, and customs of dragons. Gawaine did not distinguish himself in these studies. He had a marvelously versatile gift for forgetting things. In the afternoon he showed to better advantage, for then he would go down to the South Meadow and practice with a battle-ax. In this exercise he was truly impressive, for he had enormous strength as well as speed and grace. He even developed a deceptive display of ferocity. Old alumni say that it was a thrilling sight to see Gawaine charging across the field toward the dummy paper dragon which had been set up for his practice. As he ran he would brandish his ax and shout "A murrain on thee!" or some other vivid bit of campus slang. It never took him more than one stroke to behead the dummy dragon.

Gradually his task was made more difficult. Paper gave way to papier-mâché and finally to wood, but even the toughest of these dummy dragons had no terrors for Gawaine. One sweep of the ax always did the business. There were those who said that when the practice was protracted until dusk and the dragons threw long, fantastic shadows across the meadow, Gawaine did not charge so impetuously nor shout so loudly. It is possible there was malice in this charge. At any rate the Headmaster decided by the end of June that it was time for the test. Only the night before, a dragon had come close to the school grounds and had eaten some of the lettuce from the garden. The faculty decided that Gawaine was ready. They gave him a diploma and a new battle-ax, and the Headmaster summoned him to a private conference.

"Sit down," said the Headmaster. "Have a cigarette."

Gawaine hesitated.

"Oh, I know it's against the rules," said the Headmaster; "but, after all, you have received your preliminary degree. You are no longer a boy. You are a man. Tomorrow you will go out into the world—the great world of achievement."

Gawaine took a cigarette. The Headmaster offered him a match, but he produced one of his own and began to puff away with a dexterity which quite amazed the principal.

"Here you have learned the theories of life," continued the Headmaster, resuming the thread of his discourse; "but, after all, life is not a matter of theories. Life is a matter of facts. It calls on the young and the old alike to face these facts, even though they are hard and sometimes unpleasant. Your problem, for example, is to slay dragons."

"They say that those dragons down in the south wood are five hundred feet long," ventured Gawaine, timorously.

"Stuff and nonsense!" said the Headmaster. "The curate saw one last week from the top of Arthur's Hill. The dragon was sunning himself down in the valley. The curate didn't have an opportunity to look at him very long because he felt it was his duty to hurry back to make a report to me. He said the monster—or shall I say, the big lizard?—wasn't an inch over two hundred feet. But the size has nothing at all to do with it. You'll find the big ones even easier than the little ones. They're far slower on their feet and less aggressive, I'm told. Besides, before you go I'm going to equip you in such fashion that you need have no fear of all the dragons in the world."

"I'd like an enchanted cap," said Gawaine.

"What's that?" answered the Headmaster, testily.

"A cap to make me disappear," explained Gawaine.

The Headmaster laughed indulgently. "You mustn't believe all those old wives' stories," he said. "There isn't any such thing. A cap to make you disappear, indeed! What would you do with it? You haven't even appeared yet. Why, my boy, you could walk from here to London, and nobody would so much as look at you. You're nobody. You couldn't be more invisible than that."

Gawaine seemed dangerously close to a relapse into his old habit of whimpering. The Headmaster reassured him: "Don't worry; I'll give you something much better than an enchanted cap. I'm going to give you a magic word. All you have to do is to repeat this magic charm once and no dragon can possibly harm a hair of your head. You can cut off his head at your leisure."

He took a heavy book from the shelf behind his desk and began to run through it. "Sometimes," he said, "the charm is a whole phrase or even a sentence. I might, for instance, give you 'To make the—' No, that might not do. I think a single word would be best for dragons."

"A short word," suggested Gawaine.

"It can't be too short or it wouldn't be potent. There isn't so much hurry as all that. Here's a splendid magic word: 'Rumplesnitz.' Do you think you can learn that?"

Gawaine tried and in an hour or so he seemed to have the word well in hand. Again and again he interrupted the lesson to inquire, "And if I say 'Rumplesnitz' the dragon can't possibly hurt me?" And always the Headmaster replied, "If you only say 'Rumplesnitz,' you are perfectly safe."

Toward morning Gawaine seemed resigned to his career. At daybreak the Headmaster saw him to the edge of the forest and pointed him in the direction in which he should proceed. About a mile away to the southwest a cloud of steam hovered over an open meadow in the woods, and the Headmaster assured Gawaine that under the steam he would find a dragon. Gawaine went forward slowly. He wondered whether it would be best to approach the dragon on the run, as he did in his practice in the South Meadow, or to walk toward him, shouting "Rumplesnitz" all the way.

The problem was decided for him. No sooner had he come to the fringe of the meadow than the dragon spied him and began to charge. It was a large dragon, and yet it seemed decidedly aggressive in spite of the Headmaster's statement to the contrary. As the dragon charged, it released huge clouds of hissing steam through its nostrils. It was almost as if a gigantic teapot had gone mad. The dragon came forward so fast, and Gawaine was so frightened, that he had time to say "Rumplesnitz" only once. As he said it he swung his battle-ax, and off popped the head of the dragon. Gawaine had to admit that it was even easier to kill a real dragon than a wooden one, if only you said "Rumplesnitz."

Gawaine brought the ears home and a small section of

the tail. His schoolmates and the faculty made much of him and the Headmaster wisely kept him from being spoiled by insisting that he go on with his work. Every clear day Gawaine rose at dawn and went out to kill dragons. The Headmaster kept him at home when it rained, because he said the woods were damp and unhealthy at such times, and he didn't want the boy to run needless risks. Few good days passed in which Gawaine failed to get a dragon. On one particularly fortunate day he killed three, a husband and wife and a visiting relative. Gradually he developed a technique. Pupils who sometimes watched him from the hilltops a long way off said that he often allowed the dragon to come within a few feet before he said "Rumplesnitz." He came to say it with a mocking sneer. Occasionally he did stunts. Once when an excursion party from London was watching him he went into action with his right hand tied behind his back. The dragon's head came off just as easily.

As Gawaine's record of killings mounted higher, the Headmaster found it impossible to keep him completely in hand. He fell into the habit of stealing out at night and engaging in long drinking bouts at the village tavern. It was after such a debauch that he rose a little before dawn one fine August morning and started out after his fiftieth dragon. His head was heavy and his mind sluggish. He was heavy in other respects as well, for he had adopted the somewhat vulgar practice of wearing his medals, ribbons and all, when he went out dragon-hunting. The decorations began on his chest and ran all the way down to his abdomen. They must have weighed at least eight pounds.

Gawaine found a dragon in the same meadow where he had killed the first one. It was a fair-sized dragon but evidently an old one. Its face was wrinkled and Gawaine thought he had never seen so hideous a countenance. Much to the lad's disgust the monster refused to charge, and Gawaine was obliged to walk toward him. He whistled as he went. The dragon regarded him hopelessly but craftily. Of course it had heard of Gawaine. Even when the lad raised his battle-ax, the dragon made no move. It knew that there was no salvation in the quickest thrust of the head, for it had been informed that this hunter was protected by an enchantment. It merely waited, hoping something would turn up. Gawaine raised the battle-ax and suddenly lowered it again. He had grown very pale, and he trembled violently. The dragon suspected a trick. "What's the matter?" it asked, with false solicitude.

"I've forgotten the magic word," stammered Gawaine.

"What a pity!" said the dragon. "So that was the secret. It doesn't seem quite sporting to me, all this magic stuff, you know. Not cricket, as we used to say when I was a little dragon; but, after all, that's a matter of opinion."

Gawaine was so helpless with terror that the dragon's confidence rose immeasurably and it could not resist the temptation to show off a bit.

"Could I possibly be of any assistance?" it asked. "What's the first letter of the magic word?"

"It begins with an 'R,' " said Gawaine, weakly.

"Let's see," mused the dragon, "that doesn't tell us much, does it? What sort of a word is this? Is it an epithet, do you think?"

Gawaine could do no more than nod.

"Why, of course," exclaimed the dragon, "reactionary Republican."

Gawaine shook his head.

"Well, then," said the dragon, "we'd better get down to business. Will you surrender?"

With the suggestion of a compromise Gawaine mustered up enough courage to speak.

"What will you do if I surrender?"

"Why, I'll eat you," said the dragon.

"And if I don't surrender?"

"I'll eat you just the same."

"Then it doesn't make any difference, does it?" moaned Gawaine.

"It does to me," said the dragon with a smile. "I'd rather you didn't surrender. You'd taste much better if you didn't."

The dragon waited for a long time for Gawaine to ask "Why?" but the boy was too frightened to speak. At last the dragon had to give the explanation without his cue line. "You see," he said, "if you don't surrender, you'll taste better because you'll die game."

This was an old and ancient trick of the dragon's. By means of some such quip he was accustomed to paralyze his victims with laughter and then to destroy them. Gawaine was sufficiently paralyzed as it was, but laughter had no part in his helplessness. With the last word of the joke the dragon drew back and struck. In that second there flashed into the mind of Gawaine the magic word "Rumplesnitz," but there was no time to say it. There was time only to strike, and without a word Gawaine met the onrush of the dragon with a full swing. He put all his back and shoulders into it. The impact was terrific, and the head of the dragon flew away almost a hundred yards and landed in a thicket.

Gawaine did not remain frightened very long after the death of the dragon. His mood was one of wonder. He was enormously puzzled. He cut off the ears of the monster almost in a trance. Again and again he thought to himself, "I didn't say 'Rumplesnitz'!" He was sure of that, and yet there was no question that he had killed the dragon. In fact, he had never killed one so utterly. Never before had he driven a head for anything like the same distance. Twenty-five yards was perhaps his best previous record. All the way back to the knight school he kept rumbling about in his mind; seeking an explanation for what had occurred. He went to the Headmaster immediately and, after closing the door, told him what had happened. "I didn't say 'Rumplesnitz,'" he explained with great earnestness.

The Headmaster laughed. "I'm glad you've found out," he said. "It makes you ever so much more of a hero. Don't you see that? Now you know that it was you who killed all these dragons, and not that foolish little word 'Rumplesnitz.'"

Gawaine frowned. "Then it wasn't a magic word, after all?" he asked.

"Of course not," said the Headmaster; "you ought to be too old for such foolishness. There isn't any such thing as a magic word."

"But you told me it was magic," protested Gawaine. "You said it was magic, and now you say it isn't."

"It wasn't magic in a literal sense," answered the Headmaster, "but it was much more wonderful than that. The word gave you confidence. It took away your fears. If I hadn't told you that, you might have been killed the very first time. It was your battle-ax did the trick."

Gawaine surprised the Headmaster by his attitude. He was obviously distressed by the explanation. He interrupted a long philosophic and ethical discourse by the Headmaster with, "If I hadn't of hit 'em all mighty hard and fast any one of 'em might have crushed me like a, like a—"

He fumbled for a word.

"Eggshell," suggested the Headmaster.

"Like a eggshell," assented Gawaine and he said it many times. All through the evening meal people who sat near him heard him muttering, "Like a eggshell, like a eggshell."

The next day was clear, but Gawaine did not get up at dawn. Indeed, it was almost noon when the Headmaster found him cowering in bed, with the clothes pulled over his head. The principal called the Assistant Professor of Pleasaunce, and together they dragged the boy toward the forest.

"He'll be all right as soon as he gets a couple more dragons under his belt," explained the Headmaster.

The Assistant Professor of Pleasaunce agreed. "It would be a shame to stop such a fine run," he said. "Why, counting that one yesterday, he's killed fifty dragons."

They pushed the boy into a thicket above which hung a meager cloud of steam. It was obviously quite a small dragon. But Gawaine did not come back that night or the next. In fact, he never came back. Some weeks afterward, brave spirits from the school explored the thicket but they could find nothing to remind them of Gawaine except the metal parts of his medals. Even the ribbons had been devoured.

The Headmaster and the Assistant Professor of Pleasaunce agreed that it would be just as well not to tell the school how Gawaine had achieved his record, and still less how he came to die. They held that it might have a bad effect on school spirit. Accordingly Gawaine has lived in the memory of the school as its greatest hero. No visitor succeeds in leaving the building today without seeing a great shield which hangs on the wall of the dining hall. Fifty pairs of dragons' ears are mounted upon the shield, and underneath in gilt letters is "Gawaine le Coeur-Hardy," followed by the simple inscription, "He killed fifty dragons." The record has never been equaled.

The Interlopers

"SAKI"

Very few readers will be able to guess how "The Interlopers" will end. The story explodes in the very last word, as that remarkable storyteller, Saki, leads swiftly, step by inevitable step, to the ironical, shattering ending.

"The Interlopers" is an *original* story in the best sense of that much-abused word. It is uniquely "Saki" in its highly ingenious though somewhat contrived plottings, its clean, economical narrative line, its lightly concealed satirical thrust at paltry men and paltry motives. The final, overwhelming question of cosmic responsibility (Who is really in charge here?) is subtly posed in truly Sakian style by the climactic twist that gives this story its special bite and point.

SAKI (1870–1916), is the pen name of Hector Hugh Munro, Scottish journalist, novelist, and short story writer. He was killed in World War I at Beaumont-Hamel.

Saki's fame rests on his short stories—a unique blend of urbanity, humor, whimsy, satire, and horror. Among the best known of his collections are Reginald *(1904),* The Chronicles of Clovis *(1911), and* Beasts and Super-Beasts *(1914).*

The Interlopers

In a forest of mixed growth somewhere on the eastern spurs of the Carpathians, a man stood one winter night watching and listening, as though he waited for some beast of the woods to come within the range of his vision, and, later, of his rifle. But the game for whose presence he kept so keen an outlook was none that figured in the sportsman's calendar as lawful and proper for the chase; Ulrich von Gradwitz patrolled the dark forest in quest of a human enemy.

The forest lands of Gradwitz were of wide extent and well stocked with game; the narrow strip of precipitous woodland that lay on its outskirt was not remarkable for the game it harbored or the shooting it afforded, but it was the most jealously guarded of all its owner's territorial possessions. A famous lawsuit, in the days of his grandfather, had wrested it from the illegal possession of a neighbouring family of petty landowners; the dispossessed party had never acquiesced in the judgment of the Courts, and a long series of poaching affrays and similar scandals had embittered the relationships between the families for three generations. The neighbour feud had grown into a personal one since Ulrich had come to be head of his family; if there was a man in the world whom he detested and wished ill to it was Georg Znaeym, the inheritor of the quarrel and the tireless game-snatcher and raider of the disputed border-forest. The feud might, perhaps, have died down or been compromised if the personal ill-will of the two men had not stood in the way; as boys they had thirsted for one another's blood, as men each prayed that misfortune might fall on the other, and this wind-scourged winter night Ulrich had banded together his foresters to watch the dark forest, not in quest of four-footed quarry, but to keep a look-out for the prowling thieves whom he suspected of being afoot from across the land boundary. The roebuck, which usually kept in the sheltered hollows during a storm-wind, were running like driven things tonight, and there was movement and unrest among the creatures that were wont to sleep through the dark hours. Assuredly there was a disturbing element in the forest, and Ulrich could guess the quarter from whence it came.

He strayed away by himself from the watchers whom he had placed in ambush on the crest of the hill, and wandered far down the steep slopes amid the wild tangle of undergrowth, peering through the tree-trunks and listening through the whistling and skirling of the wind and the restless beating of the branches for sight or sound of the marauders. If only on this wild night, in this dark, lone spot, he might come across Georg Znaeym, man to man, with none to witness—that was the wish that was uppermost in his thoughts. And as he stepped round the trunk of a huge beech he came face to face with the man he sought.

The two enemies stood glaring at one another for a long silent moment. Each had a rifle in his hand, each had hate in his heart and murder uppermost in his mind. The chance had come to give full play to the passions of a lifetime. But a man who has been brought up under the code of a restraining civilization cannot easily nerve himself to shoot down his neighbour in cold blood and without word spoken, except for an offence against his hearth and honour. And before the moment of hesitation had given way to action a deed of Nature's own violence overwhelmed them both. A fierce shriek of the storm had been answered by a splitting crash over their heads, and ere they could leap aside a mass of falling beech tree had thundered down on them. Ulrich von Gradwitz found himself stretched on the ground, one arm numb beneath him and the other held almost as helplessly in a tight tangle of forked branches, while both legs were pinned beneath the fallen mass. His heavy shooting-boots had saved his feet from being crushed to pieces, but if his fractures were not as serious as they might have been, at least it was evident that he could not move from his present position till some one came to release him. The descending twigs had slashed the skin of his face, and he had to wink away some drops of blood from his eyelashes before he could take in a general view of the disaster. At his side, so near that under ordinary circumstances he could almost have touched him, lay Georg Znaeym, alive and struggling, but obviously as helplessly pinioned down as himself. All round them lay a thick-strewn wreckage of splintered branches and broken twigs.

Relief at being alive and exasperation at his captive plight brought a strange medley of pious thank-offerings and sharp curses to Ulrich's lips. Georg, who was nearly blinded with the blood which trickled across his eyes, stopped his struggling for a moment to listen, and then gave a short, snarling laugh.

"So you're not killed, as you ought to be, but you're caught, anyway," he cried; "caught fast. Ho, what a jest, Ulrich von Gradwitz snared in his stolen forest. There's real justice for you!"

And he laughed again, mockingly and savagely.

"I'm caught in my own forest-land," retorted Ulrich. "When my men come to release us you will wish, perhaps, that you were in a better plight than caught poaching on a neighbour's land, shame on you."

Georg was silent for a moment; then he answered quietly:

"Are you sure that your men will find much to release? I have men, too, in the forest tonight, close behind me, and *they* will be here first and do the releasing. When they drag me out from under these damned branches it won't need much clumsiness on their part to roll this mass of trunk right over on the top of you. Your men will find you dead under a fallen beech tree. For form's sake I shall send my condolences to your family."

"It is a useful hint," said Ulrich fiercely. "My men had orders to follow in ten minutes' time, seven of which must have gone by already, and when they get me out— I will remember the hint. Only as you will have met your death poaching on my lands I don't think I can decently send any message of condolence to your family."

"Good," snarled Georg, "good. We fight this quarrel out to the death, you and I and our foresters, with no cursed interlopers to come between us. Death and damnation to you, Ulrich von Gradwitz."

"The same to you, Georg Znaeym, forest-thief, game-snatcher."

Both men spoke with the bitterness of possible defeat before them, for each knew that it might be long before his men would seek him out or find him; it was a bare matter of chance which party would arrive first on the scene.

Both had now given up the useless struggle to free themselves from the mass of wood that held them down; Ulrich limited his endeavours to an effort to bring his one partially free arm near enough to his outer coat-pocket to draw out his wine-flask. Even when he had accomplished that operation it was long before he could manage the unscrewing of the stopper or get any of the liquid down his throat. But what a Heaven-sent draught it seemed! It was an open winter, and little snow had fallen as yet, hence the captives suffered less from the cold than might have been the case at that season of the year; nevertheless, the wine was warming and reviving to the wounded man, and he looked across with something like a throb of pity to where his enemy lay, just keeping the groans of pain and weariness from crossing his lips.

"Could you reach this flask if I threw it over to you?" asked Ulrich suddenly; "there is good wine in it, and one may as well be as comfortable as one can. Let us drink, even if tonight one of us dies."

"No, I can scarcely see anything; there is so much blood caked round my eyes," said Georg, "and in any case I don't drink wine with an enemy."

Ulrich was silent for a few minutes, and lay listening to the weary screeching of the wind. An idea was slowly forming and growing in his brain, an idea that gained strength every time that he looked across at the man who was fighting so grimly against pain and exhaustion. In the pain and languor that Ulrich himself was feeling the old fierce hatred seemed to be dying down.

"Neighbour," he said presently, "do as you please if your men come first. It was a fair compact. But as for me, I've changed my mind. If my men are the first to come you shall be the first to be helped, as though you were my guest. We have quarrelled like devils all our lives over this stupid strip of forest, where the trees can't even stand upright in a breath of wind. Lying here tonight, thinking, I've come to think we've been rather fools; there are better things in life than getting the better of a boundary dispute. Neighbour, if you will help me to bury the old quarrel I—I will ask you to be my friend."

Georg Znaeym was silent for so long that Ulrich thought, perhaps, he had fainted with the pain of his injuries. Then he spoke slowly and in jerks.

"How the whole region would stare and gabble if we rode into the market-square together. No one living can remember seeing a Znaeym and a von Gradwitz talking to one another in friendship. And what peace there would be among the forester folk if we ended our feud tonight. And if we choose to make peace among our people there is none other to interfere, no interlopers from outside. . . . You would come and keep the Sylvester night beneath my roof, and I would come and feast on some high day at your castle. . . . I would never fire a shot on your land, save when you invited me as a guest; and you should come and shoot with me down in the marshes where the wildfowl are. In all the countryside there are none that could hinder if we willed to make peace. I never thought to have wanted to do other than hate you all my life, but I think I have changed my mind about things too, this last half-hour. And you offered me your wine-flask. . . . Ulrich von Gradwitz, I will be your friend."

For a space both men were silent, turning over in their minds the wonderful changes that this dramatic reconciliation would bring about. In the cold, gloomy forest, with the wind tearing in fitful gusts through the naked branches and whistling round the tree-trunks, they lay and waited for the help that would now bring release and succour to both parties. And each prayed a private prayer that his men might be the first to arrive, so that he might be the first to show honourable attention to the enemy that had become a friend.

Presently, as the wind dropped for a moment, Ulrich broke silence.

"Let's shout for help," he said; "in this lull our voices may carry a little way."

"They won't carry far through the trees and undergrowth," said Georg, "but we can try. Together, then."

The two raised their voices in a prolonged hunting call.

"Together again," said Ulrich a few minutes later, after listening in vain for an answering halloo.

"I heard something that time, I think," said Ulrich.

"I heard nothing but the pestilential wind," said Georg hoarsely.

There was silence again for some minutes, and then Ulrich gave a joyful cry.

"I can see figures coming through the wood. They are following in the way I came down the hillside."

Both men raised their voices in as loud a shout as they could muster.

"They hear us! They've stopped. Now they see us. They're running down the hill towards us," cried Ulrich.

"How many of them are there?" asked Georg.

"I can't see distinctly," said Ulrich; "nine or ten."

"Then they are yours," said Georg; "I had only seven out with me."

"They are making all the speed they can, brave lads," said Ulrich gladly.

"Are they your men?" asked Georg. "Are they your men?" he repeated impatiently as Ulrich did not answer.

"No," said Ulrich with a laugh, the idiotic chattering laugh of a man unstrung with hideous fear.

"Who are they?" asked Georg quickly, straining his eyes to see what the other would gladly not have seen.

"Wolves."

The Fly

KATHERINE MANSFIELD

How long can a man mourn for his dead son? As long as
he has eyes to weep, the Boss had always said. But only
six years later, he sat looking at his son's picture, and
the tears would not come. He felt strangely unmoved, and
he did not know why.

Katherine Mansfield's unique narrative gifts are beautifully embodied in "The Fly." Here we see her descriptive
and analytical powers swiftly probing the deep and tangled
impulses that animate the Boss. We see her employing
with great effect one of her favorite devices: centering the
story around a small, seemingly insignificant incident in
order to light up and give significant form and meaning
to the character's motives. Few writers have managed
the illuminating incident with Miss Mansfield's consummate skill. A disciple of Chekhov, she went far beyond
her master in her ability to create mood or atmosphere.

*KATHERINE MANSFIELD (1888–1923) was born
Kathleen Beauchamp in New Zealand, and she spent her
early years there. Much of her life was plagued by marital
difficulties and illness. Her first marriage ended in divorce,*

*and in 1918 she married the critic J. Middleton Murry.
Looking for a climate that would be favorable to her
fragile health, she traveled extensively on the continent.
She died of tuberculosis in Paris in 1923.*

*Belated critical recognition came to Miss Mansfield
with the publication of* Bliss and Other Stories *(1920).*
The Garden Party *(1922) and* The Dove's Nest *(1923)
followed in quick succession. The best of her stories have
been collected in* The Short Stories of Katherine Mansfield
(1937).

*Miss Mansfield was deeply influenced by the Russian
short story master, Anton Chekhov. Her work, in turn—
particularly her use of the "crucial moment" as a
literary device—has exercised a strong influence on modern short story writers.*

The Fly

"Y'are very snug in here," piped old Mr. Woodifield, and
he peered out of the great, green leather arm-chair by
his friend, the boss's desk, as a baby peers out of its pram.
His talk was over; it was time for him to be off. But he
did not want to go. Since he had retired, since his . . .
stroke, the wife and the girls kept him boxed up in the
house every day of the week except Tuesday. On Tuesday
he was dressed up and brushed and allowed to cut back
to the City for the day. Though what he did there the
wife and girls couldn't imagine. Made a nuisance of himself to his friends, they supposed. . . . Well, perhaps
so. All the same, we cling to our last pleasures as the
tree clings to its last leaves. So there sat old Woodifield,
smoking a cigar and staring almost greedily at the boss,
who rolled in his office chair, stout, rosy, five years older
than he, and still going strong, still at the helm. It did
one good to see him.

Wistfully, admiringly, the old voice added, "It's snug
in here, upon my word!"

"Yes, it's comfortable enough," agreed the boss, and he

flipped the *Financial Times* with a paper-knife. As a matter of fact he was proud of his room; he liked to have it admired, especially by old Woodifield. It gave him a feeling of deep, solid satisfaction to be planted there in the midst of it in full view of that frail old figure in the muffler.

"I've had it done up lately," he explained, as he had explained for the past—how many?—weeks. "New carpet," and he pointed to the bright red carpet with a pattern of large white rings. "New furniture," and he nodded towards the massive bookcase and the table with legs like twisted treacle. "Electric heating!" He waved almost exultantly towards the five transparent, pearly sausages glowing so softly in the tilted copper pan.

But he did not draw old Woodifield's attention to the photograph over the table of a grave-looking boy in uniform standing in one of those spectral photographers' parks with photographers' storm-clouds behind him. It was not new. It had been there for over six years.

"There was something I wanted to tell you," said old Woodifield, and his eyes grew dim remembering. "Now what was it? I had it in my mind when I started out this morning." His hands began to tremble, and patches of red showed above his beard.

Poor old chap, he's on his last pins, thought the boss. And, feeling kindly, he winked at the old man, and said jokingly, "I tell you what. I've got a little drop of something here that'll do you good before you go out into the cold again. It's beautiful stuff. It wouldn't hurt a child." He took a key off his watch-chain, unlocked a cupboard below his desk, and drew forth a dark, squat bottle. "That's the medicine," said he. "And the man from whom I got it told me on the strict Q. T. it came from the cellars at Windsor Castle."

Old Woodifield's mouth fell open at the sight. He couldn't have looked more surprised if the boss had produced a rabbit.

"It's whisky, ain't it?" he piped, feebly.

The boss turned the bottle and lovingly showed him the label. Whisky it was.

"D'you know," said he, peering up at the boss wonderingly, "they won't let me touch it at home." And he looked as though he was going to cry.

"Ah, that's where we know a bit more than the ladies," cried the boss, swooping across for two tumblers that stood on the table with the water-bottle, and pouring a generous finger into each. "Drink it down. It'll do you good. And don't put any water with it. It's sacrilege to tamper with stuff like this. Ah!" He tossed off his, pulled out his handkerchief, hastily wiped his moustaches, and cocked an eye at old Woodifield, who was rolling his in his chaps.

The old man swallowed, was silent a moment, and then said faintly, "It's nutty!"

But it warmed him; it crept into his chill old brain—he remembered.

"That was it," he said, heaving himself out of his chair. "I thought you'd like to know. The girls were in Belgium last week having a look at poor Reggie's grave, and they happened to come across your boy's. They are quite near each other, it seems."

Old Woodifield paused, but the boss made no reply. Only a quiver of his eyelids showed that he heard.

"The girls were delighted with the way the place is kept," piped the old voice. "Beautifully looked after. Couldn't be better if they were at home. You've not been across, have yer?"

"No, no!" For various reasons the boss had not been across.

"There's miles of it," quavered old Woodifield, "and it's all as neat as a garden. Flowers growing on all the graves. Nice broad paths." It was plain from his voice how much he liked a nice broad path.

The pause came again. Then the old man brightened wonderfully.

"D'you know what the hotel made the girls pay for a pot of jam?" he piped. "Ten francs! Robbery, I call it. It was a little pot, so Gertrude says, no bigger than a half-crown. And she hadn't taken more than a spoonful when they charged her ten francs. Gertrude brought the pot away with her to teach 'em a lesson. Quite right, too; it's trading on our feelings. They think because we're over there having a look around we're ready to pay anything. That's what it is." And he turned towards the door.

"Quite right, quite right!" cried the boss, though what was quite right he hadn't the least idea. He came around by his desk, followed the shuffling footsteps to the door, and saw the old fellow out. Woodifield was gone.

For a long moment the boss stayed, staring at nothing, while the grey-haired office messenger, watching him, dodged in and out of his cubbyhole like a dog that expects to be taken for a run. Then: "I'll see nobody for half an hour, Macey," said the boss. "Understand? Nobody at all."

"Very good, sir."

The door shut, the firm, heavy steps recrossed the bright carpet, the fat body plumped down in the spring chair, and leaning forward, the boss covered his face with his hands. He wanted, he intended, he had arranged to weep. . . .

It had been a terrible shock to him when old Woodifield sprang that remark upon him about the boy's grave. It was exactly as though the earth had opened and he had seen the boy lying there with Woodifield's girls staring down at him. For it was strange. Although over six years had passed away, the boss never thought of the boy except as lying unchanged, unblemished in his uniform; asleep for ever. "My son!" groaned the boss. But no tears came yet. In the past, in the first months and even years after the boy's death, he had only to say those words to be overcome by such grief that nothing short of a violent fit of weeping could relieve him. Time, he had declared then, he had told everybody, could make no difference. Other men perhaps might recover, might live their loss down, but not he. How was it possible? His boy was an only son. Ever since his birth the boss had worked at building up this business for him; it had no other meaning if it was not for the boy. Life itself had come to have no other meaning. How on earth could he have slaved, denied himself, kept going all those years without the promise for ever before him of the boy's stepping into his shoes and carrying on where he left off?

And that promise had been so near being fulfilled.

The boy had been in the office learning the ropes for a year before the war. Every morning they had started off together; they had come back by the same train. And what congratulations he had received as the boy's father! No wonder; he had taken to it marvellously. As to his popularity with the staff, every man jack of them down to old Macey couldn't make enough of the boy. And he wasn't in the least spoiled. No, he was just his bright, natural self, with the right word for everybody, with that boyish look and his habit of saying, "Simply splendid!"

But all that was over and done with as though it never had been. The day had come when Macey had handed him the telegram that brought the whole place crashing about his head. "Deeply regret to inform you . . ." And he had left the office a broken man, with his life in ruins.

Six years ago, six years . . . How quickly time passed! It might have happened yesterday. The boss took his hands from his face; he was puzzled. Something seemed to be wrong with him. He wasn't feeling as he wanted to feel. He decided to get up and have a look at the boy's photograph. But it wasn't a favorite photograph of his; the expression was unnatural. It was cold, even stern-looking. The boy had never looked like that.

At that moment the boss noticed that a fly had fallen into his broad inkpot, and was trying feebly but desperately to clamber out again. Help! help! said those struggling legs. But the sides of the inkpot were wet and slippery; it fell back again and began to swim. The boss took up a pen, picked the fly out of the ink, and shook it on to a piece of blotting-paper. For a fraction of a second it lay still on the dark patch that oozed round it. Then the front legs waved, took hold, and, pulling its small sodden body up, it began the immense task of cleaning the ink from its wings. Over and under, over and under, went a leg along a wing, as the stone goes over and under the scythe. Then there was a pause, while the fly, seeming to stand on the tips of its toes, tried to expand first one wing and then the other. It succeeded at last, and sitting down, it began, like a minute cat, to clean its face. Now one could imagine that the little front legs rubbed against each other lightly, joyfully. The horrible danger was over; it had escaped; it was ready for life again.

But just then the boss had an idea. He plunged his pen back into the ink, leaned his thick wrist on the blotting-paper, and as the fly tried its wings, down came a great, heavy blot. What would it make of that? What indeed! The little beggar seemed absolutely cowed, stunned, and afraid to move because of what would happen next. But then, as if painfully, it dragged itself forward. The front legs waved, caught hold, and, more slowly, the task began again.

He's a plucky little devil, thought the boss, and he felt a real admiration for the fly's courage. That was the way to tackle things; that was the right spirit. Never say die; it was only a question of . . . But the fly had again finished its laborious task, and the boss had just time to refill his pen, to shake fair and square on the new-cleaned body yet another drop. What about it this time? A painful moment of suspense followed. But, behold, the front legs were again waving; the boss felt a rush of relief. He leaned over the fly and said to it tenderly. "You artful little b . . ." And he actually had the brilliant notion of breathing on it to help the drying process. All the same, there was something timid and weak about its efforts now, and the boss decided that this time should be the last, as he dipped the pen into the inkpot.

It was. The last blot fell on the soaked blotting-paper, and the draggled fly lay in it and did not stir. The back legs were stuck to the body; the front legs were not to be seen.

"Come on," said the boss. "Look sharp!" And he stirred it with his pen—in vain. Nothing happened or was likely to happen. The fly was dead.

The boss lifted the corpse on the end of the paper-knife and flung it into the waste-paper basket, but such a grinding feeling of wretchedness seized him that he felt positively frightened. He started forward and pressed the bell for Macey.

"Bring me some fresh blotting-paper," he said, sternly, "and look sharp about it." And while the old dog padded away he fell to wondering what it was he had been thinking about before. What was it? It was . . . He took out his handkerchief and passed it inside his collar. For the life of him he could not remember.

The Secret Sharer

JOSEPH CONRAD

When the fugitive outcast Leggatt climbs aboard the ship, the captain confronts "the personality every man sets up for himself secretly." Essentially, this is what "The Secret Sharer" is about—each man's lonely struggle for identity, maturity, fulfillment. Throughout the story we are witness to the captain's painful coming-of-age, and in the end, we recognize him for what he has become—"a free man, a proud swimmer striking out for a new destiny."

"The Secret Sharer" is one of the really great modern short stories. These are some of the ingredients of its greatness: Conrad's deep and sensitive probing of man's moral nature and problems, his search for meaning and design in the universe, his magnificent and richly evocative descriptions of the sea, his almost magical ability to create and sustain moods of mystery and tension, his clear and coherent handling of symbols. Blending these elements together, Conrad's sure and meticulous hand builds into "The Secret Sharer" a strange, dramatic singularity.

JOSEPH CONRAD (1857–1924) was born Teodor Jozef Konrad Korzeniowski in what was then Russian Poland.

His father was a Polish poet and revolutionary. In 1873, after waiting two years for permission to go to sea, Conrad finally signed up as an ordinary seaman on a French merchant ship, and for the next twenty years, he followed the sea. Fifteen of these years he spent on English ships, most of the time as an officer; it was during this period that he began to study the English language. By the time he became an English subject in 1886, he had acquired a superb command of English.

Three years later, Conrad was hard at work at the fantastically difficult task of writing his first novel (Almayer's Folly) in his adopted tongue. In 1894 he retired to England to devote the rest of his life to his writing. Among his major works are The Nigger of the "Narcissus" *(1897),* Lord Jim *(1900),* Heart of Darkness *(1902), and* Nostromo *(1904). "Youth," "Typhoon," and "The Secret Sharer" are among Conrad's best short stories.*

Though the sea is ever-present in Conrad's stories and novels, they are more than mere sea and adventure stories. They are profound and moving studies of human character and experience tested under great hazards and pressures, brooding analyses and explorations of moral problems and dilemmas, penetrating probings into man's isolation. Conrad is universally regarded as one of the great writers of the twentieth century and one of the finest stylists in the English language.

The Secret Sharer

I

On my right hand there were lines of fishing stakes resembling a mysterious system of half-submerged bamboo fences, incomprehensible in its division of the domain of tropical fishes, and crazy of aspect as if abandoned forever by some nomad tribe of fishermen now gone to the other end of the ocean; for there was no sign of human habitation as far as the eye could reach. To the left a group of barren islets, suggesting ruins of stone walls, towers, and blockhouses, had its foundations set in a blue sea that itself looked solid, so still and stable did it lie below my feet; even the track of light from the westering sun shone smoothly, without that animated glitter which tells of an imperceptible ripple. And when I turned my head to take a parting glance at the tug which had just left us anchored outside the bar, I saw the straight line of the flat shore joined to the stable sea, edge to edge, with a perfect and unmarked closeness, in one leveled floor half brown, half blue under the enormous dome of the sky. Corresponding in their insignificance to the islets of the sea, two small clumps of trees, one on each side of the only fault in the impeccable joint, marked the mouth of the river Meinam we had just left on the first preparatory stage of our homeward journey; and, far back on the inland level, a larger and loftier mass, the grove surrounding the great Paknam pagoda, was the only thing on which the eye could rest from the vain task of exploring the monotonous sweep of the horizon. Here and there gleams as of a few scattered pieces of silver marked the windings of the great river; and on the nearest of them, just within the bar, the tug steaming right into the land became lost to my sight, hull and funnel and masts, as though the impassive earth had swallowed her up without an effort, without a tremor. My eye followed the light cloud of her smoke, now here, now there, above the plain, according to the devious curves of the stream, but always fainter and farther away, till I lost it at last behind the miter-shaped hill of the great pagoda. And then I was left alone with my ship, anchored at the head of the Gulf of Siam.

She floated at the starting point of a long journey, very still in an immense stillness, the shadows of her spars flung far to the eastward by the setting sun. At that moment I was alone on her decks. There was not a sound in her—and around us nothing moved, nothing lived, not a canoe on the water, not a bird in the air, not a cloud in the sky. In this breathless pause at the threshold of a long passage we seemed to be measuring our fitness for a long and arduous enterprise, the appointed task of both our existences to be carried out, far from all human eyes, with only sky and sea for spectators and for judges.

There must have been some glare in the air to interfere with one's sight, because it was only just before the sun left us that my roaming eyes made out beyond the highest ridges of the principal islet of the group something which did away with the solemnity of perfect solitude. The tide of darkness flowed on swiftly; and with tropical suddenness a swarm of stars came out above the shadowy earth, while I lingered yet, my hand resting lightly on my ship's rail as if on the shoulder of a trusted friend. But, with all that multitude of celestial bodies staring down at one, the comfort of quiet communion with her was gone for good. And there were also disturbing sounds by this time —voices, footsteps forward; the steward flitted along the main-deck, a busily ministering spirit; a hand bell tinkled urgently under the poop deck. . . .

I found my two officers waiting for me near the supper table, in the lighted cuddy. We sat down at once, and as I helped the chief mate, I said:

"Are you aware that there is a ship anchored inside the islands? I saw her mastheads above the ridge as the sun went down."

He raised sharply his simple face, overcharged by a terrible growth of whisker, and emitted his usual ejaculations: "Bless my soul, sir! You don't say so!"

My second mate was a round-cheeked, silent young man, grave beyond his years, I thought; but as our eyes happened to meet I detected a slight quiver on his lips. I looked down at once. It was not my part to encourage sneering on board my ship. It must be said, too, that I knew very little of my officers. In consequence of certain events of no particular significance, except to myself, I had been appointed to the command only a fortnight before. Neither did I know much of the hands forward. All these people had been together for eighteen months or so, and my position was that of the only stranger on board. I mention this because it has some bearing on what is to follow. But what I felt most was my being a stranger to the ship; and if all the truth must be told, I was somewhat of a stranger to myself. The youngest man on board (barring the second mate), and untried as yet by a position of the fullest responsibility, I was willing to take the adequacy of the others for granted. They had simply to be equal to their tasks; but I wondered how far I should turn out faithful to that ideal conception of one's own personality every man sets up for himself secretly.

Meantime the chief mate, with an almost visible effect of collaboration on the part of his round eyes and frightful whiskers, was trying to evolve a theory of the anchored ship. His dominant trait was to take all things into earnest consideration. He was of a painstaking turn of mind. As he used to say, he "liked to account to himself" for practically everything that came in his way, down to a miserable scorpion he had found in his cabin a week before. The why and the wherefore of that scorpion —how it got on board and came to select his room rather than the pantry (which was a dark place and more what a scorpion would be partial to), and how on earth it managed to drown itself in the inkwell of his writing desk—had exercised him infinitely. The ship within the islands was much more easily accounted for; and just as we were about to rise from table he made his pronouncement. She was, he doubted not, a ship from home lately arrived. Probably she drew too much water to cross the bar except at the top of spring tides. Therefore she went into that natural harbor to wait for a few days in preference to remaining in an open roadstead.

"That's so," confirmed the second mate, suddenly, in his slightly hoarse voice. "She draws over twenty feet. She's the Liverpool ship *Sephora* with a cargo of coal. Hundred and twenty-three days from Cardiff."

We looked at him in surprise.

"The tugboat skipper told me when he came on board for your letters, sir," explained the young man. "He expects to take her up the river the day after tomorrow."

After thus overwhelming us with the extent of his information he slipped out of the cabin. The mate observed regretfully that he "could not account for that young fellow's whims." What prevented him telling us all about it at once, he wanted to know.

I detained him as he was making a move. For the last

two days the crew had had plenty of hard work, and the night before they had very little sleep. I felt painfully that I—a stranger—was doing something unusual when I directed him to let all hands turn in without setting an anchor watch. I proposed to keep on deck myself till one o'clock or thereabouts. I would get the second mate to relieve me at that hour.

"He will turn out the cook and the steward at four," I concluded, "and then give you a call. Of course at the slightest sign of any sort of wind we'll have the hands up and make a start at once."

He concealed his astonishment. "Very well, sir." Outside the cuddy he put his head in the second mate's door to inform him of my unheard-of caprice to take a five hours' anchor watch on myself. I heard the other raise his voice incredulously—"What? The Captain himself?" Then a few more murmurs, a door closed, then another. A few moments later I went on deck.

My strangeness, which had made me sleepless, had prompted that unconventional arrangement, as if I had expected in those solitary hours of the night to get on terms with the ship of which I knew nothing, manned by men of whom I knew very little more. Fast alongside a wharf, littered like any ship in port with a tangle of unrelated things, invaded by unrelated shore people, I had hardly seen her yet properly. Now, as she lay cleared for sea, the stretch of her main-deck seemed to me very fine under the stars. Very fine, very roomy for her size, and very inviting. I descended the poop and paced the waist, my mind picturing to myself the coming passage through the Malay Archipelago, down the Indian Ocean, and up the Atlantic. All its phases were familiar enough to me, every characteristic, all the alternatives which were likely to face me on the high seas—everything! . . . except the novel responsibility of command. But I took heart from the reasonable thought that the ship was like other ships, the men like other men, and that the sea was not likely to keep any special surprises expressly for my discomfiture.

Arrived at that comforting conclusion, I bethought myself of a cigar and went below to get it. All was still down there. Everybody at the after end of the ship was sleeping profoundly. I came out again on the quarterdeck, agreeably at ease in my sleeping suit on that warm breathless night, barefooted, a glowing cigar in my teeth, and, going forward, I was met by the profound silence of the fore end of the ship. Only as I passed the door of the forecastle I heard a deep, quiet, trustful sigh of some sleeper inside. And suddenly I rejoiced in the great security of the sea as compared with the unrest of the land, in my choice of that untempted life presenting no disquieting problems, invested with an elementary moral beauty by the absolute straightforwardness of its appeal and by the singleness of its purpose.

The riding light in the forerigging burned with a clear, untroubled, as if symbolic, flame, confident and bright in the mysterious shades of the night. Passing on my way aft along the other side of the ship, I observed that the rope side ladder, put over, no doubt, for the master of the tug when he came to fetch away our letters, had not been hauled in as it should have been. I became annoyed at this, for exactitude in some small matters is the very soul of discipline. Then I reflected that I had myself peremptorily dismissed my officers from duty, and by my own act had prevented the anchor watch being formally set and things properly attended to. I asked myself whether it was wise ever to interfere with the established routine of duties even from the kindest of motives. My action might have made me appear eccentric. Goodness only knew how that absurdly whiskered mate would "account" for my conduct, and what the whole ship thought of that informality of their new captain. I was vexed with myself.

Not from compunction certainly, but, as it were mechanically, I proceeded to get the ladder in myself. Now a side ladder of that sort is a light affair and comes in easily, yet my vigorous tug, which should have brought it flying on board, merely recoiled upon my body in a totally unexpected jerk. What the devil! . . . I was so astounded by the immovableness of that ladder that I remained stockstill, trying to account for it to myself like that imbecile mate of mine. In the end, of course, I put my head over the rail.

The side of the ship made an opaque belt of shadow

on the darkling glassy shimmer of the sea. But I saw at once something elongated and pale floating very close to the ladder. Before I could form a guess a faint flash of phosphorescent light, which seemed to issue suddenly from the naked body of a man, flickered in the sleeping water with the elusive, silent play of summer lightning in a night sky. With a gasp I saw revealed to my stare a pair of feet, the long legs, a broad livid back immersed right up to the neck in a greenish cadaverous glow. One hand, awash, clutched the bottom rung of the ladder. He was complete but for the head. A headless corpse! The cigar dropped out of my gaping mouth with a tiny plop and a short hiss quite audible in the absolute stillness of all things under heaven. At that I suppose he raised up his face, a dimly pale oval in the shadow of the ship's side. But even then I could only barely make out down there the shape of his black-haired head. However, it was enough for the horrid, frost-bound sensation which had gripped me about the chest to pass off. The moment of vain exclamations was past, too. I only climbed on the spare spar and leaned over the rail as far as I could, to bring my eyes nearer to that mystery floating alongside.

As he hung by the ladder, like a resting swimmer, the sea lightning played about his limbs at every stir; and he appeared in it ghastly, silvery, fishlike. He remained as mute as a fish, too. He made no motion to get out of the water, either. It was inconceivable that he should not attempt to come on board, and strangely troubling to suspect that perhaps he did not want to. And my first words were prompted by just that troubled incertitude.

"What's the matter?" I asked in my ordinary tone, speaking down to the face upturned exactly under mine.

"Cramp," it answered, no louder. Then slightly anxious, "I say, no need to call anyone."

"I was not going to," I said.

"Are you alone on deck?"

"Yes."

I had somehow the impression that he was on the point of letting go the ladder to swim away beyond my ken— mysterious as he came. But, for the moment, this being appearing as if he had risen from the bottom of the sea (it was certainly the nearest land to the ship) wanted only to know the time. I told him. And he, down there, tentatively:

"I suppose your captain's turned in?"

"I am sure he isn't," I said.

He seemed to struggle with himself, for I heard something like the low, bitter murmur of doubt. "What's the good?" His next words came out with a hesitating effort.

"Look here, my man. Could you call him out quietly?"

I thought the time had come to declare myself.

"*I* am the captain."

I heard a "By Jove!" whispered at the level of the water. The phosphorescence flashed in the swirl of the water all about his limbs, his other hand seized the ladder.

"My name's Leggatt."

The voice was calm and resolute. A good voice. The self-possession of that man had somehow induced a corresponding state in myself. It was very quietly that I remarked:

"You must be a good swimmer."

"Yes. I've been in the water practically since nine o'clock. The question for me now is whether I am to let go this ladder and go on swimming till I sink from exhaustion, or—to come on board here."

I felt this was no mere formula of desperate speech, but a real alternative in the view of a strong soul. I should have gathered from this that he was young; indeed, it is only the young who are ever confronted by such clear issues. But at the time it was pure intuition on my part. A mysterious communication was established already between us two—in the face of that silent, darkened tropical sea. I was young, too; young enough to make no comment. The man in the water began suddenly to climb up the ladder, and I hastened away from the rail to fetch some clothes.

Before entering the cabin I stood still, listening in the lobby at the foot of the stairs. A faint snore came through the closed door of the chief mate's room. The second mate's door was on the hook, but the darkness in there was absolutely soundless. He, too, was young and could sleep like a stone. Remained the steward, but he was not likely to wake up before he was called. I got a sleep-

ing suit out of my room and, coming back on deck, saw
the naked man from the sea sitting on the main hatch,
glimmering white in the darkness, his elbows on his knees
and his head in his hands. In a moment he had concealed
his damp body in a sleeping suit of the same gray-stripe
pattern as the one I was wearing and followed me like
my double on the poop. Together we moved right aft,
barefooted, silent.

"What is it?" I asked in a deadened voice, taking the
lighted lamp out of the binnacle, and raising it to his
face.

"An ugly business."

He had rather regular features; a good mouth; light
eyes under somewhat heavy, dark eyebrows; a smooth,
square forehead; no growth on his cheeks; a small, brown
mustache, and a well-shaped, round chin. His expression
was concentrated, meditative, under the inspecting light of
the lamp I held up to his face; such as a man thinking
hard in solitude might wear. My sleeping suit was just
right for his size. A well-knit young fellow of twenty-
five at most. He caught his lower lip with the edge of white,
even teeth.

"Yes," I said, replacing the lamp in the binnacle. The
warm, heavy tropical night closed upon his head again.

"There's a ship over there," he murmured.

"Yes, I know. The *Sephora*. Did you know of us?"

"Hadn't the slightest idea. I am the mate of her——"
He paused and corrected himself. "I should say I *was*."

"Aha! Something wrong?"

"Yes. Very wrong indeed. I've killed a man."

"What do you mean? Just now?"

"No, on the passage. Weeks ago. Thirty-nine south.
When I say a man——"

"Fit of temper," I suggested, confidently.

The shadowy, dark head, like mine, seemed to nod im-
perceptibly above the ghostly gray of my sleeping suit.
It was, in the night, as though I had been faced by my
own reflection in the depths of a somber and immense
mirror.

"A pretty thing to have to own up to for a Conway
boy," murmured my double, distinctly.

"You're a Conway boy?"

"I am," he said, as if startled. Then, slowly . . . "Perhaps you too——"

It was so; but being a couple of years older I had left before he joined. After a quick interchange of dates a silence fell; and I thought suddenly of my absurd mate with his terrific whiskers and the "Bless my soul—you don't say so" type of intellect. My double gave me an inkling of his thoughts by saying: "My father's a parson in Norfolk. Do you see me before a judge and jury on that charge? For myself I can't see the necessity. There are fellows that an angel from heaven—— And I am not that. He was one of those creatures that are just simmering all the time with a silly sort of wickedness. Miserable devils that have no business to live at all. He wouldn't do his duty and wouldn't let anybody else do theirs. But what's the good of talking! You know well enough the sort of ill-conditioned snarling cur——"

He appealed to me as if our experiences had been as identical as our clothes. And I knew well enough the pestiferous danger of such a character where there are no means of legal repression. And I knew well enough also that my double there was no homicidal ruffian. I did not think of asking him for details, and he told me the story roughly in brusque, disconnected sentences. I needed no more. I saw it all going on as though I were myself inside that other sleeping suit.

"It happened while we were setting a reefed foresail, at dusk. Reefed foresail! You understand the sort of weather. The only sail we had left to keep the ship running; so you may guess what it had been like for days. Anxious sort of job, that. He gave me some of his cursed insolence at the sheet. I tell you I was overdone with this terrific weather that seemed to have no end to it. Terrific, I tell you—and a deep ship. I believe the fellow himself was half crazed with funk. It was no time for gentlemanly reproof, so I turned round and felled him like an ox. He up and at me. We closed just as an awful sea made for the ship. All hands saw it coming and took to the rigging, but I had him by the throat, and went on shaking him like a rat, the men above us yelling, 'Look out! look out!' Then a crash as if the sky had fallen on my head. They say that for over ten minutes hardly anything was to be seen of the ship—just the three masts and a bit of the forecastle head and of the poop all awash driving along in a smother of foam. It was a miracle that they found us, jammed together behind the forebitts. It's clear that I meant business, because I was holding him by the throat still when they picked us up. He was black in the face. It was too much for them. It seems they rushed us aft together, gripped as we were, screaming 'Murder!' like a lot of lunatics, and broke into the cuddy. And the ship running for her life, touch and go all the time, any minute her last in a sea fit to turn your hair gray only a-looking at it. I understand that the skipper, too, started raving like the rest of them. The man had been deprived of sleep for more than a week, and to have this sprung on him at the height of a furious gale nearly drove him out of his mind. I wonder they didn't fling me overboard after getting the carcass of their precious shipmate out of my fingers. They had rather a job to separate us, I've been told. A sufficiently fierce story to make an old judge and a respectable jury sit up a bit. The first thing I heard when I came to myself was the maddening howling of that endless gale, and on that the voice of the old man. He was hanging on to my bunk, staring into my face out of his sou'wester.

"'Mr. Leggatt, you have killed a man. You can act no longer as chief mate of this ship.'"

His care to subdue his voice made it sound monotonous. He rested a hand on the end of the skylight to steady himself with, and all that time did not stir a limb, so far as I could see. "Nice little tale for a quiet tea party," he concluded in the same tone.

One of my hands, too, rested on the end of the skylight; neither did I stir a limb, so far as I knew. We stood less than a foot from each other. It occurred to me that if old "Bless my soul—you don't say so" were to put his head up the companion and catch sight of us, he would think he was seeing double, or imagine himself come upon a scene of weird witchcraft; the strange captain having a quiet confabulation by the wheel with his own gray ghost. I became very much concerned to prevent anything of the sort. I heard the other's soothing undertone.

"My father's a parson in Norfolk," it said. Evidently

he had forgotten he had told me this important fact before. Truly a nice little tale.

"You had better slip down into my stateroom now," I said, moving off stealthily. My double followed my movements; our bare feet made no sound; I let him in, closed the door with care, and, after giving a call to the second mate, returned on deck for my relief.

"Not much sign of any wind yet," I remarked when he approached.

"No, sir. Not much," he assented, sleepily, in his hoarse voice, with just enough deference, no more, and barely suppressing a yawn.

"Well, that's all you have to look out for. You have got your orders."

"Yes, sir."

I paced a turn or two on the poop and saw him take up his position face forward with his elbow in the ratlines of the mizzen rigging before I went below. The mate's faint snoring was still going on peacefully. The cuddy lamp was burning over the table on which stood a vase with flowers, a polite attention from the ship's provision merchant—the last flowers we should see for the next three months at the very least. Two bunches of bananas hung from the beam symmetrically, one on each side of the rudder casing. Everything was as before in the ship— except that two of her captain's sleeping suits were simultaneously in use, one motionless in the cuddy, the other keeping very still in the captain's stateroom.

It must be explained here that my cabin had the form of the capital letter L, the door being within the angle and opening into the short part of the letter. A couch was to the left, the bed place to the right; my writing desk and the chronometers' table faced the door. But anyone opening it, unless he stepped right inside, had no view of what I call the long (or vertical) part of the letter. It contained some lockers surmounted by a bookcase; and a few clothes, a thick jacket or two, caps, oilskin coat, and such like, hung on hooks. There was at the bottom of that part a door opening into my bathroom, which could be entered also directly from the saloon. But that way was never used.

The mysterious arrival had discovered the advantage

of this particular shape. Entering my room, lighted strongly by a big bulkhead lamp swung on gimbals above my
writing desk, I did not see him anywhere till he stepped
out quietly from behind the coats hung in the recessed
part.

"I heard somebody moving about, and went in there
at once," he whispered.

I, too, spoke under my breath.

"Nobody is likely to come in here without knocking
and getting permission."

He nodded. His face was thin and the sunburn faded,
as though he had been ill. And no wonder. He had been,
I heard presently, kept under arrest in his cabin for nearly
seven weeks. But there was nothing sickly in his eyes or
in his expression. He was not a bit like me, really; yet, as
we stood leaning over my bed place, whispering side by
side, with our dark heads together and our backs to the
door, anybody bold enough to open it stealthily would
have been treated to the uncanny sight of a double captain
busy talking in whispers with his other self.

"But all this doesn't tell me how you came to hang on
to our side ladder," I inquired, in the hardly audible murmurs we used, after he had told me something more of
the proceedings on board the *Sephora* once the bad
weather was over.

"When we sighted Java Head I had had time to think
all those matters out several times over. I had six weeks
of doing nothing else, and with only an hour or so every
evening for a tramp on the quarter-deck."

He whispered, his arms folded on the side of my bed
place, staring through the open port. And I could imagine
perfectly the manner of this thinking out—a stubborn if
not a steadfast operation; something of which I should
have been perfectly incapable.

"I reckoned it would be dark before we closed with
the land," he continued, so low that I had to strain my
hearing near as we were to each other, shoulder touching shoulder almost. "So I asked to speak to the old
man. He always seemed very sick when he came to see
me—as if he could not look me in the face. You know,
that foresail saved the ship. She was too deep to have
run long under bare poles. And it was I that managed

to set it for him. Anyway, he came. When I had him in my cabin—he stood by the door looking at me as if I had the halter round my neck already—I asked him right away to leave my cabin door unlocked at night while the ship was going through Sunda Straits. There would be the Java coast within two or three miles, off Angier Point. I wanted nothing more. I've had a prize for swimming my second year in the Conway."

"I can believe it," I breathed out.

"God only knows why they locked me in every night. To see some of their faces you'd have thought they were afraid I'd go about at night strangling people. Am I a murdering brute? Do I look it? By Jove! If I had been he wouldn't have trusted himself like that into my room. You'll say I might have chucked him aside and bolted out, there and then—it was dark already. Well, no. And for the same reason I wouldn't think of trying to smash the door. There would have been a rush to stop me at the noise, and I did not mean to get into a confounded scrimmage. Somebody else might have got killed—for I would not have broken out only to get chucked back, and I did not want any more of that work. He refused, looking more sick than ever. He was afraid of the men, and also of that old second mate of his who had been sailing with him for years—a gray-headed old humbug; and his steward, too, had been with him devil knows how long—seventeen years or more—a dogmatic sort of loafer who hated me like poison, just because I was the chief mate. No chief mate ever made more than one voyage in the *Sephora,* you know. Those two old chaps ran the ship. Devil only knows what the skipper wasn't afraid of (all his nerve went to pieces altogether in that hellish spell of bad weather we had)—of what the law would do to him—of his wife, perhaps. Oh, yes! she's on board. Though I don't think she would have meddled. She would have been only too glad to have me out of the ship in any way. The 'brand of Cain' business, don't you see. That's all right. I was ready enough to go off wandering on the face of the earth—and that was price enough to pay for an Abel of that sort. Anyhow, he wouldn't listen to me. 'This thing must take its course. I represent the law here.' He was shaking like a leaf. 'So you won't?' 'No!' 'Then I hope you will be able to sleep on that,' I said, and turned my back on him. 'I wonder that *you* can,' cries he, and locks the door.

"Well after that, I couldn't. Not very well. That was three weeks ago. We have had a slow passage through the Java Sea; drifted about Carimata for ten days. When we anchored here they thought, I suppose, it was all right. The nearest land (and that's five miles) is the ship's destination; the consul would soon set about catching me; and there would have been no object in bolting to these islets there. I don't suppose there's a drop of water on them. I don't know how it was, but tonight that steward, after bringing me my supper, went out to let me eat it, and left the door unlocked. And I ate it—all there was, too. After I had finished I strolled out on the quarterdeck. I don't know that I meant to do anything. A breath of fresh air was all I wanted, I believe. Then a sudden temptation came over me. I kicked off my slippers and was in the water before I had made up my mind fairly. Somebody heard the splash and they raised an awful hullabaloo. 'He's gone! Lower the boats! He committed suicide! No, he's swimming.' Certainly I was swimming. It's not so easy for a swimmer like me to commit suicide by drowning. I landed on the nearest islet before the boat left the ship's side. I heard them pulling about in the dark, hailing, and so on, but after a bit they gave up. Everything quieted down and the anchorage became as still as death. I sat down on a stone and began to think. I felt certain they would start searching for me at daylight. There was no place to hide on those stony things—and if there had been, what would have been the good? But now I was clear of that ship, I was not going back. So after a while I took off all my clothes, tied them up in a bundle with a stone inside, and dropped them in the deep water on the outer side of that islet. That was suicide enough for me. Let them think what they liked, but I didn't mean to drown myself. I meant to swim till I sank—but that's not the same thing. I struck out for another of these little islands, and it was from that one that I first saw your riding light. Something to swim for. I went on easily, and on the way I came upon a flat rock a foot or two above water. In the daytime, I dare say, you might make it out with a glass from your poop. I scrambled up on it and rested myself for a bit. Then I made another start. That last spell must have been over a mile."

His whisper was getting fainter and fainter, and all the time he stared straight out through the porthole, in which there was not even a star to be seen. I had not interrupted him. There was something that made comment impossible in his narrative, or perhaps in himself; a sort of feeling, a quality, which I can't find a name for. And when he ceased, all I found was a futile whisper: "So you swam for our light?"

"Yes—straight for it. It was something to swim for. I couldn't see any stars low down because the coast was in the way, and I couldn't see the land, either. The water was like glass. One might have been swimming in a confounded thousand-feet-deep cistern with no place for scrambling out anywhere; but what I didn't like was the notion of swimming round and round like a crazed bullock before I gave out; and as I didn't mean to go back . . . No. Do you see me being hauled back, stark naked, off one of these little islands by the scruff of the neck and fighting like a wild beast? Somebody would have got killed for certain, and I did not want any of that. So I went on. Then your ladder——"

"Why didn't you hail the ship?" I asked, a little louder.

He touched my shoulder lightly. Lazy footsteps came right over our heads and stopped. The second mate had crossed from the other side of the poop and might have been hanging over the rail for all we knew.

"He couldn't hear us talking—could he?" My double breathed into my very ear, anxiously.

His anxiety was an answer, a sufficient answer, to the question I had put to him. An answer containing all the difficulty of that situation. I closed the porthole quietly, to make sure. A louder word might have been overheard.

"Who's that?" he whispered then.

"My second mate. But I don't know much more of the fellow than you do."

And I told him a little about myself. I had been appointed to take charge while I least expected anything of the sort, not quite a fortnight ago. I didn't know either the ship or the people. Hadn't had the time in port to look about me or size anybody up. And as to the crew, all they knew was that I was appointed to take the ship home. For the rest, I was almost as much of a stranger on board as himself, I said. And at the moment I felt it most acutely. I felt that it would take very little to make me a suspect person in the eyes of the ship's company.

He had turned about meantime; and we, the two strangers in the ship, faced each other in identical attitudes.

"Your ladder——" he murmured, after a silence. "Who'd have thought of finding a ladder hanging over at night in a ship anchored out here! I felt just then a very unpleasant faintness. After the life I've been leading for nine weeks, anybody would have got out of condition. I wasn't capable of swimming round as far as your rudder chains. And, lo and behold! there was a ladder to get hold of. After I gripped it I said to myself, 'What's the good?' When I saw a man's head looking over I thought I would swim away presently and leave him shouting—in whatever language it was. I didn't mind being looked at. I—I liked it. And then you speaking to me so quietly—as if you had expected me—made me hold on a little longer. It had been a confounded lonely time—I don't mean while swimming. I was glad to talk a little to somebody that didn't belong to the *Sephora*. As to asking for the captain, that was a mere impulse. It could have been no use, with all the ship knowing about me and the other people pretty certain to be round here in the morning. I don't know—I wanted to be seen, to talk with somebody, before I went on. I don't know what I would have said. ... 'Fine night, isn't it?' or something of the sort."

"Do you think they will be round here presently?" I asked with some incredulity.

"Quite likely," he said, faintly.

He looked extremely haggard all of a sudden. His head rolled on his shoulders.

"H'm. We shall see then. Meantime get into that bed," I whispered. "Want help? There."

It was a rather high bed place with a set of drawers underneath. This amazing swimmer really needed the lift I gave him by seizing his leg. He tumbled in, rolled over on his back, and flung one arm across his eyes. And then, with his face nearly hidden, he must have looked exactly as I used to look in that bed. I gazed upon my other self for a while before drawing across carefully the two green serge curtains which ran on a brass rod. I thought for a moment of pinning them together for greater safety, but I sat down on the couch, and once there I felt unwilling to rise and hunt for a pin. I would do it in a moment. I was extremely tired, in a peculiarly intimate way, by the strain of stealthiness, by the effort of whispering and the general secrecy of this excitement. It was three o'clock by now and I had been on my feet since nine, but I was not sleepy; I could not have gone to sleep. I sat there, fagged out, looking at the curtains, trying to clear my mind of the confused sensation of being in two places at once, and greatly bothered by an exasperating knocking in my head. It was a relief to discover suddenly that it was not in my head at all, but on the outside of the door. Before I could collect myself the words "Come in" were out of my mouth, and the steward entered with a tray, bringing in my morning coffee. I had slept, after all, and I was so frightened that I shouted, "This way! I am here, steward," as though he had been miles away. He put down the tray on the table next the couch and only then said, very quietly, "I can see you are here, sir." I felt him give me a keen look, but I dared not meet his eyes just then. He must have wondered why I had drawn the curtains of my bed before going to sleep on the couch. He went out, hooking the door open as usual.

I heard the crew washing decks above me. I knew I would have been told at once if there had been any wind. Calm, I thought, and I was doubly vexed. Indeed, I felt dual more than ever. The steward reappeared suddenly in the doorway. I jumped up from the couch so quickly that he gave a start.

"What do you want here?"

"Close your port, sir—they are washing decks."

"It is closed," I said, reddening.

"Very well, sir." But he did not move from the doorway and returned my stare in an extraordinary, equivocal manner for a time. Then his eyes wavered, all his expression changed, and in a voice unusually gentle, almost coaxingly:

"May I come in to take the empty cup away, sir?"

"Of course!" I turned my back on him while he popped in and out. Then I unhooked and closed the door and even pushed the bolt. This sort of thing could not go on very long. The cabin was as hot as an oven, too. I took a peep at my double, and discovered that he had not moved, his arm was still over his eyes; but his chest heaved; his hair was wet; his chin glistened with perspiration. I reached over him and opened the port.

"I must show myself on deck," I reflected.

Of course, theoretically, I could do what I liked, with no one to say nay to me within the whole circle of the horizon; but to lock my cabin door and take the key away I did not dare. Directly I put my head out of the companion I saw the group of my two officers, the second mate barefooted, the chief mate in long India-rubber boots, near the break of the poop, and the steward half-way down the poop ladder talking to them eagerly. He happened to catch sight of me and dived, the second ran down on the main-deck shouting some order or other, and the chief mate came to meet me, touching his cap.

There was a sort of curiosity in his eye that I did not like. I don't know whether the steward had told them that I was "queer" only, or downright drunk, but I know the man meant to have a good look at me. I watched him coming with a smile which, as he got into point-blank range, took effect and froze his very whiskers. I did not give him time to open his lips.

"Square the yards by lifts and braces before the hands go to breakfast."

It was the first particular order I had given on board that ship; and I stayed on deck to see it executed, too. I had felt the need of asserting myself without loss of time. That sneering young cub got taken down a peg or two on that occasion, and I also seized the opportunity of having a good look at the face of every foremast man as they filed past me to go to the after braces. At breakfast time, eating nothing myself, I presided with such frigid dignity that the two mates were only too glad to escape from the cabin as soon as decency permitted; and all the time the dual working of my mind distracted me almost to the point of insanity. I was constantly watching myself, my secret self, as dependent on my actions as my own personality, sleeping in that bed, behind that door which faced me as I sat at the head of the table. It was very much like being mad, only it was worse because one was aware of it.

I had to shake him for a solid minute, but when at last he opened his eyes it was in the full possession of his senses, with an inquiring look.

"All's well so far," I whispered. "Now you must vanish into the bathroom."

He did so, as noiseless as a ghost, and then I rang for the steward, and facing him boldly, directed him to tidy up my stateroom while I was having my bath—"and be quick about it." As my tone admitted of no excuses, he said, "Yes, sir," and ran off to fetch his dustpan and brushes. I took a bath and did most of my dressing, splashing, and whistling softly for the steward's edification, while the secret sharer of my life stood drawn up bolt upright in that little space, his face looking very sunken in daylight, his eyelids lowered under the stern, dark line of his eyebrows drawn together by a slight frown.

When I left him there to go back to my room the steward was finishing dusting. I sent for the mate and engaged him in some insignificant conversation. It was, as it were, trifling with the terrific character of his whiskers; but my object was to give him an opportunity for a good look at my cabin. And then I could at last shut, with a clear conscience, the door of my stateroom and get my double back into the recessed part. There was nothing else for it. He had to sit still on a small folding stool, half smothered by the heavy coats hanging there. We listened to the steward going into the bathroom out of the saloon, filling the water bottles there, scrubbing the bath, setting things to rights, whisk, bang, clatter—out again into the saloon—turn the key—click. Such was my scheme for keeping my second self invisible. Nothing better could be contrived under the circumstances. And there we sat; I at my writing desk ready to appear busy with some papers, he behind me out of sight of the door. It would not have been prudent to talk in daytime; and I could not have stood the excitement of that queer sense of whispering to myself. Now and then, glancing over my shoulder, I saw him far back there, sitting rigidly on the low stool, his bare feet close together, his arms folded, his head hanging on his breast—and perfectly still. Anybody would have taken him for me.

I was fascinated by it myself. Every moment I had to glance over my shoulder. I was looking at him when a voice outside the door said:

"Beg pardon, sir."

"Well!" . . . I kept my eyes on him, and so when the voice outside the door announced, "There's a ship's boat coming our way, sir," I saw him give a start—the first movement he had made for hours. But he did not raise his bowed head.

"All right. Get the ladder over."

I hesitated. Should I whisper something to him? But what? His immobility seemed to have been never disturbed. What could I tell him he did not know already? . . . Finally I went on deck.

II

The skipper of the *Sephora* had a thin red whisker all round his face, and the sort of complexion that goes with hair of that color; also the particular, rather smeary shade of blue in the eyes. He was not exactly a showy figure; his shoulders were high, his stature but middling—one leg slightly more bandy than the other. He shook hands, looking vaguely around. A spiritless tenacity was his main characteristic, I judged. I behaved with a politeness which seemed to disconcert him. Perhaps he was shy. He mumbled to me as if he were ashamed of what he was saying; gave his name (it was something like Archbold—but at this distance of years I hardly am sure), his ship's name, and a few other particulars of that sort, in the manner of a criminal making a reluctant and doleful confession. He had had terrible weather on the passage out—terrible—terrible—wife aboard, too.

By this time we were seated in the cabin and the steward brought in a tray with a bottle and glasses. "Thanks! No." Never took liquor. Would have some water, though. He drank two tumblerfuls. Terrible thirsty work. Ever since daylight had been exploring the islands round his ship.

"What was that for—fun?" I asked, with an appearance of polite interest.

"No!" He sighed. "Painful duty."

As he persisted in his mumbling and I wanted my double to hear every word, I hit upon the notion of informing him that I regretted to say I was hard of hearing.

"Such a young man, too!" he nodded, keeping his smeary blue, unintelligent eyes fastened upon me. "What was the cause of it—some disease?" he inquired, without the least sympathy and as if he thought that, if so, I'd got no more than I deserved.

"Yes; disease," I admitted in a cheerful tone which seemed to shock him. But my point was gained, because he had to raise his voice to give me his tale. It is not worth while to record that version. It was just over two months since all this had happened, and he had thought so much about it that he seemed completely muddled as to its bearings, but still immensely impressed.

"What would you think of such a thing happening on board your own ship? I've had the *Sephora* for these fifteen years. I am a well-known shipmaster."

He was densely distressed—and perhaps I should have sympathized with him if I had been able to detach my mental vision from the unsuspected sharer of my cabin as though he were my second self. There he was on the other side of the bulkhead, four or five feet from us, no more, as we sat in the saloon. I looked politely at Captain Archbold (if that was his name), but it was the other I saw, in a gray sleeping suit, seated on a low stool, his bare feet close together, his arms folded, and every word said between us falling into the ears of his dark head bowed on his chest.

"I have been at sea now, man and boy, for seven-and-thirty years, and I've never heard of such a thing happening in an English ship. And that it should be my ship. Wife on board, too."

I was hardly listening to him.

"Don't you think," I said, "that the heavy sea which, you told me, came aboard just then might have killed the man? I have seen the sheer weight of a sea kill a man very neatly, by simply breaking his neck."

"Good God!" he uttered, impressively, fixing his smeary blue eyes on me. "The sea! No man killed by the sea ever looked like that." He seemed positively scandalized at my suggestion. And as I gazed at him certainly not prepared for anything original on his part, he advanced his head close to mine and thrust his tongue out at me so suddenly that I couldn't help starting back.

After scoring over my calmness in this graphic way he nodded wisely. If I had seen the sight, he assured me, I would never forget it as long as I lived. The weather was too bad to give the corpse a proper sea burial. So next day at dawn they took it up on the poop, covering its face with a bit of bunting; he read a short prayer, and then, just as it was, in its oilskins and long boots, they launched it amongst those mountainous seas that seemed ready every moment to swallow up the ship herself and the terrified lives on board of her.

"That reefed foresail saved you," I threw in.

"Under God—it did," he exclaimed fervently. "It was by a special mercy, I firmly believe, that it stood some of those hurricane squalls."

"It was the setting of that sail which——" I began.

"God's own hand in it," he interrupted me. "Nothing less could have done it. I don't mind telling you that I hardly dared give the order. It seemed impossible that we could touch anything without losing it, and then our last hope would have been gone."

The terror of that gale was on him yet. I let him go on for a bit, then said, casually—as if returning to a minor subject:

"You were very anxious to give up your mate to the shore people, I believe?"

He was. To the law. His obscure tenacity on that point had in it something incomprehensible and a little awful; something, as it were, mystical, quite apart from his anxiety that he should not be suspected of "countenancing any doings of that sort." Seven-and-thirty virtuous years at sea, of which over twenty of immaculate command, and the last fifteen in the *Sephora,* seemed to have laid him under some pitiless obligation.

"And you know," he went on, groping shame-facedly amongst his feelings, "I did not engage that young fellow. His people had some interest with my owners. I was in a way forced to take him on. He looked very smart, very gentlemanly, and all that. But do you know—I never liked him, somehow. I am a plain man. You see, he wasn't exactly the sort for the chief mate of a ship like the *Sephora.*"

I had become so connected in thoughts and impressions with the secret sharer of my cabin that I felt as if I, personally, were being given to understand that I, too, was not the sort that would have done for the chief mate of a ship like the *Sephora.* I had no doubt of it in my mind.

"Not at all the style of man. You understand," he insisted, superfluously, looking hard at me.

I smiled urbanely. He seemed at a loss for a while.

"I suppose I must report a suicide."

"Beg pardon?"

"Sui-cide! That's what I'll have to write to my owners directly I get in."

"Unless you manage to recover him before tomorrow," I assented, dispassionately. . . . . "I mean, alive."

He mumbled something which I really did not catch, and I turned my ear to him in a puzzled manner. He fairly bawled:

"The land—I say, the mainland is at least seven miles off my anchorage."

"About that."

My lack of excitement, of curiosity, of surprise, of any sort of pronounced interest, began to arouse his distrust. But except for the felicitous pretense of deafness I had not tried to pretend anything. I had felt utterly incapable of playing the part of ignorance properly, and therefore was afraid to try. It is also certain that he had brought some ready-made suspicions with him, and that he viewed my politeness as a strange and unnatural phenomenon. And yet how else could I have received him? Not heartily! That was impossible for psychological reasons, which I need not state here. My only object was to keep off his inquiries. Surlily? Yes, but surliness might have provoked a point-blank question. From its novelty to him and from its nature, punctilious courtesy was the manner best calculated to restrain the man. But there was the danger of his breaking through my defense bluntly. I could not, I think, have met him by a direct lie, also for psychological (not moral) reasons. If he had only known how afraid I was of his putting my feeling of identity with the other to the test! But, strangely enough—(I thought of it only afterwards)—I believe that he was not a little disconcerted by the reverse side of that weird situation, by something in me that reminded him of the man he was seeking—suggested a mysterious similitude to the young fellow he had distrusted and disliked from the first.

However that might have been, the silence was not very prolonged. He took another oblique step.

"I reckon I had no more than a two-mile pull to your ship. Not a bit more."

"And quite enough, too, in this awful heat," I said.

Another pause full of mistrust followed. Necessity, they say, is mother of invention, but fear, too, is not barren of ingenious suggestions. And I was afraid he would ask me point-blank for news of my other self.

"Nice little saloon, isn't it?" I remarked, as if noticing for the first time the way his eyes roamed from one closed door to the other. "And very well fitted out, too. Here, for instance," I continued, reaching over the back of my seat negligently and flinging the door open, "is my bathroom."

He made an eager movement, but hardly gave it a glance. I got up, shut the door of the bathroom, and invited him to have a look round, as if I were very proud of my accommodation. He had to rise and be shown round, but he went through the business without any raptures whatever.

"And now we'll have a look at my stateroom," I declared, in a voice as loud as I dared to make it, crossing the cabin to the starboard side with purposely heavy steps.

He followed me in and gazed around. My intelligent double had vanished. I played my part.

"Very convenient—isn't it?"

"Very nice. Very comf . . ." He didn't finish and went out brusquely as if to escape from some unrighteous wiles of mine. But it was not to be. I had been too frightened not to feel vengeful; I felt I had him on the run, and I meant to keep him on the run. My polite insistence must have had something menacing in it, because he gave in suddenly. And I did not let him off a single item; mate's room, pantry, storerooms, the very sail locker which was also under the poop—he had to look into them all. When at last I showed him out on the quarter-deck he drew a long, spiritless sigh, and mumbled dismally that he must really be going back to his ship now. I desired my mate, who had joined us, to see to the captain's boat.

The man of whiskers gave a blast on the whistle which he used to wear hanging round his neck, and yelled, "*Sephora's* away!" My double down there in my cabin must have heard, and certainly could not feel more relieved than I. Four fellows came running out from somewhere forward and went over the side, while my own men, appearing on deck too, lined the rail. I escorted my visitor to the gangway ceremoniously, and nearly overdid it. He was a tenacious beast. On the very ladder he lingered, and in that unique, guiltily conscientious manner of sticking to the point:

"I say . . . you . . . you don't think that——"

I covered his voice loudly:

"Certainly not. . . . I am delighted. Good-by."

I had an idea of what he meant to say, and just saved myself by the privilege of defective hearing. He was too shaken generally to insist, but my mate, close witness of that parting, looked mystified and his face took on a thoughtful cast. As I did not want to appear as if I wished to avoid all communication with my officers, he had the opportunity to address me.

"Seems a very nice man. His boat's crew told our chaps a very extraordinary story, if what I am told by the steward is true. I suppose you had it from the captain, sir?"

"Yes. I had a story from the captain."

"A very horrible affair—isn't it, sir?"

"It is."

"Beats all these tales we hear about murders in Yankee ships."

"I don't think it beats them. I don't think it resembles them in the least."

"Bless my soul—you don't say so! But of course I've no acquaintance whatever with American ships, not I, so I couldn't go against your knowledge. It's horrible enough for me. . . . But the queerest part is that those fellows seemed to have some idea the man was hidden aboard here. They had really. Did you ever hear of such a thing?"

"Preposterous—isn't it?"

We were walking to and fro athwart the quarter-deck. No one of the crew forward could be seen (the day was Sunday), and the mate pursued:

"There was some little dispute about it. Our chaps took offense. 'As if we would harbor a thing like that,' they said. 'Wouldn't you like to look for him in our coal-hole?' Quite a tiff. But they made it up in the end. I suppose he did drown himself. Don't you, sir?"

"I don't suppose anything."

"You have no doubt in the matter, sir?"

"None whatever."

I left him suddenly. I felt I was producing a bad impression, but with my double down there it was most trying to be on deck. And it was almost as trying to be below. Altogether a nerve-trying situation. But on the whole I felt less torn in two when I was with him. There was no one in the whole ship whom I dared take into my confidence. Since the hands had got to know his story. it would have been impossible to pass him off for anyone else, and an accidental discovery was to be dreaded now more than ever. . . .

The steward being engaged in laying the table for dinner, we could talk only with our eyes when I first went down. Later in the afternoon we had a cautious try at whispering. The Sunday quietness of the ship was against us; the stillness of air and water around her was against us; the elements, the men were against us—everything was against us in our secret partnership; time itself—for this could not go on forever. The very trust in Providence was, I suppose, denied to his guilt. Shall I confess that this thought cast me down very much? And as to the chapter of accidents which counts for so much in the book of success, I could only hope that it was closed. For what favorable accident could be expected?

"Did you hear everything?" were my first words as soon as we took up our position side by side, leaning over my bed place.

He had. And the proof of it was his earnest whisper, "The man told you he hardly dared to give the order."

I understood the reference to be to that saving foresail.

"Yes. He was afraid of it being lost in the setting."

"I assure you he never gave the order. He may think he did, but he never gave it. He stood there with me on the break of the poop after the main topsail blew away, and whimpered about our last hope—positively whimpered about it and nothing else—and the night coming on! To hear one's skipper go on like that in such weather was enough to drive any fellow out of his mind. It worked me up into a sort of desperation. I just took it into my own hands and went away from him, boiling, and—— But what's the use telling you? *You* know! . . . Do you think that if I had not been pretty fierce with them I should have got the men to do anything? Not I! The bo's'n perhaps? Perhaps! It wasn't a heavy sea—it was a sea gone mad! I suppose the end of the world will be something like that; and a man may have the heart to see it coming once and be done with it—but to have to face it day after day—— I don't blame anybody. I was precious little better than the rest. Only—I was an officer of that old coal wagon, anyhow——"

"I quite understand," I conveyed that sincere assurance into his ear. He was out of breath with whispering; I could hear him pant slightly. It was all very simple. The same strung-up force which had given twenty-four men a chance, at least, for their lives, had, in a sort of recoil, crushed an unworthy mutinous existence.

But I had no leisure to weigh the merits of the matter—footsteps in the saloon, a heavy knock. "There's enough wind to get under way with, sir." Here was the call of a new claim upon my thoughts and even upon my feelings.

"Turn the hands up," I cried through the door. "I'll be on deck directly."

I was going out to make the acquaintance of my ship. Before I left the cabin our eyes met—the eyes of the only two strangers on board. I pointed to the recessed part where the little campstool awaited him and laid my finger on my lips. He made a gesture—somewhat vague—a little mysterious, accompanied by a faint smile, as if of regret.

This is not the place to enlarge upon the sensations of a man who feels for the first time a ship move under his feet to his own independent word. In my case they were not unalloyed. I was not wholly alone with my command; for there was that stranger in my cabin. Or rather, I was not completely and wholly with her. Part of me was absent. That mental feeling of being in two places at once affected me physically as if the mood of secrecy had penetrated my very soul. Before an hour had elapsed since the ship had begun to move, having occasion to ask the mate (he stood by my side) to take a compass bearing of the pagoda, I caught myself reaching up to his ear in whispers. I say I caught myself, but enough had escaped to startle the man. I can't describe it otherwise than by saying that he shied. A grave, preoccupied manner, as though he were in possession of some perplexing intelligence, did not leave him henceforth. A little later I moved away from the rail to look at the compass with such a stealthy gait that the helmsman noticed it—and I could not help noticing the unusual roundness of his eyes. These are trifling instances, though it's to no commander's advantage to be suspected of ludicrous eccentricities. But I was also more seriously affected. There are to a seaman certain words, gestures, that should in given conditions come as naturally, as instinctively as the winking of a menaced eye. A certain order should spring on to his lips without thinking; a certain sign should get itself made, so to speak, without reflection. But all unconscious alertness had abandoned me. I had to make an effort of will to recall myself back (from the cabin) to the conditions of the moment. I felt that I was appearing an irresolute commander to those people who were watching me more or less critically.

And, besides, there were the scares. On the second

day out, for instance, coming off the deck in the afternoon (I had straw slippers on my bare feet) I stopped at the open pantry door and spoke to the steward. He was doing something there with his back to me. At the sound of my voice he nearly jumped out of his skin, as the saying is, and incidentally broke a cup.

"What on earth's the matter with you?" I asked, astonished.

He was extremely confused. "Beg your pardon, sir. I made sure you were in your cabin."

"You see I wasn't."

"No, sir. I could have sworn I had heard you moving in there not a moment ago. It's most extraordinary . . . very sorry, sir."

I passed on with an inward shudder. I was so identified with my secret double that I did not even mention the fact in those scanty, fearful whispers we exchanged. I suppose he had made some slight noise of some kind or other. It would have been miraculous if he hadn't at one time or another. And yet, haggard as he appeared, he looked always perfectly self-controlled, more than calm—almost invulnerable. On my suggestion he remained almost entirely in the bathroom, which, upon the whole, was the safest place. There could be really no shadow of an excuse for anyone ever wanting to go in there, once the steward had done with it. It was a very tiny place. Sometimes he reclined on the floor, his legs bent, his head sustained on one elbow. At others I would find him on the campstool, sitting in his gray sleeping suit and with his cropped dark hair like a patient, unmoved convict. At night I would smuggle him into my bed place, and we would whisper together, with the regular footfalls of the officer of the watch passing and repassing over our heads. It was an infinitely miserable time. It was lucky that some tins of fine preserves were stowed in a locker in my stateroom; hard bread I could always get hold of; and so he lived on stewed chicken, *pâté de foie gras,* asparagus, cooked oysters, sardines—on all sorts of abominable sham delicacies out of tins. My early-morning coffee he always drank; and it was all I dared do for him in that respect.

Every day there was the horrible maneuvering to go

through so that my room and then the bathroom should be done in the usual way. I came to hate the sight of the steward, to abhor the voice of that harmless -man. I felt that it was he who would bring on the disaster of discovery. It hung like a sword over our heads.

The fourth day out, I think (we were then working down the east side of the Gulf of Siam, tack for tack, in light winds and smooth water)—the fourth day, I say, of this miserable juggling with the unavoidable, as we sat at our evening meal, that man, whose slightest movement I dreaded, after putting down the dishes ran up on deck busily. This could not be dangerous. Presently he came down again; and then it appeared that he had remembered a coat of mine which I had thrown over a rail to dry after having been wetted in a shower which had passed over the ship in the afternoon. Sitting stolidly at the head of the table I became terrified at the sight of the garment on his arm. Of course he made for my door. There was no time to lose.

"Steward," I thundered. My nerves were so shaken that I could not govern my voice and conceal my agitation. This was the sort of thing that made my terrifically whiskered mate tap his forehead with his forefinger. I had detected him using that gesture while talking on deck with a confidential air to the carpenter. It was too far to hear a word, but I had no doubt that this pantomime could only refer to the strange new captain.

"Yes, sir," the pale-faced steward turned resignedly to me. It was this maddening course of being shouted at, checked without rhyme or reason, arbitrarily chased out of my cabin, suddenly called into it, sent flying out of his pantry on incomprehensible errands, that accounted for the growing wretchedness of his expression.

"Where are you going with that coat?"

"To your room, sir."

"Is there another shower coming?"

"I'm sure I don't know, sir. Shall I go up again and see, sir?"

"No! never mind."

My object was attained, as of course my other self in there would have heard everything that passed. During this interlude my two officers never raised their eyes off their respective plates; but the lip of that confounded cub, the second mate, quivered visibly.

I expected the steward to hook my coat on and come out at once. He was very slow about it; but I dominated my nervousness sufficiently not to shout after him. Suddenly I became aware (it could be heard plainly enough) that the fellow for some reason or other was opening the door of the bathroom. It was the end. The place was literally not big enough to swing a cat in. My voice died in my throat and I went stony all over. I expected to hear a yell of surprise and terror, and made a movement, but had not the strength to get on my legs. Everything remained still. Had my second self taken the poor wretch by the throat? I don't know what I could have done next moment if I had not seen the steward come out of my room, close the door, and then stand quietly by the sideboard.

"Saved," I thought. "But, no! Lost! Gone! He was gone!"

I laid my knife and fork down and leaned back in my chair. My head swam. After a while, when sufficiently recovered to speak in a steady voice, I instructed my mate to put the ship round at eight o'clock himself.

"I won't come on deck," I went on. "I think I'll turn in, and unless the wind shifts I don't want to be disturbed before midnight. I feel a bit seedy."

"You did look middling bad a little while ago," the chief mate remarked without showing any great concern.

They both went out, and I stared at the steward clearing the table. There was nothing to be read on that wretched man's face. But why did he avoid my eyes, I asked myself. Then I thought I should like to hear the sound of his voice.

"Steward!"

"Sir!" Startled as usual.

"Where did you hang up that coat?"

"In the bathroom, sir." The usual anxious tone. "It's not quite dry yet, sir."

For some time longer I sat in the cuddy. Had my double vanished as he had come? But of his coming there was an explanation, whereas his disappearance would be inexplicable. . . . I went slowly into my dark room, shut the door, lighted the lamp, and for a time dared not turn round. When at last I did I saw him standing bolt-upright in the narrow recessed part. It would not be true to say I had a shock, but an irresistible doubt of his bodily existence flitted through my mind. Can it be, I asked myself, that he is not visible to other eyes than mine? It was like being haunted. Motionless, with a grave face, he raised his hands slightly at me in a gesture which meant clearly, "Heavens! what a narrow escape!" Narrow indeed. I think I had come creeping quietly as near insanity as any man who has not actually gone over the border. That gesture restrained me, so to speak.

The mate with the terrific whiskers was now putting the ship on the other tack. In the moment of profound silence which follows upon the hands going to their stations I heard on the poop his raised voice: "Hard alee!" and the distant shout of the order repeated on the main-deck. The sails, in that light breeze, made but a faint fluttering noise. It ceased. The ship was coming round slowly: I held my breath in the renewed stillness of expectation; one wouldn't have thought that there was a single living soul on her decks. A sudden brisk shout, "Mainsail haul!" broke the spell, and in the noisy cries and rush overhead of the men running away with the main brace we two, down in my cabin, came together in our usual position by the bed place.

He did not wait for my question. "I heard him fumbling here and just managed to squat myself down in the bath," he whispered to me. "The fellow only opened the door and put his arm in to hang the coat up. All the same——"

"I never thought of that," I whispered back, even more appalled than before at the closeness of the shave, and marveling at that something unyielding in his character which was carrying him through so finely. There was no agitation in his whisper. Whoever was being driven distracted, it was not he. He was sane. And the proof of his sanity was continued when he took up the whispering again.

"It would never do for me to come to life again."

It was something that a ghost might have said. But what he was alluding to was his old captains's reluctant admission of the theory of suicide. It would obviously serve his turn—if I had understood at all the view which seemed to govern the unalterable purpose of his action.

"You must maroon me as soon as ever you can get amongst these islands off the Cambodge shore," he went on.

"Maroon you! We are not living in a boy's adventure tale," I protested. His scornful whispering took me up.

"We aren't indeed! There's nothing of a boy's tale in this. But there's nothing else for it. I want no more. You don't suppose I am afraid of what can be done to me? Prison or gallows or whatever they may please. But you don't see me coming back to explain such things to an old fellow in a wig and twelve respectable tradesmen, do you? What can they know whether I am guilty or not—or of *what* I am guilty, either? That's my affair. What does the Bible say? 'Driven off the face of the earth.' Very well, I am off the face of the earth now. As I came at night so I shall go."

"Impossible!" I murmured. "You can't."

"Can't? . . . Not naked like a soul on the Day of Judgment. I shall freeze on to this sleeping suit. The Last Day is not yet—and . . . you have understood thoroughly. Didn't you?"

I felt suddenly ashamed of myself. I may say truly that I understood—and my hesitation in letting that man swim away from my ship's side had been a mere sham sentiment, a sort of cowardice.

"It can't be done now till next night," I breathed out. "The ship is on the off-shore tack and the wind may fail us."

"As long as I know that you understand," he whispered. "But of course you do. It's a great satisfaction to have got somebody to understand. You seem to have been there on purpose." And in the same whisper, as if we two whenever we talked had to say things to each other which were not fit for the world to hear, he added, "It's very wonderful."

We remained side by side talking in our secret way— but sometimes silent or just exchanging a whispered word or two at long intervals. And as usual he stared through the port. A breath of wind came now and again into our faces. The ship might have been moored in dock, so gently and on an even keel she slipped through the water, that did not murmur even at our passage, shadowy and silent like a phantom sea.

At midnight I went on deck, and to my mate's great surprise put the ship round on the other tack. His terrible whiskers flitted round me in silent criticism. I certainly should not have done it if it had been only a question of getting out of that sleepy gulf as quickly as possible. I believe he told the second mate, who relieved him, that it was a great want of judgment. The other only yawned. That intolerable cub shuffled about so sleepily and lolled against the rails in such a slack, improper fashion that I came down on him sharply.

"Aren't you properly awake yet?"

"Yes, sir! I am awake."

"Well, then, be good enough to hold yourself as if you were. And keep a lookout. If there's any current we'll be closing with some islands before daylight."

The east side of the gulf is fringed with islands, some solitary, others in groups. On the blue background of the high coast they seem to float, on silvery patches of calm water, arid and gray, or dark green and rounded like clumps of evergreen bushes, with the larger ones, a mile or two long, showing the outlines of ridges, ribs of gray rock under the dank mantle of matted leafage. Unknown to trade, to travel, almost to geography, the manner of life they harbor is an unsolved secret. There must be villages—settlements of fishermen at least—on the largest of them, and some communication with the world is probably kept up by native craft. But all that forenoon, as we headed for them, fanned along by the faintest of breezes, I saw no sign of man or canoe in the field of the telescope I kept on pointing at the scattered group.

At noon I gave no orders for a change of course, and the mate's whiskers became much concerned and seemed to be offering themselves unduly to my notice. At last I said:

"I am going to stand right in. Quite in—as far as I can take her."

The stare of extreme surprise imparted an air of ferocity also to his eyes, and he looked truly terrific for a moment.

"We're not doing well in the middle of the gulf," I continued, casually. "I am going to look for the land breezes tonight."

"Bless my soul! Do you mean, sir, in the dark amongst the lot of all them islands and reefs and shoals?"

"Well—if there are any regular land breezes at all on this coast one must get close inshore to find them, mustn't one?"

"Bless my soul!" he exclaimed again under his breath. All that afternoon he wore a dreamy, contemplative appearance which in him was a mark of perplexity. After dinner I went into my stateroom as if I meant to take some rest. There we two bent our dark heads over a half-unrolled chart lying on my bed.

"There," I said. "It's got to be Koh-ring. I've been looking at it ever since sunrise. It has got two hills and a low point. It must be inhabited. And on the coast opposite there is what looks like the mouth of a biggish river—with some towns, no doubt, not far up. It's the best chance for you that I can see."

"Anything. Koh-ring let it be."

He looked thoughtfully at the chart as if surveying chances and distances from a lofty height—and following with his eyes his own figure wandering on the blank land of Cochin-China, and then passing off that piece of paper clean out of sight into uncharted regions. And it was as if the ship had two captains to plan her course for her. I had been so worried and restless running up and down that I had not had the patience to dress that day. I had remained in my sleeping suit, with straw slippers and a soft floppy hat. The closeness of the heat in the gulf had been most oppressive, and the crew were used to seeing me wandering in that airy attire.

"She will clear the south point as she heads now," I whispered into his ear. "Goodness only knows when, though, but certainly after dark. I'll edge her in to half a mile, as far as I may be able to judge in the dark——"

"Be careful," he murmured, warningly—and I realized suddenly that all my future, the only future for which I was fit, would perhaps go irretrievably to pieces in any mishap to my first command.

I could not stop a moment longer in the room. I motioned him to get out of sight and made my way on the poop. That unplayful cub had the watch. I walked up and down for a while thinking things out, then beckoned him over.

"Send a couple of hands to open the two quarter-deck ports," I said, mildly.

He actually had the impudence, or else so forgot himself in his wonder at such an incomprehensible order, as to repeat:

"Open the quarter-deck ports! What for, sir?"

"The only reason you need concern yourself about is because I tell you to do so. Have them open wide and fastened properly."

He reddened and went off, but I believe made some jeering remark to the carpenter as to the sensible practice of ventilating a ship's quarter-deck. I know he popped into the mate's cabin to impart the fact to him because the whiskers came on deck, as it were by chance, and stole glances at me from below—for signs of lunacy or drunkenness, I suppose.

A little before supper, feeling more restless than ever, I rejoined, for a moment, my second self. And to find him sitting so quietly was surprising, like something against nature, inhuman.

I developed my plan in a hurried whisper.

"I shall stand in as close as I dare and then put her round. I will presently find means to smuggle you out of here into the sail locker, which communicates with the lobby. But there is an opening, a sort of square for hauling the sails out, which gives straight on the quarter-deck and which is never closed in fine weather, so as to give air to the sails. When the ship's way is deadened in stays and all the hands are aft at the main braces, you will have a clear road to slip out and get overboard through the open quarter-deck port. I've had them both fastened up. Use a rope's end to lower yourself into the water so as to avoid a splash—you know. It could be heard and cause some beastly complication."

He kept silent for a while, then whispered, "I understand."

"I won't be there to see you go," I began with an effort. "The rest . . . I only hope I have understood, too."

"You have. From first to last"—and for the first time there seemed to be a faltering, something strained in his whisper. He caught hold of my arm, but the ringing of the supper bell made me start. He didn't though; he only released his grip.

After supper I didn't come below again till well past eight o'clock. The faint, steady breeze was loaded with dew; and the wet, darkened sails held all there was of propelling power in it. The night, clear and starry, sparkled darkly, and the opaque, lightless patches shifting slowly against the low stars were the drifting islets. On the port bow there was a big one more distant and shadowily imposing by the great space of sky it eclipsed.

On opening the door I had a back view of my very own self looking at a chart. He had come out of the recess and was standing near the table.

"Quite dark enough," I whispered.

He stepped back and leaned against my bed with a level, quiet glance. I sat on the couch. We had nothing to say to each other. Over our heads the officer of the watch moved here and there. Then I heard him move quickly. I knew what that meant. He was making for the companion; and presently his voice was outside my door.

"We are drawing in pretty fast, sir. Land looks rather close."

"Very well," I answered. "I am coming on deck directly."

I waited till he was gone out of the cuddy, then rose. My double moved too. The time had come to exchange our last whispers, for neither of us was ever to hear each other's natural voice.

"Look here!" I opened a drawer and took out three sovereigns. "Take this anyhow. I've got six and I'd give you the lot, only I must keep a little money to buy some fruit and vegetables for the crew from native boats as we go through Sunda Straits."

He shook his head.

"Take it," I urged him, whispering desperately. "No one can tell what——"

He smiled and slapped meaningly the only pocket of the sleeping jacket. It was not safe, certainly. But I produced a large old silk handkerchief of mine, and tying the three pieces of gold in a corner, pressed it on him. He was touched, I supposed, because he took it at last and tied it quickly round his waist under the jacket, on his bare skin.

Our eyes met; several seconds elapsed, till, our glances still mingled, I extended my hand and turned the lamp out. Then I passed through the cuddy, leaving the door of my room wide open. . . . "Steward!"

He was still lingering in the pantry in the greatness of his zeal, giving a rub-up to a plated cruet stand the last thing before going to bed. Being careful not to wake up the mate, whose room was opposite, I spoke in an undertone.

He looked round anxiously, "Sir!"

"Can you get me a little hot water from the galley?"

"I am afraid, sir, the galley fire's been out for some time now."

"Go and see."

He flew up the stairs.

"Now," I whispered, loudly, into the saloon—too loudly, perhaps, but I was afraid I couldn't make a sound. He was by my side in an instant—the double captain slipped past the stairs—through a tiny dark passage . . . a sliding door. We were in the sail locker, scrambling on our knees over the sails. A sudden thought struck me. I saw myself wandering barefooted, bareheaded, the sun beating on my dark poll. I snatched off my floppy hat and tried hurriedly in the dark to ram it on my other self. He dodged and fended off silently. I wonder what he thought had come to me before he understood and suddenly desisted. Our hands met gropingly, lingered united in a steady, motionless clasp for a second. . . . No word was breathed by either of us when they separated.

I was standing quietly by the pantry door when the steward returned.

"Sorry, sir. Kettle barely warm. Shall I light the spirit lamp?"

"Never mind."

I came out on deck slowly. It was now a matter of conscience to shave the land as close as possible—for now he must go overboard whenever the ship was put in stays. Must! There could be no going back for him. After a moment I walked over to leeward and my heart flew into my mouth at the nearness of the land on the bow. Under any other circumstances I would not have held on a minute longer. The second mate had followed me anxiously.

I looked on till I felt I could command my voice.

"She will weather," I said then in a quiet tone.

"Are you going to try that, sir?" he stammered out incredulously.

I took no notice of him and raised my tone just enough to be heard by the helmsman.

"Keep her good full."

"Good full, sir."

The wind fanned my cheek, the sails slept, the world was silent. The strain of watching the dark loom of the land grow bigger and denser was too much for me. I had shut my eyes—because the ship must go closer. She must! The stillness was intolerable. Were we standing still?

When I opened my eyes the second view started my heart with a thump. The black southern hill of Koh-ring seemed to hang right over the ship like a towering fragment of the ever-lasting night. On that enormous mass of blackness there was not a gleam to be seen, not a sound to be heard. It was gliding irresistibly towards us and yet seemed already within reach of the hand. I saw the vague figures of the watch grouped in the waist, gazing in awed silence.

"Are you going on, sir?" inquired an unsteady voice at my elbow.

I ignored it. I had to go on.

"Keep her full. Don't check her way. That won't do now," I said, warningly.

"I can't see the sails very well," the helmsman answered me, in strange, quavering tones.

Was she close enough? Already she was, I won't say in the shadow of the land, but in the very blackness of it,

already swallowed up as it were, gone too close to be recalled, gone from me altogether.

"Give the mate a call," I said to the young man who
stood at my elbow as still as death. "And turn all hands
up."

My tone had a borrowed loudness reverberated from
the height of the land. Several voices cried out together:
"We are all on deck, sir."

Then stillness again, with the great shadow gliding
closer, towering higher, without a light, without a sound.
Such a hush had fallen on the ship that she might have
been a bark of the dead floating in slowly under the very
gate of Erebus.

"My God! Where are we?"

It was the mate moaning at my elbow. He was thunder-
struck, and as it were deprived of the moral support of
his whiskers. He clapped his hands and absolutely cried
out, "Lost!"

"Be quiet," I said, sternly.

He lowered his tone, but I saw the shadowy gesture
of his despair. "What are we doing here?"

"Looking for the land wind."

He made as if to tear his hair, and addressed me
recklessly.

"She will never get out. You have done it, sir. I knew
it'd end in something like this. She will never weather, and
you are too close now to stay. She'll drift ashore before
she's round. O my God!"

I caught his arm as he was raising it to batter his poor
devoted head, and shook it violently.

"She's ashore already," he wailed, trying to tear himself away.

"Is she? . . . Keep good full there!"

"Good full, sir," cried the helmsman in a frightened,
thin, childlike voice.

I hadn't let go the mate's arm and went on shaking it.
"Ready about, do you hear? You go forward"—shake—
"and stop there"—shake—"and hold your noise"—shake
—"and see these head-sheets properly overhauled"—
shake, shake—shake.

And all the time I dared not look towards the land lest

my heart should fail me. I released my grip at last and he ran forward as if fleeing for dear life.

I wondered what my double there in the sail locker thought of this commotion. He was able to hear every-thing—and perhaps he was able to understand why, on my conscience, it had to be thus close—no less. My first order "Hard alee!" re-echoed ominously under the tower-ing shadow of Koh-ring as if I had shouted in a moun-tain gorge. And then I watched the land intently. In that smooth water and light wind it was impossible to feel the ship coming-to. No! I could not feel her. And my second self was making now ready to ship out and lower himself overboard. Perhaps he was gone already . . . ?

The great black mass brooding over our very mast-heads began to pivot away from the ship's side silently. And now I forgot the secret stranger ready to depart, and remembered only that I was a total stranger to the ship. I did not know her. Would she do it? How was she to be handled?

I swung the mainyard and waited helplessly. She was perhaps stopped, and her very fate hung in the balance, with the black mass of Koh-ring like the gate of the everlasting night towering over her taffrail. What would she do now? Had she way on her yet? I stepped to the side swiftly, and on the shadowy water I could see noth-ing except a faint phosphorescent flash revealing the glassy smoothness of the sleeping surface. It was impossible to tell—and I had not learned yet the feel of my ship. Was she moving? What I needed was something easily seen, a piece of paper, which I could throw overboard and watch. I had nothing on me. To run down for it I didn't dare. There was no time. All at once my strained, yearning stare distinguished a white object floating with-in a yard of the ship's side. White on the black water. A phosphorescent flash passed under it. What was that thing? . . . I recognized my own floppy hat. It must have fallen off his head . . . and he didn't bother. Now I had what I wanted—the saving mark for my eyes. But I hardly thought of my other self, now gone from the ship, to be hidden forever from all friendly faces, to be a fugitive and a vagabond on the earth, with no brand of the curse on his sane forehead to stay a slaying hand . . . too proud to explain.

And I watched the hat—the expression of my sudden pity for his mere flesh. It had been meant to save his homeless head from the dangers of the sun. And now—behold—it was saving the ship, by serving me for a mark to help out the ignorance of my strangeness. Ha! It was drifting forward, warning me just in time that the ship had gathered sternway.

"Shift the helm," I said in a low voice to the seaman standing still like a statue.

The man's eyes glistened wildly in the binnacle light as he jumped round to the other side and spun round the wheel.

I walked to the break of the poop. On the over-shadowed deck all hands stood by the forebraces waiting for my order. The stars ahead seemed to be gliding from right to left. And all was so still in the world that I heard the quiet remark, "She's round," passed in a tone of intense relief between two seamen.

"Let go and haul."

The foreyards ran round with a great noise, amidst cheery cries. And now the frightful whiskers made themselves heard giving various orders. Already the ship was drawing ahead. And I was alone with her. Nothing! no one in the world should stand now between us, throwing a shadow on the way of silent knowledge and mute affection, the perfect communion of a seaman with his first command.

Walking to the taffrail, I was in time to make out, on the very edge of a darkness thrown by a towering black mass like the very gateway of Erebus—yes, I was in time to catch an evanescent glimpse of my white hat left behind to mark the spot where the secret sharer of my cabin and of my thoughts, as though he were my second self, had lowered himself into the water to take his punishment: a free man, a proud swimmer striking out for a new destiny.